Who Committed The Deadliest Sin?

JOHANNES HUMBRECHT—A lost soul at the Church of the Good Shepherd, he lived in squalor, but he owned a Bible so rare, the price of possessing it was murder.

MR. "JONES"—A powerful Mafia chieftain, he believed the priceless Bible could buy him a place in heaven...even if he killed to get it.

J. J. KNOX—Senior partner in a law firm known for its integrity, he swore no one knew about Humbrecht's will...but did something make him lie?

FATHER PRIOR SIMON—A jolly monk and scholar, he loved books with a religious zeal...but did he also have a sinful passion?

ROBIN ELDER—Dapper attorney in J. J. Knox's office, he had three ex-wives, three alimony payments, and three good reasons to need some extra cash.

DR. JOYCE COMPTON—Representative of the Chicago Art Institute, she fervently believed the Bible belonged in her museum...but did she also believe in murder?

"A detective story that plays fair with the reader, providing scrupulous clues...and strong motives. When you add the insight into a clergyman's life, and the sparks of irreverent humor, you come up with a solidly appealing evening's reading."

Detroit Free Press

"Readers will enjoy this crafty mystery."

People

Other Avon Books by
Charles Merrill Smith

REVEREND RANDOLLPH AND THE AVENGING ANGEL
REVEREND RANDOLLPH AND THE FALL FROM GRACE
REVEREND RANDOLLPH AND THE HOLY TERROR
REVEREND RANDOLLPH AND THE WAGES OF SIN

REVEREND RANDOLLPH AND THE UNHOLY BIBLE

CHARLES MERRILL SMITH

AVON
PUBLISHERS OF BARD, CAMELOT, DISCUS AND FLARE BOOKS

AVON BOOKS
A division of
The Hearst Corporation
1790 Broadway
New York, New York 10019

Published by arrangement with G. P. Putnam's Sons
Library of Congress Catalog Card Number: 82-18125
ISBN: 0-380-67660-5

The G. P. Putnam's Sons edition contains the following Library of Congress Cataloging in Publication Data:

Smith, Charles Merrill.
Reverend Randollph and the unholy Bible.
I. Title.
PS3569.M5156R44 1983 813'.54 82-18125
ISBN 0-399-12796-8

First Avon Printing, March 1984

Printed in the U. S. A.

WFH 10 9 8 7 6 5 4 3 2 1

Acknowledgments

I am indebted to Herb Raiser, master bookbinder, and Father Joe Kelly, who told me much I needed to know but didn't before writing this book. I am also indebted to the Illinois State University Library for making available to me a facsimile of the Gutenberg Bible, and also to Ina Danenberger, one of the few people in the world who can read my handwriting, who typed the manuscript.

This is another one for Betty
My Samantha Stack

REVEREND RANDOLLPH AND THE UNHOLY BIBLE

1

RANDOLLPH HAD never seen a freshly slaughtered human carcass before. His experience with dead bodies had been confined mostly to waxed and polished examples of the mortician's craft, with muted Muzak whispering sweet Jesus hymns to the viewers, all designed to assure that none of this was real, that death wasn't such a bad deal when handled by experienced professionals.

But Johannes Humbrecht was real. And he was unmistakably dead, half-sprawled across the rickety table at which Randollph had sat with the old man many times, drinking the strong and unpalatable tea Humbrecht always served him. Humbrecht, in the spasms of death, had knocked his own cup and saucer on the floor, Randollph saw, as one sees trivial things in the midst of shock. Another cup, still full of tea, sat at the opposite end of the table.

Humbrecht was face down, making it simple for Randollph to see the cause of death. The entire back of

Humbrecht's skull was smashed in, a mess of blood and brains and bone.

Randollph shook himself out of shock and looked for a telephone. Then he remembered that Humbrecht's rotting old mansion had no phone—at least, not one in service. There might be a telephone somewhere amid the unbelievable accumulation of debris which filled the rooms of the large house, but Randollph needed a phone that worked. That meant finding a pay phone, probably among the small collection of expensive boutiques, hairdressers' establishments and restaurants three or four blocks up the street. He needed to call homicide, and particularly Lieutenant Michael Casey if Casey was available.

He reached for the doorknob, then jerked his hand back as if he had suddenly remembered the knob was scorching hot. He had not touched the inside knob, and there might be fingerprints. He'd been around Lieutenant Casey enough to know about the importance of fingerprints. Using his handkerchief as insulation, he twisted open the doorknob by its shank. His fingerprints were on the outside knob, of course. When Humbrecht hadn't answered his knock, Randollph had pushed in the partially opened door by the knob. No point in messing it up further. He carefully pulled the door closed, again using his handkerchief and the shank of the knob.

He headed rapidly for the little business district catering to the expensive needs of people who could afford to live near the lake. At the periphery of his consciousness he was aware that this was a brisk and beautiful September day—cool for so early, but with the sun ducking out now and then shedding a brief warmth as if summer were reluctant to depart. There was a fair amount of street traffic up ahead. He couldn't make out their features, but people were playing the scenes he supposed were staged here every day. A man in a dark suit was assisting a mink-cloaked lady into a Rolls-Royce, while her uniformed chauffeur was putting packages into the trunk. Another man studied what Randollph guessed was the menu taped to the window of a small French restaurant as if estimating his resources and wondering if they would permit him to invite a lady to dinner. The hairdressers' establishments were both receiving and discharging customers. A dumpy woman in a long coat and hood hurried toward the el station carrying two unmatched bags which appeared too heavy for her.

Randollph wondered if his eye recorded this normal scene so as to smudge the grisly sight that it had witnessed moments ago.

He saw a young woman with a newly clipped poodle on a leash abandon a phone booth, and he grabbed it.

In his haste to find a phone, Randollph had not noticed a dark Buick sedan with three men sitting in it just parking across the street from Humbrecht's house. As soon as Randollph was a block away one of the men, sixtyish, gray hair cut by the kind of barber who advertised himself as a hair stylist, and dressed in a dark three-piece suit said, "Let's go. Put your gloves on. Remember, we may need to persuade the old man to answer some questions, but no real rough stuff. He may have a weak heart. He's no good to me dead."

"Mr. Jones, why did that guy just left use a handkerchief to close the door?"

"How the hell should I know?" the older man snapped. "Maybe he's got a thing about germs. I don't pay you to ask dumb questions, Junior."

"Sure, Mr. Jones," the big young man said. "C'mon, Pack." Pack was not as large as Junior, but younger and well muscled. They both wore jeans and sweaters.

"No bell," Junior reported after inspecting Humbrecht's door.

"Then knock, you damn fool," the older man said.

Junior knocked.

"Knock harder," the older man said irritably. Junior banged on the door.

"Try the door. It may be unlocked. We'll pick it if we have to. He's got to be in there. He just had a visitor."

Junior opened the door. "There you are, boss," he said as he stood aside to let the older man enter. He looked pleased with himself, as if he'd just done something clever.

"God, the place stinks!" Pack said. "And look at this mess! Looks like a junkyard. The old guy some kind of weirdo?"

"Jesus H. Christ!" Junior yelled. "Would you look at this, Mr. Jones!"

But the older man had already spotted the mortal remains of Johannes Humbrecht. He swore softly in a foreign language.

"Ya wanna search the place?" Junior asked. "Tell us what we're lookin' for, we'll search."

The older man clouted Junior across the face with the back of his gloved hand. "You idiot, it'd take months to search this place. What I want is to get the hell out before someone finds us here."

Lieutenant Michael Casey inspected possible places to sit down—limited to three chairs of uncertain stability and crusted with grime of unknown origin but capable of transferring itself to his beige gabardine slacks—and said, "This place stinks. Let's go sit in my car and talk while the technical crew finishes up."

"Good idea," Randollph agreed. He'd had enough of Humbrecht's house for one day.

Casey got into the driver's side of the blue unmarked Pontiac police car, Randollph on the passenger side.

"Now, Doctor, how did you happen to find the old man? Why were you here? Why did you go into the house when no one answered your knock? Who was this old guy—"

Randollph held up a restraining hand. "Slow down, Lieutenant. I'll tell all—but let's get it into some kind of order."

Casey smiled. "I stand rebuked. Policemen always want to find out everything in a hurry. Occupational disease. Tell it your way."

Randollph thought again that Casey didn't look much like a policeman. He always dressed like a young executive in a business that permitted a subdued flair in the garb of its employees. Randollph meditated briefly on his relationship with the lieutenant. They'd known each other awhile. They'd been thrown together by circumstances. Casey had been best man at Randollph's recent wedding, mostly because Randollph hadn't been in Chicago long enough to accumulate any close male friends. Yet they still addressed each other by title rather than name.

"I was paying a pastoral call," Randollph began.

This surprised Casey. "On that old geezer? I thought the Church of the Good Shepherd didn't admit the lower classes."

"Come on, Lieutenant, just because we have a fair number of prestigious old Chicago families on our rolls doesn't mean we exclude anyone. We're a church, not a club."

"And this Humbrecht was a member of your church?"

"Came every Sunday."

"Do you call on all your members?"

"No. That would be next to impossible. Our members are scattered over the city, suburbs mostly. We have other clergy on the staff who do pastoral calling."

"Then why did you bother with Humbrecht? He couldn't have been high enough on your totem pole to rate calls from the head guy. Why didn't you have one of your flunk—" he caught himself—"one of your assistants do it? That's what my pastor at St. Aloysius does. He's got a flock of assistants, and you can tell how you stand by which one calls on you. The least important members usually get the newest and greenest assistant."

Randollph was tempted to ask Casey what grade of curate called on him, but thought better of it.

"I suppose we do a little of that, too," he said, "although it's certainly not policy."

"So why did you call on Humbrecht?"

Randollph pondered his answer. "I'm not sure I can tell you."

"Can't or won't?" Casey's tone was sharper.

"Can't. But I'll try if you wish."

"Try."

"Because it was both an onerous chore and a genuine joy."

Casey snorted. "What kind of an answer is that?"

"I'll try to explain. I suspect I have feelings of guilt being the well-paid pastor to comfortable, well-to-do people. I live in a luxurious penthouse, employ a chef-majordomo, and—because I'm senior pastor of the Church of the Good Shepherd—am cultivated by the business and political leaders of the city."

"Doesn't hurt that you're a famous ex-pro football star, either," Casey said dryly.

"I don't trade on that," Randollph replied, irritation creeping into his voice.

"Sorry," Casey said.

"Anyway," Randollph continued, "I get these guilt feelings. Did St. Peter hobnob with the mayor—not that that's any fun. What would St. Paul think of my penthouse parsonage? So visiting Johannes Humbrecht—poor, a Collier-brothers type who collected and filled his house with all kinds of worthless junk, a man no one cared about, devoid of friends or relatives—visiting him made me feel a little more like a true pastor. Pastors are supposed to visit the poor. I suppose Johannes Humbrecht was my token poor parishioner. Can you understand that?"

"I think so."

"It was a chore. It was a repugnant task. As you know, the place stinks something awful. And he always served me that nasty tea he favored. But about once a month I'd screw up my courage and visit him. And I always came away lifted in mind and spirit."

"That doesn't make sense."

"Oh, but it does," Randolph assured him.

"Why?"

"Because Humbrecht had a very well-stocked mind. You find so few people today with well-stocked minds. He had taught history at Northwestern University for many years, and church history is my field. So we had a common affection and respect for history. But he also knew philosophy and theology—another thing we had in common. He was, I would say, a genuine expert in the fields of art and music. I'm untutored in art and music, but he delighted in trying to teach me. He was also an avid sports fan."

"Jesus, a queer one. So today you came to visit." Casey was anxious to get on with it. "Why did you go on in when he didn't answer your knock?"

"Because he hardly ever went anywhere in the afternoon. And because the door was ajar. That was most unusual. I thought something might be wrong."

"And something sure as hell was wrong. Then?"

"I looked for the phone, then remembered Humbrecht didn't have one. So I rushed out to find a pay phone."

"How long did all this take?"

Randollph thought about it. "That's hard to say. I was shocked, dazed, by the sight of Humbrecht. Say it took me a minute or two to collect myself. I then had sense enough to use a handkerchief to open the door carefully by the shank, not the knob—"

"For which the Chicago Police Department extends you its gratitude," Casey said. "We might find something on the knob."

"I shut it the same way on the outside," Randollph added. "Though, of course, my fingerprints will be on the outside knob. Then I took off for the small business district up there." He indicated the area to Casey.

"Did you run?"

"No. I walked rapidly."

"So you phoned me maybe fifteen to twenty minutes after you discovered Humbrecht?"

"That would be close."

Casey opened the car door. "Let's go see what the tech crew's got. They ought to be about done by now. By the way, isn't your beautiful wife giving a dinner party tonight to which Liz and I are invited? Or do I have my dates mixed up?"

Randollph stopped short. "I'd completely forgotten." He smiled. "She said it's a party just for people she especially likes. It will be a cheerful ending to a rather cheerless day."

"I look forward to Clarence's cooking and the company of nice people," Casey said. "But this is not a cheerless day for me. Just routine." Randollph thought he detected a small edge of spiritual pride in Casey's voice.

Inside, the fingerprint man, the photographer, and the two detectives who had come with Casey were getting ready to leave. The police surgeon was a pleasant-looking young chap who couldn't have been too long out of medical school. He was still examining Humbrecht's body and whistling "Some Enchanted Evening."

"What can you tell me, Al?" Casey asked the doctor.

"Dead two hours or so, no more, probably less."

"Then you couldn't have been far behind the killer, Doctor," Casey said.

"Who me? I wasn't anywhere near here," the police surgeon protested.

"Oh, sorry, I meant Dr. Randollph. He discovered the body. Dr. Randollph, this is Dr. Al Emerson."

"I know," the police surgeon said. "You're Con Randollph—at least that's what they called you when you played with the Rams. Quick hands and the mind of a confidence man, right? Do they still call you that?"

"I hope not," Randollph said. "Only my former teammates."

"Wouldn't do in your present profession," Dr. Emerson said. "Although it would fit some of the Bible-thumpers around here."

"If you can interrupt your discussion of the state of religion, Al, I'd like to ask somebody if the murder weapon's been located."

"Sure, Mike," one of the detectives answered. He held up a glassine bag with a badly stained baseball bat in it.

"Johnny Mize model," the police doctor volunteered.

"Forty-two ounces," Randollph said. "Ted Williams once tried it and said it was like swinging a telephone pole."

"Now how would you know that?" Dr. Emerson asked. "I thought football was your game."

"I like most sports. I was a good enough catcher in college that I got a few offers from the professionals. Maybe I should have signed. On the whole, baseball is a better game than football."

"Knock it off," Casey ordered. "This is a murder investigation, not a sports seminar. Al, would it take much of a blow from that bat to cave in his skull?"

"Not too much, Mike."

"What I want to know is if those wounds could have been inflicted by someone of only ordinary strength?"

"Sure, Like Dr. Randollph said, that's a heavy bat. Designed to hit a baseball out of sight—or crack skulls." He began to stuff his instruments into a black suitcase fitted to receive them. "I'm done. You'll want an autopsy?"

"Of course," Casey said.

"Waste of time. Well, as far as I'm concerned he's ready for the meat wagon." He resumed whistling "Some Enchanted Evening" as he left.

2

CASEY OFFERED Randollph a ride back to the church. Randollph usually walked home from his visits to Humbrecht because he got precious little exercise except when he could find the time to work out at the Chicago Athletic Club where the church maintained a membership for its pastor—a perquisite of position just like those handed out by secular corporations to executives who had risen to high positions. Randollph occasionally wondered whether there was any essential difference between being pastor of a large church and president of a company. The pastor's pay, though generous by sacred standards, was negligible when compared to the compensation of a company president. There were no stock options for a pastor other than those collectible in heaven. But a pastor, like the corporation executive, was the head of a business which had to remain solvent. So, like a good executive, Randollph decided he'd better duck into the church office before going home.

"See you tonight," Casey said as he let Randollph off in front of the church. "Black tie, isn't it?"

"Yes. It pleases Clarence. I suspect he feels that we should dress for dinner every evening. And it pleases Sammy."

"I don't mind," Casey replied. "I don't get too many opportunities to wear a dinner jacket."

"You will when you become police commissioner," Randollph said, and headed for the church door.

During the week, the church door served mostly as the entry to the high-rise office building in which the church was encapsulated. It admitted lawyers, clerks, and people bent on buying and selling this and that rather than worshipers. True, the doors were heavy brass and looked as if they belonged to some vast and ancient Gothic edifice. And there was a discreet metal plaque set in the masonry beside the doors announcing that this was the Church of the Good Shepherd and listing the clergy employed by the church to combat the world, the flesh, and the devil, all of which, presumably, had powerful forces at work in Chicago's Loop.

But the church doors did not open on a hushed and prayerful narthex. They opened on a corridor with banks of elevators on each side, a press of people waiting to ride up, and cars full of people who had just ridden down and were shoving their way out. One had to follow the corridor to another set of brass doors to find the church.

The idea of a church in an office building and hotel (separate entrance) had shocked some of the members when, some decades ago, it had been proposed by the trustees. For one thing, they already had an adequate building—a sturdy Romanesque structure squatting on the corner of what was fast becoming one of the busiest areas of the Loop. It was on the site of the log hut which had been a mission to the Indians inhabiting the frontier area around the great waters. The Indians, though, had been recalcitrant about becoming Christians. They couldn't see that Christianity was any improvement over the religion they already had. Also, the missionaries preached against the consumption of firewater, which the Indians considered the one true blessing the white man had bestowed upon them.

So the log cabin mission was torn down and replaced by a modest frame chapel catering to the spiritual requirements of the increasing number of white settlers.

Soon a larger frame church in the New England congregational style was built on the same site. This attracted the better class of settlers, meaning the more prosperous. By the time Chicago was old enough to have old families and something resembling social distinctions, the church had a corner on the upper-class ecclesiastical market.

So the trustees said: "This is the age of progress. We've got to keep up with the times." They tore down the New England-style frame church, hired an architect who favored Romanesque, and erected a gloomy but impressive new church—thus attracting an even larger share of the better classes, who wished to worship the Lord in a building befitting their standing in the community. But when the price of real estate per front foot kept going up like a soprano straining for a high C, the trustees said: "This is the age of progress. We've got to keep up with the times," and proposed wrecking the Romanesque temple devoted solely to the worship of God and replacing it with a church concealed in the bowels of an office building-cum-hotel. Some of the members grumbled that this was a spiritually unhealthy mixture of piety and commerce. But when it was pointed out that such a building would produce sufficient revenues to relieve present and future parishioners of the necessity of excessive contributions, the opponents of the plan were able to see that their objections had been perhaps ill-conceived, and that a church ensconced in a large business enterprise might be an even more effective witness to the faith than a church separated from the world of commerce.

One stubborn trustee insisted that "we've got to do something to make it look like a church." So when the building was topped out, it was capped with a huge Gothic tower culminating in a pinnacle, complete with gargoyles and other readily recognizable Christian symbols. And though it looked like a church at the top where no hymns were sung and no petitions to the Almighty uttered, and looked like a business building below where prayers were raised and sacraments administered, people were able to worship in good conscience because of the spiritually comforting presence of a genuine church tower, though it was separated from them by stories of offices, ramming its medieval snout into the Chicago sky.

More than a quarter century prior to Randollph's incumbency his predecessor, The Reverend Dr. Arthur Hartshorne—who had been named pastor because his sermons were comprised of funny, nostalgic and heart-tugging stories unencumbered by theology or biblical references, and because he was young and full of beans—had proposed that the church utilize the vast empty space in the Gothic tower atop it by building in it a "suitable parsonage for the senior pastor." This would have the advantage of having the pastor housed right in the building only an elevator ride away from his office, thus saving the inconvenience of commuting. It would be an economy, too, he pointed out, since the church already owned the space.

The trustees agreed, though they had second thoughts about the economy argument when the bills came in. Matilda Hartshorne's tastes, if not downright sybaritic, were ultra-luxurious. She laid on the best of everything and plenty of it. Thus, though he served a master who often had no place to lay his head, Randollph came to inhabit a penthouse that was superior to most of the habitations along Chicago's gold coast.

Randollph took the elevator to the third floor where the church offices were located. The elevator opened into a spacious waiting room which Randollph saw was blessedly empty. Since it was so near to closing time, he doubted there would be anyone still seeking him this afternoon. He went into Miss Adelaide Windfall's office. Miss Windfall's employment as church secretary had predated Arthur Hartshorne's ministry. Her power in the Church of the Good Shepherd had grown with the years and her weight. She was a formidable woman in size and demeanor, and had the personality of one who knows where all the bodies are buried.

She nodded to Randollph, a gesture which, though courteous, carried a reproof for his overlong absence from the office.

"We've just lost a good member of our church," Randollph announced. That ought to startle the old girl, he thought. "Good member" to Miss Windfall meant someone of wealth and status.

"Not Mr. Castle," she said, concern in her voice. "Why, he was reported doing just fine this morning."

Mr. Castle, from a "fine old family," was the only good member of Good Shepherd being hotly pursued, at the moment, by the grim reaper.

"No. Mr. Johannes Humbrecht."

Miss Windfall brightened considerably.

"Oh? How?" The question was rhetorical. Miss Windfall considered Johannes Humbrecht to be socially unworthy of membership in Good Shepherd. Because he didn't bathe, he stunk, and Miss Windfall was convinced that anyone whose body odor was offensive ought never be admitted to membership in the first place.

"He was murdered," Randollph said. "Back of his head bashed in by a baseball bat. I found him. That's why I'm so late getting back."

This did shock Miss Windfall.

"There'll be unpleasant publicity. The church will be involved in an unsavory way. Your name will be all over the papers, too, won't it?" It was not a question but a reproof. Good Shepherd and its pastors shouldn't be mentioned in the papers except as having launched some prominent young couple up the shoal-strewn stream of matrimony, or as dispatching some worthy citizen on his way to heaven or wherever. Certainly members of Good Shepherd shouldn't have the bad taste to get themselves murdered. Even more unthinkable was for the pastor to discover the body.

But Miss Windfall did not mourn Mr. Humbrecht's messy passing, nor let a mere murder divert her from her responsibilities.

"Here is the list of your phone calls." She handed Randollph a paper. "The ones requiring a return call today are noted. Here is the agenda for the monthly board meeting." She handed him another piece of paper. "If you could read it and initial it now there is still time for the girls to make copies today and get them in the mail."

Randollph pretended to inspect the agenda, then initialed it. He hadn't read a word of it, and he knew that Miss Windfall knew that he hadn't. The agenda for board meetings was pretty much engraved on stone tablets. Randollph doubted the board members ever glanced at it, so familiar was the routine. Occasionally some items provoked a debate, but they would provoke it whether Randollph initialed the paper or not. He supposed this was the sort of thing executives were hired to do. He wondered what life was like for executives who spent their days initialing agendas, reports, memos, writing reports for other executives to read and initial, attending meetings at which reports were read and discussed, dictating letters to secretaries or recording devices. Some people must like it, apparently, because millions of people did it. If they liked it, fine. People ought to do what they liked, though Randollph's powers of imagination were insufficient to comprehend that anyone could by choice spend the precious hours of their lives in that way.

Some people did it for money. Some for power. Some because there was no convenient way to escape doing it, especially with someone like Adelaide Windfall hovering over them to see that lazy, procrastinating pastors who consistently avoided their paper work did it.

Miss Windfall took the initialed agenda. "There's time to return those calls before offices close for the day," she reminded him.

"Yes, of course." He clutched the list. "I think I'll make them from the parsonage," he lied.

Miss Windfall sniffed. It was her way of stating that she knew he was going to play hooky.

3

RANDOLLPH HAD TO take the elevator back down to the building's business lobby, elbow his way out the doors, then walk ten steps to the hotel entrance. Access to the penthouse parsonage was from the hotel, which the church leased to something called Luxury Inns of America. It thrived on housing conventions and selling booze. Only hotel elevator number eight went all the way to the penthouse. It opened into a small foyer, then three steps brought you to the door of the penthouse. Randollph used his key to unbolt the sturdy lock. It would not be easy to break into this apartment.

This, he reflected, was a part of the day that always picked him up. Downtown Chicago was just another city—busy, grubby streets packed with people rushing to perform duties or complete errands that made little difference in the total scheme of things. True, there was a current of vitality running through this city. He supposed that it was generated by the crowds, the traffic, the seemingly constant noise of buildings being built or destroyed. As he moved about on Chicago's streets

Randollph was a contributor, however small, to the busyness and confusion and vitality.

But in the penthouse his perspective changed.

For one thing, the view was stunning. Because of the octagonal configuration of the Gothic tower, the rooms of the penthouse were oddly shaped. But they were spacious, because no building speculator had to figure ways to cut costs when the apartment had been built. There were two floors. The first floor included a living room, dining room, a kitchen whose space and equipment would have pleased even the world's most demanding chefs, and a study where the pastor could delve into the *Summa Theologica* and other exciting and relevant holy tomes. Upstairs were bedrooms: a master suite, somewhat smaller but not ungenerous accommodations now occupied by Clarence Higbee, and a guest room. All the outside walls were glass. Randollph could look out over the conglomeration of towers and slabs of buildings—some thick and heavy as a matron's middle, others spiky and graceful—and realize the vastness of the city. And beyond the buildings there was Lake Michigan, an inland sea of changing moods specked with graceful sailboats and power boats, and graceless but useful freighters, with occasional planes and helicopters darting about overhead like birds inspecting the waters for some fish they fancied for dinner.

Randollph never tired of this scene. He always took a little time to contemplate it when he came home, day's work done. Though he had done nothing to make what he saw, he thought he knew how God must have felt when, creation completed, He looked upon it and pronounced it good.

Clarence Higbee, assisted by a pretty young girl in a maid's uniform, pushed a portable bar into the living room.

"Good evening, Dr. Randollph," he said. "This is Annette, who will be helping me this evening."

Randollph could tell that Clarence was happy, even though his demeanor was, as always, that of the English servant who knew exactly the relationship between employer and majordomo. But Clarence liked dinner parties. They gave him a wider audience for his art. And they gave him an excuse to wear his tailcoat and white tie. No matter that the guests would be wearing dinner jackets. A proper butler always wore tails when serving a dinner party.

"Madam asks that you join her as soon as possible," Clarence informed him. Randollph translated this to mean that Sammy wanted him ready in plenty of time to greet the arriving guests.

The master suite of the penthouse was done in green and gold and white because Matilda Hartshorne liked green and gold and white. The sitting room had a long sofa, a long coffee table, two large chairs and several smaller ones. The bedroom offered a king-sized bed, lounge chairs and two dressing rooms. The bath, with sunken tub and a separate glass case for showering, was of a size and quality not often seen in a private residence. Randollph often wondered what Francis of Assisi, who probably didn't bathe too often, would have thought of it. Dan Gantry said the master suite looked like a high-class whorehouse.

"I'm in here." Sammy's voice came from her dressing room. "I read all about it on the news ticker before I left the studio. That poor old man! Did it shake you up, Randollph?"

"The answer is yes, it shook me up. But I dislike conversing with a disembodied voice. Whey don't you come on out of there?"

"Because I'm naked."

"We're married. It would not be a novel experience for me to see you naked."

"No, but you always react the same way."

"How?"

"Lustfully."

"So I do, come to think of it. But there is nothing in Holy Scriptures or Christian theology forbidding a man to feel passion for his wife."

"For which I am profoundly grateful." Sammy came out of her dressing room smoothing a slip over her hips. "But you can't be dallying, even with your wife, while dinner guests wait below. So get a move on, buster." She gave him a quick kiss, spun deftly from his grasp, and retreated to her dressing room.

Randollph pondered the mystery of love. He'd known

many beautiful women. Some of them were bright. Some were charming. Some were witty. Some aroused his interest as well as his passion. He'd even thought he'd been in love, more or less, with a couple of them.

When he had met Samantha Stack on his first day of duty at Good Shepherd, he hadn't been overwhelmed. Dan Gantry, who knew her well, had brought her in. Dan had been associate pastor at Good Shepherd since graduating from seminary, and he seemed to know everyone.

Dan had said, "Dr. Randollph, this is Sam Stack. Isn't she gorgeous? For an older dame, that is."

Randollph saw that she was a tallish, expensively dressed woman of about thirty. She had flaming red hair. And she'd tried to shock him by announcing that she was an atheist.

"An atheist isn't a bad thing to be," Randollph had answered her. "The classic definition of an atheist is one who refuses to worship the popular gods of current culture. Many early Christians were executed on the charge that they were atheists."

Randollph remembered well the startled look that came across Samantha Stack's face. She appealed to Dan Gantry. "Is he telling the truth or kidding me?"

"Beats me," Dan had replied. "But he's a professor of church history, he ought to know."

"Oh, hell, that takes all the fun out of being an atheist," she'd said. Then, having lost that round, she'd come right back with "You're a big, healthy-looking guy even though you must be pushing forty—or are those little flecks of gray in that handsome dark hair premature? But Danny Boy says you're single. Have you taken a vow of celibacy? Are you gay?"

Randollph remembered that he'd smiled sweetly at her. "You haven't exhausted my options, Mrs. Stack."

She'd been bested, but she liked it. "You do have an elegant way of talking, good doctor," she'd said. "I have the most popular television talk show in Chicago, if you don't count Phil Donahue, and he's really national rather than local. I'd like to have you as a guest on my show. That's why I beat Danny Boy over the head to introduce us—so I'd get first crack at you."

That's how it had started. He was a gentleman who

preferred blondes, and she was a redhead. He'd never been attracted to brash females, and Sam Stack was brash. Therefore it came as a shock and a revelation to him when he realized that he felt about Samantha Stack as he'd never felt about any other woman. He couldn't account for it. He couldn't explain it. Had he drawn up a profile of the kind of woman he'd want to marry, it would have in no way resembled Samantha. All he knew was that in the few months they had been married his life had been enhanced and completed in ways he would not have believed possible.

Sammy came out of her dressing room wearing a hostess gown in white crepe de chine around which she was fastening a wide belt made up of rows of tiny silver beads.

"Shsh, go!" She pushed Randollph toward the bathroom. "A quick shower, and then try to set a new record getting into your dinner clothes."

The bishop and his wife, Violet—an old-fashioned name for a very up-to-date lady, Randollph thought—were the first guests to be admitted by Clarence.

"You've had quite a day, C.P., if the news reports are to be believed," the bishop said.

"I haven't heard the news, Freddie—" (he must remember not to call the bishop Freddie when the other guests were present) "—but it isn't every day you pay a pastoral call and find that one of your parishioners has quite recently been done in with a baseball bat."

"How awful for you!" the bishop's wife said and patted Randollph's hand.

The other guests were not long in arriving. Sammy had a rule that members of the staff of Good Shepherd were entertained separately from her parties for "people I like a lot." But Dan Gantry was the exception to the rule. He'd been her friend for a long time, had introduced her to Randollph, and—unlike some of Good Shepherd's employees—he always pepped up the party. He was wearing a maroon Edwardian-style dinner jacket.

"I thought Edwardian was out of style," Sammy twitted him.

"It is," Dan said, "but I'm a man whose own excellent

taste is not influenced by the whims of the tailor. Edwardian becomes me. May I present Leah Aspinwall? Leah, Dr. and Mrs. C. P. Randollph." Leah was a petite and self-assured brunette who said to Sammy, "You're even more beautiful in person than on television," and to Randollph, "According to Dan you are one of the greatest men alive today."

"I paid her to say that," Dan said. "Where's the booze?"

Lieutenant Michael Casey, looking as elegant in a dinner jacket as he did in his working clothes, arrived next with his bouncy blond wife, Liz, closely followed by Lamarr and Louise Henderson. Sticky Henderson, tall and black, had been Randollph's favorite receiver and best friend when they had played for the Rams. Sticky had lost a step or two in speed but was still good enough to play for the Chicago Bears. Louise Henderson was large, beautiful and looked like a lady who sat under sun lamps to keep a nice warm tan.

Last to arrive were Thea Mason and a man Randollph judged to be about his own age, several inches less than six feet, with thinning brown hair and intelligent eyes.

"You must be Father Richard Purdy," Randollph greeted him, "though I see no Roman collar. I'm C. P. Randollph."

"Yes, I know." Purdy had a surprisingly firm handshake for a small, thin man. "I hardly ever wear one. One of the blessings of being an editor instead of a pastor. I know your beautiful wife from several appearances on her show. And I've been associated with Miss Mason through our common profession."

"Not much similarity between a gossip column and a Catholic newspaper," Thea Mason said. Randollph was glad to see that Thea had bypassed her customary semitopless evening gowns for a relatively modest number in orange and white. Her skin was darker than Louise Henderson's, achieved no doubt under the sun lamp that Louise Henderson didn't need. Her dark hair and long earrings gave Thea the look of a prosperous gypsy.

"Oh, I don't know, Thea," Father Purdy said. "I think the editor of a Catholic newspaper and a gossip columnist have a lot in common. We just gossip about different subjects."

Randollph thought he was going to like Father Purdy.

Annette served the guests, now at table, plates of cold red ham sliced very thin, accompanied by a crescent of golden melon.

"For once, Clarence, I don't have to ask what's in a dish. Prosciutto and melon," the bishop said. "One of my favorites."

"One of Dr. Randollph's favorites, too, m'lord. I was able to obtain prosciutto of unusual quality from one of my purveyors. The melon is from Spain. I'm sure you'll enjoy it." He left Annette to finish with the first course and returned to the kitchen.

"I'm full of questions," Leah Aspinwall said. "Would it be rude of me to ask some of them?"

"Ask and ye shall receive, seek and ye shall find," Dan Gantry said.

"Well, you see, Dan hadn't prepared me for any of this. He just said, 'How'd you like to go to a dinner party with me, long dress, at my boss's place? His wife's Sam Stack.'" She looked reprovingly at Dan. "Of course I didn't want to pass up an opportunity to meet the famous Sam Stack. I haven't been going out with Dan very long. I knew he was a clergyman, that's about all—although I must say he doesn't fit my image of the Protestant clergy. He doesn't talk or behave like—"

"Enough," Dan said. "No personal revelations permitted."

"I'd be interested in hearing them," Sammy said.

"I'll tell you sometime when he's not around. You see, I'm Jewish, and I kind of had the idea that the Christian clergy is poor. So Dan brings me to this absolutely glorious penthouse—I've never seen anything like the view. And there's butler, or chef, and a maid—well, I don't get it."

"I can understand your confusion," the bishop said kindly. "Your image of the Protestant clergy is correct, or nearly so. Most of them are grossly underpaid for what they are asked to do. The Church of the Good Shepherd is an exception. It has been here a long time, has accumulated about ten million dollars in endowments, and owns the office building and hotel in which it is located. This parsonage, this penthouse that dazzles you, is part of the church building."

"But a majordomo or chef? I belong to a large temple and our head rabbi is very well paid. But he doesn't have anything like this. Why'd he call you 'm'lord'?"

"Because," the bishop explained, "Clarence is English. He is also a loyal adherent to the Church of England. It is the custom to address Church of England bishops as 'your lordship' or 'm'lord.' Clarence insists on so addressing me, though in his eyes I am not a bishop of the one true church. He would address Father Purdy's bishop the same way, though by his lights the Roman Catholic Church is merely another nonconformist sect. I must say it is good for my ego to be addressed as m'lord."

"I sometimes wonder if we aren't just another Christian sect," Father Purdy said. "My cardinal archbishop accuses me of thinking it, anyway."

"I'm a Baptist," Sticky Henderson said. "I wouldn't know, but the way I hear it you have to do what your bishop says. How come he doesn't just fire you?"

"My word, Sticky, you have certainly changed your idiom. What happened to the locker room jive, the black patois?" Randollph asked.

Sticky grinned at him. "I'm getting ready to enter the world of culture and business. I'm a college man, remember? The kind of people I plan to be dealing with wouldn't appreciate the way I used to talk."

"He's improving his manners generally," Louise Henderson commented.

"What part of the world of culture and business are you planning to enter?" Randollph asked.

"Announcement to come later," the big black man said. "I want to hear why Father Purdy's bishop doesn't fire him. Even a Baptist hears this cardinal archbishop runs things kind of like old Adolf ran Germany."

Father Purdy laughed, a sort of joyous cackle, Randollph thought. "I'd dearly love to quote that in *The Catholic Reporter.*"

"Don't use my name," Sticky said. "I expect to have a lot of mackerel-snappers—sorry, Father, R.C.s—as customers. Don't want to offend them."

"The answer to your question, Mr. Henderson, is that politics keeps him from sending me to some obscure parish in Catholic Siberia. *The Catholic Reporter* is not a diocesan paper. It is independent. It is, like Dr. Randollph's church, endowed. And it has a board of directors which, according to our bylaws, has sole responsibility for hiring and firing the editor. Also, we have a large circulation for which I get credit whether I deserve it or not. We were established after Vatican II, and are what you might call the voice of the liberal Catholics. The consequences of summarily removing me would be more unpleasant for His Eminence than the pain of tolerating me. So he makes do with snubbing me personally and ordering the editor of the diocesan paper to say something nasty about my paper in almost every issue. He is too bullheaded to realize that these attacks help our circulation."

"Sounds like a mean cat, His Eminence," Sticky said.

"Lamarr," Louise reproved him, "watch how you talk."

"Yeah," Sticky said. "His Eminence would appear to be an authoritative and vindictive person. That better?"

"Much," Louise said.

"That pretty well describes him," Father Purdy said. "Half our priests are in rebellion against him."

"We have some bishops like the cardinal in our denomination," the bishop added.

Annette came in pushing a serving cart carrying a silver soup tureen and began ladling a brownish liquid into exquisite ceramic bowls. When she served the bishop she said shyly, "Clarence said you would ask about the soup, sir. It is chestnut soup. It contains chopped carrots, leeks, celery, and onions browned in olive oil. Then chestnuts, chicken stock, parsley and cloves are added. After simmering until the vegetables are soft, the soup is pureed, cream and brandy are added, and everything is brought to a boil."

"I don't need to know what's in it to know that it is delicious," Lieutenant Casey said.

"Second that," Liz Casey said.

"Perhaps I am of a curious nature, but dining on Clarence's cuisine is, for me, educational as well as fattening." The bishop glanced down at his plump belly straining the cummerbund obviously purchased in slimmer years.

"You haven't said anything about that body you found this afternoon," Thea Mason accused Randollph. "I'm expecting something from you for tommorrow's column."

"*Verboten!*" Sammy snapped. "Not a subject for dinner table conversation. Ask him after dinner."

"Yes, mine hostess." Thea exaggerated her contrition. "But ask him I will. After all, I was maid of honor at his wedding. That should entitle me to something."

"I'll give you an item for your column, Thea, as long as you don't attribute it to me." Randollph observed that Father Purdy knew how to divert a conversation headed for murky waters back into clear and rippling streams.

"Shoot, Reverend Father," Thea said.

"It's this. His Eminence the cardinal archbishop is planning a twenty-one-gun, don't-spare-the-ammunition campaign to grab some tax money for parochial schools."

"So what's new about that? He's always yammering away about that," Thea replied.

"What's new is that he's formed a coalition with the Association of Christian Academies."

"You mean those schools the Fundamentalists are starting?" asked Thea.

"Not starting. Well, yes, new ones pop up every day. But you'd be amazed at how many of them there are. They're already big business. They print textbooks. They have brigades of consultants who—for a fee, of course—will advise and help you to start a Christian academy. And they lobby hard for tax money. The cardinal figures why not join them. It would remove the onus of a Roman Catholic raid on tax funds—there's still plenty of anti-Roman feeling around. But if you include the Protestants, you lend an aura of ecumenicity to the campaign."

"Clever, very clever," the bishop said.

"Parochial schools are a pain in the-ah-neck," Lieutenant Casy said. "I went to one. Too much catechism—which was just a way of teaching bad theology by rote.

And too much worship of football, begging your pardon, Dr. Randollph."

"But you're still a Catholic?" Father Purdy inquired.

"Yes, I hung in there from habit. Then at the university I was lucky to have some teachers who made sense out of Catholic belief." Randollph suppressed a grin. Casey wanted people to know he was a college man and not just another dumb Irish cop. A forgivable spiritual pride.

"Oh, don't be so holy, Mike," Liz Casey chided him. "You may understand Catholic theology, but I have trouble every Sunday getting you up in time for Mass."

"You have me there, Liz." Casey was smiling. "But you know as well as I do that our pastor is an old bore. Who'd be anxious to get out of a warm bed to hear the same old sermon every week—don't miss Mass, don't miss your weekly payments, don't miss confession, don't practice birth control...." Casey shook his head as if wearied by the thought of what an enlightened Catholic layman had to endure.

Clarence and Annette pushed in a cart heavy with large covered platters. Clarence, with the brisk but almost negligent motions of a man who knew precisely what he was doing, began filling plates and passing them to Annette to serve. As she served the bishop, Clarence said: "Herbed veal chops, m'lord. A simple dish, really. Thick chops, dredged lightly in flour, sautéed in butter. Remove the chops, add white wine to the stock in the pan, cook over high heat. Then add chives, tarragon and parsley—chopped, of course—swirl in a bit more butter, then pour the sauce over the chops. I've accompanied the chop with green noodles tossed in butter. The bland taste of the noodles is a nice counterpoint to the seasoned veal. I have a high regard for veal—proper veal, that is. Not the young cow so often sold in the markets as veal." Clarence let a little contempt into his voice. "Fortunately, I know a purveyor who does his own butchering. He has not failed me yet."

"He hasn't failed you this time," the bishop assured Clarence. "I doubt that the tables in heaven could improve on this."

"Thank you, m'lord." He began to pour red wine from a crystal decanter. "I've decanted the wine, but have determined that it is of excellent quality. It is from a small California vineyard, but has the character of a good French Beaujolais, and, in my opinion, is the equal of the French product. There are extra chops in the kitchen. Mr. Gantry usually requests a second helping. Others may wish to join him."

"Count me in," Sticky Henderson said.

"Me too," Casey said.

"You've but to ring when you wish them served," Clarence replied as he and Annette left for the kitchen.

"I can't get over it, I just can't get over it," Leah Aspinwall said, more to herself than to the others. "That tiny bald-headed man, brown as an Indian, talks like an English duke and prepares food that only a few restaurants in Chicago could match."

"Well, we both work," Sammy told her, "and I never know when I'll get home. Someone has to look after us, feed us."

"Dan, will you marry me?" Leah asked. "Of course, I'll expect a penthouse and a Clarence."

"Plenty of penthouses around, dear girl," Dan answered between bites, "but only one Clarence. You'll just have to make do with my handsome appearance, charming personality, and brilliant mind. What more could any girl ask?"

"Well, I couldn't marry you anyway. You're a Christian and I'm a Jew—a liberal Jew, but not liberal enough to convert to Christianity."

"Maybe I could become a rabbi," Dan said. "I'd make a great rabbi. All Christians are Jews, anyway."

"Now what does that mean?"

"Ask the boss. I'm just quoting from one of his recent sermons."

When Leah looked at Randollph questioningly, he said to her: "It means just what it says, Miss Aspinwall. Jesus was a Jew. His religion was the Jewish faith. Everything he said and taught had its source in Judaism. He had no intention of starting a new religion. He wanted his own people to understand and practice the faith of Israel as it was meant to be understood and practiced."

"Then why did Christianity become a separate religion?"

"It didn't at first." Randollph was enjoying this, but supposed that he sounded like a stuffy old pedant to Leah Aspinwall's young ears. Well, she'd asked for information, so he might as well give it to her. "Christianity was originally a Jewish sect in Asia Minor. It recognized Jesus as the promised Messiah, but it never caught on in Asia. It found its real growth when it turned west. It had a tremendous appeal to the gentiles, to the Greeks and the Romans."

"And they separated Christianity from Judaism?" She seemed genuinely interested, Randollph thought.

"They tried. There was a movement to discard the Jewish scriptures, the Old Testament, and make Christianity over into a gentile religion."

"And?"

"Fortunately, it failed. The church fathers said that the Jewish scriptures were too precious, too much a part of the Christian faith to be discarded. They sensed that there was no way to understand Jesus apart from the faith which produced him. And that, Miss Aspinwall, is why all Christians are Jews—spiritual Jews."

Leah Aspinwall continued to look amazed. "Dan told me you were once a famous professional football player—I don't know anything about football, I think it's boring—so I expected you to talk like those athletes who—"

"Jocks for Jesus," Dan said.

"And you don't talk like them at all. I thank you for making something clear to me that I've never understood."

"He didn't always talk like a scholar and gentleman, miss," Sticky Henderson said. "Why, when I'd drop an easy pass, he'd chew my—he spoke harshly to me. He used words that would curl your pretty little ears, old Con here did. The mind of a confidence man and the tongue of a sailor, that's what the sportswriters said about him."

"Then let him be an example for you, Lamarr. If Dr. Randollph could put all that—that football talk behind him and learn to speak like a scholar and a gentleman, so can you." Louise Henderson, Randollph could see, was enjoying herself. Her gentle, husky voice took the sting out of her words.

"I'm tryin', I'm tryin', Louise honey. I am not a scholar, but I sure as—but I aspire to be a gentleman. At least talk like one."

Sammy announced: "We do not follow the barbaric custom of the ladies withdrawing after dinner, leaving the men to cigars and port—not in this house." She rang for Clarence, who came in quickly. He whisked glasses and bottles from the recesses of a cabinet.

"I can offer cognac and an assortment of liqueurs, as well as an excellent port, of course."

"I'll have the strong stuff," Dan Gantry announced.

"I'll join him," Casey said.

"Port," the bishop said. "Ah, this takes me back to my days at Oxford."

Thea and Dan lit cigarettes. Clarence said, "I have a selection of English market cigars if any of you gentlemen would care for one."

"I never smoke except here," the bishop said. "But I do enjoy one of Clarence's cigars."

"The bishop prefers a maduro, as do I." Clarence offered a box of dark panatelas to the bishop. "They appear to the eye as perhaps extrastrong, but they are not. I fancy a good cigar myself. I have claros also."

"My daddy was a strict Baptist preacher, and he'd want you Christian gentlemen to ask yourselves, 'Would Jesus smoke a cigar?'" Thea Mason said as she lit another cigarette.

"Well, would he, Reverend Randollph?" There was a bit of the imp in Leah Aspinwall, Randollph decided.

"The boss won't answer you if you call him reverend," Dan Gantry told her.

"Why not? He's a reverend, isn't he?"

"Reverend is an adjective, not a title, he says. It's Reverend Mister, or Reverend Doctor, or Reverend Father."

"My, this is an educational evening for a Jewish girl," Leah said.

"Just one of the lost causes for which I continue to battle bravely," Randollph said. "Not an issue crucial to the survival of the faith." He sniffed the long dark cigar Clarence had given him. "Would Jesus smoke this? You've asked a doctrinal question, Miss Aspinwall."

"I have? I didn't mean to."

"It's hard to ask questions that don't have their answers in doctrines and theologies, especially if one takes his religion at all seriously. The answer to your question, for a Christian, depends on your view of Jesus."

"Don't all Christians have the same view of Jesus?"

"By no means. The traditional, the orthodox view is that Jesus was God. There are all kinds of variations within this concept of Jesus. But if you believe that the first and fundamental truth about Jesus is the incarnation—that he was God—well, people have difficulty thinking of God as smoking a cigar."

"My pastor at St. Aloysius would be shocked at the very idea, though he is seldom without a cigar in his mouth," Casey said.

"You don't believe Jesus was God incarnate, Doctor?" Father Purdy asked.

Randollph pondered his answer. "I have some difficulty with it, especially as it is usually presented in creeds and doctrinal statements. If I am permitted to define 'incarnation' and 'son of God,' then I can believe it, although it is utterly beyond proof. It has to be accepted as an article of faith."

"You theologians just mess up Christianity," Dan Gantry said. "Jesus said he came to help the poor, free the captives and liberate those who are oppressed. That's what Christianity is all about. Don't need a lot of doctrine to understand that."

The bishop added, "Perhaps Miss Aspinwall would be interested to know that Jesus was quoting from the book of Isaiah when he said that."

"I told you I'd make a good rabbi," Dan said.

"That's nice, but I'd still like to know if Jesus would smoke a cigar," she persisted.

"I'll have to oversimplify to give you an answer." Randollph felt a little foolish talking Christian doctrine at a dinner party. "The other half of the orthodox view of Jesus is that he is not only fully God but fully man—fully human. Throughout its history, the Christian church has had little trouble accepting Jesus as God. But it has all sorts of difficulties with the idea that he was human. Yet the synoptic gospels—"

"The what?" Leah asked.

"Matthew, Mark and Luke," Dan Gantry told her. "Called that because they all tell the same story."

"You practicin'—practicing to become a scholar, Elmer?"

"I am a scholar, Sticky my man. I sweated three long years to earn a Master of Divinity degree, and I've got the sheepskin to prove it."

"Why does he call you Elmer?" Thea Mason asked.

"He had to read *Elmer Gantry* to pass some English course. He thinks it's cute to call me Elmer."

"I expect you get a lot of that," Father Purdy remarked.

"All the time. I let Sticky get away with it because he's bigger than I am."

"Sorry," Sticky said. "Let's get back to the cigar. Con, pray continue. I'd like to know the answer myself."

"The synoptic gospels, while they contain plenty of material reinforcing the idea that Jesus was the Messiah and the son of God, show us his humanity. They are honest about his convivial habits, and that the Pharisees said he liked food and wine too well. So the human Jesus, who enjoyed God's created world—if the gospels are accurate—yes, I think he would enjoy not only one of Clarence's dinners, but also one of Clarence's cigars."

"I wish my daddy could have heard that," Thea Mason said. "I may quote you in my column—'prominent pastor says Jesus would enjoy a good cigar.'"

"Raise a howl from the Christers," Dan said.

"The what?" Leah asked.

"That's what we call the super-pious Jesus-worshipers," Dan informed her. "Very prickly people."

"Well, maybe I won't quote him, but I'd like something on that old man you found murdered. The news said you were paying a pastoral call."

Randollph told the story of his visits to Johannes Humbrecht. "And that's all I really know about him," he added.

"I've found out a few things about him," Lieutenant Casey said.

"Like what?" Thea asked. "Do you mind if I take notes, Sam?"

"Of course not."

Thea excavated a notebook and ball-point pen from her large purse. "Ready when you are, Mike."

"Tomorrow's papers will tell you that Humbrecht—Dr. Humbrecht, he had a doctorate from the University of Tübingen—was eighty-five years old, had taught history at Northwestern for many years. Modern European history was his field. And that there is no apparent motive for the murder. Murders without motive are the hardest kind to solve," he added.

"Give me some inside stuff if you have it, Mike. I'm a columnist, not a reporter."

"O.K. We've asked around—neighbors, shopkeepers, people who have lived there or operated businesses in that area for years."

"And?"

"The papers will have stories about him being a recluse, about the junk-filled house—we've sealed it, but eventually we'll have to search it. I don't envy anyone that job."

"You mean you won't be doing the searching, Mike?" Thea was making rapid notes.

"A good executive knows how to delegate work."

"He sure does," Liz Casey added. "He'd delegate all the dishwashing, cleaning, shopping, and errand-running to me if I'd let him."

"As I was saying before this beautiful lady interrupted me with her irrelevant comments, the papers will have stories about Humbrecht being like one of the Collier brothers. What they won't have is that he wasn't like that until about twenty years ago."

"What happened twenty years ago?"

"He reached the age for mandatory retirement from his teaching post, and his wife died. After these two events, coming close together, he changed, seldom left his mansion except on foraging trips to collect the junk—twenty years' collection that we'll have to sift through."

"Did he have any money?"

"Apparently only his pension, probably Social Security. Can't keep up a mansion on that. Curious thing, though. He wife was wealthy in her own name—inherited money. But she left every nickel to a small Catholic order. She was an ardent Catholic, and he so Dr. Randollph tells me—was very loyal to the Church of the Good Shepherd."

"Funny name for a church in the middle of a city," Leah Aspinwall said. "How many of your members have ever been nearer a sheep than a roast leg of lamb?"

"Hush, child, I'll explain it to you later, you're interrupting Mike's story," Dan said.

"Are you intimating that the shock of having his wife leave her fortune to charity and nothing to him made him go bonkers?" Thea asked.

"Maybe," Casey answered. "But here's a strange thing. Everyone who knew them said the Humbrechts were very much devoted to each other. They had no children."

"That's the kind of stuff I'm looking for," Thea said with satisfaction. "What was she like, Mrs. Humbrecht? Anybody tell you that?"

"Not me personally. But a couple of my men found people who'd known them. Mrs. Humbrecht had a sparkling personality, was witty and extremely bright."

Randollph added, "He often spoke of her to me. Always with love and affection."

"Then here we have a mystery." Thea scribbled rapidly. "Why did loving and devoted wife cut her loving and devoted husband out of her will? I love a mystery. My readers love a mystery. Thanks, Mike. May I quote you by name?"

"I don't see why not." Randollph realized that Casey was not at all bashful about having his name in the press these days. Was he bucking for a promotion?

"You'll be conducting Humbrecht's funeral, C.P.?" the bishop asked.

Randollph hadn't thought about it. "I suppose so, when Lieutenant Casey releases the body."

"Couple of days."

"What does the C.P. stand for?" Leah Aspinwall asked.

"Cesare Paul," Randollph answered.

"Cesare sounds sinister."

"I expect my mother had been reading romantic novels when she picked that name. She balanced it with a solid saint's name." He thought about the Christian disposal of Johannes Humbrecht's remains. There were no living relatives, or so Humbrecht had told him. If he'd left a will, who'd find it in that debris-crammed house? Since there were no relatives, and since there was little likelihood of a will turning up, Randollph supposed it was incumbent on him to make the arrangements as well as to conduct the rites. And, no doubt, pay the bills. He didn't mind. He wasn't going to let his friend be buried by the county.

4

BUT JOHANNES HUMBRECHT had left a will. It surfaced the day after Sam's dinner party.

It was Friday. Randollph's sermon for Sunday was finished. He'd go over it, tighten and polish it a bit on Saturday. Then, before breakfast on Sunday morning, he'd go over it two more times, scribble in an additional sentence here, delete one there, be sure he had it well in mind.

But he had a rule, frequently broken by an exceptionally busy week or an unanticipated demand on his time, that Sunday's sermon be in manuscript form by the end of Thursday. If he didn't have Thursday as a personal deadline, he wound up scratching around frantically on Saturday finding something to say that would get him by, at least, on Sunday morning.

During his days as a teacher at the seminary, informing future bishops, ecclesiastical bureaucrats, and managers of sacred institutions why St. Augustine renounced the pleasures of the flesh for the joys of piety, or that Charlemagne maybe wasn't as surprised to be crowned the first Holy Roman Emperor as he let on, life had been vastly different. For one thing, seminary professors didn't have to fabricate a fresh homily every week. You mastered your field, you knew your material, and you taught the same courses year after year. It kept you on your toes a bit. If you were at all conscientious you had to keep up your reading in your field. But church history was made up of what was accepted as established facts. Randollph suspected that like any kind of history the facts weren't entirely factual. The ancients were notoriously careless about accurate dating. And being no different in nature from modern historians, they shaded the facts for or against a person or a movement or a reform to suit their personal prejudices.

At any rate, teaching church history to seminarians who probably thought their time would be better employed studying money raising, organizational skills, and public relations techniques was a relaxed kind of job compared to the business of being pastor of a church. A professor didn't have to deal with budgets—that was Dean Freddie's responsibility, or had been until he became a bishop.

And a professor had a power over the students that was built into the structure of the profession. Randollph had always tried to make his lectures interesting, to communicate his own fascination with the history of the Christian faith—its high moments and its low moments, its saints and scoundrels, its martyrs and its blackguards. It was a complex and tightly woven tapestry, this story that ran all the way from Jesus to the latest imbecilities of the church militant. But whether his students caught his enthusiasm or not, they had to listen. They had to attend class for a reasonable amount of time, because Professor Randollph gave exams and made out their grades.

No one, though, had to attend upon the Reverend Dr. Randollph's preaching. Whatever the reason they came—to worship God, to hear the superb music Good Shepherd provided, to see and hear a famous ex-pro quarterback preach—their coming was a voluntary act. They weren't there to pass a course and gain a credit. The kind of people who believed that faithful attendance upon divine worship would help some when they shuffled off this mortal coil were unlikely to be in the congregation at Good Shepherd. So the preacher was under pressure to turn out a cracking good sermon Sunday after Sunday, or he'd get himself classified as a bore. People would say, "Who wants to hear him? We've only got this one Sunday in town, let's not waste it. I hear the preacher at Fourth Presbyterian has a beautiful Welsh accent."

So Randollph tried to set aside one day per week to work on sermons scheduled for some Sundays hence. When he got to his office that morning he told Miss Windfall he'd be busy working on sermons, which meant that she was to intercept any interruptions, whether by phone or by a visitor who could just as well drop by another time. Randollph was aware that Miss Windfall considered the time he spent on sermon preparation as unnecessary, and even a mark of inadequate professional competence. She looked upon Dr. Arthur Hartshorne, Randollph's predecessor, as the very model of a modern clergyman, and Dr. Hartshorne had never wasted time in sermon preparation.

"Old Artie just told stories, mostly about himself," Dan Gantry told Randolph. "Made 'em up, probably. He'd start out with some stupid little moral, then smother it in stories. Told the stories real well, though."

But though she might disapprove of his use of time just as she probably disapproved of his haberdashery as too fashionable for a clergyman, Miss Windfall would protect him. She had an unerring knowledge of who rated the right of interruption and who should be shooed off to call again another day.

He was planning a series of sermons, The Seven Deadly Sins. With an introductory sermon, that would take eight Sundays—just enough to squeeze in the series before the Christian calendar changed to Advent. Each sermon had to hold up by itself, because much of the congregation that packed Good Shepherd every Sunday was made up of one-timers: tourists and conventioneers collecting one more experience from their visit to the big city to take home to Altoona or Grand Forks or Dodge City.

He jotted down the deadly sins on a piece of scratch

paper: pride, avarice, sloth, gluttony, envy, anger and lust. He'd have to start with pride, because pride was the parent of all the other sins. That's what the Bible said. That's what sound Christian theology had always claimed. Perhaps he could—

The imperfectly wired intercom crackled into life. He said, "Yes, Miss Windfall," trying to keep the annoyance out of his voice.

"Mr. J. J. Knox is calling you."

Miss Windfall did not explain that Mr. Knox claimed his business was urgent. Even though Mr. Knox's pedigree as a member of Good Shepherd stretched back through enough ancestors to meet Miss Windfall's exacting standards for the top layer of church and Chicago society, she would have ascertained that he hadn't called on some frivolous matter.

Randollph punched the plastic button winking at him from the base of the phone, and at the same time recalled his information about J. J. Knox. He was the senior partner in Knox, Knox, and Elder, a prosperous and highly regarded law firm with a reputation for competence and integrity. He was a member of Good Shepherd's governing board, and he acted as usher at Sunday service once a month. Though he had frequent contact with the man, Randollph didn't know him well. He doubted that anyone did.

"Good morning, Mr. Knox, it is an unexpected pleasure to hear from you," Randollph lied. It probably wasn't even a lie, Randollph reflected. It would be understood in heaven, though not conforming exactly to the truth, as the kind of prevarication a busy and conscientious pastor needed to employ from time to time for the greater good of Christ's church.

"Good morning, Dr. Randollph." The precise accents were neither friendly nor unfriendly. "I have a rather peculiar piece of information for you. I've read about the passing of Mr. Johannes Humbrecht. We were his attorneys."

Why, Randollph wondered, did Humbrecht need an attorney? Mr. Knox supplied the answer immediately.

"We are in possession of Humbrecht's last will and testament."

"Oh, you drew his will. I can't imagine that he had

much to leave, considering the way he lived. There's the house, of course, such as it is."

"We have no idea what's in the will," replied Knox.

"Oh, I thought—"

"That we drafted it? No, we are in possession of it."

Randollph didn't know what to say. Knox sought to enlighten him. "Mr. Humbrecht came to us a year ago. He stated that he had chosen us because we—I—am a member of Good Shepherd. And because we have a name for integrity. He stated that he didn't trust lawyers as a profession, but that everyone said Knox, Knox, and Elder was entirely trustworthy."

"It pleased you to hear that, I'm sure." Randollph thought that Mr. J. J. Knox was suffering from a small case of spiritual pride.

"Yes," Knox continued. "We place a high value on our reputation. Mr. Humbrecht had a document which he wanted us to certify as his last will and testament. It was typed and clipped in a binder. He wanted to sign it, have it notarized, and leave it in our possession against the day of his death. Considering his age, he was realistic enough to know that day couldn't be far distant. But he didn't want us to read it."

"That's unusual."

"Yes, but we are seldom surprised by extraordinary requests by clients. I suspect it was the facet of his personality that had turned him into a recluse which prompted the request."

Randollph began to wonder what all this had to do with him.

"He had us place it in an extra-heavy manila envelope and seal it with wax with the firm's imprint on it. And that's why we have no idea what's in the will. We do know, however, the names of those individuals and institutions it names as beneficiaries."

"I confess that I'm confused."

"It's quite simple. He left in our care another envelope with instructions that we open it immediately upon learning of his death. We opened it this morning. It contains the list of beneficiaries." Knox paused, then said: "You are named as a beneficiary, Dr. Randollph, as is the Church of the Good Shepherd."

Randollph was speechless.

"Would it be convenient for you to attend the reading of the will at our offices on Monday morning at ten o'clock?"

It passed through Randollph's mind that there went another morning of study and sermon preparation shot to hell. "Of course. I'll be there," he said politely.

"Thank you. And by the way, Humbrecht also left instructions for the conduct of his funeral. You're to be in charge. I'll send the instructions to your office by messenger." Knox hung up.

Randollph tilted back in the commodious and expensive executive chair purchased to accommodate the generous posterior of Dr. Arthur Hartshorne, and tried to make sense out of the fact that Humbrecht had left a will—or rather, that he had left a will and named a number of beneficiaries. Though Randollph always found Humbrecht lucid of mind and capable of sprightly discourse on any number of subjects, he supposed that the old gentleman was, by definition, addled. Only someone with something missing in mind or personality would become a recluse and hoard mountains of junk as if it were piles of gold or rubies. Perhaps Humbrecht had actually believed that this debris was worth millions, and he must dispose of it through a will! Well, he'd find out Monday morning. He sighed and resumed his work.

But this was not Randollph's day to write sermons about sin. The intercom sputtered again. "The bishop is here to see you," Miss Windfall announced. Bishops, Miss Windfall believed, took precedence over governors, captains of industry, and even movie stars. People like that had to make appointments. But not a bishop.

"Good morning, C.P.," the bishop greeted Randollph as he selected the most comfortable chair available. "I always think how convenient it is to have the episcopal office in this building. I don't even have to put on a hat when I wish to see you. Are you busy?"

"Of course I'm busy, Freddie." Randollph thought that the bishop didn't look much like people expected a bishop to look. He looked like a well-fed aging cherub. "I'm busy planning a series of sermons on the seven deadly sins."

"Sin is not a popular pulpit subject these days," the

bishop said. "Except, of course, with the Fundamentalists, though they haven't the remotest idea of what they're talking about. Good people, sincere people, at least some of them. But too many of them equate sin with failure to follow the culture patterns they deem to be good, indulgence in habits they frown on, refusal to assent to some creedal statement, or the lack of some emotional experience by which Jesus consents to come into your heart."

"Maybe you could write these sermons for me, Freddie," Randollph suggested.

"Oh, I expect I could. I did my share of preaching on the subject in my days as a pastor. People listened then."

"They don't listen now?"

"Let me put it this way, C.P. If you asked the average seminary student today how he rated the importance of preaching in the professional skills he hopes to acquire, he'd reply with 'preaching's not where it's at today,' or with some equally abominable phrase. The day of great preaching is, for the moment at least, in eclipse."

"You discourage me, Freddie. Miss Windfall thinks I spend an inordinate amount of time on my sermons. I take it you agree with her."

"Oh, not at all." The bishop crossed one short plump leg over the other and slumped into a more comfortable position. "Though as an administrator I'm usually inclined to flow with the tide of things as they are at the moment, and even encourage my pastors to do the same, I'm quite aware that the high spots in the history of the faith were brought about mostly by stubborn spirits who insisted on marching to their own drum, whether it was in tune with the times or not. But I didn't come here to lecture on homiletics. I had a call from J. J. Knox this morning. It seems that your late Mr. Humbrecht left a will and named me as a beneficiary. I thought you might be able to shed some light. I never met the man, yet he evidently bequeathed me something. I was under the impression that he was a pauper."

"So was I, Freddie. I also had a call from Mr. Knox. I, too, am a beneficiary, as is the Church of the Good Shepherd. Mr. Knox indicated that other institutions are also named. He didn't enlighten me as to who they are or how many."

"Knox only tells you what you need to know—an admirable trait in an attorney, though not personally endearing."

"You know him, Freddie?"

"Yes. We've used his firm for years as attorneys for the denomination. One does not need to feel affection for one's lawyer so long as he serves one well."

"You don't like him?"

"I didn't say that," the bishop protested. "I confess he puts me off a bit with his starchy uprightness. He gets it across to you in so many subtle ways that no moral blemish has ever smirched either the family or the firm's escutcheons."

"Why, Freddie, a good bishop ought to applaud righteousness wherever he finds it."

"Oh, I do applaud it, C.P., especially in an attorney—a profession that has had a reputation for sleazy practices at least since Shakespeare's day. Mr. Knox's integrity contributes to the stability of society and the public good, just as the Pharisees' strict adherence to the law no doubt contributed to the stability of Israel. Yet I am not personally drawn to the Pharisees. I do not wish to emulate them. I feel the same way about Mr. Knox." The bishop stood up and smoothed the wrinkles from the knees of his trousers. "Well, I suppose all will be revealed Monday morning. I'll let you get back to contemplating the causes and varieties of human sinfulness."

After the bishop had gone, Randollph made what he considered an honest effort to get his mind back on sin. But it was no go. The gas was out of the balloon. Whatever inspiration he'd summoned had departed.

Unless he had a luncheon engagement Randollph went to the penthouse at noon to be fed by Clarence. His only alternatives were a flavorless sandwich in the hotel coffee shop, or a heavy mediocre meal in the hotel dining room. Also, he looked forward to what Clarence would set before him. He never knew what it would be, but he knew that it would be delicious.

Today it was something in a generous pastry shell.

"Scallops, Dr. Randollph," Clarence explained. "I cook them in clam broth and butter flavored with Worcestershire sauce, celery, salt, and dry mustard. When the scallops have cooked for about five minutes, I stir in tomato puree, bring to a boil, then add a bit of heavy cream. The salad is beets with a spiced dressing, my own recipe. I mix the vinegar, oil, and spices, heat it and pour it over the beets, then chill thoroughly before serving. Some people don't care for beets, but I know that you like them."

"Clarence, I know that you are a Christian man."

"I try to be, Dr. Randollph. None of us ever achieves the perfection of attitudes and behavior we strive for. What you would call a perfect state of grace."

"That's good theology. Now I want to ask you a theological question."

"Me, sir? That is your field of competence. Why do you ask me?"

"Because it has to do with your field of competence."

"In what way, sir?"

"Let me put it this way. Until you came into my household, I had what you would call no palate and didn't even think much about what I ate. Now I think about it. I anticipate my meals. I speculate about what you will be serving. I like to hear you describe a dish. Isn't this a spiritually unhealthy preoccupation with food?"

"Oh, not at all, sir. I should think just the opposite."

"You'll have to explain that to me, Clarence."

"Quite easily, sir. A person who voluntarily eats ill-prepared food is showing disrespect for God's creation. If I may say so, sir, what the average American restaurant serves constitutes blasphemy."

"Oh?" Randollph was surprised at the contempt in Clarence's voice.

"If I understand the story of creation in the book of Genesis—or the two creation stories in Genesis—the point is that what we have, all that we have, is a gift from God to us. And that we are to enjoy it. That means we are to treat the gift with reverence. You and madam work hard at your vocations. You try to do the best work possible. Am I not correct?"

"Correct." Randollph thought that anyone who did

not know Clarence would consider this short, completely bald Englishman, whose skin had been burned a permanent tan by the sun over the many seas he had sailed as a ship's chef, an unlikely source for theological insight.

"It is my vocation to look to your domestic needs," Clarence continued. "I try to provide quality food, well prepared and attractive. Eating is something we do every day to sustain life. If the food I serve you not only sustains the life of the body but at the same time lifts your spirits, then I have succeeded at my vocation. May I say, sir, that I take your interest in what I prepare as a great compliment." He cleared away the now empty dishes in front of Randollph. Then, as if he had expressed personal opinions more freely than was proper for a domestic, he said: "I have lemon pudding cake for dessert. I'm sure you will find it satisfactory."

Randollph went back to the office manfully determined to let Miss Windfall bully him into cleaning up the paper work that had been accumulating all week. He supposed it was some weakness in his genes that tempted him to put off doing work for which he had no appetite. When he was a teacher he'd been the same way about making out grades, and he always put off reading term papers which all too often were hastily thrown together or cribbed outright.

He arrived at the office almost simultaneously with Lieutenant Casey.

"Can we talk for a few minutes?" Casey asked.

"Of course," Randollph said. "Miss Windfall, see that we aren't disturbed." Miss Windfall's pleasant "Yes, Dr. Randollph" told Randollph that while she fully understood that he welcomed this temporary detour around his manifest duty, she rather liked Lieutenant Casey.

"Nice office, this," Casey said as he slumped into the scruffy brown leather sofa left over from the days of the Reverend Dr. Arthur Hartshorne. "Has that slightly tatty but expensive look you find in an English gentlemen's club." Casey had recently been to London on one of those trips on which the policemen from one country study the police methods of another country and was happy for opportunities to allude to it. "A Humbrecht will has turned up. That could be a break. Might supply a motive. That is, if the old boy really had some money. I hate murders without any motive, any apparent motive. Those are the ones that don't get solved." Casey sounded as if murders without apparent motive were designed to offend him personally.

"Perhaps I'll become a suspect," Randollph said. "Or maybe you prefer Freddie—the bishop. He had a motive too."

Casey sat up straight. "What are you talking about?"

"I'm named as beneficiary in the will. So is the bishop. I assume there are others as well."

"Now how in the world could you know that? You been holding out on me?"

Randollph laughed. Not a tactful thing to do, he supposed. But he didn't have too many opportunities to go one up on Casey.

"Mr. Knox called me, as I assume he called you, Lieutenant. He said that I was a beneficiary, as is the church, and invited me to the reading Monday morning. The bishop told me that he got the same kind of call from Mr. Knox."

"Well I'll be damned. Did he have anything to leave besides that house full of junk? How much are you down for?"

"I have no idea." Randollph told Casey about the sealed will.

"So that's it. I asked Knox about the beneficiaries and the terms of the will. You know what he said?"

"I expect he said something like 'that will be revealed Monday morning.'"

"Almost his words. You know the guy?"

"He's a member of Good Shepherd."

"I've half a notion to get a court order and force Knox to open the will today."

"I'd discard that half-notion if I were you, Lieutenant."

"Why?"

"Come, now, Lieutenant, a moment's reflection would tell you why. You're the chap they always send out when someone of political or social importance is involved. You have the manners and the education. You have the touch to deal with people like that. Well, Mr.

J. J. Knox is that kind of person. If you try to push him around, he'll shove back. He would know how to do it. He would have the political connections."

Casey stared glumly at his black patent loafers with little gold buckles across the front. "I don't like these shoes. I don't know why in hell I ever bought them." He sighed as if he had just given up on a cherished enterprise. "You knew Humbrecht better than anyone. You had any more thoughts about who did it or why? Anything."

"I assume you noticed the teacups. Humbrecht's shattered, the other one still on the table?"

"Of course. Tested the full cup for prints. Only Humbrecht's. We assume Humbrecht served that tea to a visitor. You don't serve tea to a stranger."

"Humbrecht would have," Randollph said. "But I also assumed that he'd had a visitor whom he knew. He always served me that special tea of his. I thought it tasted awful. And I wasn't too keen on drinking out of one of his cups. I think he'd just rinse them in cold water, that's about as far as he'd go. Whether the visitor was the murderer or not, I wouldn't know. I'm inclined to think so. And that it was someone he thought of as a friend, or at least someone with whom he was acquainted."

"So do we," Casey agreed. "Otherwise we'd put it down to some punks who probably heard the old man had a lot of money hidden in the house. People always believe that about a recluse, you know. It gets around. The probable treasure grows in each telling. Wonder someone hadn't tried it before."

"That's a rather good neighborhood where he lived," Randollph observed. "Old, but still respectable."

"Yes, but not many blocks away you get into pretty scummy places. They're full of young toughs who'd kill the Virgin Mary for a quarter." Casey meditated again on the shoes he wished he hadn't bought. "You have any idea how many people Humbrecht would have known well enough to invite in for a cup of tea?" He reached in his jacket pocket and brought out a pack of cigarettes. Randollph got up hastily from the old brown leather chair that matched the sofa and rummaged in a desk drawer for an ashtray. But Casey said, "Don't bother, Doctor. I'm quitting cigarettes," and put the pack back into his pocket. "Don't have the character to do it cold turkey."

Randollph sat down again. "I should think that at one time Humbrecht had an extensive circle of acquaintances. He often talked of people who served on the faculty with him at Northwestern. And there were his wife's friends. I gather that the Humbrechts had a busy social life. After her death he apparently cut himself off from former friends and acquaintances. But if someone, some acquaintance from the past, presented himself at the door he would invite him in. He was a gentleman, with European habits of hospitality. He'd insist on serving them something—that vile tea. And he wouldn't explain or even refer to the filthy conditions in which he lived. He never explained it to me, anyway. He never apologized for it, or indicated that it was in any way abnormal."

Casey looked gloomy. "That means we'll have to dig into his past, talk to people who knew him. Tedious work. You sure you never heard him mention any enemies, anyone who might have had it in for him?"

"No, none. Despite his abrupt change from one kind of person into another kind of person, he was a pleasant and polite man. A gracious man. It's hard to believe that he ever had an enemy, not one hostile enough to murder him."

"That baseball bat, the one the killer used to clobber him, would it have been in that junk in his house?"

"Very likely. He was an avid sports fan. European football was his favorite game—"

"You mean soccer?"

"Yes. He regretted it was not highly popular here. But he liked our football too, followed the Bears."

"Discouraging business, being a Bears fan."

"But baseball was his favorite American game. Claimed it was a derivative of cricket. He was a Cubs fan—"

"A real masochist," Casey said. "A Bears fan and a Cubs fan. I'd call it suicide if there was any way for him to have bopped himself with that bat."

"I expect you'll find all sorts of sports equipment when you go through all that junk, Lieutenant. I remember seeing footballs, soccer balls, tennis racquets—he had a high opinion of tennis. I don't recall ever having seen that baseball bat, but it was probably there. Every time I called on him the junk was different, or at least shifted around."

"You know what you're saying, don't you?"

Randollph knew, but he thought it would cheer Casey a little if he pretended ignorance. "What am I saying, Lieutenant?"

"You're saying that the killer knew the bat would be there, or something equally effective, to do the job. That is, if the murder was premeditated. Whoever did it had been there before. People planning to bash somebody's head in don't come to the door lugging a baseball bat."

"You know, you're right about that."

Casey was beginning to perk up. "The other possibility is that whoever did it hadn't planned to, but decided on the spur of the moment and the bat was handy."

"It's difficult to think of a third possibility," Randollph said.

"The second possibility would fit fine with the theory of young punks on a treasure hunt if it weren't for that damned tea. Some jokers break in and say where's the money, you don't say would you like a nice cup of tea." Casey got up to go. "Well, we'll start digging into Humbrecht's past. See you Monday morning—Knox at least had the courtesy to invite me to the reading of the will. And, Doctor, thanks for calming me down."

As he ushered Casey out of the study, Miss Windfall said, "A Father Richard Purdy asked that you call him as soon as possible." Miss Windfall didn't know who Father Richard Purdy was, so she couldn't calculate his importance rating. Therefore, she hadn't been able to brush off his call. That would be exceeding the limits of her authority, and Miss Windfall knew exactly where those boundary lines were located.

"Thank you, Miss Windfall. Will you ring him for me please?" Randollph went back to his office-study and shut the door, leaving Miss Windfall uninformed as to the standing and status of Father Purdy.

When he picked up the phone he said: "Father Purdy? Nice of you to call." How often, he wondered, did he utter such pleasant banalities each day? They were expected. They were useful in concealing irritation, or frustration, or any number of antisocial impulses. The banalities greased the wheels of human relationships, short-circuited rudeness, and helped keep people from strangling each other. But in this case Randollph meant it. He liked Father Richard Purdy.

"You may not appreciate my call all that much when you hear what it's about," Father Purdy said. "You remember what I told you—or rather, told Thea, last night at your dinner party? Which, by the way, was one of the most amazing and delightful evenings I've had in a long time. I mentioned the cardinal's campaign for tax funds for parochial schools?"

"I remember."

"Well, I thought at the time that the opening guns were to be fired in two or three weeks. His Eminence is an impatient man. Tomorrow's the day."

"That's very interesting," Randollph replied to the priest. He wondered what this had to do with him.

"I thought it wouldn't hurt to warn you," Father Purdy explained. "Two reporters just grilled me, and they are headed for your office. They said you are chairman of the Chicago Alliance of Churches' Committee on Ecumenical Concerns—"

"So I am," Randollph said. He had completely forgotten. The committee functioned at a sluggish pace. It mostly formulated pious statements for public consumption on the subject of church unity. These statements either deplored the disunity of Christ's church, or expressed holy optimism about that blessed day, soon to come it was hoped, when all Christians would be one in faith, one in hope and one in organizational unity. Everyone on the committee always voted for this longed-for spiritual utopia. They all knew, of course, that none of this meant a damned thing, and promptly went back to their parishes to resume the intense competition with the other churches in their parish areas. It had never occurred to Randollph that his committee would ever be called upon to pronounce on some current and controversial issue.

"And," Father Purdy continued, "they want an opinion from you on this campaign. They left here about twenty minutes ago. That would put them at your place in another ten or fifteen minutes."

"I appreciate the warning. It will give me time to collect my thoughts. Of course I can't speak for the committee." Randollph realized that he'd have to call a committee meeting, whether it contributed anything to the ushering in of Christ's Kingdom or not. He doubted that it would.

Father Purdy chuckled. "Oh, the reporters don't care about the committee. They just want a good story. They're grateful to have an excuse to interview the best-known Protestant pastor in town."

"Would you mind telling me how you handled them?" Randollph asked.

"Very, very carefully. I'm not looking for a confrontation with the cardinal on this one. He's awfully impulsive, and he doesn't intend to fail in this. If I came out square against it he might blow sky high and have my hide."

"You didn't endorse the campaign, surely?"

"No. I'm not that big a hypocrite. I didn't say anything against it. I pointed out that we—the editorial we—needed to clear up the legal problems that might arise, that neither I nor the cardinal would want to violate the Constitution. Of course, the part about the cardinal was a lie, and I shall be properly contrite when I make my next confession." Father Purdy's voice didn't sound as if this sin was weighing heavily on his Catholic conscience. "If they quote me on that, His Eminence will be much irritated with me, but he can't come out and say that he'd gladly violate the Constitution."

Randollph's respect for Father Richard Purdy went up a notch. He knew how to be the loyal opposition.

"Thanks again," Randollph said. "And, Father, keep in touch, will you?"

"Glad to. You do the same."

When the reporters arrived Miss Windfall sent them right in. She was always gracious to reporters. She believed that the press never did the Church of the Good Shepherd any good, but that it could do it a lot of harm. Reporters were to be handled with care.

There were two of them. A young black man dressed

in the style Lieutenant Casey favored. He introduced himself as Gordon Hickman of the *Trib*.

"This is Allie Stone, of the *Sun-Times*," he said. "Normally we're competitors, but we figured we had to have our stories for tomorrow and that the people we'd want to interview wouldn't stand for several reporters individually taking up their whole day. So we, along with some of the suburban papers, decided we'd better pool our efforts."

"You know what we want to talk about?" Allie Stone asked. She was a little older than Hickman, Randollph judged, and not so particular about her grooming. But she had an intelligent look about her. He doubted that anyone slipped anything by her.

"I have an inkling," Randollph answered her.

"You know about the cardinal's coalition with private Protestant schools to get tax funding?"

"I've heard rumors."

"Wants the city to pay parochial and Protestant schools the same amount per pupil as it spends to educate a student in the public schools. What do you think of that, Dr. Randollph?" Allie Stone was, apparently, the more aggressive of the two reporters. Or maybe they just took turns with the interviewees. But Randollph saw the trap in her question.

"What do I think of what, Miss Stone? What do I think of parochial schools, or what do I think of the cardinal's proposed method for financing them?"

"Would you endorse the plan, now that Protestant schools are included?"

"No."

"Even though it can be shown—or so the cardinal and the Protestant school administrators claim—that they do a much better job of educating the students than the public schools?"

"Perhaps they do, I don't know," Randollph said. "But the quality of their educational program is irrelevant."

Both Hickman and Stone scribbled in their notebooks. "May we quote you on that?" Hickman asked.

"If you get it straight. Don't make it come out that I said the quality of education in our schools is not important."

"Isn't that what you just said?" Hickman pressed him.

Randollph sighed. "Perhaps I wasn't entirely clear. What I want to say, what you may quote, is that the quality of education provided by parochial schools has nothing to do with the issue."

"Then what is the issue?" Allie Stone wrested control of the interview from Hickman.

"The issue, the only issue, is the Constitution of the United States. The Constitution makes it plain, or so it seems to me, that the state may not support any religion or religious endeavor no matter that the putative benefits of the endeavor would be a blessing to society."

"Whew!" Hickman said, "I hope I got that all down."

"I got it, Hick," Allie Stone said. "Then may we quote you, Doctor, as being unchangeably opposed to this proposal?"

"I suppose," Randollph said, "that anyone is foolish to say they will never change their minds. But, yes, you may quote me that I can't imagine any circumstances that would cause me to alter my position on this issue."

"Well," Hickman said, "at last we found a preacher who took a firm stand against the cardinal."

"It was about time," Allie Stone said.

5

THE GRAY-HAIRED MAN, expensively dressed and carefully groomed, was pacing up and down the large living room and swearing softly. He'd been doing this since last evening. Junior and Pack did their best to stay out of his sight.

The man's name was Christopher Bart. He'd started life on the island of Sicily as Cristoforo Bartelione. But as a young man, now a resident of the United States, he had seen the advantages of a classy-sounding native American name. It was easy to anglicize his real name, recorded in the parish records of the Sicilian village where he had been born.

Bart thought about how he'd patiently tracked this treasure of treasures for years. About the money he'd spent on detectives and specialists in tracing family trees, though the money didn't matter much to him. About the false leads and blind alleys. And always, of course, the chance that he was chasing a dream, a rumor, a legend born of someone's imagination stimulated by too much wine.

Bart had included these uncertainties in his calculations when he'd started the search. But the possibility that the story was true was worth the effort and the money. Now he was certain that the treasure of treasures actually existed. A man had been murdered for it. He'd seen the murderer. He'd seen him use a handkerchief to shut the door so as not to leave any fingerprints. A big man, six feet two inches or thereabouts. Dark hair, well-barbered, flecks of gray in it. Somewhere around forty, give or take a couple of years. Looked fit and strong. He could have tapped the old guy's skull with that heavy-looking bat using only one hand.

Bart would have seen the irony in the situation had he not been involved. If it had been someone else chasing a precious, very precious object for years, then—victory in sight—he'd arrived about fifteen minutes too late, just in time to witness the exit of the murderer and thief, Bart would have laughed and laughed and laughed.

Bart had not intended to kill the old man. Make him a reasonable offer for the treasure, even an unreasonably high offer. Or, if the old man was stubborn, persuade him. Bart knew how to persuade people. If the old guy kicked up too much of a fuss, he'd have killed him—after he had the treasure. Generally, though, killing was not good business. He'd done plenty of it, but only when it was the wisest alternative. Only when it was good business. He despised the stupid thugs who thought killing was the answer to every problem. He despised even more the brainless savages, some of whom he employed from time to time, who killed for the thrill, the pure sadistic pleasure they got out of it.

This fellow who had undoubtedly killed the old guy didn't look like the kill-for-the-fun-of-it type. He looked more like a successful businessman. Bart had trained himself to size up people quickly. It would have helped to talk to this fellow—people told you a lot about themselves by the way they talked. But he did have a clear photograph of the murderer printed on his mind. He'd been wearing a medium-gray, single-breasted three-piece suit, and a white shirt with broad blue stripes, plain blue tie. The suit jacket had the Brooks Brothers natural cut, no padding in the shoulders. But this chap had big shoulders, so Bart assumed the suit was the product of a good bespoke tailor.

But who was he? Not a banker or corporation executive. Bankers and corporation executives didn't wear that kind of shirt. A lawyer maybe. Or connected with an advertising agency. Or maybe some rich bastard who didn't work for a living.

But how to go about discovering who he was? It had to be done, but how? He'd murdered old Humbrecht for that priceless treasure the old man possessed. He'd beaten Bart to it by fifteen minutes or so, and Bart didn't like to lose—ever. And he was particularly enraged at losing this one, this enterprise, this chase, all those years of patient tracking. Success, the possession of the treasure, had become an obsession with him. He had to have it. Bart knew himself well enough to be aware that he was obsessed with it. He couldn't help it.

He began to think about ways to find out who had killed old Humbrecht and stolen the treasure. Private detectives? They might find out, but it would take them weeks, months. That wouldn't do him any good. Bart had plenty of connections among both the legitimate and not-so-legitimate. Maybe the police knew something. Well, he could find out.

Bart went into a little study off the living room. It had a phone that was checked every day for bugs. He looked up the number of a certain police station and punched it out. "Sergeant Hollister, please," he said to the policewoman on the switchboard.

"Hollister."

"I'm Harry's friend," Bart stated. "I'd like to talk. It will be helpful to you."

Anyone at the station listening in would have to conclude that this was one of Hollister's stoolies. Hollister, of course, knew exactly what it meant—that he was to call a certain number within fifteen minutes. Call from a public phone.

"I'll take care of it," Hollister said. Bart could hear the greed in his voice.

Fourteen minutes later the unlisted, bug-free phone rang. "Hollister," the caller said.

"I need information about the Humbrecht murder."

"The what?"

"The old man that was killed yesterday in his house on the north side, the old recluse."

"Oh, yeah, I heard a little about that. He was a nobody, so there isn't any excitement about it. What you need to know?"

"Who's handling the investigation?"

"That would be Mike Casey, Lieutenant Michael Casey."

"You know him?"

"Yeah. We're not intimate friends, if that's what you mean. He's one of the new breed on the force. Went to college." Hollister's tone implied that a cop who had gone to college automatically had a black mark against him.

"I want to know," Bart said, "what he knows about who killed the old guy. I also want to know what he finds out about this murder before he tells anyone else. Will ten bills be enough to, ah, to insure his cooperation?"

There was silence on the other end of the line.

"Well?" Bart asked impatiently.

"You want me to bribe Casey?"

Bart was exasperated. "What the hell you think I'm talking about? Isn't this the kind of job Harry pays you for? Pays well, too."

"Yeah, sure." His voice was nervous now. Bart could hear the uncertainty in it.

"Then what the hell's the problem? Won't he cooperate for the ten? I'll go higher if necessary, but try him for ten."

Hollister had no idea to whom he was talking. "Harry's friend" was the code that guaranteed the status of the caller and confirmed the number for him to call. All he knew was that anyone who identified himself as "Harry's friend" was to be obeyed. And that whoever it was was likely to be a cruel and impatient man. Sometimes he wished he'd never gotten mixed up with all this. Over the years he'd collected a nice pile—part stashed away in safe-deposit boxes, part in Panamanian banks. But he'd also collected ulcers and many sleepless nights when he thought about the various things that could happen to him if he ever got caught—all of them extremely unpleasant.

"Look," Hollister said, "you've got to know something about Casey. He's the fair-haired boy at homicide. He's the one always deals with important people. He's ambitious. He thinks he's going to be commissioner someday, and he probably will."

"What's your point?"

"He's not going to risk his future for a lousy ten grand. Also, he's got a reputation for being hard-nosed honest."

"Nonsense. There never was such a thing as an honest cop. It's just a matter of price. I want that information."

"Let me tell you a story. A while back, when Casey was just a detective, there was this drug dealer got knocked off. He had a big inventory. Well, Casey and his partner—guy by the name of Brown—got to the drug dealer's stash before the heisters. Brown says why don't we take a little of this stuff in for evidence, sell the rest and split the take? Casey says O.K. So Brown takes it, then meets with Casey for the split. They chat about how easy it was, how maybe they'd get lucky again. Brown says since it was his idea he ought to have a bigger share, and they discuss terms—"

"Get on with it," Bart snarled. "I didn't call you to listen to stories."

"Yeah, but this will tell you something about Casey. Seems Casey was wearing a little transmitter and it was all being broadcast and recorded in the next room. Casey turned him in, passed up about a hundred fifty grand, and testified against his partner. Brown's still in the slam."

"So you're telling me there's nothing you can do for me?"

Hollister thought about it. "Maybe I can get something out of Casey's captain—Captain John Manahan. He's a regular fellow. I've slipped him a few bills now and then. And he hates Casey. Doesn't let on. Makes it look like he's sure proud because Casey's good, and he's in solid up above, and he makes Manahan, who ain't too bright anyway, look like he's running a, an efficient department. I try to bribe Casey, he'd have my ass. Manahan, I can handle. Maybe for one bill even."

Bart knew this was the best he was going to get, and he was not a man to waste emotional energy over the difference between what he'd like and what was possible.

"All right," he agreed. "Get what you can out of Manahan. Start him out with a thousand, and tell him there's plenty more where that came from if he gets me anything I can use. But make this clear to him—if they find the fellow who murdered Humbrecht, I get the name before they make an arrest. I'll get the money to you in the usual way." He hung up.

Bart returned to the living room. He thought again about how ugly it was. It was a beautifully proportioned room, but it had been furnished by someone with more money than taste. The furniture was too heavy and there was too much of it. The paintings were mediocre reproductions, mostly seascapes and pastoral scenes. He'd be glad when he concluded his business and got out of this house. It depressed him.

He had to get hold of himself. He was letting frustration, disappointment, and anger distort his thinking. He had trained himself over the years never to make decisions based on emotion. If you expected to succeed in his or any other business, you made decisions and took action only when you had assembled all the information you were likely to get on the problems at hand.

That was the trouble. He didn't have much to go on. He didn't have too much confidence in what Hollister would produce. This hadn't been an important murder by Chicago standards. Chicago had so many homicides that unless the victim was a prominent citizen, they rated only a paragraph sandwiched between ads on one of the back pages. Humbrecht's murder had gotten a little more attention in the morning papers and even a mention on the local TV news because of the human interest angle. People liked stories about an old recluse who got himself killed amid the accumulated junk that filled a once lovely but now decaying mansion. It helped too that he had once been a genteel and respected professor in a highly regarded university. And the odd fact that he'd been found by his pastor who called on the old gent regularly.

It had all happened just yesterday afternoon. But Bart knew that time was working against him. The murderer might even be out of the country by now. That would make Bart's job much, much more difficult. He'd find him eventually, of course. The idea that he could fail was intolerable. If he was still in the country, if he hadn't disposed of the treasure yet, then the task would be simple. But first he had to find out who it was, who had done the job on Humbrecht.

"Junior! Pack!" he yelled, "get in here."

Junior and Pack came in a hurry. They looked scared. They were local hoodlums Bart had hired temporarily through an intermediary, and they didn't even know his name. He had told them his name was Mr. Jones. They didn't ask questions. The less they knew the better for them.

"Sit down," Bart ordered. "I want to talk to you. I want you to think back to yesterday, when we sat there in the car and watched that fellow come out of the house and use his handkerchief to shut the door behind him, and then get the hell out of there like a scalded cat. Now put everything else out of your mind except that. Concentrate on that picture. Got it?"

"Yes, Mr. Jones," Pack said. He couldn't see any reason for this, but Mr. Jones was a real smart guy, so he'd have a reason that made sense.

"Sure, Mr. Jones." Junior, whose wits were next to inactive, didn't speculate at all about the boss's purpose.

"Now what I want, fellows, is to see if you can remember something, anything, that could give us a clue as to who that fellow was." Bart made his voice soft and friendly. He didn't want these two thugs nervous and scared. If they felt they had to come up with answers or suffer his wrath, they'd only make up something. At least that's what Pack would do. Bart doubted that Junior had enough imagination to make up anything. He considered offering a cash incentive if they could remember anything significant, but that would have the same effect as scaring them. Pack wasn't stupid, but he was greedy.

Bart watched them. Junior frowned as if the effort

of recall was downright painful. Bart didn't have much confidence that this little exercise would produce anything helpful, but experience had taught him to explore every possibility when analyzing a problem.

"Never saw him before," Junior mumbled.

Bart could see that Pack was really trying to concentrate. After a couple of minutes he said: "Ya know, Mr. Jones, I thought there was something, well, ya know, familiar about the guy. I mean, well, it wasn't much, an' I didn't have time to think about it, we went right in the house and found the old guy, an' then got out fast. It's like, well, it's like—" Pack struggled to express what he meant "—it's like you saw somebody years ago, then you don't see 'em, then you see 'em again, and they've changed some but there's something familiar about 'em, you know you know who they are but you can't exactly place 'em."

Bart wanted to scream at him, "Think, you bastard, remember who it was or I'll—" But he knew better. He couldn't beat Pack into remembering. That might dissipate Pack's wispy memory altogether. Be gentle. Coax it out of him.

"You remember him, he's probably some football player," Junior said. "Football players, that's all you know about."

"Yeah, you might be right," Pack said, ignoring Junior's sarcasm.

Bart said, "Let's take it step by step. Maybe he was with Green Bay at one time."

"Nah, I'd know him for sure. I know everybody played for the Pack the last ten, fifteen years. He didn't play for them."

Bart forced himself to be patient. A little flattery might make Pack think harder.

"Pack, you are the best-informed person on the subject of pro football I've ever met. I'll bet you could guess what position he played. That would narrow down the possibilities."

"Well, he's 'bout six-two, weighed prob'ly 'bout two hunnert. Too small for interior line. Could be a tight end. They're usually heavier, though." He sorted out the possibilities. "I'd say a corner back or free safety if he's defense. If he's offense he'd be a running back or a quarterback."

"Now," Bart said, "how old would you say he is?"

"'Bout forty."

"That would mean he'd quit playing about when?" Bart asked.

Pack reflected. "Could a played up to maybe five years ago he stay in good shape, don't get busted up. Unless he was a quarterback. Quarterbacks can play like forever they don't get hurt. He looked like he was in good shape, hadn't any belly like a lot of 'em get soon's they quit."

"Then if he's a quarterback he could still be playing?"

"Don't think so. I know every quarterback in the league playin' now."

Bart was disappointed, but hid it. "What would be the best way to go about figuring out who he is—that is, if he was a pro?"

"Well," Pack said, "back at my room, I don't mean here, where I live, I got sports magazines an' pro football magazines from as far as twenty years ago. I prob'ly got the best collection in Chicago. I could go look through 'em, prob'ly find him if he ever played much."

"Do it," Bart said. "Do it now. And, Pack—"

"Yeah, Mr. Jones?"

"If you find him, don't take the time to come back and tell me. Phone me."

After Pack had gone Bart resumed his pacing. Anxiety mixed with excitement, impatience, and anticipation had his blood racing. This was not characteristic. He'd spent his adult lifetime learning how to curb his emotions. They called him Chris the Cool, or the Iceman, didn't they? He liked those names, even though nobody used them in his presence. His coolness was his edge. Early on he'd seen how smart people, intelligent people, people capable of thinking through a problem to its solution, had been undone by letting a sudden anger or a burst of passion contradict their better judgment. Bart decided as a young man to let his mind control his actions at all times and without exception. He had an excellent mind, a superior intelligence. He knew this. He trusted his mind. He also believed that feelings and emotions were, by their very nature, untrustworthy.

But he'd never wanted anything so badly as he wanted this. He'd trained himself never to need anything so badly that the need was an all-consuming thing. He'd seen men who needed a certain woman so badly that it distorted their judgment about the woman and everything else. No good ever came from this kind of compelling need.

But he needed Humbrecht's treasure, needed it so desperately that he knew he was in danger of falling into the error he so despised in other men. He had to get hold of himself. He forced himself to sit down. He commanded himself to read the novel he'd started last night when he couldn't calm down enough to sleep. It was a novel that made the Mafia look like pretty good guys after all.

It was two hours before Pack called. "Found him," he said.

"Who is he?" Bart asked with a calmness he did not feel.

"Con Randollph. Played for L.A., the Rams. I guessed quarterback, and started looking them up, and I guessed right," Pack said proudly.

"Is he still playing?"

"No. Quit when he was about thirty. I found this big article about him quitting when he was at the top an' makin' the big bucks. Nobody unnerstood why. He just said, this article here says, that it was time to move on to something else."

"I remember him. You could make a lot of money betting the Rams when he was quarterback. What's he doing now?"

"Well, Mr. Jones, I happen to know that because, see, I read the sports pages every day. An' you ain't gonna believe this. He's a preacher, some big church right here in Chicago. There was this article about him, maybe a year ago, little longer."

Bart was momentarily stunned. Randollph. He remembered now. That was the name of the pastor who had discovered Humbrecht's body. He recalled that he'd never seen the name Randollph spelled with two l's.

"So I guess it couldn't be him." Pack's voice carried

disappointment. "I mean, a preacher wouldn't have snuffed the old guy."

Bart's mind raced over the facts he had. "Of course he could have done it. A preacher would have a special reason for doing it." Bart, a practicing Roman Catholic who was the largest contributor to his parish church, still had the Sicilian's dislike for the clergy. He knew about immoral priests, venal bishops, hard, unrighteous clerics. The Church held the keys to heaven, but often in soiled and bloody hands.

"Is he a priest?"

"Whatcha mean?"

"I mean is he a Roman Catholic?"

"I dunno. I remember seein' an article a while back that he got married," Pack said. "It was on the sports page," he added unnecessarily. "Priests don't get married, do they?" Pack's grasp of sectarian rules and taboos was obviously limited.

"You don't remember the name of the church where he's pastor? Oh, never mind, I can look it up. Hang on, I may have some instructions for you."

Bart quickly leafed through Chicago's cumbersome phone book to the listing for names beginning with R. Reverend C. P. Randollph was the first listing under that name. There was only one Randollph spelled with two l's. Bart read Pack the address. "That's right downtown," Pack said. "Nobody lives there unless he lives in a hotel."

"What I want you to do," ordered Bart, "is to hustle down there and find out exactly where he lives, the lay of the land. Pretend you're a football fan and you want to get his autograph. Phone me as soon as you find out anything. And, Pack—"

"Yes, Mr. Jones."

"At least put on a clean sweat shirt."

Bart was certain that Randollph was the murderer. This explained something that had been puzzling him. It was hard for him to believe that anyone else could have gotten wind of this very special treasure. Of course, some of his sources of information could have decided to move in and take it themselves. But he doubted it. They knew with whom they were dealing. They only knew him as Mr. Jones, but they understood what he represented. They were aware of how much he wanted this. And, in polite terms, he had described how he dealt with people who double-crossed him.

But what was more natural than for old Humbrecht to show his special treasure to his pastor? A pastor would know its value well. Bart knew the power of his own obsession. He was convinced that Randollph had been under the same power. How clever of him to call the police and report the discovery of the old man's body. He'd had a perfect excuse for being there. No one would think to suspect him. The average American had this strange idea that the clergy was different from other people—better, more moral, above committing crimes, especially violent crimes. But Bart knew better. A priest had special powers conferred upon him by God at his ordination, guaranteed by the apostolic succession. But ordination didn't carry with it a guarantee of goodness. And Randollph wasn't even a true priest, so his ordination didn't count anyway. The only thing Bart couldn't figure out was why Randollph went to the trouble of keeping his fingerprints off the doorknob. Since he'd gone in on the pretext of paying one of his regular pastoral calls there was every reason for his fingerprints being on the knob. Oh well, there was probably some reason why he did it. He'd ask Randollph about it when he had him.

Pack finally called. It seemed to Bart that it had taken the young hood an extraordinary amount of time. But when he looked at his watch he realized that it was his own anxieties that had slowed down the clock.

"Randollph lives in a hotel, like I thought," Pack reported. "Only he doesn't exactly live in the hotel."

"Don't talk in riddles." Bart was curt in spite of his determination not to be. He ought to be grateful to Pack, but gratitude was foreign to him. Someone did you a favor, you squared it with money or a return favor. He'd see that Pack got a nice bonus.

"You got to let me explain," Pack pleaded. "This is the damndest setup you ever saw."

"Take your time," Bart said gently.

"Well, this church where Randollph's the preacher, it's called the Church of the Good Shepherd. But it isn't like a church. I mean, it is a church, but it's in a great big building which is part an office building an' part a hotel. Randollph lives in the hotel, sort of. This building has got a great big tower on top of it, and Randollph lives in that tower. Mr. Montoya called it a penthouse, which I thought was just the name for a magazine. I guess it's a real classy apartment—"

"I know what a penthouse is. Who's Mr. Montoya?"

"Oh yeah, I forgot to tell you, he's the doorman at the hotel. He's a big fan of Randollph's an' when I said I'd been a Randollph fan all my life he opened up. Promised to ask Randollph if I could get his autograph. He said there's no point in trying to see Randollph in his penthouse because only special friends ever get in it. No way to get at him there. It's like a fort Mr. Montoya says."

"He's got to come out sometime. Or I'll figure a way to entice him out. Come on back."

As soon as he'd broken the connection Bart consulted an address book, then punched out a number.

"Angelo's Body Repair, whatcha want?" a voice answered.

"This is Harry's friend. I need a taxi, properly licensed, of course, and a reliable driver."

"When you need it?" The voice was respectful now.

"Tonight. And I may need it for several days. I'll call in a couple of hours with instructions." Bart hung up.

The discoveries, decisions, and actions of the day had soothed his spirit. He was reasonably sure that Randollph had not yet had time to dispose of the treasure, and now Bart could see to it that he didn't have the chance. He picked up his novel about the Mafia being the good guys and settled down to read.

6

RANDOLLPH NEVER DID get back to planning sermons on sin that Friday. The afternoon trickled away from him. After the reporters had gone he disposed of the fragments of paper work accumulated through a week of neglecting them. He was always amazed at the amount of correspondence that, under the watchful eye of Miss Windfall, he had to answer each week. Always, week in and week out, a batch of invitations to speak. He supposed he should be flattered. But pride was largely mitigated by the absence of any honorarium attached to most invitations. Luncheon clubs were the worst offenders. Every Rotary, Kiwanis, Optimist Club, and various other civic booster organizations in the city and northern third of the state assumed that he would be thrilled to prepare a speech, take the time, and spend his own money to travel to them and entertain them without compensation. This he considered the moral equivalent of theft. He was glad, or at least willing, to speak sans fee for an organization or cause which merited support, and often did. But he was not willing to waste his time filling the schedule of speakers for some luncheon club, even though these clubs engaged in a certain number of good works. He had given Miss Windfall a standard reply to these requests. "Dear Mr. ———: I regret that my schedule will not permit me to accept your gracious invitation. . . ." All he had to do was write "no" on these letters and Miss Windfall knew how to answer.

Then he had piles of pleas for money. The ones that were obviously prepared by slick, highly paid money-raising professionals went to the wastebasket. But the legitimate requests from denominational and ecumenical agencies had to be dealt with. He had worked out a system for handling them, too—another form letter. "Dear ———: I have put your letter in the hands of The Reverend Mr. O. Bertram Smelser, who handles all financial matters for our church. . . ." Randollph had a feeling that Bertie Smelser, a colorless personality, but reliable guardian of Good Shepherd's expenditures, heartlessly recommended against most of these requests.

The more difficult letters to dispose of were the requests for appointments. But Miss Windfall had an infallible sense about which of these requests disguised the writer's wish to see Randollph in order to sell him (or his church) something; which ones just wanted to meet and bat the breeze with a famous pro athlete; and which ones were worthy of serious attention. Randollph relied on her judgment as to how these requests should be answered.

As Miss Windfall departed clutching sheaves of paper and a sense of moral superiority common to all those who have managed to do their duty against superable but difficult odds, Dan Gantry came in.

"Hi, Addie, I see you got the boss to play executive," Dan said. Miss Windfall smiled benignly on Dan and sailed out. Miss Windfall's genial acceptance and even affection for Dan Gantry was a continuing mystery to Randollph. Dan was everything in a clergyman that Miss Windfall should have loathed. He had no clerical dignity. He didn't respect wealth and social position. He was often involved in controversial crusades against outrages attempted or committed by various political and corporate establishments against the defenseless minorities, the poor, the publicly unpopular segments of society. But Miss Windfall seemed to find no fault in him. Randollph had given up trying to understand this. He let it serve to remind him of the uncertainty of predicting human behavior, and that even the most rigid of personalities is likely to confound you occasionally by an improbable attitude or action.

"Answering correspondence, huh? Dull business," Dan commented.

"Mostly turning down invitations to speak."

"You know, boss, you could do it like old Artie Hartshorne and make a pile."

"How's that?"

"He got bookings through a speakers' bureau. Spent most weeks between Sundays making speeches for five hundred bucks a shot. You could get double that, what with inflation and your name. Maybe more."

"No thanks. What's on your mind?"

Dan shook a cigarette from a nearly empty pack, and for the second time that afternoon Randollph found an ashtray. He had to have one handy. Many of the people who came to him for counseling wouldn't articulate their problem without a cigarette going.

"You ought to quit those things," Randollph said. "Lieutenant Casey was in earlier, and he's trying to quit."

"Yeah," Dan said, taking a lungful of smoke, "I'm planning to quit. But I got so many things to worry about right now I figure I'll wait till my nerves are calmer."

"What's troubling you?" Randollph asked. "I didn't think anything ever bothered you."

"Most things don't. But Leah Aspinwall is bothering me." He puffed on his cigarette.

Randollph asked, "Oh? How?"

"Because I'm beginning to feel about her a different way from how a man feels toward most pretty girls—I mean, I have a normal, healthy, horny feeling toward her. But I feel that about a lot of girls. This is different."

"How is it different?" Randollph knew from personal experience how it was different, but Dan needed to sort it out himself.

"We agree on, well, we're both for the Equal Rights Amendment, she even marches in their parades, carries banners. We're both against nuclear power. We both think our stupid government spends, wastes, mind-blowing amounts of money on arms and not enough, nowhere near enough, on helping people. Things like that."

"You must know other pretty girls who agree with you too."

Dan considered that. "Yeah, you're right. I guess I was just trying to talk myself into believing that was what attracted me to her."

"Believe me, it hasn't much of anything to do with it," Randollph said, feeling like a patriarch dispensing wisdom to the young. "Samantha and I have profound disagreements about some things. How many Christian ministers have an atheist, or at least an agnostic, for a wife? But I feel for her what—if I understand what you are saying—you feel, or are beginning to feel for Leah Aspinwall."

"You mean I'm really falling in love?" Dan looked as if he were depressed by the idea.

"I expect so. Why so gloomy?"

"Because she's a Jew, that's why."

Randollph pretended to be shocked. "Dan, I never expected to hear anti-Semitic sentences from your mouth."

"Oh hell, boss, you know it isn't that." Dan reached for another cigarette but the pack was empty. He crushed it and hurled it at Randollph's wastebasket, missing by a good two feet. "I'm beginning to have, uh, honorable intentions. I think I might want to marry this girl."

"Then marry her."

"But I don't want to give up the ministry. I ought to be willing to chuck it for love, but I'm not. I want to do what I'm doing now. I don't think I could chuck it, even for Leah, and not—not feel that part of me was missing. That's no way to start a marriage. And you heard her say she has no intention of converting to Christianity."

"For which I honored her."

"Well, what's bothering me, bugging the hell out of me, is can I marry a Jewish girl who's always going to be a Jewish girl, and keep on being a Christian minister? I mean, will a congregation put up with it? Lotta anti-Semites in most congregations. Don't admit it. 'Some of my best friends are Jews' types. But that's what they are. I'm even afraid to ask the bishop about it. God, I wish I had a cigarette."

"I'm ashamed of you, Dan." Randollph consciously put a firm tone into his voice. "You ought to have more confidence in the bishop than that."

"What do you think he'd say?"

"I can tell you exactly what he would say. 'If this is the girl you love, then marry her if she'll have you. I won't say that an interfaith marriage will be free of problems for you. As long as you remain at Good Shepherd the difficulties, if any, will be minor. On the other hand, if you were named pastor of a suburban church, or a small-town parish, you'd need to be prepared for some friction. However, if I were you, I'd marry the girl and cross those career bridges later.' Five will get you ten that this is the substance of what the bishop will say."

Dan brightened considerably. "You're on, and I hope I lose. I think I'll go ask him now."

As Dan was about to leave, Randollph said, "And, Dan, I think this girl is capable of holding her own with you. She's as strong-minded as you are—and, of course, much prettier."

Friday night was the best night of the week for Randollph. There were never any committee meetings on Friday night. He avoided all duties but the absolutely unavoidable. Clarence usually took the night off, though he provided food for Randollph and Sam unless they were dining out. Friday night was when Randollph wound down from the week so that on Saturday he could begin to wind up for Sunday.

Sam was already home by the time Randollph got to the penthouse. She was wearing a lime-colored housecoat with several unfastened buttons at top and bottom.

Randollph kissed her, held her, began running his hands over her. She broke away. "Keep your distance for the nonce," she ordered. "I need to get laid—oh, how

I need to get laid—and if you start fooling around now it'll mess up the evening's agenda."

"What's so important about an agenda that it can't be altered for good and sufficient reason?" He moved toward her.

"Nope," she said firmly. "I am the chairperson, and I rule you out of order. First, you go slip into something comfortable—the woman always says that's what she's going to do, doesn't she? But why shouldn't the man do the same thing?"

"It's the age of equality," Randollph answered. "And then?"

"Then I'll have dinner ready. Aren't you interested in what Clarence has for us?"

"I'm more interested in satisfying other carnal appetites," he said.

"Randollph, you've got to learn the joys of anticipation."

"I've been anticipating all day, whenever I had a moment to think about it."

"That's not what I mean. You should anticipate things in order."

"You smell good."

"For what I paid for that bath oil I ought to," Sam replied. "Now, first we anticipate dinner. I told Clarence to fix something substantial enough to satisfy you, but not too heavy because I expected to make love—"

"You what? You said that to Clarence? Wasn't he shocked? He—"

"Oh, don't get so excited," Sam said as she poked around in the refrigerator. "Clarence is no prude."

"But—"

"Want to guess what he said?"

"I do not look upon myself as devoid of imagination, but I confess at this moment it fails me."

"He said: 'Quite so, madam. A heavy meal does inhibit amorous activity. I'll prepare something appropriate.' That's what he said."

Randollph was speechless.

"Let's see, he left me this note. 'Madam, the baking dish in the oven contains chicken salad whose ingredients are diced cooked chicken, celery sliced, coarsely chopped walnuts, lemon juice, and chopped onion. If you will sprinkle a generous handful of croutons on it and bake (450° oven) for fifteen minutes, it should be ready. There is a simple salad of romaine, red-tipped, and Boston lettuce in the fridge, which I suggest you take out when you begin baking the chicken salad (along with the oil, vinegar, and herb dressing). In the freezer you will find rhubarb sherbet (my own recipe). Or, if you prefer, there are freshly baked chocolate eclairs in the fridge. I suggest they be set out at room temperature for several minutes before eating. There is a chilled bottle of a good domestic rosé in the usual rack in the fridge. Bon appétit. Clarence H.' I like that little touch, the *bon appétit*. He doesn't say which appetite he means. Probably both."

"How does Clarence spend his Friday evenings?" Randollph asked, imagining dimensions to Clarence's tastes and behavior that had never before occurred to him.

"Not what you're thinking, Randollph. He told me that he and some of his professional buddies, good chefs, have set out to try all the highly rated reataurants in Chicago, greater Chicago. They do this on Friday evenings, and sooner or later they'll publish a book with their ratings and comments. Now be off and change clothes. Dinner will be ready by the time you get back. Look forward to it. Anticipate it. Then I'm expecting a nice, long, slow roll in the hay. Make me squeal and groan."

Randollph kissed her lightly. "You can look forward to it, lady. I do have a suggestion."

"I'll bet you do."

"We might want to skip dessert."

Sammy sighed with contentment. She hoisted herself on one elbow and looked at a naked and somnolent Randollph.

"Randollph?"

"Mm, yes?"

"Do you suppose I love you just for your body?"

"In bad novels the woman says 'You just love me for my body.' That's part of it, though. The old prayer book version of the marriage ceremony had both bride and groom say to each other 'With my body I thee worship.' Elizabethan England wasn't prissy about the body."

"I brought the subject up," Sammy said, "so I could tell you how much I love you for other reasons too."

"I'd like to hear more on that subject."

"Well, I can't add it up like a list of virtues. You're a fine figure of a man, isn't that how the phrase goes? A little beat-up in places from all that football, but that just reminds me that I caught a famous athlete."

"You sure took your time catching me. How many times did I propose?"

"I didn't count. But all the time I was resisting—and for good reasons, not wanting to be a preacher's wife or the seminary professor's dear little spouse, or giving up my career, my identity, to name a few—I knew I was going to marry you eventually."

"You might have told me," Randollph said. "Think of the wear and tear it would have saved my nervous system."

"No, seriously. I wish I could tell you exactly why I love you. But apart from superficial reasons, I can't. It's a total thing. I'm incomplete without you. I can't imagine life without you. I got along very well without you until you came along. I couldn't now."

Randollph put his arms around her. "Tell me—"

The phone rang. Randollph used some language more appropriate to his football days than to the pastor of a distinguished church.

Sam giggled. "Answer it, Randollph. You'll just fret about maybe it was important if you don't. Then go wash your mouth out with soap and come back to bed."

"Randollph residence," he said to the phone, hoping it was a wrong number, and thinking what a ridiculous sight he must be answering the phone in the nude, and how dependent we are on clothes to give us a sense of security and invulnerability.

"Dr. Randollph?"

"Yes." Randollph hoped he didn't sound as irritated as he felt.

"This is Chaplain Mel Craig at Wesley Memorial Hospital."

"Yes, Mel." As soon as the caller had identified himself Randollph knew it was no insignificant matter. If Mel Craig called at this hour it could only be bad news.

"You have a family in your church named Kline? Pat and Linda Kline, and a boy, seventeen, Ben?"

Randollph quickly scavenged through his memory. He was miles short of every pastor's goal of knowing all of the members of his congregation by face and name. But he managed to come up with a picture of the Klines, an attractive couple about his age. Pat Kline was an architect, a partner in some large firm that designed uninspired but cost-effective apartment buildings. Linda was active in various charitable organizations. Benny, Randollph had heard, possessed an intelligence quotient in the genius range. A couple for whom the American dream had come true.

"Their son Benny's been in a bad accident," Randollph heard Chaplain Craig say. "He was riding in a car that got hit by a drunk driver. Killed the guy driving the car Benny was in. Doctors don't give Benny much chance. The drunk has a few bruises," the chaplain added with disgust. "I think you'd better come out here. The parents are still in shock, but when they begin to come out of it, they're going to need all the help they can get."

"I'll be there as soon as I can," Randollph said. "I thank you for letting me know."

He told Sammy about it as he got dressed. "Oh, how awful!" Sammy said. "I know Linda Kline. She often gets television exposure promoting one of her charities. All wrapped up in that boy. He's an only child."

"Tell me about her." Randollph was fastening a clerical collar to a collarless black shirt. "Curse these collar buttons!" The bishop had told him, at the beginning of his pastorate at Good Shepherd, that it was a good idea to wear clericals when visiting in the hospital. You could get one of those little badges at the front desk that said "Visiting Clergy" of course, and no one would question your right to be wandering around the halls after visiting hours. But the bishop felt the badges were kind of tacky. The clerical was better, too, because it made you instantly identifiable, proclaimed you for what you were, and, unlike the badge, didn't remind people of a delegate to a convention.

Collar finally secure, Randollph put on a dark-gray flannel suit, as Sammy said: "She's outgoing, enthusiastic about her causes, speaks well—that's why she's the one whose causes are always put on TV. No raving beauty, her face is too long. Good figure. Knows how to dress. Wholesome I guess is the word to describe her. What will you say to them, Randollph? How do you go about comforting them?"

"I don't know. I'm new at this. I'll have to wait till I get there to decide." He went over to the bed and kissed her. "Go to sleep. This may be an all-night vigil."

There were always taxis at the hotel door. Randollph got in the first one. "Wesley Hospital," he instructed the driver.

"Right, Reverend," the driver said without enthusiasm. He was resigned, Randollph supposed, to a small tip. Downtown Chicago, for all the bright neon tubing and flashing signs, was nearly deserted. The cab driver, who probably knew the quickest route to any spot in the city, worked his way north by a series of secondary and almost empty streets.

"I don't know if it means anything," he said to Randollph, "but there's a car following us."

"I can't imagine why," Randollph replied. His mind was on the situation he was likely to find at the hospital.

"Another cab," the driver supplied. "He was at the back of the line at the hotel. When we pulled out, he pulled out. He thinks he's far enough back I won't notice. Been in this game a long time. I can always spot a car following me, don't matter how good he is."

"I can't imagine why anyone would want to follow me."

The cab driver launched a long story about how he once evaded a car driven by a detective ("a real pro") tracking a wayward husband. Randollph barely listened.

At the hospital Randollph shocked the driver by his generosity. He knew he usually overtipped, and he wasn't sure why he did it. Perhaps to reassure himself that he was a kindhearted and generous man. Perhaps as a sign of his gratitude not to the recipient but to a gracious providence that had exempted him from the kind of work in which gratuities made up a significant slice of one's income. Or maybe it just made him feel good.

Of all the tasks attached to the office of pastor the most difficult by far, so Randollph thought, was dealing with tragedy. Death sometimes hovered on the wings of an angel over the long-stricken, over those in severe and incurable pain, over those who had passed beyond the boundaries of medical science's wisdom and technologies; over those who had had their portion of earthly joys and for whom life was complete.

But the case of a little child snatched away by some freak accident or swift disease; or a sturdy athlete whose fragile and unrepairable spinal cord is severed; or as tonight, when a bright and promising young life is blighted by the moral irresponsibility of a man who never calculated the possible consequences of driving while drunk—these were Randollph's severest trials.

Chaplain Craig was waiting for Randollph in the hospital foyer. "I'll take you to them," he said. "I've been with them constantly. It's a rough deal for them." He guided Randollph to an elevator. "They're in a waiting room on the third floor."

"How's Benny?"

"Touch and go. Still in surgery. The wife had hysterics but she's past that now—at least I think so. The husband isn't saying much."

"Did they ask for me?"

"The wife did. I told her I'd already called you and you were on your way. She thanked me. That shows she has at least some hold on herself."

Randollph thought what a ghostly place a hospital was in the middle of the night. No cheerful clatter of visitors bringing presents or flowers or magazines or just themselves to a friend or a family member who was healing on schedule. No press of doctors and clergy making rounds. No banging and clanging of dinner trays. Just the white figures of nurses hurrying silently to answer a patient's call light, or bearing medicine that had to be given at regular intervals, or carrying the injection that would ease unbearable pain. Now and then the silence was broken by a sharp cry of agony, or the groans of a restless sleeper dreaming bad dreams. A hospital late at night, Randollph thought, testified both to the strength and the fragility of the human species.

"Here we are," Chaplain Craig said, stopping by a closed door. "I'll take you in and then leave. If you need me, have the nurses' station ring me. I have the night duty. They can find me." He opened the door. "Mr. and Mrs. Kline, Dr. Randollph's here," he said, and left, closing the door quietly.

"Oh, Dr. Randollph, I'm so glad you've come!" Linda Kline exclaimed, grabbing him as if she could draw strength from him. Pat Kline hardly noticed Randollph. He was looking both stricken and hostile, and kept pounding his fist into the palm of his hand and muttering, "I'll kill the son of a bitch! I'll kill that murderous bastard!"

Linda Kline clung to Randollph and began sobbing. "Why did it have to happen to Benny? Why, why, why? He's such a good boy."

"I don't have any easy answers to that question." Randollph said gently.

"If Benny—if he—he doesn't make it," Pat Kline said, "I'll curse God. We've been good Christians all our lives. We go to church. We live decently. And then God lets this happen to us. What kind of a God would—could let that rotten drunk run into Benny, a boy like Benny, and—well, that drunken bastard hardly gets a scratch. I don't have any use for that kind of a God!"

Randollph knew the answer to that. Pat's hostile and disillusioned cry was rooted in the popular notion that you could earn God's special care and protection by virtuous living. *Quid pro quo* theology. Refuted by the book of Job in the Old Testament centuries before Christ. Denied by human experience over the ages. Anyone who took the trouble to read history, or the Bible, or the daily paper couldn't help but observe that the wicked frequently prospered and sailed through the years with a minimum of difficulty and discomfort, while many a saint was pummeled bloody by life's arbitrary and unaimed blows.

But it wasn't the moment to explain his faulty theology to Pat Kline. The bishop had warned him against talking too much in situations like this.

"When I was dean of the seminary," he had told Randollph, "I proposed a course for the curriculum of practical theology to be called The Value of Silence. Its aim was to teach pastors, at the beginning of their ministry, when to shut up. Preachers talk too much. They ruin a service by commenting on everything. They comment on the hymns and on the anthems and on anything that pops into their minds. And they comment on their comments. They seem to be afraid of silence. At least they don't appreciate the value of silence. One section of my proposal was to be on what not to say to the grief-stricken."

"What shouldn't I say?" Randollph inquired.

"Never say, 'accept it as the will of God.' When they have time to reflect on it, the grief-stricken will realize that you have said God has the character of a heartless monster."

"What else shouldn't I say?"

"Never say to people who have suffered the loss of a loved one, especially one whose death is tragic and untimely, that their loved one is now living in a far better place than this world. I'll bet there are a thousand funeral sermons a week preached on that theme. No one is anxious to get to that better place, as the next world is reputed to be, so why should the idea that their loved one is already there be a comfort?"

"Was the proposal accepted?"

"No, the faculty voted it down. Teachers make their living by talking so they have a professional prejudice against silence. But knowing when to be quiet can be more healing than anything you can say."

Pat Kline suddenly quit his angry talk. It was as if some internal switch had been thrown. He put his head in his hands and sobbed quietly but continuously. Randollph was grateful for the bishop's counsel. This was a time for him to keep quiet. He sat with the family for more than an hour. They finally talked, more or less calmly. They clung to hope, but they knew there wasn't much hope, and Randollph didn't encourage them to believe Benny would be all right. That was another thing the bishop had told him. "Don't tell people everything's going to be fine when you're fairly sure it won't." He prayed with them. When he saw that he had done what he could, for the moment at least, he took his leave. He felt his own inadequacy to minister to them, and was almost embarrassed by their gratitude for his coming.

Downstairs, he asked the girl at the desk to phone for a taxi. Then, wanting to be done with the hospital and knowing that cabs directed by a radio dispatcher often arrived quickly, he stepped outside, appreciating the cool September air. It wasn't long until a cab pulled up. "That was quick," Randollph thought. When he was about at the cab, the rear door opened quickly and a young fellow in a sweat shirt and green-and-yellow Zelan jacket came out fast. "This is a gun, here in my pocket," he said. "If it goes off it will hurt you bad. Get in quiet, no funny stuff. Mr. Jones wants to see you."

Randollph was wedged between Junior and Pack in the back seat of the taxi. It was a tight fit because Junior was big, Randollph was a large man, and Pack, while smaller, wasn't a little man.

"Get going," Pack ordered the driver. "And don't speed, don't run any stop signs. I wouldn't wanna explain to no cop what we're doing."

"Relax, sonny," the driver said. "I been drivin' since you was in diapers. I don't make no mistakes."

"O.K., O.K., just makin' sure. Mr. Jones, he don't like it if things get fouled up. An' when Mr. Jones don't like somethin', it ain't no fun for who screwed things up."

Randollph finally managed to speak. It had all happened so suddenly that he hadn't had time to be afraid. "I think you've made a mistake," he said. "There is no possible advantage to anyone in kidnapping me."

"You Con Randollph? I know you are. You don't talk like no football player, but I know you are. Mr. Jones just said for us to go get Randollph, he don't say why, none of our business why. He says get you, we do what he says."

Randollph frantically searched his mind for some clue as to what was happening. This had the smell of a professional job. Who was Mr. Jones? Why would anyone want to kidnap him? He'd saved some money from his high-salaried days as a pro quarterback, but not nearly enough to tempt well-organized professional criminals to hold him for ransom. Did they know the Church of the Good Shepherd had large endowments and were counting on it to ransom him? Not likely. Then why? He felt the icy breath of fear chilling him.

"Gotta blindfold you now," Pack said. "Mr. Jones said make it look like a bandage, we get stopped, which we goddam well better not, we say our friend, meanin' you, has a bad infection in both eyes. Don't try anything. Mr. Jones says we get in any kind of trouble we shoot our way out. He don't want nothin' to happen to you, he's anxious to talk to you like I said. But shootin' starts, you can't tell where bullets might end up. Might end up in you. You unnerstand?"

Randollph said he understood. He was glad to hear that Mr. Jones, whoever he was, didn't want him hurt.

"I'm doin' this," Pack explained as he applied gauze blinders over Randollph's eyes, "'cause it's best for you not to know where you're goin' or where you been. Mr. Jones told me to say that he expected all to go well, and that you wouldn't be detained long—detained, that's the word he used." Pack seemed unsure of just what it meant. Randollph felt a little better.

Randollph tried to estimate the time it took to get to wherever they were going. He thought it was forty-five minutes, or maybe an hour. The driver wasn't hurrying, he could tell that. They stopped frequently, probably for red lights. Finally they stopped, and he heard a new voice. It said: "Mr. Jones said there's only three of you I should let you in." Randollph heard the clang of metal and what sounded like gates being opened.

"You got them damned dogs penned up?" he heard Junior ask. "I don' want no piece tore out of my ass by one of them Dobermans."

"They're penned," the new voice said. "Won't let 'em out till you get your big ass inside the house." The taxi drove on. When it stopped, Pack said: "Soon's we get inside I'll take the bandages off. We gotta go up some steps. I'll take your arm and tell you what to do." He guided the blind Randollph up nine steps. "Now it's level to the door, jus' walk natural." Five paces later:

"Now stop. I gotta ring the bell." The door opened almost immediately. "Come on," Pack instructed Randollph. Randollph heard the door shut. "Now we take off the bandages. Might hurt just a little." He ripped off the tape that had secured the blindfold. Randollph winced, but said nothing.

As his eyes became accustomed to the light, he could see that he was in a large room that looked like a replica of what someone imagined a medieval castle must have looked like. It was a long room with vaulted ceiling. The floor was rough stone with oriental carpets scattered here and there, islets of color on a gray granite sea. At the end of the room opposite the door was a fireplace higher than a tall man's head and wide enough to accommodate an enormous log. The hall was cluttered with artifacts, whether real or reproductions Randollph couldn't tell, left over from the days when knighthood was in flower. There were suits of armor, broadswords, lances, and even a prie-dieu where, presumably, noble warriors had knelt to petition the favor and protection of the Almighty before they set out to slay the enemy.

"Hideous, isn't it?" Randollph had not noticed the opening of one of the many doors that entered the hall. The voice was soft and cultured; Randollph turned quickly toward it. The man was wearing a red silk smoking jacket with black velvet lapels and a red and black ascot. Randollph had never seen anyone actually dressed in a smoking jacket except in movies. The man had carefully trimmed gray hair, full but not long, which glinted silver when the light bounced off it at certain angles. He was not large, no more than five seven or eight, and slender. His nose, too long and narrow for his face, and dark eyes under heavy black brows gave him the look of a predatory hawk, Randollph thought.

"I welcome you to this house, Doctor, though I will not insult you by offering my hand in friendship. I confess my invitation for you to visit me was abrupt and unconventional. I will try to make amends. Let us go into the parlor or living room, which is as tasteless as this hall, but more comfortable." He indicated the open door. Randollph preceded him into the overcrowded living room, also of outsized proportions but so stuffed with sofas, tables, chairs, lamps, and other furniture that the effect was to diminish its spaciousness. It was as if the person who had furnished it had been afraid that unoccupied space would be interpreted as a badge of poverty.

"I'm Mr. Jones," the gray-haired man said. "Of course that is not my name, but it will serve. It's better for both of us that you don't know my real name. Will you join me in a brandy?"

Randollph was about to refuse. One does not drink with his kidnapper. Then he thought a refusal would be silly. He needed something to pull his badly shattered nerves together again.

"Thank you, yes," he said.

Mr. Jones went to a heavy, ornate cabinet, took out two brandy snifters and a bottle. "This is a very fine old cognac," he said as he poured a generous slug in each glass and handed one to Randollph. "Here's to a quick and agreeable conclusion of our business."

"I'll drink to that," Randollph replied, "though I haven't the remotest idea of what our business is." He knew he should sip the amber liquid, but he gulped at it. It felt like a stream of fire all the way to his stomach. He wondered briefly why what should be a painful sensation was so pleasant.

Mr. Jones clasped the bowl of his snifter for a moment, inhaling the fumes of the liquor intensified by the warmth of his hands. "Oh, I think you can imagine why I have, ah, invited you here."

"I'm afraid you will need to enlighten me."

Mr. Jones took a delicate sip from his glass and said: "Ah, glorious. Sit in this chair opposite me, Dr. Randollph. We can face each other and have a frank discussion."

Randollph sat down. Mr. Jones continued: "What I want, Dr. Randollph, as you have probably already guessed, is the Bible."

Randollph couldn't believe he had heard correctly. "A Bible?"

"Not *a* Bible, Doctor, *the* Bible. I know that you have it, or know where it is."

"Mr. Jones," Randollph said, "I'm completely mystified."

Mr. Jones sighed. "All right, if you want to play dumb I'll humor you. I'll pretend that you don't know what I'm talking about, so I'll explain. I want that Gutenberg Bible."

Randollph wondered if Mr. Jones was some kind of madman. "Mr. Jones, there are only forty-seven surviving copies or partial volumes of the Gutenberg Bible extant. They are all in museums, all accounted for. To my knowledge none of them has been stolen or sold. How in heaven's name would I come into possession of a Gutenberg Bible?"

"I see that you have done your homework," Jones said complacently, sipping again at his brandy. "That is one more piece of evidence that you are lying. Why would you know the exact number of surviving copies unless you had been doing some recent research into the matter? How many people in the world could tell you offhand the exact number of surviving copies?"

"Not too many, of course. But, Mr. Jones, you haven't done your homework. Prior to my advent as pastor at the Church of the Good Shepherd I was a seminary professor. My field is church history. I hold a doctorate in the subject."

Jones thought about this for a moment, then dismissed it. "Even so, you would be unlikely to remember the exact number of copies unless you had recently refreshed your memory. And you know as well as I do that the number of surviving copies is forty-eight, not forty-seven."

"I have no such knowledge."

Mr. Jones sighed again. "You are a persistent and accomplished liar, Doctor."

"Mr. Jones, you are obviously not without education—"

"A bachelor's from Fordham and an M.B.A.—that's Master of Business Administration—from Wharton," Jones said proudly.

"Impressive," Randollph told him, "but not the kind of education to make you an expert on incunabula."

"Incunabula?"

"A Latin word meaning 'things from the cradle.' It is applied today to early examples of the printer's craft."

"What's your point?"

"How would you, unequipped by the scholarly training necessary to research the kind of material which would indicate that there is a forty-eighth extant copy of Gutenberg's Bible, how would you come into possession of this knowledge? Did some slick confidence man sell you information, phony information, that such a Bible existed?"

Randollph expected Mr. Jones to be irritated, perhaps even become very angry at this denigration of his business acumen. Mr. Jones smiled genially.

"They called you Con when you played for the Rams, didn't they? They said you had the mind of a confidence man, the way you called plays. By the way, I won a lot of money betting on the Rams when you were their quarterback. I bet on you, really. I see that you still have the mind of a con man. You're doing a good job trying to convince me that there isn't any Bible, that I have been taken. A guess, but not a bad guess under the circumstances. I admire that kind of cunning. You, of course, know the history of the Bible. But you couldn't know how I know it."

"I'd be pleased if you would tell me."

"All right. It's such a fascinating story I'd like to talk about it. I haven't had the opportunity to talk about it to anyone who has the background to understand what a thrilling—yes, thrilling—story it is." Mr. Jones inhaled brandy fumes, settled in his chair, and began.

"First, I must tell you something about myself."

"I'll be interested," Randollph assured him.

"You will be. You are right. I am not a scholar. I knew nothing about, what was that word you used, about examples of early printing?"

"Incunabula."

"I must remember it. To get on with it, I am a businessman, a very rich businessman. I do not live in this area. This ugly house I have on temporary loan from a business associate who, shall we say, owes me a favor. I needed a secure headquarters while I found the Bible—which I had traced to Chicago." He looked around the room. "I'll be glad to get out of this place. The owner has money, but no taste, no taste whatever."

"We do agree on that," Randollph said.

"I might as well tell you, since you have or will guess,

that my business is connected with, is, well, some people, the public, think of it as illegitimate."

"Organized crime?"

"It is called that. Or the Mafia, or Cosa Nostra, or the mob."

"Yes, I'd guessed that," Randollph said.

"I was born in Sicily," Mr. Jones continued. "When I was seven years old my parents moved to New York. We were poor, but my father's older brother had been in New York for years, and had done well. Yes, as a member of a powerful Mafia family. He brought us over. He gave my father a job in his organization. Not a very important job, but compared to our life in Sicily we were rich. Well, to shorten the story, my uncle—Uncle Ricco—took a special liking to me. He had no sons, the great sorrow of his life, so he treated me like a son. He hired a tutor to teach me English and get rid of my foreign accent. He saw to it that I went to college. Uncle Ricco was a remarkable man." Mr. Jones paused, lost for a moment in affectionate memories. "He was of the old school, what you've heard called a Mustache Pete. But he'd figured out one thing that most of his associates didn't understand. Do you know what that was?"

Randollph didn't know.

"He'd figured out that all business—all big business, big corporations—is also organized crime. Only big legitimate business uses creative bookkeeping instead of hit men. It bribes policemen and judges and buys politicians instead of killing them. It uses clever tax lawyers instead of submachine guns. Safer, less trouble, and more profitable than gang wars. Oh, the legitimate businesses sometimes kill someone. I could cite you instances. But only when absolutely necessary. Uncle Ricco saw that the future of the Mafia, or whatever you want to call it, was with adapting the methods of legitimate business. And that's why he insisted I get a master's in business administration. And that's why I've done so well."

"I still hear about gang wars and mob figures being gunned down," Randollph said.

"That's true. Some people are too stupid or too violent to learn. But the ones that stay out of jail are the ones that operate as I do. Not that I haven't killed people, and ordered people killed," he added dispassionately, "but only as a sound business procedure. Sometimes it is the only sensible option you have."

Randollph gulped his brandy.

"But you understand that, don't you, Doctor? I don't suppose you wanted to kill that old man, but it must have been your only way to get possession of the Bible."

Randollph came up out of his chair. "What in God's name are you talking about?" he shouted.

"Calm down, calm down," Mr. Jones admonished him. "I'm not blaming you. I'm not going to report you to the police. The Bible is well worth a murder—many murders. Any sensible man would have done the same thing."

"But I didn't, how did—"

"I was sitting across the street in a car when you came out of the house and used a handkerchief to shut the door, and took off like a bat out of hell."

"But, but, that wasn't the way it was at all!" Randollph heard himself sputtering. He was sure he sounded guilty to Mr. Jones's ears. He tried to collect his wits. "Whatever made you think that that poor old man possessed a priceless Gutenberg Bible?"

"I don't think, I know," Mr. Jones said with assurance. "I have spent three years and hundreds of thousands of dollars tracing it. I had it almost in my grasp. You beat me to it by a matter of minutes, really. I suppose I should hate you for that, but I'm a man who appreciates irony. And if I'm so determined to possess that Bible, why should I blame you for the same determination?"

Randollph was sure he was living through some giant hallucination. This couldn't possibly be real. Mr. Jones was the kind of person who inhabited bad dreams. He'd wake up in a moment and find himself in bed, Sammy snoozing comfortably at his side.

But he knew that this scene, however bizarre, was real. He knew he had to play his part as best he could.

"Mr. Jones," he said, "if you will forgive me, I fail to see why you are so obsessed by this Bible. You are, by your own admission, a businessman, a very successful businessman. Granted that a Gutenberg Bible would command a fine price, there must be easier ways for you to make money."

"A good point, Doctor. But you see, just making money finally becomes boring to a sensitive man. And I am a sensitive man. I became bored with it many years ago. It is so easy to make money when you know how. Some of my business associates find making money enough. Some of them are so greedy that success in a million-dollar deal gives them the equivalent of a giant orgasm. It feels so good they can hardly wait to repeat the experience."

"But not you?"

"No. They are brutes without culture, barely human, no appreciation for the finer things of life."

"And what are the finer things of life, as you put it?" Randollph, in spite of himself, was fascinated by Mr. Jones.

"For me, it is beauty, beauty, particularly great art. I do not claim to be an expert, but I'm learning. That is the excitement of it. There is so much to know, so much to learn. When you begin to see, in a painting or a sculpture, what you had not seen before. When you can tell by looking at two paintings and immediately know that one is splendid and one is mediocre, ah, that is excitement. And to own, to possess great art, to live with it, to be surrounded by it—" Mr. Jones must have realized he was letting himself be carried away. He stopped, smiled, then said, "For me, Doctor, that is the great orgasm. Like sex, one wishes to repeat the experience as frequently as possible." Mr. Jones stared into his brandy glass. "I have a fine collection of paintings in my home. I've been helped and taught by a reputable dealer, a true expert. You would be impressed by my collection."

Randollph, whose knowledge of art was sketchy, said, "I'm sure I would."

Mr. Jones went on talking as if Randollph had not spoken. "A little more than three years ago an agent of mine was in Frankfurt, Germany. Rummaging around in a dusty old antique shop he found a painting of no particular worth, but thought it was painted over another painting that might be valuable. He bought it for a small amount. Well, it turned out that there was a painting underneath, but it wasn't any good either. However, when the wood backing of the painting was removed, the restorer found a letter. Does the name Peter Schoeffer mean anything to you?"

"Yes. He was foreman of Gutenberg's printing business when the Bible was produced. When Johann Fust, the businessman who had financed the Bible project, drove Gutenberg out of the business, Peter Schoeffer became Fust's partner. He also became Fust's son-in-law."

"You really have done your homework, Doctor. Out of idle curiosity I had the letter translated. He had to find a scholar in Germany who understood this particular dialect. It turned out to be a letter from Peter Schoeffer, to one Else Humbrecht. Do you know who she was?"

"Yes. Gutenberg's niece and his heir. He never married."

Mr. Jones shook his head in amazement. "This letter is dated February 4, 1468."

"The day after Gutenberg died," Randollph commented. "Let me guess what it said."

It was Mr. Jones who was fascinated now. "Guess," he said.

"It probably praised Gutenberg, said the world would long remember him, and apologized or begged forgiveness for his part in pushing her uncle out of the business. He probably pointed out that he could hardly have sided against his prospective father-in-law."

Mr. Jones stared intently at Randollph with his hard, dark eyes. "How in hell could you have known that?"

"Just an informed guess, Mr. Jones."

"Informed by what?"

"By my knowledge of Gutenberg's life."

"You'll have to explain that."

"All right. Peter Schoeffer was an artisan of some skill when he persuaded Gutenberg to hire him. There is every indication that they were personally fond of each other. I'm guessing that Schoeffer was astute enough to realize that Johann Fust was an old crook, who waited until most or all of the printing of the Bible was completed and he didn't need Gutenberg's expertise any longer. Then he foreclosed the mortgage he held on Gutenberg's shop so that all the profits would accrue to him."

"Just good business," Mr. Jones said.

"Bad ethics, but I suppose you are right."

"If he had a mortgage and Gutenberg couldn't pay, why not foreclose so as to collect the best possible profit from the deal? Ethics has nothing to do with business. If it's legal, it's ethical. But go on."

"I'm guessing that Schoeffer had a bad conscience. And people with a bad conscience usually try to rationalize their acts which they view as ugly and dishonorable. I'm guessing that when Gutenberg died, Schoeffer had an attack of remorse over his part in cheating his friend and mentor. So he wrote a letter to Gutenberg's nearest relative to praise Gutenberg and get his guilt off his chest."

"Doctor, you are a most interesting man. I could never have figured that out. I don't understand why anyone should have a bad conscience over an entirely legal business transaction. But yes, you have very accurately described a part of the letter."

"There's more?"

"Oh yes, the important part. It was a long letter, and went into detail about a Bible Schoeffer helped Gutenberg print. Gutenberg planned a very special copy, his personal copy. Schoeffer didn't tell Fust about it, and he helped Gutenberg get it out of the shop—"

"That would be the unbound sheets."

"Of course. This Bible was printed on a special paper, a paper that Gutenberg had imported from Cathay, as Schoeffer called it—the ancient name for China. He says to the niece that Gutenberg planned to have it illuminated and richly bound. It was to be handed down, from generation to generation, through the Gutenberg family. It was never to be sold—he had a priest pronounce a curse on whoever sold it. It was to be a perpetual monument to his invention. According to Schoeffer, Gutenberg planned to leave detailed instructions for preserving the Bible and make it an obligation to whatever family member owned it at any time. According to Schoeffer's letter the Bible would remain in excellent condition if these instructions were faithfully followed."

"Ah," Randollph said, "I am beginning to understand your determination to possess this Bible."

This seemed to please Mr. Jones. "I'm glad you can feel for it what I feel, Doctor."

"You no doubt know, Mr. Jones, that all critics have long agreed that no piece of printing since the forty-two-line Mainz Bible has ever equaled it in beauty or perfection. It still remains the finest example of the craft—in this case craft raised to an art form."

"Yes, I know that."

"So you would possess the finest example of the finest achievement in the history of printing. The only one of its kind."

"Precisely. It would bring me the supreme spiritual orgasm. I must possess it." He poured himself another finger of brancy. Randollph said that he had enough. "Now I'm a fair man, Doctor. I do not intend to take the Bible away from you. After all, you went to a lot of trouble and committed a murder, which would no doubt bother you more than it would bother me. I am prepared to pay you a handsome price—say five hundred thousand dollars in cash, tax-free. I know the Bible is worth much more than that."

"If it exists, it would be priceless."

"We can haggle over the price later."

"You traced the Bible to Johannes Humbrecht?" Randollph asked.

"Yes, and it wasn't cheap or easy. What a coincidence that he bears the same name as the niece who first inherited it. He is—was—by the way, the last of the Gutenberg line descending from her branch of the family. He had the Bible. I'm convinced."

Randollph realized he was dealing with a man who was so obsessed that he had to believe that Humbrecht had been killed for the Bible and that Randollph had done theft and murder to get his hands on it. Mr. Jones, however cool and analytical in running his business, however shrewd and logical in conducting his normal affairs, was—so far as his convictions about Randollph's guilt—a genuine fanatic. He would be impervious to reason. Like all true believers he would reject any evidence, any persuasion which contradicted his faith. And Randollph was too weary of body and soul to argue further.

"I can only state once more that I do not have the Bible," he said.

"I expected you to be stubborn, Doctor, though I had hoped we could conclude our business this evening. However, it is late and we are both tired."

"I know I am."

"So we'll continue our discussion in the morning. You'll be my overnight guest. There is a comfortable guest suite on the third floor. I hope you won't take it into your mind to leave without saying goodbye. Your door will be locked from the outside. It would do you no good to climb out the window, because if you didn't fall and break your neck, one of the Dobermans would attack you and do a lot of damage before the guard could call him off. This place is escape proof, as well as being safe against unwelcome visitors. And by the way, the household staff belongs to the owner of the house. They are instructed to follow my orders. No point in trying to bribe them to help you escape." Mr. Jones set his now empty glass on a table by his chair, yawned and got up. "I'm retiring now. The butler will show you to your suite. I wish you a good rest."

7

AFTER RANDOLLPH LEFT for the hospital Sammy realized that she felt as good as a woman can feel. Suffused by a post-lovemaking languor and the remembered though interrupted pleasure of articulating her feelings about him, she drifted off in a reverie of their life together.

She recalled that she had been attracted to him when they first met, more as a curiosity, she admitted, than as a potential friend or husband. He had not been at all what she had expected. She was familiar with what Dan Gantry called "jocks for Jesus." She'd had several of them on her talk show. In all fairness she had to give them credit for sincerity. Every last one, she was convinced, believed that God was an important ingredient in raising his batting average fifty points, or connecting on that Hail Mary touchdown pass that won the championship in the last desperate seconds of the game, or the sudden second wind, when on the ropes, to come back and beat an opponent into bloody oblivion.

She believed that they believed. But she found their

simplistic and essentially self-centered theology tasteless and pathetic. And, being an atheist herself, she was not much taken by their eager piety.

She had expected Randollph to be some version of this type, even worse, perhaps, because he had taken their sweaty Christianity a step further and become a clergyman. However, the Church of the Good Shepherd was an important Chicago institution. And Cesare Paul Randollph had been a highly publicized quarterback for the Los Angeles Rams. He was the kind of guest that inspired people to tune in to her show.

So she'd persuaded Dan Gantry, a good friend, to get her in to see Randollph his first day on the job in order to wangle a commitment from him to be a guest on her show before her competitors got at him.

And Randollph had been a surprise. At the very least she'd expected a hearty, extroverted type who used his reputation as an athlete to promote his theology and his church. Instead, she'd found a man who dressed like a successful businessman with expensive and semiconservative tastes, and who talked with suave precision. He was sharp. He parried her every attempt to shock him, and impaled her neatly each time.

At the time of that first meeting Sammy had no man in her life. She admitted to herself that she was a little soured on men. She'd married, almost on impulse it seemed now, a good-looking boob who was a lush. After finally giving up on him, she found that she had more propositions than proposals. She put it down to her success in a man's world. A lot of guys, married and unmarried, apparently wanted to hang her scalp from the belt of their sexual accomplishments. But none of them fancied being married to a career woman—at least not one so prominent and competent as Sam Stack.

When circumstances intensified her acquaintance with Randollph into friendship, she tried to stifle her emotions. He had a reserved charm. He was not an extrovert like most of the men she worked with. Nor was he an introvert. She classified him as introspective. And she surely didn't mind being seen in public with a big, "fine figure of a man" as she had called him.

But fall in love with him? Ridiculous! To begin with, he was a preacher and she was an atheist. At the time, he had been serving as interim pastor at Good Shepherd while the bishop searched for a suitable successor to that pleasant old windbag Arthur Hartshorne. Then, the year up, he would forsake the godawful Chicago climate and return to his teaching post at the seminary washed by the more benevolent weather of California. And she wasn't going to give up her well-established career to play housewife.

But she had married him. The bishop had planned all along to keep Randollph at Good Shepherd. Randollph wasn't so certain he was cut out to be a pastor, but he was certain that he was cut out to be Sam Stack's husband.

She had said, "But you're a Christian preacher and I'm an atheist, agnostic anyway," and he had replied, "Samantha, I'm not marrying you for your theology."

Anyway, it had worked. Any wise marriage counselor would have advised against it. He was not the kind of man a popular TV talk-show hostess should be marrying. And for sure, no pastor of a prestigious church, or any kind of church, should be marrying a girl who had no real interest in his work, and who frequently used words best not heard from the mouth of a pastor's wife.

But it had worked. The answer to why it worked eluded her. It was as if their two lives spilled over into each other. They were still the same people, separate individuals, each a person with his and her identity intact. Neither was diminished by their union. But this spillage of one life into another created something new in both of them. By being joined, their lives were intensified. She had been wary of the word "love," so easy to utter and so hard to achieve, since the failure of her first marriage, which had begun with a fleeting infatuation and ended in bitter disillusion. She had never doubted her capacity for deep and biding love for a man. But that was behind her. These were things she had wanted to tell Randollph, and later she would.

Sammy sighed with contentment and picked up a book whose author was scheduled to be one of the guests on her show next week. He was a survivalist, one of that breed who counseled finding a refuge in some wilderness, stocking it with food, guns, ammunition, and waiting for the crash of the American economy, due any day now. She'd have to make a lot of notes and try to turn what promised to be a dull, dull program into something that would keep viewers from spinning the dial.

Sammy didn't awaken until nine o'clock the next morning. Saturdays were free days for her unless some celebrity was in town only that day and she had to tape an interview, or a sizable disaster smote the city and the station required more experienced reporters than the second team working the weekend shift. She yawned and stretched, in the pleasant knowledge that she didn't have to propel herself into her normal working day's furious activity. Then she noticed that the other side of the huge bed was empty. Well, that wasn't unusual. On Saturdays Randollph was often full of Clarence's always superb breakfast and in his study polishing his sermon before she awakened. She hadn't heard him come in, but supposed that it had been very late and that he'd taken extra care not to waken her. He should have slept late, she thought. She wondered if the Kline boy had died.

She took her time in the shower, then dressed in black slacks and a fawn-colored knit top. As she went down the steps she paused to appreciate the graceful curve of the free-hanging open stairway; the generous proportions and odd but not unpleasing shape of the living room; the handsome and expensive if somewhat standard-looking furniture; the expanse of Chicago sky-line lighted by a mellow late-September sun and appearing more like a vast mural than a reality viewed through the glass wall of this house so high in the sky. It was one of those moments when mind, body, spirit, the felicitous conditions of one's life at present, and the shining prospect for the future fused into a state she supposed was happiness—only happiness wasn't a strong enough word to describe it.

She'd like to have gone into Randollph's study and persuaded him to come out and have a cup of coffee with her while she ate breakfast. She knew, though, that he'd be polishing up his sermon and wouldn't appreciate the interruption. He'd explained to her that this semifinal processing of the sermon consisted of ironing out wrinkled sentences; excising adjectives that had looked green and healthy when written but had turned weak and purple on a second reading; killing of clichés that, like cockroaches, crept in despite efforts to keep them out; exchanging a pallid verb for a vigorous verb; and trading off the almost right word for exactly the right word.

She'd once commented that this seemed a lot of hard work which wasn't really necessary anyway since most of his congregation talked in banalities, redundancies, and wouldn't know a split infinitive if they met one face-to-face.

"But it is necessary for me, Samantha," he'd replied. "I'm no fussy grammarian. I never can remember the definition of a gerundive or how it differs from a participle. But I'm trying to communicate something to people that I believe is important. So I have to do all that I can to communicate it with precision and grace. If you want people to understand precisely what you are saying, you have to say it with precision. And if you want them to be moved by what you say, you must say it with a grace that will linger in the mind. This is the mark of a good teacher, and of a good preacher. I have to feel, come Sunday morning, that I have done all I can through careful preparation to justify my listeners' investment of their time in hearing what I have to say. Do I sound stuffy?"

"No," she'd said. "But you'd not last long in my game. You have to churn out the words fast and constantly. No time to worry about precision and grace in the television business."

Anyway, she knew that he didn't like to be disturbed during his Saturday morning time for shining up his sermon. He liked to get it done by lunch so that he could watch a game on the tube. At this time of year he'd have a choice between college football or major-league baseball. So she'd breakfast alone, take her time, read the paper, and then go to the kitchen and talk with Clarence. Clarence, she thought, worked with precision and grace at his profession. But unlike Randollph, he was able to chat while he worked at it. Come to think of it, Clarence also talked with precision and grace. Since Clarence had been raised in a Church of England orphanage, he'd been exposed early to the cadences of Cranmer's Book of Common Prayer and the King James Bible. This exposure to the best the English language had to offer apparently had erased the colorful but imprecise and graceless cockney idiom that had been his linguistic heritage.

Sammy seldom took much time to eat breakfast, and she knew that distressed Clarence. Saturdays, though, were different. It was her day to dawdle over breakfast, and Clarence always prepared something he knew she especially liked. Maybe it would be baked mushroom caps stuffed with seasoned bread crumbs and bacon. Or rice fritters with chopped almonds and raisins and grated lemon rind encased in delicate golden-fried nuggets which Clarence always served with apricot jam. She didn't know where Clarence purchased jams and jellies, but they were of a flavor and quality she'd never tasted before. She saw that the dining room table had two place settings. That was odd. Randollph should have breakfasted earlier. Perhaps he'd just had coffee and planned to breakfast with her. That would be nice.

"Good morning, madam." Clarence came in with two silver bowls containing glasses of orange juice bedded in shaved ice. "I take it Dr. Randollph will be joining you shortly."

Sammy suddenly lost her appetite. "You—you mean you haven't seen him this morning?"

"No, madam." Clarence caught the anxiety in her voice. "I assumed he was sleeping late."

"No. He was called to the hospital last night. A serious accident. He thought he might be late."

"Perhaps he is still there." Clarence's voice lacked conviction, but he took hold of the problem with the same orderly method he employed in preparing a meal. "Permit me to call the hospital and ascertain if he is still there. To which hospital was he called?"

"Wesley."

"And did he mention the name of the patient?"

"Benjamin Kline. Son of Pat and Linda Kline. He was injured badly in an auto accident," Sammy added irrelevantly.

"If you will excuse me I'll make immediate inquiries."

Sammy's mind was a froth of imagined explanations for Randollph's absence. She hoped he had been detained all night by the parents' need for comfort, and immediately hated herself for hoping it. Were that the case, it would mean the boy was still lingering at the edge of death or had already died. But she knew that if this were the case Randollph would have found a moment to call. Had he been mugged and was lying undiscovered somewhere seriously injured or dead? Things like that happened all the time in Chicago, and he would have left the hospital very late. Had he suffered an attack of amnesia? She fought a rising panic. Hold onto yourself, don't give way to hysterics, try to get the facts. There is probably some simple and reasonable explanation.

Clarence's return stopped her grim speculations. "Dr. Randollph is not at the hospital, madam. The lady at the information desk paged him several times. She knows Dr. Randollph by sight, but has not seen him leave. Of course, she didn't come on duty till eight o'clock this morning. I requested the name and phone number of the person on the night shift, but it is against hospital regulations to give out that information. The Kline boy died at approximately three o'clock this morning, and the parents have left the hospital."

"O God," Sammy said, her voice heightened by anxiety, "what do I do now?"

"May I suggest that a call to Lieutenant Casey would be in order? He has the authority and facilities to assemble the facts as expeditiously as possible."

Lieutenant Casey parked the unmarked blue Pontiac in a no-parking zone as near to the hospital's front doors as he could get. He hurried in to the hospital and went directly to the information desk. The girl behind the desk was talking on the phone, apparently having a chat with a friend. She glanced at Casey without interest and went on with her conversation. "So I says to him, where do you think you get the right to paw me—"

Casey slapped his police identification in front of her

and said: "Will you interrupt your call, please? This is police business."

The girl muttered "Call ya' back" and hastily hung up.

"I want the name, address, and phone number of the person who was on duty at this desk from midnight on last night."

"We're not allowed to give out—"

"Lady, I'm a policeman and I don't have time to fool with your hospital red tape. Unless I have that information in thirty seconds I'll see to it that you spend time in jail for refusing the lawful order of a police officer." Casey knew he was being nasty to an unimportant employee trying to follow organizational regulations. But she wasn't very bright, and the not-very-bright of this world were often stubborn and perverse. The quickest way to get action out of them was to put the fear of God into them.

Thoroughly frightened now, the girl nervously wrote out the information he wanted. He gave her a curt thank you and headed for a nearby bank of public phones.

Mrs. Emily Curtis answered the phone with a sleepy hello. Casey quickly told her the information he needed, hoping that she was more intelligent and amiable than the girl on the information desk now. She was.

"Yes, Lieutenant, I saw Dr. Randollph leave last night, or this morning actually. He asked me to phone for a cab."

"Which company?"

"Yellow."

"And then?"

"He went on out front to wait. People often do that. They send cabs by radio, you know, and can get here quick. Funny thing, tough."

"What was that?"

"About fifteen minutes later a cab driver came in and said where was the passenger I'd phoned for. I said he'd gone out to wait. Well, there's no one out there, he said. Probably some other cab came by and he thought it was the one looking for him and left in it, I said. It happens now and then. That's piracy, the driver said, and he used a swear word I won't repeat and left."

"Thank you," Casey said, "you've been a big help."

"What's this all about?" the woman asked. "Has something happened to Dr. Randollph?"

"We're just conducting a routine investigation," Casey answered, realizing how silly this must have sounded. "Thank you again." He hung up.

Casey hated to call Sammy. He needed to sound reassuring with nothing to reassure her. He'd try to minimize the seriousness of the situation, and he'd be lying. He'd have to tell her that he was turning it over to Missing Persons, not only because it belonged to that department but because they had the experience, skill, and manpower to conduct a thorough search for Randollph. One thing he could do was get them cracking. Though egalitarian in theory, any police department operated on a policy more congruent with an aristocracy. The anonymous citizens of Chicago who had disappeared either by volition or against their wills would wait the attention of Missing Persons until Randollph's disappearance had been cleared up. Randollph was a prominent citizen. He was the chief operating officer of a prominent and powerful Chicago institution. He was nationally known, familiar to millions as Con Randollph the pro football star. If Missing Persons didn't find a lost husband or a runaway teenager, no one except the immediate family would know or care. But it had damn well better locate Randollph, and quickly, or it was in for a bad press. Casey knew this really wasn't right in a proper democracy, but it was the way things were, always had been, and always would be. Also, Randollph was Casey's friend. He'd make it clear to Missing Persons that there was a fraternal aspect to this search. Policemen looked after their own with a zeal not always manifest in cases unconnected to the department. This was an instance of the rights of one taxpayer taking precedence over the rights of other taxpayers. Casey often deplored the far-from-evenhanded dispensation of police resources and efforts, but not this time. This time it involved someone who meant something to him personally, and Casey had the influence to command the best effort of which Missing Persons was capable. It all depended, as Martin Luther had said, on whose ox is being gored.

He'd picked up that quote, he remembered, from Randollph.

But turning it over to Missing Persons meant publicity. It might be delayed for a day or two, but it wouldn't take long for the police reporters to find out. You couldn't conduct the search for a prominent citizen in secret. Then Sammy would be hounded and harassed by the media. She was a member of the media, so she would know what she was in for.

Casey's first guess was that Randollph had been mugged, probably by some junkie. Hospitals attracted junkies. Hospitals always had plenty of drugs around and had the constant problem of drug theft by employees who were either users or part-time pushers. Casey guessed that Randollph had run afoul of some junkie—or maybe more than one—who figured that late at night they could get away with bashing even this big guy. So what if he was a priest? He'd have some money on him, probably some jewelry. For some reason they'd thought it wise to conceal the body. If no place else was available they could have stuffed him into the trunk of a nearby car. It was possible, Casey thought, that someone was driving around Chicago right now not knowing that he was hauling the body of The Reverend Dr. Cesare Paul Randollph in his trunk.

Casey couldn't think of any other reasonable explanation for Randollph's disappearance. If Randollph had been a wealthy man Casey would have guessed kidnapping. But no one could have any motive that Casey could imagine for kidnapping Randollph. If Sammy asked him for his estimate of what had happened to her husband, and if he answered her honestly, he'd say I think he's dead. But of course he wouldn't say that. He'd try to sound cheerful and optimistic. But it wouldn't be easy.

He called her. Best to get it over with. And he found it easier than he had thought. After he told her what he had found out and what he intended to do, she said: "I know it doesn't look too hopeful, Mike, but I'm going to be hopeful. I've gotten hold of myself. I'm not going to have hysterics. Do what you think best. Just tell me anything you know as soon as you find out. You don't have to baby me. I'm a big girl."

But she didn't feel like a big girl. How could her life taste so sweet one moment and so bitter the next? Love, she realized, made you vulnerable to pain. She thought briefly of Pat and Linda Kline. They had invested so much of themselves in Benny and lost it all. Having someone you loved totally and without condition unexpectedly and irrevocably snatched from you left you spiritually bankrupt.

"O God," she whispered, "please make Randollph safe and bring him back to me." It never occurred to her that she didn't believe in God or prayer.

8

THE ANCIENT and uncommunicative butler who led Randollph up a broad stairway covered by carpeting the color of old blood was dressed in a plain black suit, soft white shirt, and black tie. Clarence would give the fellow low marks, Randollph thought, for wearing improper attire while on duty. They trudged up to the third floor. The butler led Randollph down a long hall, unlocked a door and said, "Your quarters, sir. You'll find everything you need in its proper place. Good night, sir." The old man shut the door behind him, and Randollph heard the thunk of a heavy metal bolt being shot home.

Randollph inspected his prison. He was in a large sitting room furnished in the same tasteless and overcrowded style as the parlor three floors below. The bedroom, equally large, was dominated by a canopied king-sized bed. The bathroom, gaudy with gold fixtures and slabs of glass and marble, was also large. Whatever Mr. Jones had in mind for him, physical privation did not seem to be a part of it.

Randollph was suddenly and completely exhausted. What with comforting the Klines and holding himself together through the bizarre experience of being kidnapped, he had used up his supply of nervous energy. He just wanted to collapse. He pushed open the sliding door to a roomy clothes closet. Plenty of hangers, lots of shelf space, a few garments pushed to one end of the closet. He was too tired to examine them. He quickly shucked his clothes, hanging them carefully from habit. Pajamas of an unpleasant green color were folded on the turned-back covers of the canopied bed. They were a fair fit. Randollph wondered where the butler had found them on short notice but was too weary to care.

The bathroom had toothpaste, toothbrush, shaving gear, and an assortment of mouthwashes and lotions all laid out. Randollph brushed his teeth with what seemed his remaining strength, then fell into bed.

But he didn't fall asleep. He tried to clear his mind, make it an empty space vulnerable to the invasion of slumber. But he couldn't do it. Too much to think about.

Was Johannes Humbrecht, in fact, the last of the Else Humbrecht branch of the Gutenberg family? Had Johannes Gutenberg, in fact, printed—with the secretive help of Peter Schoeffer—this best and most durable copy of his forty-two-line Bible? Had it been well-preserved down through the centuries? Had Johannes Humbrecht inherited it? Where would be have kept it in his trash-filled old mansion? Why had he never alluded to the Bible in the many conversations he'd had with his pastor and—Randollph believed—good friend? If the Bible did turn up, who would own it now? Would Humbrecht have bequeathed it to some art museum? It would be an item in Humbrecht's will, no doubt. Randollph remembered that he was supposed to attend the reading of Humbrecht's will at ten o'clock Monday morning. He wondered if he would be free by then. What did Mr. Jones have in store for him? If Jones persisted in his obsession that Randollph had killed Humbrecht and stolen the Bible, there was no way that Randollph could satisfy him. Randollph knew something about obsessive personalities, if mainly by reading about them. The Christian church had, over the centuries, its share of people obsessed with beliefs and ideas. Sometimes the ideas and beliefs were good, sometimes bad, or just plain nutty. But good or bad, nothing ever seemed to deter these obsessed people. They were impervious to reason, logic, facts, other people's opinions. They were true believers. The true believer, Randollph knew, did not dare entertain the thought that he might just possibly be wrong. To doubt was to risk unraveling his personality. He needed to believe to save his sanity—such as it was—or his soul.

Was Mr. Jones a true believer? Randollph tried to recall their conversation for clues. Jones had exhibited pride in his cold, analytical approach to business. He obviously despised his hot-blooded associates who thought violence was the answer to every problem. But the man's personality changed when he talked about the Bible. It was something he wanted too badly. He had invested his soul in finding it. He was convinced both consciously and somewhere several layers below his conscious need that he must have that Bible, that were he to fail in his quest, life would be insupportable. He had to believe in the Bible, its existence, its availability.

Randollph knew he could never fully understand a true believer. He believed a number of things. Some of them he believed passionately. Some of them he would fight for, suffer for, maybe even die for if it came to that. But those things in which he believed, though they involved his emotions, had their true roots in his mind. He admitted to himself that he believed in the truth of several ideas and doctrines he could not prove, indeed were beyond proof. They were articles of faith and that is how he classified them. He was a firm believer in the doctrine of salvation by grace through faith, though he was aware there was no way to prove it on this side of heaven. But the doctrine did not offend reason or good sense. To believe it did not demand that he abandon the processes of the mind. It did not require that he accept what was patently absurd.

Now and then Randollph concluded that something vital was missing from the structure of his personality. Whatever it was that drove people to commit themselves utterly to some cause, however goofy, and fire others to follow them in the crusade was left out of his makeup, was absent from his genes. He'd never know the ecstasy, the bliss, the certainty beyond question that what he wanted was what God wanted. Louis the Pious and Joan of Arc had apparently found this bliss, this ecstasy more than enough reward for enduring dungeon, fire, and sword. No doubt they deserved sainthood, but people like that made him nervous.

Mr. Jones made Randollph nervous. He was afraid that the good judgment and analytical approach to problems characteristic of Jones in his business dealings would desert him in the matter of the Bible. When it came to Gutenberg's special and unique Bible, Mr. Jones was a true believer. And Randollph didn't trust true believers. Would Jones kill him? Not if Jones followed his credo that killing was seldom the answer to a problem. But that was Jones, the businessman. Jones, the true believer, angry and frustrated, might very well kill a Randollph who refused to confess killing Humbrecht and the theft of the Bible. Randollph shuddered.

His thoughts drifted back to the events of the evening prior to his kidnapping. The brief time with Sammy had been one of his life's luminous moments. It was so easy to believe in the goodness of God when you are in the arms of the woman you love and listening to her tell you how much she loves you. Was so much happiness more than any human had a right to? Was there something in the nature of the universe that when it gave you so much it had to balance the scales by penalizing you? He was sure the Klines thought so. Randollph knew it was a silly and unsupported idea, but he had a little more sympathy for Pat Kline's grief-stricken hostility toward the unfathomable ways of the Almighty than he had had earlier in the evening. After all, there was no certainty that he would ever see Sammy again. He was chiding himself for such negative thinking when he finally dropped off to sleep.

Randollph was awakened by the sound of the door being unlocked. The white-haired butler, wearing the same semi-uniform he had worn last night, came in bearing a silver tray with a silver coffeepot and a fragile-looking blue and white china cup. "Good morning, sir," he said, putting the tray on an end table beside a heavy overstuffed chair. "I thought perhaps you would like a cup of coffee. Mr. Jones hopes you'll be able to join him for breakfast in the dining room in a half hour." He poured a cup of coffee and handed it to Randollph. "While you shave and bathe, sir, I'll lay out a few things for you. There's clean underwear and socks. Mr. Jones thought you might be more comfortable in a casual shirt. I'm afraid you'll have to make do with your own trousers."

Randollph finished the coffee and went to the bathroom. He decided not to think about anything until brain and body were stabbed awake by hot, then cold high-pressure spray. He would have preferred a scratchier towel for its abrasive and stimulating sensation over the giant down-soft towels provided, then rebuked himself for what he regarded as an over-concern for sensual pleasure. St. Luke, on his journeys with Paul, probably was grateful for any kind of towel.

After showering, Randollph hastened through shaving, finishing up by sloshing his face and body with generous palmsful of a spicy but subtle bay rum. Then, wrapping one of the large soft towels around himself, he went back into the bedroom. The old butler was preparing to leave. "When you've dressed, sir," he instructed Randollph, "just come down the stairs to the main hall. The first door on the left opens into the dining room."

So they're only going to lock me in at night, Randollph thought. That meant that they weren't really worried about the possibility of an escape. Jones just didn't want him wandering the house in the middle of the night trying to escape and inconveniencing everyone. Not a cheering thought with which to start the day. He planned to survey the possibility of an escape. But it didn't sound too promising.

The dining room was enormous. Mr. Jones was sitting about halfway down a dining table which, Randollph estimated, would accommodate at least forty people. Jones, wearing a dressing gown that looked like it was made of pale green damask, was sipping coffee.

"Ah, good morning, Doctor," he said pleasantly. "Please sit opposite me." He must have pressed a button with his foot, Randollph guessed, because the butler appeared almost instantly. "What do you have to offer us this morning, Anthony?" Jones asked the butler.

"A honeydew melon to start, Mr. Jones," the butler said. "Then whatever you wish, though cook does a nice eggs Benedict; I recommend it."

"Sounds good," Jones said. "How about you, Doctor?"

"Eggs Benedict is a favorite of mine," Randollph replied.

"Thank you, Anthony, we'll have that." Jones dismissed the butler, who was back shortly with two large crescents of melon.

"Ah, delicious," Jones said after scooping out a chunk of the yellow-green melon and devouring it. Randollph thought the honeydew had been insufficiently ripened and indifferently served. It should have been on a bed of ice and accompanied by a slice of fresh lime. Clarence, he knew, would have considered the melon unworthy, and would have been offended by its poor presentation.

When the eggs Benedict arrived, Jones dug into his plate hungrily. "Heavenly!" he sighed. "Anthony was right. Cook does this dish well."

"My chef does it much better." Randollph took malicious pleasure in the startled look with which Jones reacted.

"Your what?"

"His name is Clarence, Clarence Higbee. He's English. He runs our household. My wife works, we need someone to look after us, feed us. Clarence," Randollph added, "is widely respected in culinary circles as one of the finest chefs in the Chicago area."

Mr. Jones carefully laid his knife and fork on his plate. "Are you a wealthy man, Doctor?"

"No, not at all," Randollph assured him. "I am paid quite well. My wife is a well-known Chicago television personality, so she also is well paid. I managed to save a few dollars from the days when I was greatly overpaid for playing football. You could say that we live comfortably."

"If you are able to afford your personal chef, I'd say that you live more than comfortably."

Randollph thought about it. "Perhaps you are right. Even though Clarence's salary is modest compared to what he could command, and our housing is furnished by the church, we do live on the edge of luxury. It bothers my conscience sometimes."

Mr. Jones looked puzzled. "I don't understand that at all. If you can afford luxury, then enjoy luxury."

Randollph decided it would be too complicated to explain to Mr. Jones the biblical and theological arguments against a Christian minister affecting a fancy life-style. Jones had lost interest in the subject anyway. He turned the direction of the conversation back to the eggs Benedict.

"In what way, Doctor, would your chef improve on this dish? I find it most tasty."

"I didn't say it wasn't good," Randollph answered. "But Clarence would consider the hollandaise sauce too bland. And your cook has used flavorless ham straight from the supermarket meat case. Clarence would have used ham or Canadian bacon cured to his own specifications by one of what he calls his purveyors. Your cook is competent," Randollph added. "Clarence is an artist."

Randollph thought he might be pushing Mr. Jones too hard. But he wanted to challenge the man, disagree with him, cross him. It salvaged some of the self-respect damaged by the pushing around he'd endured at the hands of Jones's two hoods.

But Jones laughed. "He isn't my cook, just part of the staff loaned to me by the owner of this house. He and his family are on a trip abroad." Jones topped up Randollph's coffee cup, poured some for himself, then offered Randollph a thin black cigar.

"No, thank you, I hardly ever smoke."

"Perhaps my cigars don't meet your standards." Jones was sarcastic.

"Since I am not familiar with them, I couldn't say. On the rare occasion I do indulge myself, it is with one from Clarence's English Market selection."

"Those are Cuban, you know. You and Clarence are breaking the law. Purchase and possession of Cuban tobacco is illegal. You aren't above breaking the law, then, are you, Doctor?" Jones lit his cigar, satisfied that he'd scored a point. "And if you do not hesitate to break one law for your own pleasure and benefit, then you'd probably have no qualms about breaking other laws if the benefit to be gained was very great the possession of the finest example of the printer's art ever created, for example."

"Are you a legalist, Mr. Jones?" Randollph asked.

"Meaning what?"

"A legalist," Randollph explained, "is concerned with the letter of the law. He does not distinguish between a good law or a bad law. He does not care if the breaking of one law is of no real consequence, while the breaking of another law has very serious consequences for another person or for society. In his eyes, it is the infraction that is wrong, not the consequences."

"You are saying that it is all right to break one law, but not another?"

"Not exactly. But, if I understand you correctly, you were saying that a person who would smoke an illegal cigar would also commit theft and murder. The one is a peccadillo—"

"A what?"

"A small fault. Not entirely defensible, perhaps, but not to be compared with theft, or with the most serious of crimes, murder."

Jones tapped the ash from his cigar into a large jade bowl. "I'm just trying to figure out how you think, Doctor. To answer your question, no, I'm not a legalist."

"I judged that you were not." Randollph was unable to repress a smile when he said it, but Jones didn't seem to notice.

"I have nothing but contempt for all laws," Jones continued. "If it is necessary to my purposes, I break the law, any law. My preference, though, is to use the law to achieve my purposes. I come from a country with a long history of suffering under the law. I don't remember it, of course, but my parents and my uncle Ricco taught me that in the old country laws were used to benefit the rich and oppress the poor." Jones looked into the oily blue smoke floating above his head as if expecting a vision to emerge from it. "So, Doctor, contempt for law is part of my heritage. That is why I have no difficulty believing that you killed old man Humbrecht and stole the Bible. After all, you have admitted you have contempt for one law—and if for one, why not all laws? I think you have that Bible, and I mean to get it. I hope we can reach a mutually beneficial agreement—that is the best way to do business. No unpleasantness, no problems. But if we can't do that, I'm prepared to make it unpleasant for you—unpleasant enough that you will be glad to cooperate with me. I've done a lot of business that way, too." Jones spoke calmly and without any menace in his voice. But Randollph didn't doubt that Jones would do something very painful to him if he didn't get the answers he wanted.

"Mr. Jones," Randollph said, "are you governed by any moral law whatever?"

"No."

"There is nothing too awful, too hideous that you would not resort to in order to achieve a purpose, realize a goal?"

"I can't think what it would be," Jones replied pleasantly, filling Randollph's coffee cup again.

"You must have been raised a Roman Catholic," Randollph persisted.

"I was and I still am a Roman Catholic, a good one. I've been to Mass already today. I never miss my Sunday duty." Randollph reflected that he'd missed his Sunday duty today. He wondered who had filled his pulpit, how his absence had been explained. "I am very generous with my contributions to my church," Jones went on. "I go to confession. I keep the rules." He said it proudly.

Randollph wished Lieutenant Casey could hear this. Jones represented the kind of superstitious, credulous Catholicism from which Casey considered himself blessedly liberated. It wasn't so much different, Randollph realized, from superstitious, credulous Protestantism.

"You have told me that you recognize no moral law and that you have stolen and killed without pain to your conscience," Randollph said. "Do you have no fear of hell?" Maybe, just maybe, he could use Jones's primitive religious beliefs to advantage.

"I expect to spend some time in purgatory, of course," Jones answered. "Everyone but the most saintly have to do that. But I have kept the rules. I hope my stay in purgatory will be short. That is one reason I must have that Bible."

Randollph, who had been sipping coffee, almost choked. "What did you say?"

"I want to possess that Bible," Jones explained. "Then I shall will it to the Pope. I am very sure that by giving it to the Holy Father I shall receive a remission for every sin I have ever committed. And," he added, "there are many of them." He smiled. "This is how I expect to escape purgatory after a short visit. So, Doctor, I have a double reason for wanting that Bible. I want to enjoy it in this life. And I expect it to get me into heaven."

Randollph now had no doubt that in the matter of the Bible Jones was a true believer. He knew he had little hope of changing Jones's mind. How could you appeal to a person whose twisted theology told him that by donating the Gutenberg Bible to his church, even though he had come by the Bible through theft or murder, he could count on the Pearly Gates swinging wide for him? Randollph knew that you couldn't. But he had to try.

"You said earlier, Mr. Jones, that you wanted to discover how I think."

"Yes."

"Would you like me to tell you?"

"Of course, Doctor," Jones replied, with what Randollph took to be an amused smile. "Of course, I'll have to make allowances for some exaggeration in your own favor, won't I?"

Randollph smiled. "I suppose so. All of us tend to be self-serving when justifying our own behavior. I'll do my best to be honest."

"Go ahead."

"What you really want to know about me," Randollph said, "is if I am capable of theft and murder."

"I've already decided that you are."

"But you aren't entirely sure, otherwise you wouldn't care about how I think." Randollph was trying hard to plant a seed of doubt in Jones's mind, hoping it would grow fast enough to shake his certainty about who had the Bible.

"I can understand your feelings about the law," Randollph hastened on. "No doubt many laws are bad laws, designed to help those who have the power to pass them. But I do not share your contempt for the law. It is the rule of law that makes a free society possible. How I think and how you think differ most in our view of the moral law."

"How so?"

"You have no regard for law, including moral law."

"That's right."

"I, on the other hand, am convinced that 'Thou shalt not kill' is a restriction on my behavior sanctioned by God Himself. Oh, I can envision situations in which I might kill another human being. But not many. I believe, I am sure that even if I wanted that Gutenberg Bible with all my heart, I am incapable of killing anyone for it. I devoutly hope that I am."

Jones smiled tolerantly. "That doesn't prove anything, Doctor."

"No, of course it doesn't. I'm just trying to describe how I think."

"Go on."

"Also, I believe it is sinful to covet what belongs to someone else." Randollph thought of the preliminary notes on his series of sermons about the seven deadly sins. Would he ever get to preach those sermons? If he did he'd have some firsthand exposure to deadly sins behind him. "You've heard that greed is one of the seven deadly sins, haven't you?"

"Of course," Jones answered impatiently. "I told you I was a loyal Catholic."

"Your passion to possess that Bible is a form of greed. And greed is one of the seven deadly sins. It has you in its grip. It is difficult for you to understand that I do not covet that Bible as you covet it. You are projecting your own feelings, your own state of mind, on me. But I have no passion to possess that Bible."

Jones almost sneered. "So you say."

"So I say. Oh, I am not free of wanting things. I am addicted to expensive clothes. I spend too much for them. I would miss my lovely penthouse and Clarence's superb cooking. I am a sinner too. But wanting to possess something like that Bible isn't one of my particular desires."

"Nonsense! Anyone would want it."

"You are making the common mistake of supposing that everyone feels exactly as you feel."

Jones puffed on his cigar thoughtfully. Randollph let the silence hang between them. Jones finally spoke. "You have said that you are not a rich man, Doctor. You could sell the Bible and be a wealthy man. You would never have to worry about money again."

"But, Mr. Jones, I don't worry about money now. I have more money than I need. I'm sure I could live a happy—and I hope useful—life on much less money."

Again Jones turned sarcastic. "You are painting the portrait of a saint, Doctor. I doubt that you are a saint."

Randollph realized that he had pictured himself as better than most of his fellow creatures. He phrased his answer carefully. "Your criticism may well be valid, Mr. Jones. I do not retract my claim that I have no desire to possess the Bible. That is the truth. But, while I am not guilty of the sin of greed, I am guilty of another and more serious of the deadly sins."

"Oh, what is that?" Jones was interested.

"I am proud of the fact that I am not guilty of the sin of greed. That makes me guilty of the sin of pride. I am a victim of spiritual pride. And the Bible says that is a more serious sin than greed." Randollph thought what a weird scene this was—a kidnapper and his prisoner breaking bread together and debating the nature of sin. Mr. Jones was affable and personable and treated Randollph with respect. This, Randollph was aware, obscured the seriousness of his predicament. Randollph found himself liking Mr. Jones. He'd heard that the hostages in a plane hijacking often formed some kind of sympathetic relationship with their captors. He'd have to be careful to avoid liking Mr. Jones. He must remember that Jones, despite his amiability and veneer of culture, was a vicious, amoral hoodlum.

Jones stubbed out his cigar in the jade bowl. "You are an interesting man, Doctor. I've enjoyed our talk. I seldom have the opportunity to talk with an intelligent and thoughtful man. My associates, I regret to say, do not have stimulating minds." Jones got up from the table. "I'm afraid, though, that we'll have to conclude this fascinating discussion. As I told you, my business interests are not in the Chicago area. Far from here, in fact. So I have some phone calls to make. A business does not run itself."

Randollph wondered about how well his holy corporation would operate in his absence. The office routine would continue as usual under the firm guidance of Adelaide Windfall. She'd be concerned that the mysterious disappearance of the senior pastor would bring scandal to the ornate doors of Good Shepherd, but she would continue to run things as she had for so many years. The Reverend O. Bertram Smelser would go on counting and investing Good Shepherd's money as usual. Dan Gantry, he was sure, would be upset but would stretch himself to do his own job and as much of Randollph's as he could handle. And the bishop would contribute his steadying presence in the crisis. Randolph had a gloomy feeling that his business could run itself in his absence, then mentally scolded himself because he recognized that this sense of not being absolutely essential was just another manifestation of spiritual pride.

Jones paused at the door. "Perhaps you'd like to read about your mysterious disappearance, Doctor. The Sunday *Trib* is across the hall in that overstuffed parlor. Then, if you'd like some exercise, you are free to roam around the backyard. It's quite large. I believe Pack and Junior are out there throwing a football around. Pack never tires of football, and would be thrilled, I'm sure, to toss the ball around with a famous professional star. Junior will be grateful to you because he's lazy and only plays because Pack insists."

"I do need some exercise," Randollph said.

"You're likely to think about escaping, the kind of man you are. I strongly advise against it. The owner of this house has gone to some lengths to prevent, shall we say, unwanted guests from surprising him. His precautions not only keep people out, but keep people in. The brick wall that encloses the backyard is topped with electrified barbed wire. Pack and Junior both carry guns and know how to use them. They have orders to use them if you try to escape. They won't kill you. You're no good to me dead. But they know how to incapacitate you. I hope they won't need to do that."

"I'd be glad to escape, of course," Randollph told Jones. "But I'm no fool."

"I didn't think that you were," Jones said. "I'll see you at lunch, then." He closed the door after him.

WHERE IS CON RANDOLLPH?

This was the headline on a story that ran across the entire bottom third of the Sunday *Tribune*.

> —The Tribune has learned [Randollph read] that the Reverend Dr. C. P. Randollph, pastor of the Loop's Church of the Good Shepherd, is being sought by the police Bureau of Missing Persons. Dr. Randollph, known to sports fans as Con, former quarterback of the Los Angeles Rams, was last seen leaving Wesley Memorial Hospital around 12:30 A.M. Saturday morning.

The story went on to tell of his emergency pastoral visit, the calling for a taxi, and the belated detection of his disappearance. Randollph's eye scanned the story rapidly looking for something about Sammy. He had to turn the pages to the continuation of the story to find it.

> —Mrs. Randollph [it read], who is known professionally as Sam Stack, television news reporter and hostess of the popular talk show *Sam Stack's Chicago,* permitted us to interview her though she was obviously under great strain. She said she knew of no enemies who wished her husband harm, and that he had been in excellent spirits prior to being called to the hospital....

Damn Jones's eyes! Randollph thought. Curse the son of a bitch for causing Sammy so much pain and anxiety! He'd told Jones that he believed Thou Shalt Not Kill was a divine mandate. But at the moment he felt that he'd gladly strangle the smug bastard.

"Captain Wilbur Hotchkiss of Missing Persons," the story went on, "refused to speculate on what may have happened to Dr. Randollph. 'We have failed to uncover one clue, any indication,' Captain Hotchkiss said, 'but then, we haven't had much time. There are so many possibilities, and they all have to be checked out.'"

Randollph threw the paper aside. He was angry, and

he knew he mustn't permit himself the luxury of anger if he wanted to get himself out of this ridiculous predicament. He decided that the best antidote for his anger was to go outside and throw the football around as Mr. Jones had suggested.

The backyard ran the length of the house and was at least forty feet deep. Even the twelve-foot-high solid brick wall, topped by six strands of barbed wire, which enclosed the yard did not diminish it. There was a terrace of flagstones jutting out from the back of the house, ending at the edge of a kidney-shaped swimming pool. Most of the backyard was a closely clipped carpet of some durable variety of grass.

Pack had on the green-and-gold jacket he'd worn last night. Randollph could see the bulge of what was probably a gun in the right jacket pocket. Junior had on a sweatshirt covered with a heavy wool sweater. Junior bulged in so many places it was difficult to spot his gun, but Randollph did not doubt that he carried one.

Pack was exhorting Junior to "throw the damn football as far as you can," then took off from an imaginary line of scrimmage. Junior heaved a high wobbly pass which Pack timed and caught with a deftness that surprised Randollph.

"That'd been intercepted, you fat schmuck," Pack yelled at Junior. "Ya gotta throw it more on a line. Ya gotta imagine there's two or three defensive backs are tryin' to pick it off."

"Nag, nag, nag," Junior complained. "Ya act like you think you're my wife."

"Who'd marry you, ya tub of lard," Pack jeered. "You ain't got no wife an' you ain't ever goin' to have one." It was obvious that though Junior was older and larger, Pack was the dominant personality.

"Mind if I get in the game?" Randollph asked. They handn't seen him come out of the house, and both looked up startled. "Mr. Jones said it was O.K.," Randollph added to reassure them.

"Can you throw a football?" Junior asked. "I'm tired a this jerk bitching at me. Take my job."

"Can he throw a football?" Pack said contemptuously. "Don'tcha know this is Con Randollph, mebbe one of the four or five best pro quarterbacks ever lived?"

"How'm I supposed to know that?" Junior complained. "You know I don' give a shit 'bout football."

"Well, ya ought to." Randollph thought Pack sounded like a Sunday School teacher reprimanding a pupil for failing to memorize his quota of Bible verses.

Junior tossed the football to Randollph and flopped on the grass.

"Wanna throw me some passes, Con?" Pack was suddenly shy, deferential. The only gods in his pantheon were the great players, present and past, of professional football. Randollph was one of the great ones. He may have shoved a gun in the ribs of this deity last night, but then he was merely an extension of Mr. Jones. Today, on his own, something approaching reverence was the proper attitude. "Can I call you Con?"

"Sure, why not." A plan, still amorphous and requiring time to give it definition and refinement, was floating around in some corner of Randollph's mind. All he knew was that it involved Pack, so it was important to cultivate him, win his good will.

"All right," Randollph said, "let's make this as realistic as possible. Junior, would you center the ball?"

"Oh shit," Junior groaned, but dragged himself to his feet.

"Now," Randollph said, "we've just been penalized ten yards. It's third and seventeen. Pack, you're a wide receiver. See those French doors on the house?"

"Yea."

"We'll say that's where the yard marker is. You've got to get beyond those doors for a first down."

"Gotcha!" Pack was caught up in the game, excited.

"Now this is going to be a down-and-in route. You've got to get in the seam of the zone coverage."

"Yea, yea."

"So you cut straight down the field, juke to the outside toward the wall, then cut back toward the middle. Got it?"

"Got it."

"I'm a little rusty," Randollph said. "Haven't thrown a ball in quite a while. But I'll try to see that the ball is there when you've taken six steps on your cut toward the middle."

"Yea, yea!" Pack was hopping up and down with excitement.

"Now, let's line up. Junior, cover the ball. We'll go on the count of three. I'll call a string of numbers, then three huts. Like this—hut-pause-then hut, hut. On the third hut you just put the ball in my hands, Junior, and Pack, you take off. All right, line up."

Junior groaned as he bent over the ball, but passed it to Randollph on the third hut. Randollph dropped back, gripped the ball, and as Pack started his cut to the inside, threw it on a flat trajectory. When Pack turned toward Randollph, the ball was almost to him. He reached out and caught it, then laughed in sheer joy.

"Great pass, Con! How'd I do?" he said as he trotted back.

"Your moves were good. You had the first down, all right. But you forgot to wrap up the ball."

"What?"

"You've got to remember," Randollph explained patiently, "that as soon as you catch a pass like that you're more than likely going to get hit by the corner back you've faked out, or a safety, or probably both. They'll try to strip the ball when they hit you. Good receivers tuck the ball in with both arms wrapped around it as soon as they catch it. That way, they don't fumble."

"Oh. Yea. I know that. I just didn't think."

"Let's try it again," Randollph ordered. He kept throwing passes to Pack for some time. The kid just couldn't seem to get enough of it. Randollph had been cold in his borrowed sport shirt when they started, but was warming up now. It wasn't quite October yet, but it felt like an October day—crisp and chilly but with the promise of warmth to come. The exercise and the climbing sun were making Randollph sweat. Pack, he noticed, had discarded his jacket. Something in Randollph's mind told him that this was important, an item to be filed away for future reference. But it didn't tell him why it was important.

The game had to be called when Anthony came out on the terrace and said, "Luncheon is served, sir." He ignored the two young hoodlums.

"Could we play some more after lunch?" Pack asked eagerly.

"Sure," Randollph said. "Mr. Jones and I have some business to discuss, but if it doesn't take too long, I'll be glad to have another go at it."

"We'll be out here," Pack assured him.

"I'll wager that your Clarence doesn't make a better fettucini than this," Mr. Jones said, wrapping strands of the long thin pasta around his fork.

"I don't recall that he has ever served us fettucini," Randollph answered. "But I doubt that he could surpass this." He believed that Clarence, were he of a mind to prepare it, could easily produce a better example of fettucini, but thought it wise to mollify Mr. Jones.

"I dislike discussing unpleasant topics during a good meal, Doctor, but we're going to have to talk about the Bible. Time is important to me. I'm needed back in—where my business is located. And my patience is wearing thin." He replenished his wine-glass. "An excellent Chianti, none of that dago red that comes wrapped in raffia. But about the Bible. I've gone over it again in my mind, and the only reasonable explanation of Humbrecht's murder is that you did it for the Bible."

"I had no knowledge of the Bible and still have none beyond what you have told me."

"The newspapers said you were Humbrecht's friend, pastor, and regular visitor. Do you expect me to believe that he would not have shown you the Bible?"

"I'll admit that if he indeed possessed this fabulous Bible—if there was or is, in fact, such a Bible—I would think he might have shown it to me."

"I'm sure that he did. And that you stole it."

"Mr. Jones, are you aware that a Gutenberg Bible is always bound in at least two volumes—folio volumes, huge volumes?" Randollph tried to keep the exasperation out of his voice. "They are bulky. They are heavy. You can't tuck them in your jacket pocket."

"So?"

"You saw me come out of Humbrecht's house, and not long after he was murdered. Did you see me carrying two large volumes, or carrying something large enough to contain two big books?"

"No," Jones admitted. "But I've figured that out."

"Then enlighten me."

"You knew where the Bible—Bibles—was. Humbrecht showed you. You stole it days, weeks maybe, before you killed him. That day I saw you, Humbrecht had found the Bible gone, and besides himself you were the only one who knew where he kept it. You had to be the thief. So he accused you, threatened to turn you in, and you killed him." Jones sat back with the self-satisfied smile of a theologian who has just clarified an arcane dogma for a congregation of laymen.

Randollph felt his spirit sag under the weight of discouragement. True believers, like Mr. Jones, could always find a justification for their incredible beliefs.

"And I have the Bible hidden away somewhere?" Randollph asked.

"Probably in that penthouse you live in. Who's going to find it there?"

"And what do I intend to do with it?"

Jones shrugged. "How should I know? Keep it. Possess it. Enjoy it. Sell it. You being a priest, well, kind of a priest, would want this Bible, want to own it, more than the average person."

"I wouldn't even be able to read it."

"You don't read German?"

"It isn't printed in German, Mr. Jones."

"Gutenberg was a German. It was printed in Germany."

"True. But what Gutenberg printed was the Vulgate."

"The what?"

For a man willing to kill in order to own this Gutenberg Bible, Jones, Randollph thought, knew surprisingly little about it.

"The Vulgate, Mr. Jones, was a translation of the Bible into Latin, authorized by the church fathers sometime late in the fourth century. The translator was the great scholar of the day, Hieronymous—or as we know him—St. Jerome."

"The guy El Greco painted?"

"The same. His Latin translation, the Vulgate, was the Bible of the Middle Ages. Gutenberg somehow obtained an almost perfect copy of the Vulgate and used that as the text of his printed Bible." Maybe, Randollph thought, if he could knock a little of that know-it-all cockiness out of Jones he could shake the fellow's unshakable conviction that Randollph had the Bible. "The Vulgate," he added, "is still the official Bible of the Roman Catholic Church."

Jones waved his hand as if dismissing a servant. "I don't care about that. I don't care what language it's in. I value it because Humbrecht's copy is undoubtedly a great work of art, and because it is unique."

"I admit that I'd like to see it," Randollph said, watching Jones closely. Did he detect a flicker of doubt in those dark eyes, or was it a projection of his hope?

"Doctor, I like you. You are charming and interesting. But I do not let sentiment interfere with my business. I still believe you have the Bible. As you can imagine, I have ways of, shall we say, encouraging people to talk. It is not pleasant for them."

Randollph shivered.

"The sensible thing for me to do is to apply those methods to you right now, Doctor. It is perhaps a sign of weakness in me that I do not. But, because you are a kind of priest I am going to permit myself a weakness. I have a source who might be able to discover if there is a possible alternative to my theory. I think he will discover that there is not. But I shall be fair to you and try." He added, "I am never fair in my business dealings unless it is to my advantage. So I am breaking one of my own rules to be fair to you."

"I appreciate it," Randollph said with feeling. He guessed that Jones was deceiving himself. Somehow the seed of doubt had been planted and had borne fruit. Now, Jones wasn't so completely convinced that he was right. But like all true believers, he didn't dare admit to himself that he might be in error. So he called his doubt by a different name—in this case it wore the mask of fairness.

Jones pushed back his chair. "It will take me most of the afternoon to make my investigation," he informed Randollph. "Maybe you'd like to play some more football to pass the time. I'll be away for several hours, but remember, Doctor, any attempt to escape is sure to fail as well as having painful consequences for you." He said it with a menace which, Randollph guessed, was to reassure himself that he really hadn't gone soft after all.

After Jones had gone, Randollph sat at the table for a while trying to give shape to the nebulous plan for escape that had flickered into his mind earlier. The temporary absence of Jones must be counted a bonus. It occurred to him that this was a mental process much like that of writing a sermon. You began with an idea that seemed to have possibilities. You then sketched it out, at the same time probing for weaknesses and inconsistencies. Then you subtracted those parts which didn't hold up on examination. After that you buttressed your manuscript with planks of ideas calculated to give it shape and definition. Finally, you scrutinized the finished product, polished away any rough spots, and went with it.

He arranged the steps in his plan in chronological sequence. Everything had to fit, every step had to be completed successfully or he would end up, at best, a cripple. If Mr. Jones returned and found that Randollph had tried to escape and failed—well, that wasn't pleasant to contemplate. But the alternative was probably more dangerous in the end. He did not doubt that Jones, failing to find some plausible explanation for Humbrecht's murder and the theft of the Bible, would torture him. Then, if he lived through that, it was more than likely that Jones would kill him.

Randollph reviewed his plan once more. He memorized the sequence of events that he had to bring about if it was to succeed. Then he got up and headed for the backyard.

9

ALBERT VAN CAMP didn't look like a detective. He was short and slim, and wore thick-lensed spectacles in clear plastic frames. People who liked to guess at other people's occupations would have put him down as a schoolteacher or maybe an accountant. His clothes were neat but unremarkable. He had the inoffensive look of a man who habitually took orders from others and tried not to make trouble. Most people didn't notice him at all. It was a look, a personality he cultivated when he'd started his one-man office and had to follow errant husbands and other miscreants whom someone wanted under surveillance and was willing to pay him to do it. Now, as owner of a large and successful private agency, he never did that sort of work. But the long-cultivated knack of being inconspicuous had stuck.

Van Camp arrived at the west side German restaurant ahead of Jones. He always arrived ahead of clients he met outside the office. The restaurant was large and noisy with late Sunday lunchers. Husky waitresses in bright Bavarian costumes hustled among the crowded tables with plates of sauerbraten, knackwurst and kraut, and oversized steins of beer. The place was saturated with the smell of kraut and beer. Van Camp, who came here often, supposed the smell had soaked into the dark wood paneling over the years. He liked it. He liked busy, noisy places for meeting clients who didn't want to come to his office.

"Hello, Mr. Van Camp," the hostess said with a smile reserved for the best customers. She knew his name. She didn't know what he did for a living. He'd not told her and she'd not asked.

"Hello, Emily, a booth toward the back if you have one. I'm expecting a friend."

"For you I can find one. Come along."

The booth was large and dark, illuminated by a shaded low-wattage bulb in a bracket set just high enough to shed light over the large menu. "I'll wait to order until my friend comes," he told the waitress. "No, on second thought, bring me a stein of dark."

He wondered what Jones wanted of him. He'd put in a lot of hours tracing Humbrecht for Jones, earned a lot of money, too. Jones didn't object to stiff fees. He didn't know who Jones was, but he had a good idea of *what* he was. Van Camp had built a reputation for honest dealing and rigidly confidential treatment of whatever a client told him. That, he supposed, is why Jones had come to him. He didn't even know why Jones wanted to find the descendant of an Else Gensfleisch who had married one Henne Humbrecht in Mainz, Germany, and who had died in Frankfurt-on-Main, Germany, in 1475. Van Camp had just done it, because he knew how to do things like that and made plenty of money doing it. But he'd read about Johannes Humbrecht's murder. He read about every crime the newspapers reported. And he was nervous. The coincidence of having traced Humbrecht for a client only to have him murdered shortly after was too much of a coincidence. Van Camp didn't believe in coincidence, at least not one like this. If the police did a thorough investigation of Humbrecht's murder, they were bound to discover that the Van Camp agency had been interested in Humbrecht. Van Camp had a good reputation with the police, but murder was murder. All he could tell them was that

Mr. Jones, who had volunteered neither his first name nor address, had employed him to trace this latter-day descendant of Else Gensfleisch Humbrecht who, Jones believed, lived in Chicago. Jones, he reflected, must have spent a lot of money following a family tree from fifteenth-century Germany to Chicago. He had to have a powerful motivation for finding Else's descendant. Oh well, the police probably wouldn't bother much with the murder of a penniless old recluse. Too many murders in Chicago, too few homicide detectives. Chicago was a good place for a murderer. His chances of getting caught were minimal unless he knocked off someone rich, prominent and important.

Van Camp reflected on his dealings with Jones. A hundred to one he was in organized crime. High up. But not from the Chicago area. Van Camp knew by sight every top hoodlum in Chicago, Detroit, Cleveland, and St. Louis. Jones covered it well. He was cultured, soft-spoken, obviously educated. But the signs were there if you knew what to look for. A certain deadliness about the eyes. A hint of cruelty in the lips. The casual care he took not to give the detective one ounce of information beyond what he needed to know.

Van Camp was about to order another beer when Mr. Jones slid into the seat across from him. "Good afternoon, Mr. Van Camp," he said, "thank you for meeting me on a Sunday afternoon."

"We try to accommodate our good clients," Van Camp answered. "May I order something for you?"

"I've had lunch. If you haven't eaten, please do. I'll have a glass of wine."

Van Camp summoned a waitress. "Please bring this gentleman a glass of the special Pfalz. I'll have sauerbraten and kartoffel, and another stein of dark. I think you'll enjoy the Pfalz," he said when the waitress had gone. "It is a rich, somewhat sweet Rhine with an aroma and flavor the Germans prize. They get it in limited amounts so it doesn't appear on the wine list." It didn't hurt to let a client like Mr. Jones know he was getting royal treatment.

"I'm sure I'll enjoy it. I suppose you've heard about the untimely passing of Mr. Humbrecht?"

"I have."

"For me, his murder was a disaster."

"I'm sorry to hear that. I know you must have gone to great trouble and expense to trace him."

"Yes. I had a business proposition to discuss with him—a very important piece of business. But by the time I got there he was already dead." Jones paused as the waitress set a glass of white wine in a green-tinted glass in front of him, and a plate of sliced beef in a heavy brown gravy before Van Camp. Then he continued, choosing his words carefully. "There is a possibility that I can still complete this business transaction. To do so will require some discreet inquiries."

Van Camp forked up a chunk of sauerbraten, then followed it with a swallow of brown beer. Having your mouth full was a good reason to keep quiet, let Jones do the talking. Jones sipped his wine and said, "Excellent," but Van Camp could tell that he hadn't really tasted it. "Let us assume," Jones said, putting down his glass and pushing it aside, "that a rare and expensive painting or sculpture or manuscript—like, let us say, a first-edition Shakespeare—had been obtained, er, illegally by someone who wanted to sell it. Would you know the—the dealer—or maybe dealers—here in Chicago who could find a buyer for that kind of merchandise?"

Van Camp tore a thick slice of pumpernickel in half and began to butter it. "Yes," he said.

"Good! What I need to know is if anyone is offering a special, a one-of-a-kind Gutenberg Bible for sale. Or, if one has been sold recently, who is the buyer. And if it is still on the market, who is the seller."

Van Camp mopped up thick brown gravy with pumpernickel before answering. "I can probably get you the information you want—if it is to be had. Nothing illegal about obtaining information and passing it along. I have to assume that you want to buy the Bible."

"Correct. And I'm willing to pay top price."

"What would be illegal, Mr. Jones, would be for me to act as your agent in negotiations or purchase. I could lose my license, my agency, for doing that."

"Yes, yes, of course," Jones said impatiently. "I'm not asking you to do that. Just get me the information. What I do with it is my problem."

"One more thing."

"Yes, what?"

"I take it you want to deal with the seller directly."

"Yes. I'm in a hurry. I can't afford the time to haggle through a middleman."

"Then I'll have to personally guarantee that the middleman, the dealer, will get his commission. Otherwise, I can't get the name of the seller."

"The dealer will take your guarantee?"

"I have a reputation for keeping my word. I'm in a business full of crummy operators. If you can afford to be honest, and I can, it's very very good for business."

"Of course I'll guarantee the dealer's commission," Jones said impatiently. "But are you willing to take my word for it?"

Van Camp chewed thoughtfully before answering. "I judge you to be a man who, once he gives his word, considers it a matter of honor to keep it," he answered. "And," he added, "I didn't get to the top of my profession by misreading character."

"Thank you," Jones said, obviously appreciating the compliment. "You haven't misread mine. How soon can you get this information? Time is a very important factor in this deal."

Van Camp finished his sauerbraten, wiped his mouth with his napkin, and said, "With luck, right away." He slid out of the booth. "If you will excuse me I'll make a phone call."

While Van Camp was gone, Jones sipped at his wine without enjoying it. He didn't expect anything to come from Van Camp's inquiries. He was still almost sure that Randollph was guilty. But Randollph had shaken his certainty just a little. Randollph had had the opportunity and the means to kill Humbrecht and steal the Bible. The Bible itself was motive enough for murder. In fact, if Van Camp uncovered any information Jones expected that Randollph would turn out to be the seller. He hoped that's what Van Camp would discover. He'd gone to a lot of trouble to kidnap Randollph. He didn't want to waste time dealing with someone else. At the same time, he admitted to himself, he would be just a little disappointed to have his convictions about Randollph confirmed. He liked Randollph. He'd enjoyed his company and their conversations. Jones had no illusions about the goodness of the human species. He looked on everyone as corrupt or corruptible. Yet there was some kind of sincerity about this Randollph that came through as genuine. Probably just a well-perfected act, Jones thought. The clergy, even the worst of them—and Jones had known some pretty bad ones—had to pretend to be good, sincere, righteous. It was their stock-in-trade. Randollph was probably just better at it than most.

Van Camp was sitting across from him again before Jones, deep in his thoughts, noticed that the little detective had returned. Van Camp had to clear his throat before Jones looked up from his wine-glass.

"I have the information," he announced in a flat, matter-of-fact tone. "A seller got in touch with this dealer a couple of weeks ago. Said he wanted a buyer for what he described as a one-of-a-kind Gutenberg Bible, prime condition. Gutenberg's personal Bible, handed down through his family. Asking price, two million cash, no checks."

Jones felt the excitement rising in him. "Cheap at that price."

"A little out of my price range," Van Camp said dryly. "There are some interested buyers. A couple of South American millionaires, fellows who probably own half a country. One dictator of a banana republic who wants it as portable wealth if things get too hot for him and he has to leave in a hurry."

"But no deal has been made?"

"Not yet. The dealer thinks the seller hopes to jack up the price if enough possible buyers get to bidding against one another."

"Does the dealer have the Bible?"

"No. The seller says it is in a safe place, and he can deliver in forty-eight hours."

"Did you get the name of the seller?"

"Yes. That was the hard part. The dealer didn't want to tell me, but he trusts me and my assurance about his commission. One thing."

"Yes, what is it?" Jones hardly realized his voice had become harsh and raspy.

"I promised him there would be no rough stuff, no attempt to injure the seller and steal the Bible."

Jones knew it was a question. "You have my word," he said.

"All right, I'll take that." Van Camp explored his jacket pocket and came up with a piece of paper. He handed it to Jones. "This is the name of the seller and his address."

Jones clutched at the paper. He glanced at it and said softly, "Well, I'll be damned! Who is he?"

"Never heard of him."

"How'd he get his hands on the Bible?" Jones asked the question more of himself than of Van Camp.

"I have no idea, and I don't want to know," Van Camp said. "Waitress." The girl hurried over. Van Camp was known as a generous tipper. "Would you bring me a slice of Black Forest torte and a cup of coffee? Black."

So, Jones thought, I was wrong about Randollph. Jones didn't like to be wrong. He'd succeeded in business, had risen to a position of dominance by being right. In his line of work if you were wrong very often you ended up dead. Jones was as severely analytical of himself as he was of others. He just didn't make mistakes, he knew, when he obeyed his own rule of excluding emotion from the decision-making process. He also knew that his obsession with the Gutenberg Bible, his need to possess it, to enjoy it and to use it for the salvation of his sin-blackened immortal soul had served to dim his wits. He was in the grip of something he couldn't shake. Nothing in his adult life had been so exciting as the search for the last of the Gutenbergs and the Bible. No prize had ever seemed so worth pursuing.

Now he had a double problem. He had to get in touch with and deal with the seller of the Bible. And he had to decide what to do about Randollph. He'd feel better if he could figure out some way to compensate Randollph for the indignities to which he had been subjected. Jones owed him that, and he was a man who didn't like to be in anyone's debt. But that was the counsel of his emotions. His unsentimental judgment was that it would be a mistake to let Randollph go. Free, Randollph was a threat to Jones. He could identify him. Though he'd never been in jail, the police would have mug shots of Cristoforo Bartelione. The thought of standing trial for kidnapping a prominent pastor and sports hero was most unattractive. Instinct and emotionless calculation convinced Jones that his wisest option was to kill Randollph.

Jones forced his mind back to the moment. He pulled an envelope from the inside pocket of his jacket and laid it by Van Camp's plate. "There's five thousand dollars in the envelope," he said. "Will that cover your fee for your work today?"

Van Camp pocketed the envelope. "That will cover it very nicely," he said. "May I order you something more?"

"No, thank you, I must be going."

"If you don't mind, I think I'll stay and have another slice of this delicious torte," Van Camp said. He had a rule that he never left with a client.

10

WHEN RANDOLLPH went out into the backyard after lunch, he found Pack and Junior sitting in a shady spot by the wall. It wasn't warm yet. He could feel the chill through his borrowed sports shirt. But it was warming up. Much warmer than this morning. He hoped the sun would hurry up with its work. The sun was essential to his plan. He was counting on a cooperative providence to keep the clouds away.

When Pack saw Randollph he came to his feet in a hurry. "Hey, Con," he yelled, "catch." He threw a wobbly and not too accurate pass to Randollph, who let the ball settle into his large hands.

"Ole blubber butt here quit on me," Pack explained. "Says he's tired."

"Well, I am," Junior complained.

"You were born tired."

"Besides, I want to watch TV. Why do I gotta play football with you all the time?"

"Oh, let him go watch television," Randollph said, hoping he didn't sound too eager. Getting rid of Junior was step number one in his plan. "I thought I'd show you a few moves a wide receiver needs. We don't need him for that."

"O.K., the man says you can go watch your stupid TV," Pack said, "so get the hell out of here and leave the field to us athletes."

"You're a sweet guy, Pack, you know that?" Junior said sarcastically, and trotted toward the house.

Now for step number two, Randollph thought, and hoped it would be as easy as step number one.

"Let me throw you a few, get myself warmed up," he said. He had to get that jacket off Pack if possible. If Pack didn't shed it, the job would be more dangerous, but he'd have to manage some way.

"Sure, Con." Pack was almost reverent.

Randollph started the young hood out with a few short, easy passes. Then he had him running longer and longer routes. After a fifty-yard fly pattern, Pack came dragging back to the imaginary line of scrimmage.

"I'm pooped," he said, flopping on the ground. "Sure is nifty, though, the way I turn where you tell me an' the ball's right there. Soon's I catch my breath, how about you show me some of them moves you said you would?"

"Whenever you're ready," Randollph said. "Getting hot, isn't it? If this were a real game and you were in uniform you'd be sweating like a pig." He hoped there was something to the power of suggestion.

"I am anyway," Pack said. "I'm gonna get rid of this damn jacket." Randollph tried not to watch as Pack unzipped his jacket, shucked it off, and dropped it. Randollph did note that the pocket containing the gun was on the underside next to the ground. Good! That meant that Pack was so absorbed in the game he'd forgotten he was supposed to be guarding a prisoner.

"All right, you're the wide receiver and I'm the defensive man you've got to get by and get open," Randollph instructed. "I can give you a bump, just one. I'll try to do it so as to upset your timing, make you take too long to run your route. That way the quarterback has to eat the ball, get sacked or try to find another receiver open. Or, if he's throwing to a spot and you can't get to the spot in time, it's either incomplete or an interception. But you know all that, don't you?"

"Yeh, I know."

"Then let's try it. Line up. Now make up your mind how you plan to fake me out and get by me. I'll try to bump you, throw you off stride. I'll do it easy; but I'm not going to let you get by me without a bump—not if I can help it, that is."

"Sure, I want you to make it tough for me, Con. Ready when you are."

Randollph was careful to establish an area not too far from the discarded jacket from which Pack would take off.

"Now," he told Pack, "go when I say hut."

"O.K."

"Hut!"

Pack took a half-step right, then left, then right. It was what Randollph expected him to do. He knew that most players run better and more naturally to their right, especially if they are right-handed. So Randollph gave him a gentle bump before letting him by. They went through the same routine several times, until Randollph could make an accurate guess as to how Pack would move each time. Like some professionals, Pack unconsciously followed a sequence of four or five different moves. If Pack stuck to his pattern, his next routine would be the right-left-right fake.

"Now this time you chuck me a little harder if I manage to get in your way," Randollph told Pack. He wanted Pack to have extra momentum when he started his moves.

"If you say so."

"Ready?"

"Yea."

"All right, hut!"

As Randollph had anticipated, Pack took a step to the right, then left, then drove hard back to his right. Randollph got in front of him, and just as Pack bowled into him locked his hands together, brought them up hard under Pack's chin while simultaneously driving a knee into Pack's stomach. Randollph quickly ascertained that the hoodlum was out cold, then grabbed the green-and-gold jacket and snatched the gun from its pocket. It looked like the gun Lieutenant Casey carried. Randollph made sure the safety was on, then flipped the still unconscious Pack face down on the ground. He bound Pack's hands behind him, using the sleeves of the jacket for a rope. It wasn't the most secure of bindings, but it would have to do and probably would. He then turned Pack face up, took his own handkerchief and stuffed it into Pack's mouth. By now Pack was regaining consciousness. He looked at Randollph with glazed eyes.

"Now listen carefully," Randollph said. "I want you to understand that I don't intend to wait around here for Mr. Jones. Sooner or later he's going to kill me. So I'm desperate. If I have to kill you, I'll do it." He saw a flicker of fear in Pack's eyes. "You're going to help me. I know you don't want to, but helping me is better than being dead, which is what you'll be if you don't do exactly as I say. I hope you don't doubt that I'll shoot you if you give me trouble." The fear in Pack's eyes was more palpable now.

"Here's what we're going to do," Randollph continued. "We're going to walk into the house, me behind you with this gun in your back. Then we're going to surprise Junior. You're going to help me tie him up. Now if I were in your place and had any ideas about trying to get away from me, that's when I would try it. So I'm going to be very alert, and I'm going to be very quick with the gun. I'm handy with a gun. I was the champion marksman on my college team." Randollph wondered if he'd ever told a bigger lie, and couldn't think of one. He disliked guns and knew little about them. He'd have to hope that he sounded sure of himself. "I could take both you and Junior out before you could get at me. On your feet. Let's go."

There was a large television set in the parlor or living room, Randollph remembered. He quietly opened the door that led from the medieval hall into the living room, prodding Pack to precede him. The television set was blaring a singing commercial for a detergent. Junior was stretched out on one of the sofas sound asleep.

Randollph had figured in advance that the most likely material at hand for tying up Junior would be the wire by which the many pictures on the wall were hung.

Keeping the gun on Pack with one hand, he managed to take down two of the paintings with his free hand. Now came a difficult step. He had to keep watching both hoodlums while twisting loose the screw eyes holding the wire to the picture frames. He made Pack lie face down on the floor. Junior slept on. Randollph soon had two lengths of braided picture wire free from the frames. He quickly found a poker by the fireplace where he'd remembered seeing it. Then he untied Pack's hands and softly ordered him to his feet.

"Take this," he whispered to Pack, handing him one of the strands of wire, "and go stand by Junior's feet. I'll be at his head with the gun on him. I want you to get that wire around his feet as quick as you can and twist it tight. He'll probably wake up while you're doing it, but I'll keep him quiet. If he gets rowdy, I'll clout him with this poker. And if you get any ideas, well, you're too far away to hit with the poker, so I'll just have to shoot you. Understand?" Pack nodded. "And get that wire tight fast. I'll be testing it. If you leave it loose, I'll assume you did it on purpose and punish you."

When they were both positioned, Randollph nodded to Pack. He was surprised by the swiftness with which Pack bound Junior's feet together and twisted the wire. Pack had good hands. Junior grunted, opened his eyes, and said, "What the hell you think you're doin'—" Randollph cut him off by pressing the point of the poker into Junior's Adam's apple. "Be quiet and you won't get hurt," Randollph said in the toughest tones he could muster. "If you cause any trouble, I'll clout you across the throat with this poker. It'll hurt like hell and you won't talk again for a long time, if ever. If you try to get up, this gun I'm pressing against your head will go off. I don't want that to happen. It would splatter blood and brains all over me and I'd be a mess." He hoped that Junior's dim, sleep-befuddled wits could comprehend the situation. He quickly patted the bulges around Junior's belly, located the gun, took it, and shoved it into his belt.

"Now, Junior," Randollph said, "Pack is going to roll you over on your face. Pack isn't doing this because he wants to. He's doing it because I'll shoot him if he doesn't. And if you don't cooperate, I'll shoot you, too. You two thugs kidnapped me and put my life in danger. It would be a pleasure to shoot you both. So don't tempt me." Randollph was surprised at the feeling that surged through him as he saw the fear in both faces. He was master. He had the gun. They'd pushed him around, now he was pushing them around. They'd humiliated him. Now he was visiting the same indignities on them. An eye for an eye, a tooth for a tooth.

"I gotta go to the crapper," Junior whined.

"You'll have to solve that problem as you think best," Randollph told him coldly. "When Pack gets you rolled over on your face he's going to tie your hands with this piece of wire. Then he's going to take this table scarf here and tie it around your mouth. Remember, I'll be standing here with the gun on you. If I were you, I wouldn't even twitch. Also, after we leave, you might try to roll off the sofa and make a lot of noise. I wouldn't. You'd most likely break a kneecap, or maybe your nose. Break your nose and you'd choke to death on your own blood." Randollph didn't know if this was true or not, but he was sure Junior would believe it. "All right, Pack, get busy."

When Junior was face down, trussed and gagged, Randollph ordered Pack to lie face down on the floor, then quickly checked Junior's binding. The wires were secure. If Junior tried to work them loose, he'd only succeed in giving himself intense pain. Randollph guessed that Junior didn't care much for pain.

"Now, Pack, get up and take the gag out of your mouth. You know enough not to yell or raise a fuss, don't you?" Pack nodded dumbly and did as he was told.

"What cars are in the garage?" Randollph asked.

Pack tried to speak, but at first no sound came. Then, in a shaky voice he said, "Mr. Jones, he prob'ly took the Buick." He wrinkled his brow as if it hurt to think. "That leaves a Caddy sedan, a Mercedes station wagon, a Jag XJ, and a Rolls convertible."

"My, my, the owner of this house must be in a profitable line of business," Randollph commented. "You have access to the keys?"

"What?"

"Do you know where the keys to the cars are kept?"

"Sure. In a box in the garage."

"We'll take the Rolls. It's harder to see into the back of a convertible. You ever drive it?"

"Yeah. It's a sweetheart. Wish it was mine."

Pack, Randollph could see, was returning to something like normal. He'd better figure a way to put the fear of God back into him.

"What's the procedure when someone drives out?"

"I don't getcha."

"Does the guard at the gate check the car? Don't lie to me. I'm going out of here, and you're going to drive me. In a minute I'll describe what is going to happen to you if you try to cross me. It might not kill you, but you'd wish you were dead."

"We phone the gate," Pack said in a subdued voice. "We tell the guy who's comin' out and what car. That way he opens the gate so's the car don't hafta stop. Mr. Jones, he don' like to hafta stop."

"How do you get to the garage?"

"Through the kitchen."

"Will anyone be in the kitchen now?"

"Proly not."

"Let's hope not. I don't want to shoot innocent people. Shooting you I don't mind. You aren't innocent." Randollph grinned what he intended to be an evil grin at Pack. "Come to think of it, I can't kill you. I need you to drive me out of here. I could bang you up some, though. Hurt you plenty."

Pack almost cowered. "I ain't gonna give you no trouble, Con."

"Dr. Randollph to you, you little creep." He motioned with the gun. "Lead the way."

There was no one in the kitchen. Pack preceded Randollph to the door that opened into the garage. The garage was nearly as clean as the kitchen. The expensive cars gave it the look of a dealership in a posh suburb.

"Where are the keys?"

"In that box." Pack pointed to a rectangular green steel box fixed to the wall by the kitchen door.

"Open it slowly, get the keys to the Rolls, and toss them to me carefully."

Randollph caught the keys. "I see there's a telephone

by the key box. Now here is what I want you to do. Call the gate. Tell the guard—does he have a name?"

"Pete. That's all I know. He's on now. Harry's night guard."

"You tell him Mr. Jones called you. He wants the Rolls. You're supposed to take it to him, bring the Buick back. Got it?"

"Sure."

"Then you're going to drive out that gate. I'll be in the back, stretched out on the floor. If you drive right out, Pete won't see me. If you decide to stop at the gate, I'll shoot both you and Pete before either of you can do anything. Remember, I've got two guns now."

"I ain't gonna try anything, Con—Dr. Randollph."

"Now, when you are out of the gate, I want you to turn toward town—Chicago. Which way?"

"Left."

"Then drive a couple of blocks, just be sure you're out of sight of the gate, and pull over and park. And, Pack."

"Yea?"

"Convertibles have bucket seats."

"I know." Pack looked puzzled.

"If anything funny happens, I'll shove the back of your seat forward and shoot you through the crack of the seat. Got that?"

"Yea. You'd shoot me in the ass."

"More than that," Randollph said.

Pack cringed. "You'd shoot off my balls and my dick? That's awful!"

"Yes, that would be awful. No more girls, ever, for the rest of your life. I don't like to do a thing like that even to a jerk like you. But I will if necessary. I tell you this so that you will have no doubts about the pain and suffering you will endure if you try anything. I have nothing to lose. If I don't get out, I'm almost sure to be a dead man. You understand me?"

"Yea." Pack was trembling. He was more afraid of being desexed than of being dead.

"All right. Call the gate. No unnecessary chitchat with Pete."

Pack, his hand shaking, picked the phone from its cradle and punched one of the plastic buttons. "Pete?

Pack. Mr. Jones called. He wants the Rolls, wants me to bring it to him an' bring the Buick back. Why? How the hell should I know why. He don' tell me, I don' ask. Be out in three minutes or so."

"You did good," Randollph told him as he hung up. "The garage door open with an electric switch?"

"Yea. Each door has its own switch. Ya just punch that little button on the thing in the glove compartment."

"All right. Get in the car. I'll get in and hand you the keys. Then you open the garage door, back out, close the door, and drive out. Not too fast, not too slow."

"I usually toot the horn as I pass Pete, pass the gatehouse. He proly won't even come out. Gates work on electricity too."

"Toot at him then, if that's what you usually do." Randollph settled himself as best he could on the floor behind the front seat. He wished the Rolls had a front-drive transmission because it was not easy to lie across the hump down the middle of the floor which accommodated the driveshaft. "Let's go."

Randollph could hear the garage door slide up, then the soft, even sound of the big motor as it came to life. He could feel the car move slowly backward, then stop. Was Pack trying something?

"Why are you stopping?" he barked.

"Jus' to put the door down, like you tol' me."

"Yes, all right, get it done." I'm getting awfully jumpy, Randollph thought. Better calm down, keep my wits about me. The car began to move again. He heard the quick toot-toot of the horn, barely felt the dip as the big car came off the driveway and onto the street. Then a left turn. It wasn't long before it slowed, then stopped.

"Keep both hands on the wheel," Randollph ordered, and struggled upright. He pushed the back of the passenger seat forward, unlatched the door and swung it open, then scrambled out and back into the passenger seat. He pushed the nose of the gun into Pack's side. "Now, head for downtown Chicago, the Loop."

"Sure." Pack pulled onto the street. So far as Randollph could tell there was no fight in him, but that was no reason to relax. He did notice the car, though. It was a bright, shimmery metallic-blue color. How many hand-rubbed coats of paint had it taken to achieve the depth and richness of that color? And how many cows had died to provide this buttery leather upholstery that smelled so expensive? Randollph couldn't imagine anyone paying in excess of a hundred and fifty thousand dollars for this car, lovely as it was. They were buying more than luxurious transportation, of course. They were buying status. They were reinforcing their egos, reassuring themselves that they were important people. Their sinfully costly car said to the world, "Look at me. Look and envy my success. Look and realize that I am one of the very special few. There aren't many people in the world who can afford this car." People who bought cars like this Rolls-Royce were, by Randollph's lights, guilty of wanton extravagance—which, he reflected, was a child of spiritual pride. He wondered if, on a lesser scale, he was guilty of the same sin when he thought nothing of spending five hundred dollars or more for a suit. Did the monetary difference between the Rolls-Royce owner's extravagance and his mitigate his sin of squandering money on clothes? Randollph realized that he didn't care about cars. He did care about clothes. It occurred to him that he might have some uncomfortable moments when he got back to writing those sermons on the seven deadly sins.

Randollph hadn't noticed the blue and white police cruiser behind them until he heard the sudden howl of the siren. The cruiser accelerated, drew parallel with the Rolls. The officer waved them toward the curb. "Do as he says," Randollph ordered Pack, jabbing him in the ribs with the gun.

The officer sauntered up to the driver's side of the car. "Put your window down," Randollph said to Pack. Pack pushed the little switch that lowered the window. "May I see your driver's license, sir?" the officer asked Pack. Then he noticed the gun Randollph was pressing into Pack's side. He had his own gun out very fast. "O.K., buddy," he said, "drop it on the floor and put your hands on the dashboard."

"Gladly, officer," Randollph answered, dropping the gun.

"Hey, let me look at you—you're—you're Reverend

Randollph, everybody's looking for you. Pictures in every precinct station. Sweet Jesus!—oh, sorry, Reverend."

"Under the circumstances we'll consider it a prayer of thanksgiving. Yes, I'm C. P. Randollph. I'd like to charge this fellow—I don't even know his name—with kidnapping, along with a couple of his accomplices. I also need to call my wife and Lieutenant Casey—"

"Mike Casey?"

"Know him?"

"Know of him. We'd better handcuff sonny boy here and get to the station." He opened the door. "Outside, punk. Face the car, spread your feet, and put your hands behind your back." He quickly cuffed a meek and unresisting Pack. "I'll just call for a little help," he told Randollph, "then you can follow me to the station."

"How did you happen to stop us?" Randollph asked.

"I noticed this crummy-looking kid driving a Rolls—well, people that drive a Rolls, you know, he just isn't the type. Thought I'd better check it out." He looked admiringly at the Rolls. "Beautiful car. Where'd you get it, Reverend?"

"I stole it," Randollph said.

Mr. Jones sensed that something was wrong an instant before he saw that the iron gates were wide open and there was no one in the gatehouse. He felt a spurt of fear but quickly quelled it. He curbed his reaction to speed up and get the hell out of there, maintaining a normal speed as he drove by. When he glimpsed the three police cars in front of the house he knew something very bad for him had happened. He wondered momentarily what it could have been, and cursed his luck. But he wasted little time on speculation or swearing. He'd learned one of life's important lessons—that even the most careful plans get screwed up now and then by the unexpected, by some event even Solomon couldn't anticipate. Therefore, the wise man always had a fallback position prepared, a contingency plan laid out. He'd also learned that only stupid people indulged themselves by raging at the Fates when they aren't smiling on you.

He turned at the next block and headed toward the expressway. He knew there was nothing back at the house to connect him with it. Even his wardrobe had the labels snipped out. He had to assume, though, that Pack and Junior were in police custody, and they could identify the car he was driving. He'd have to ditch it soon. He'd had the foresight to lease a small furnished duplex on the near north side. It was in an area where no one knew or cared who his neighbors were. It was stocked with food, clothes, and—very important—an anonymous Ford sedan in the garage. It was also within walking distance of an el stop. After he got rid of the Buick, he'd have to get to an elevated station by taxi. Mr. Jones didn't welcome all the inconvenience, but he expected to complete his business in a few days and be gone. After all, he now knew who had the Bible.

11

THEA MASON had come. The bishop and his wife had come. Mike and Liz Casey had come. Dan Gantry had come. Sammy was both glad and sorry they were all there. Glad because they kept her from being alone with her tormenting thoughts. Sorry because they made her feel like a widow at her husband's wake. She was more glad than sorry, she decided. After all, these were people who cared for her. Cared for Randollph. They were anxious as she was anxious. They hurt too. The strong girders of their affection supported her. She knew that if some good news about Randollph didn't come in soon, she was bound to fall apart emotionally. The presence of these friends helped her postpone that moment. She wondered what people who had no friends, no one who cared about them, did when overtaken by crisis and potential tragedy.

Clarence Higbee believed proper servants, even a majordomo, always communicated with their employers in an emotionless voice and demeanor. Announcing either that dinner is served or that the house is burning down was done in the same tone and manner. But as he came into the large odd-shaped living room, he was unable to conceal completely his glad excitement.

"A call for you, madam," he announced to Sammy. "It's Dr. Randollph. He's safe and in good health."

A cheer went up from the assembled friends. Sammy felt suddenly faint as if the inner steel with which she had braced herself had collapsed under the strain. Then she came out of her seat fast and ran from the room.

"I wonder whatever could have happened to him," the bishop's wife said.

"There is little point in speculating, Violet," the bishop said gently. "In the absence of any information, speculation is fruitless. Presumably we shall know shortly."

Sammy came back into the room. "He was kidnapped," she said. "He escaped. He'll be here soon. Mike, he wants to talk to you. I told him you were here." Sammy's voice trembled. She wasn't quite under control yet.

"Would you like us to leave, Sam?" Dan Gantry asked with uncharacteristic gentleness.

"No. Oh no. He'll want to see you, tell you about it."

Clarence cleared his throat. "May I suggest, madam, that a small celebration is in order? I can chill some champagne and prepare a collation."

Sammy clapped her hands. "That sounds just right!"

"My nerves are frazzled, Clarence, I need a shot of real hooch to calm them. Just for medicinal purposes, you understand," Dan Gantry said.

"Me too," Thea Mason said.

"Mr. Gantry, you know our liquor stock. Perhaps you would care for your needs and those of the guests while I prepare for the celebration."

"Sure, Clarence, glad to. Orders now being taken." He walked over to Sammy, bent down and kissed her on top of her head. "You first, sweetheart."

"Danny Boy, I'm so high right now, any more and I'd go right through the roof."

"I'll not point out, then, that alcohol is a depressant. Used moderately it is a salve for the wounded spirit, lifts the mind above the cares of the day, and tastes damn good. Used immoderately it turns people into disgusting drunks and raises merry hell with their lives. There, that's my temperance sermon."

"A good sermon, Dan, but her soul is singing a Te Deum. That's even better than booze," the bishop commented.

When the door chimes rang, Sammy flew to the foyer. The others could hear conversation and quiet sobbing. Then Sammy led a somewhat disheveled Randollph into the living room and everyone was pumping his hand, kissing him, laughing, and pounding him on the back. Finally Randollph said, "I feel like the Prodigal Son must have felt when he at last returned home from a far country."

"And we want to hear of your adventures," the bishop said.

"Make a deal with you," Randollph replied. "I need a bath and a change of clothes. I'll be quick about it. Then I'll tell you all about it."

"I'll come along and scrub your back," Sammy volunteered.

"A simple meal hurriedly prepared, but I'm sure no one need go hungry," Clarence said as he began to unload the serving cart. "There are pâté sandwiches, my own pâté. Virginia ham sandwiches. And these browned round ones consist of a layer of sliced chicken breast and white truffles and a layer of grated Emmenthal cheese mixed with heavy cream and brandy, then dipped in beaten eggs and browned in hot butter. This plate," he explained as he transferred it to the table, "is chutney eggs. Sliced hard-cooked eggs with a sauce of chutney, gooseberry jam, and a bit of lemon and orange juice and grated orange rind. Since Dr. Randollph is especially fond of gooseberry jam—and you, too, m'lord—I wanted to serve a dish that contained it. There is hot German-style potato salad, sliced yellow tomatoes and cucumbers in French mustard dressing. And, presently, ice cream with rum sauce. Did your, ah, captors feed you adequately, Dr. Randollph?"

"Adequately, but not splendidly. I had occasion to criticize the hollandaise sauce on the eggs Benedict at breakfast. Told my host that you did it much better, Clarence. He was not pleased."

"Not everyone can turn out a decent hollandaise."

"It seems to me, C.P., that a prisoner who is served eggs Benedict has little reason to complain about the cuisine," the bishop said.

"I wanted to irritate him. He is a proud and haughty man, albeit likable enough when he wants to be. I know how anxious you all are to know what happened. I might talk with my mouth full, but I'll go right ahead and tell you about it."

"May I record it?" Thea asked. "After all, I'm a newspaper person."

"Yes, but you'll have to agree to some rules I lay down. You probably can't get it in your paper till Tuesday morning. You'll see why in a minute. Agreed?"

"Agreed."

Randollph told them the story.

"You see, Thea," he concluded, "we don't want to start talk about this Gutenberg Bible until we have more evidence that it actually exists, or ever existed."

"How will you find out?"

"Humbrecht's will is to be opened and read tomorrow morning. If, in fact, he actually owned such a Bible, he undoubtedly made provision for its disposal in his will."

"Do you believe he did have it?"

"I don't know, Thea. Mr. Jones—whoever he is—was convinced."

"I devoutly hope that Mr. Jones was right," Casey said.

"Why, Mike?" Thea asked.

"Because then I'd have a bottled-in-bond motive for Humbrecht's murder. It's hell working on a murder when you haven't a clue to the motive behind it. But with a motive established, we can be pretty certain we'll solve it."

Thea turned to Randollph. "If it turns out there is a Bible that Gutenberg made up for himself, well, I need to know something about it. All I know is that Gutenberg invented printing—for which I should be grateful, since I make a dandy living out of being printed—and that he printed the Bible. Can you tell me anything about him, human interest stuff, that'll pep up the story—that is, if it turns out to be the story?"

"Well," Randollph said, "we could begin with the fact that his name wasn't Gutenberg."

"Come on!"

"His family name was Gensfleisch. As best anyone can tell, he was born just before the fourteenth century turned to the fifteenth—say about 1395. Johannes or Henne Gensfleisch was a son of Frilo Gensfleisch, a patrician of Mainz, whose family home was known as Gutenberg. For some reason, Johannes chose to be known as Gutenberg rather than Gensfleisch."

"Easier to pronounce," Dan Gantry said.

"Also, if you want to be accurate, don't say he invented printing."

"I don't get it. All the history books say he did."

"Printing with carved wooden blocks had been done for centuries before Gutenberg. There is even some evidence that the Koreans and maybe the Chinese had done some experimenting with printing using ceramic symbols before Gutenberg's time."

"Then what did he do?"

"He invented printing with movable metal type. For all practical purposes that was the invention of printing. His methods with some modification and improvements, of course—remained fundamentally unchanged for over four hundred years."

"How I'd love to see that Bible," the bishop said. "If it is as your Mr. Jones said, it must be a thing of exquisite beauty. If I remember correctly, Gutenberg set out to print a Bible that looked like a medieval hand-illuminated manuscript—and succeeded."

"You're right," Randollph said. "He even tried to invent color printing so that the initials and chapter headings could be in red and blue. But he failed. So he left those spaces blank to be filled in by hand. Purchasers got only the unbound pages. They would then commission a monk or someone who knew how to do it to fill in the initials and chapter headings in color, and to illuminate the manuscript. Then the purchaser had to have it bound—usually in two volumes, sometimes three."

"You couldn't just sneak it out of the house under your coat, then?" Casey asked. "Whoever stole it from old man Humbrecht would have come prepared with something to carry them in."

"I suppose you could walk out with one volume under each arm," Randollph answered, "but I doubt if anyone would. Too risky. You might drop one—or both—and damage them. If we assume this murderer and thief planned to sell the Bible, he'd be careful to protect them."

"I want to play up your escape," Thea said. "That's the most exciting part of the story. Con Randollph overpowers kidnappers and uses their own guns to effect his escape."

"No!" Randollph startled himself with the ferocity of his answer.

"Why not? I don't see—"

"Sorry I yelled, Thea. I'll tell you why not. I feel, well, ashamed of myself for that particular part of the story."

"It's the best part."

"Not for me. It's complicated."

"Perhaps, C.P.," the bishop said, "you realized that you haven't as yet reached that state of grace in which you willingly turn the other cheek."

"There's that, Freddie. I could live with that, though. I could rationalize it on the grounds that I was doing the only thing I could to save my life."

"Then what's the problem?"

"It's this. When I had that gun in my hand, I felt a sense of power I'd never felt before. I could make those two young hoods do my bidding, I could push them around. When I told them I would gladly shoot them for the way they had humiliated and degraded me, I suddenly realized that I meant it. I think if Jones had come in I might well have shot him just from rage. The worst thing about it was that I actually enjoyed this feeling. I found out something about myself that I hadn't known, that I have in me—me, a Christian preacher—the potential for violence."

"Best argument I've heard yet for banning hand guns," Dan said.

"I hated finding this out about myself," Randollph continued. "When I'd calmed down, I felt dirty, soiled by the same filth that covers those two young hoods, or Mr. Jones. I thought better of myself than that. I hadn't known I was that kind of person, and I hated finding out that I could be that kind of person."

"But, C.P., you're a good enough theologian to know that we are all—at least potentially—that kind of person," the bishop said. "The Christian's life is filled with ambiguities. Christian ethics so often has to tell us not to do what we are naturally inclined to do. Why should you be exempt from the general condition of the human race?"

"I don't know. I thought I was above the temptation to wield power and visit violence on others—above enjoying it, anyway."

Lieutenant Casey spoke up. "I seem to remember that St. Augustine said there are three Christian virtues. The first is humility, the second is humility, and the third is humility." Casey did his best to avoid looking like a man who has just made a hole-in-one.

"A cop that quotes St. Augustine. Hear, hear!" Dan Gantry said. "How does that go over down at the station house?"

"Never tried it. They'd think I was putting on airs."

"Are you, Mike?" Liz Casey asked slyly.

Casey laughed. "Maybe Dr. Randollph and I both need a lesson in humility."

"I expect I do. I know I do," Randollph said. "I'll take it that way. Then I can salvage something from the experience. I'm upset because my self-image is damaged. I'm not as good as I thought I was. I suppose we all need to be reminded of that now and then."

"I seem to recall that you are preparing a series of sermons on the seven deadly sins," the bishop said. "You are collecting plenty of material, especially about the sin of pride."

"True. And it's much more comfortable to research it in books. Anyway, Thea, I hope you see why I don't want you to picture me as a hero."

"Con Randollph the sharpshooter rides again," Dan said.

"Dan's right, you know," Thea answered him. "No matter what you want, that's how the media is going to play it. It's too good an angle to pass up. You believe in the first amendment to the Constitution?"

"You know I do." Randollph could see what was coming.

"Then you believe in freedom of the press, but in this instance you want to dictate how the press portrays you. That's what politicians always do. They yell that they believe in freedom of the press, then get mad if they get what they think is unfavorable publicity."

Randollph smiled ruefully. "This seems to be my day for lessons in humility. O.K., write it the way you want to. It's going to make me uncomfortable, but I'd better practice what I preach."

"Publish tomorrow? And tell about the Bible?"

"You'd better ask the lieutenant."

Randollph could see that Casey was struggling with the problem. Casey the detective wanted to postpone any revelation about the Gutenberg Bible, giving himself extra time to work before the murderer knew the motive had been discovered. Casey the ambitious young police officer wanted to be perceived as open and cooperative with the press. Randollph, wondering if he was adding cynicism to his other sins, made a mental bet that the ambitious Casey would prevail over the detective Casey.

"Sure, Thea, publish it the way you want to. It would be more convenient for me if you left out the part about the Bible, but I'm not going to try to manage the news—now or ever." Casey's little speech carried the clear implication that the detective confidently expected to be in a better position to manage the news in days to come, but that even when he climbed to the top of the police pyramid he'd still be the same friendly guy who always leveled with the media. Randollph choked back a chuckle.

Thea turned to Randollph. "C.P., can you give me anything else about Gutenberg that would make my story more interesting, pep it up?"

"Well, he died broke."

"When, and how come? I guess I could look it up, but I don't have much time."

"His business partner, who loaned Gutenberg quite a bit of money, foreclosed when most of the work on the Bible had been completed."

"Dirty business?"

"It would seem so. The partner, one Johann Fust, had a reputation of being, well, a sharp businessman."

"A crook," Dan Gantry said.

"Gutenberg died in 1468, supported in his last years by a grant in the form of an appointment as courtier of the Archbishop of Mainz."

"I didn't know that," the bishop said. "It's nice to know that the ecclesiastical establishment performed a good work like that."

"Then you'll also be glad to know, Freddie, that when Gutenberg first published printed material, printing was called a black art and Gutenberg was accused of being in league with the devil. The Archbishop of Mainz defended Gutenberg and put a stop to that nonsense."

"I wish it were that easy for modern bishops to put a stop to nonsense. It would make the discharge of my administrative responsibilities much, much simpler."

"C.P., is there a Gutenberg Bible in Chicago?" Thea asked. "When this story breaks, people are going to want to see one."

"No. Of the forty-seven extant copies of the Bible, nine are in the United States. The best, most nearly perfect copy—although it is far from perfect—is in the Library of Congress. The one nearest to the Chicago area, I believe, is at Indiana University in Bloomington, Indiana."

"How do you happen to know so much about the Gutenberg Bible?"

"Church history is my field, remember."

"Oh come on. Nobody remembers that much about one incident in two thousand years. Not even a learned man like you."

"That's what Mr. Jones claimed. He said my, ah, extraordinary knowledge of the Bible's history was evidence that I'd recently been researching the subject and this strengthened his conviction that I'd murdered Humbrecht and stolen the Bible."

"Well, did you? Research it recently, I mean?"

"No. I did my master's thesis on religious incunabula, that is, fifteenth-century examples of the printer's art devoted to religious subjects. I didn't tell Mr. Jones."

"And the Bible was the first example?"

"No. The oldest example of any of Gutenberg's printing is a twenty-eight-page quarto volume. It is a poem in German called 'The Last Judgment.' In addition to secular incunabula, such as calendars and Latin grammars, Gutenberg also printed a broadsheet prayer, a list of all the bishoprics in the world, and a German translation of a papal bull before he printed the Bible."

"This is kind of interesting," Thea said. "But I'll be doing a column on this as well as the news story. My readers like the human interest stuff. What kind of guy was Gutenberg? A drunk? A woman chaser?"

"I can't give you exact answers to your questions," Randollph answered. "Records show that he was in the habit of laying down two thousand liters of wine each year. The records don't say whether it was all for his personal consumption. Maybe he gave a lot of parties."

"That's a hell of a lot of booze," Dan said in an awed voice. "Guy could stay pickled on that permanently, not to mention ruining his liver."

"And women?"

"He never married. He was sued for breach of promise by a patrician lady of Strasbourg."

"Why Strasbourg?"

"He lived there for about ten years. The artisans gained control of Mainz and drove the patricians into exile for a while. Gutenberg settled in Strasbourg."

"How'd the lady's suit come out?" Dan asked.

"There's no record of the decision. All we know about the trial is that Gutenberg called one of the witnesses against him a perjurer and the witness sued him for slander. There's no record of how that trial turned out, either."

"I'll bet the lawyers made out all right, they always do," Dan said.

"What did he do in Strasbourg besides make promises to a lady which he didn't keep?" Thea asked.

"Strangely enough, he was a master goldsmith, an expert polisher of precious stones, as well as inventor of a process for the manufacture of mirrors."

"Why strangely?"

"Because he was a patrician. By law, patricians were prohibited from performing the work of artisans. He also developed his ideas for printing from movable metallic type while in Strasbourg."

"Busy chap," Casey commented. "I hate to interrupt this learned lecture—"

"Sorry about the lecture," Randollph interrupted. "When you ask a teacher a question about his own field, you have to risk a lecture. Blame Thea."

"It's just that I have to get to work," Casey finished. "I'd like you to look at some mug shots of top mobsters. I gather that's what your Mr. Jones is."

"Tonight?" Randollph let his reluctance show.

"No, I guess tomorrow'll be soon enough. We've got his description. He hasn't shown up at that place where he had you or I'd have been notified. Probably won't. Something's warned him off."

"Lieutenant, has that house been searched thoroughly?"

"Probably going on right now. I took the liberty of using your phone to order it done, done thoroughly."

"Would you mind asking your men to look in the bedroom closet in the suite on the third floor. There should be a dark-gray single-breasted suit jacket in it."

"Yours? Sure, no trouble."

"It will save me the expense of buying a new suit," Randollph explained. He'd been planning to replace that suit with a new one soon. But the decision to wear it for a while gave him the sense of virtue which is the reward of those who successfully resist temptation, even a small temptation. Randollph thought that today he needed a feeling that he could be virtuous more than he needed a new suit.

12

THE OFFICES OF KNOX, Knox, and Elder, attorneys-at-law, were located in a building not far from the Church of the Good Shepherd, so Randollph and the bishop walked. Randollph had to accommodate his pace to the bishop's stubby legs.

"Should get out and walk more," the bishop said, panting slightly. "I'm out of shape. Penalty of a sedentary job. Modern bishops don't stand up for Jesus. They sit down for him. Sit at a desk. Sit in board and committee meetings. Sit on airplanes. Sit, sit, sit."

"You could resign, Freddie, if your suffering becomes unbearable." Randollph didn't think it was good for the bishop's soul to complain about his lot in life.

"Oh, I've thought about it, C.P. I expect most bishops with any sense think about it now and then. Go back to teaching in a seminary or find a nice parish in which to serve out our declining years."

"Not that I want you to, but if the prospect of resigning is so attractive, why don't you?"

"It's the prestige and power, I expect." The bishop

was puffing now, and Randollph slowed his pace even more. "We tell ourselves that an all-wise providence chose us for this role in life. We tell ourselves we have a duty, however onerous at times, to discharge faithfully the responsibilities heaped on us. But it's the power and prestige that keeps us at it."

"Actually, I hope you continue your willingness to shoulder your heavy burdens whatever your reasons."

"Oh? Tell me why. And don't hesitate to flatter me. I've a number of difficult problems and decisions on my plate at the moment. My spirit needs sustenance."

Randollph laughed. "Freddie, Freddie, you know you're happiest when dealing with difficulties. I'll tell you why. I'd hate to see you resign—apart from having a dear friend as my bishop. It's because you're fair. My experience with bishops is limited, but I gather that fairness is not a universal characteristic of the breed. Now you may be devious and subtle; you may rule with an iron hand in that thick, soft velvet glove you wear. But you're fair."

The bishop seemed touched. "Thank you, C.P. I try to be. Ah, here we are." He stopped in front of a substantial old building that looked as if it might have been designed by Louis Sullivan. They pressed through a revolving door into a large lobby heavy with ornate tile and a gilt-ribbed ceiling.

"Place looks built to last," Randollph observed. "Wonder why the developers haven't torn it down."

"I rather suspect that J. J. Knox owns it," the bishop answered. "He more or less intimated to me that he did. J. J. Knox," he added, "is a man who does not like change. They still have uniformed elevator operators here, though an automatic system would save loads of money in wages."

"Is Knox a spendthrift?"

"Oh no, quite the contrary. He grew up when all elevators were run by operators. Perhaps he doesn't quite trust an elevator to take him where he wants to go if it can be operated by mere passengers. Perhaps he is unable to believe that a high-rise building is properly run without uniformed elevator operators."

"Perhaps he just hates to fire the operators," Randollph suggested.

"Oh no, that isn't it," the bishop assured Randollph. "J. J. Knox is quite capable of firing his grandmother if he thought Grandma deserved it. Good Christian man that he is—or I hope he is—Knox doesn't let sentiment cloud his judgment."

The law firm occupied the top two floors of the building. Randollph counted the names of eleven attorneys painted on the pebbly glass double doors leading to the firm's offices. Inside, the reception room was plain, not over-large, and sparsely furnished. The walls were paneled in a honey-colored pine. The chairs for the convenience of clients waiting to be admitted to whichever attorney would solve their legal problems were simple and straight-backed but were upholstered in genuine leather. There wasn't a bit of chrome in the room. The ashtrays were solid-looking ceramic. A small table offered copies of *Forbes, Business Week, Fortune,* and *The Wall Street Journal.* Plainly, Knox, Knox, and Elder did not approve of frivolous reading material. The office stated that Knox, Knox, and Elder was a firm of quality, serious purpose, and so well established it had no need to impress prospective clients with lush carpeting, designer furniture, or the taste of an expensive interior decorator. A thin woman in a severe gray dress, who might have been sixty, Randollph guessed, though her dark hair pulled back into a bun might have added a few years to her appearance, was sitting behind a desk. A skinny Miss Windfall, he thought. She'd probably been with the firm long enough to appropriate the power exercised by the Miss Windfalls of this world.

"May I help you?" she inquired courteously but without cordiality. Randollph gave their names and said that Mr. J. J. Knox senior was expecting them. If she'd read the morning paper containing Thea Mason's story about Randollph's kidnapping, she gave no sign of it. She punched a button on her phone, muttered something into it, then said, "Mr. Knox will be right out. Please be seated."

They'd hardly sat down when Knox appeared. "Good morning, Bishop, Dr. Randollph." He shook hands with them firmly but conveying no warmth. "We're meeting in the conference room. If you'll follow me." He led them down a hall, past several doors behind which, Randollph supposed, wills were being drawn, tax avoidance plotted, papers severing marital ties prepared, and various human predicaments requiring legal counsel were being untangled. Randollph thought being a lawyer must be a dull job. He wondered if everyone who liked his work or profession as he liked his thought other people had dull jobs, and decided that they probably did. Every one of those lawyers behind the doors they passed no doubt thought being a preacher was an unrewarding task and couldn't imagine why anyone would be so foolish as to choose it.

The conference room conveyed a feeling of spartan elegance. It, too, was paneled in honey-colored pine. The polished wide-plank hardwood floor was fastened down with dowels, or appeared to be. The dowels might have been fake, the kind so popular with people who wanted an Early American look but couldn't, or didn't want to pay for the real thing—though Randollph bet that J. J. Knox wouldn't settle for any kind of imitation. A long plain walnut table sat on an enormous hooked rug. Several small hooked rugs were scattered about, little puddles of red and green and blue. The walls showed off a magnificent picture of a three-masted ship in full sail, and several paintings in the style of Andrew Wyeth. The place had the flavor of New England about it—integrity and understated success. Randollph guessed that this was exactly what J. J. Knox had in mind when he furnished the room.

There were two people sitting at the conference table. They rose as Knox, the bishop, and Randollph came into the room. One was Lieutenant Casey. The other was a short, stout man in a brown monk's habit.

"You both know Lieutenant Michael Casey, I believe," Knox said. "This other gentleman is Father Prior Simon of the Order of St. Thomas Aquinas. The order is a beneficiary in Mr. Humbrecht's will."

Prior Simon reminded Randollph of Friar Tuck in Robin Hood—or at least as the movies had pictured the Friar, a jolly, thickset cleric who was confessor to Robin's band of noble outlaws, and who consumed his share of nut-brown ale and the king's venison.

"Ah, the famous Dr. Randollph," the prior said,

grasping Randollph's hand. "You've had a bad time recently, haven't you?"

"It wasn't fun."

"I was genuinely concerned for you when I heard you'd been kidnapped. Though I had never met you, I feel that I know you. I'm a football fan, you see. Does that sound strange coming from a monk?"

"I might not have guessed it."

"No, of course not. But St. Thomas Aquinas is not a contemplative order, nor are we withdrawn from the world. We have television sets. You'd be surprised how many of the brothers are sports fans."

Randollph was surprised. "I wouldn't have guessed that, either."

"I think it is because our order is devoted to scholarship. The life of the scholar doesn't involve physical activity. We have to engage in strenuous sports vicariously if at all. I've seen you on television many times. When you threw a pass, I threw it too. When you were sacked, not often, of course, you were very agile—"

"I had a strong offensive line."

"You were very agile. But when they sacked you, I hurt too. You are one of the favored few who have participated in combative sports and the life of scholarship too. I envy you that, even though envy is one of the seven deadly sins. I must make a note to include it in my next confession." Randollph thought that he'd enjoy spending some time with Prior Simon.

"The others should be here soon," Knox said, looking at his watch impatiently.

"We're early," the bishop said. "Tell me, Father Prior, does your order specialize in a certain field?"

"No. We do a little of everything. We're very strong in medieval theology. We work in church history, biblical studies, worship, among other endeavors. We do a contract business."

"A contract business?"

The prior smiled. "Sounds like we're a branch of the Mafia, doesn't it?" He turned to Randollph. "Football isn't the only thing we watch on television. We watch the cop shows, too. The contracts are from, oh, a bishop who wants to present a learned paper or write a scholarly dissertation for his diocesan newspaper and doesn't have time to do the research himself. Or an order wants to print a book on its history, or the life of its founder. We contract to do that sort of thing. We also publish our research in various scholarly journals, sometimes even a book."

Knox, who apparently was bored with the topic of sacred scholarship, said, "I am intrigued by what the paper reported about Humbrecht's Gutenberg Bible. I assume that if it exists, his will tells of it. It occurs to me that the Bible may be the reason he drew a will. From all appearances, he had little of value to dispose of. I suppose that such a Bible is very valuable."

"Priceless," Prior Simon said. "I don't mind admitting that when I read the story in the paper I hoped that Professor Humbrecht had such a Bible, and that he has bequeathed it to the Order of St. Thomas Aquinas. I trust this doesn't make me guilty of the deadly sin of greed. I don't think my confessor could handle two deadly sins in the same confession. He'd have me saying Hail Marys and Pater Nosters for years." Randollph noted that the prior's plain round face became most attractive when he smiled.

A phone on the conference table made a discreet chirping sound. Knox picked it up and said, "Are they all here, Esther? Good. I'll be right out." He cradled the phone. "Representatives of the other beneficiaries have arrived. May I ask if anyone objects to having my two partners sit in on the reading? One partner is my son; the other, Mr. Robin Elder, is the son of one of the founders of this firm. Their presence is not necessary, of course, but since the story in the morning paper, they are curious. If the will contains anything about a Gutenberg Bible, then this would be a historic moment, wouldn't it? We don't have many opportunities in a lifetime to participate in a historic moment. My partners would like to be in on it."

"I have no objection, Mr. Knox," the bishop said.

"Nor I," Randollph said.

"I surely don't blame them, bring them in," Prior Simon agreed.

"I'll ask the other beneficiaries," Knox said. "If you'll excuse me."

After Knox had gone Casey growled, "I wish they'd

get on with it. I'd like to know if I've got a motive or not."

"A motive, Lieutenant?" Prior Simon asked.

"For the murder of Johannes Humbrecht."

"Oh, yes, of course."

"You knew him," Casey said. "Can you think of any reason why anyone would want to kill that harmless old man?"

"I knew him slightly," the prior replied. "And that was while his wife was still living. She was our benefactor, you know. Our order was just getting started. We had little money, inadequate quarters. Our late abbot, God rest his soul, knew Mrs. Humbrecht. She purchased a disused seminary building near the campus of the University of Chicago—" he showed his charming smile to Randollph and the bishop "—a Protestant seminary that had gone out of business, I'm afraid, gentlemen."

"I'm happy that it is being put to good use," the bishop said. "After all, scholarship, true scholarship, is ecumenical."

"So it is. With suitable remodeling the building was ideal for our purposes. Mrs. Humbrecht bought it, paid for the remodeling, and established a generous endowment for the order. A most remarkable lady. Charming, too. In those days Dr. Humbrecht would occasionally visit us with his wife."

"He approved of her gifts to your order?" Casey asked.

"So far as I could tell. I remember him as a bright and interesting man. He was a recognized scholar, you know, and I'm sure his own respect for scholarship predisposed him in favor of his wife's project—even though he was a staunch Protestant. I'm sure he believed—as you put it, Bishop—that scholarship is ecumenical."

"You've been with the order a long time, then."

"Yes, Bishop, from its beginning. As a postulant I indicated an interest in New Testament studies. Our late abbot—again, God rest his soul, he was a kind and understanding man—saw to it that I studied for my doctorate in the field. Do you know why I chose the name Simon?"

"After one of Jesus' disciples, I imagine. There were two Simons among the twelve, weren't there?" Casey said it in an offhand manner as if he could come up with learned information anytime without effort.

"Remarkable! So few people remember that."

"I had a good Catholic education." With what had cost him an effort, Randollph guessed, Casey managed to sound modest.

"Simon who is called Peter everyone knows. But how many recall the name of Simon the Canaanite?"

"Not many, I imagine," Randollph answered. "I'm curious as to why you picked the name of so obscure a disciple."

"I was hoping you'd ask." Again the gentle, charming smile. "I discovered during my studies that most authorities reject the idea that Jesus had a Canaanite as a disciple. They say that the word translated 'Canaanite' is probably not Greek but an Aramaic word meaning zealous. Simon, the theory goes, perhaps got the name because he was zealous for the law. I let my imagination run and concluded that if Simon was zealous for the law, the Torah, it would be likely that he had a scholar's passion for it. I had a passion for my studies. Thus I took the name of the disciple who might well have been a scholar."

J. J. Knox led a parade of four men and one woman into the room. He quickly introduced his covey by name and the beneficiary they represented. The only name Randollph caught was "Dr. Joyce Compton, Chicago Art Institute." She was a plain woman of about fifty. Two of the men represented Northwestern University and Chicago University.

This task accomplished, Knox took his time about introducing his partners. Randollph was more interested in them than the others. J. J. Knox senior had white hair in abundance. J. J. Knox junior had brown hair which was already deserting him, especially on the crown, though he couldn't have been more than thirty-five. J. J. Knox senior wore a navy blue three-piece suit, white shirt (he'd show his white hair to better advantage with a colored shirt, Randollph thought) and black lace-up oxfords. Junior was dressed in a brown herringbone vestless suit, white shirt with short rounded collar, and laceless brown oxfords. Robin Elder, about forty-five, Randollph estimated, was just short of spiffy in a gray double-breasted unfinished worsted with pronounced and widely spaced chalk stripes, a white-on-white shirt and maroon silk tie. Randollph knew he depended too much on the clothes a person wore to get a reading on his character. J. J. Knox senior, he thought, proclaimed with his plain but well-cut conservative uniform that he was a man of established integrity and fixed values. You can trust me not to do anything rash or extraordinary, his haberdashery said. J. J. Knox junior, Randollph suspected, showed a weak and tentative rebellion against his father by the way he dressed. He felt certain that Knox senior would not approve of shoes without laces or a short rounded shirt collar even though the shirt was white. And he probably thought that a brown herringbone suit was appropriate only for leisure moments or a weekend in the country. Knox junior may have been rebelling against parental authority, but it was a rebellion calculated not to go too far.

Randollph decided that Robin Elder didn't give a damn one way or the other what Knox senior thought or preferred. Secure in his inherited partnership, he dressed and lived to suit himself. His plumage, including a rather startling droopy blond mustache, fairly shouted "Hey, girls, notice me." Randollph wondered if there was a Mrs. Elder. Robin Elder didn't look like husband material.

J. J. Knox senior cleared his throat. "Now that we are all here, we can proceed. Junior, would you get the Humbrecht file for us?" Randollph noticed Junior wince slightly, then quickly suppress it. "Yes, Father," he said, and left the room. Randollph wondered what it must be like to have a father like J. J. Knox. Sturdier spirits than Junior would have rebelled by adopting a blatantly unconventional life-style. Junior obviously wasn't strong enough for that. But what must it do to a man not much on the sunny side of middle age to endure constantly the kind of small indignity just visited upon him? Nothing good, Randollph was certain.

"You are all aware of the circumstances under which we accepted Mr. Humbrecht as a client," J. J. Knox said. "We witnessed his will and sealed it in his presence. But he did not want us to read it, so of course we didn't. I should tell you that your time in coming may have been wasted because there is nothing to indicate that he had anything of great value to dispose of." He paused to let this sink in. "Of course, you have all read the story in the morning paper about the possibility that Humbrecht may have owned a unique Gutenberg Bible."

"You could sell it for enough that, split five or six ways, it would be well worth a trip downtown," the man from one of the universities said.

Dr. Compton set her small mouth in a rigid line. "I should think that Mr. Humbrecht would have left such a rare piece of art to the Art Institute," she snapped. "That's the proper place for it."

"And I'm hoping that he left it to the Order of St. Thomas Aquinas," Father Simon said genially, trying to defuse a budding unpleasantness.

"We'll soon know," Knox said as his son came in and laid a file on the table. "Thank you, Junior." He fished in the file and brought out an envelope made of heavy cream-colored paper which Randollph estimated to be about twelve by eighteen inches. There was a blotch of dark red on one side. Knox held it up. "This is the standard envelope which we use for wills." He pointed to the red blotch. "This is the wax seal we closed it with at Mr. Humbrecht's request." He reached into an inside pocket of his jacket and brought out a pair of half-moon glasses which he adjusted to the tip of his nose. Randollph thought half-moon glasses an affectation. Apparently J. J. Knox had his own little vanities. Knox peered at the wax seal curiously and for longer than seemed necessary, then said, "As you can see, the seal is unbroken. I'll now break it." He took a letter opener and used the point to pry under the seal until the brittle wax crumbled. He then opened the flap and removed several sheets of legal-size stationery. Randollph could feel the tension in the room.

"Let's see what we have. Mm. I, Johannes Humbrecht, being of sound mind, etc.," Knox mumbled through the preamble. "Quite properly drawn. I'll skip the legal jargon. Now—" he flipped to the second page. "It says, 'For many years I have been investing in the stock market, and with success or luck have accumulated a sizable fortune. A list of my holdings, and the safe deposits where the certificates are kept, is attached.'" Knox pushed his glasses up a bit, then riffled through the will. "Ah, here it is." He looked at the list for a moment, then emitted a low whistle. Knox, Randollph thought, was not the kind of man to emit low whistles.

"How much?" A man from one of the universities asked. The man from the other university licked his lips.

Knox looked up from the paper, carefully removed his glasses, and laid them on the table. "I can't give you an exact figure, of course. That will have to be computed at today's market. But. . . ." He paused as if doing mental sums.

"Give us a ball-park estimate," the man who'd asked how much demanded.

Knox looked at him coldly. "It is well up in the millions. From a cursory glance at the list Humbrecht had an uncanny instinct for companies that were destined to prosper spectacularly. Is that a sufficient answer?" He said it in a tone which implied it had damn well better be.

"If we get a good cut," the man said.

Knox stared at him contemptuously, then put his glasses on and turned back to the will. "Mm. Bishop, you're mentioned first. He leaves you a million dollars to be used for 'good works' at your discretion."

"What a nice surprise. It will indeed be welcome," the bishop said. "We always have more good works that need doing than we have money with which to do them."

Knox peered at the will again. "Mm. Interesting." He looked up. "Humbrecht describes what he calls his library and art room. It's in the basement of his house. It is kept at a constant temperature and is fireproof and theft-proof. It has a steel door with a combination lock set in a thick concrete wall. Amazing! He gives the combination here." He looked at the lady from the Art Institute. "Dr. Compton, he leaves his collection of paintings to the Institute. Here is the list of what you should find in that room." He handed her a paper.

Dr. Compton looked at the list, stiffened, and said, "My God!"

"A good list?" Knox inquired. "I don't know much about paintings."

"Fabulous!" she replied, "though you'd need to know a little about paintings to realize just how fabulous."

"He says," Knox continued, "that over the years he has collected a very respectable library in many fields of scholarship." Here Knox began reading. "'Some of the books and manuscripts are quite rare. Because of my late wife's interest in the Order of St. Thomas Aquinas, and because of my high regard for the work to which it is dedicated, I bequeath my library to the Order.'" Knox shuffled through the papers again and said, "Here it is. Father Prior, I hand you the list of what you may expect to find." He passed several sheets of legal-size pages to the prior.

There was a stillness in the room. Everyone, Randollph guessed, was thinking the same thing—is the Gutenberg Bible on the list? If it was there, in fact did exist, then Dr. Compton wouldn't be getting it for the Art Institute, and the men from the universities wouldn't be able to haggle over their cut of its sale.

Prior Simon fumbled in his brown monk's habit that looked like an old-fashioned dress with a hood attached and found a pocket case for spectacles. He pulled out a pair of surprisingly fashionable glasses rimmed in heavy dark plastic. Little vanities, Randollph reflected, take unusual forms. He wondered if the fact that J. J. Knox wore a sort of uniform and Prior Simon was committed by the custom of his order to always appear in a uniform prompted them to seek some device, such as the selection of incongruous eyeglasses, to say to the world: "Don't take me for granted. I observe the conventions of my segment of society, but I'm still a person with my own tastes and convictions and values and opinions." In most people, he surmised, there was always this small battle between a need to identify with the prevailing style in clothes and thought and a desire to be a person who dared to be himself and defy his culture. He believed that on the whole it was a healthy battle. Too much dedication to being like everyone else produced a bland and boring person. Too much passion to be different begat the bizarre and strident personality which ended up being as predictable as the strict conformist.

The prior ran his eye rapidly down the page, then flipped it. "Extraordinary!" he said softly from time to time. He flipped another page. "Ah, it would be here," he muttered.

"Well?" one of the university representatives demanded, the one who had the habit of licking his lips, Randollph noted.

The prior looked up. "Sir?"

"Well, is the Bible on the list?"

Prior Simon removed his glasses and did not hurry to answer the rude question. At last he said, "The list is long and, like Dr. Compton's bequest, remarkable. The items are listed in categories. I've just finished reading the items under Bibles and Biblical Studies. No, the Gutenberg is not listed." He sighed. "This bequest will be a splendid addition to our order's library. I should be rejoicing. But I confess I feel mainly disappointed." He looked at Randollph. "It looks as if that rascal who kidnapped you, Doctor, was misinformed. If the Bible existed it surely would be listed here."

"Yes, I expect that it would," J. J. Knox said. "Well, let's get on with it. Hmm. 'To my dear friend and pastor, the Reverend Dr. Cesare Paul Randollph, I leave, without condition, the sum of one million dollars,'" Knox read, then turned to the next page. Randollph was so stunned that he almost missed what came next as Knox continued reading. "'I, too, am the beneficiary of an inheritance. Few, if anyone, know that I am a descendant of Else Vitztum, sister of Johannes Gensfleisch, known as Johannes or Henne Gutenberg. Her daughter, also named Else, married a patrician named Henne Humbrecht. Else Gensfleisch Humbrecht was thus niece to Johannes Gutenberg and became his heir. Herr Gutenberg was forced out of his printing business when he had completed all or most of his work. His partner and financier, Johann Fust, was an unscrupulous man who demanded repayment of the moneys he'd advanced Gutenberg before Gutenberg had a chance to raise any cash from the sale of his Bible. Like so many of mankind's greatest benefactors, he died a pauper, supported in his last years by the benevolence of the Church.'" Knox looked up from his reading. "I didn't know that." Then he went on reading. "'But Gutenberg, with the help of Peter Schoeffer, and perhaps one or two other close friends employed in his shop, printed a unique Bible for himself. What records we have indicate that Gutenberg's shop printed approximately 150 copies on paper and 35 on vellum. This Bible, which he printed for himself, was printed on a carefully made Chinese rice paper. Chinese rice paper is neutral—neither acid nor alkaline. Properly cared for it will last indefinitely. Gutenberg then took the loose sheets to a curate at St. Stephen's Collegiate Church of Mainz by the name of Heinrich Cremer who was expert at the illumination of medieval manuscripts. All Gutenberg Bibles left space at both margins and between the two columns of print for illumination. Also, space was left for headings and initials to be done by hand in color. Just as Gutenberg designed the type-face for printing the Bible, he designed the style of letters for the headings and initials of his personal Bible, and also laid out for Curate Cremer the general design and colors to be used in the marginal illumination. When the art work was completed, he commissioned the curate to bind the Bible in two volumes. The binding material was the hide of Morrocan highland goat, which is the finest leather in the world. He then prepared detailed instructions, along with the history of its manufacture, on how to preserve the Bible from insects, foxing, etc. and how to renew the leather binding. He wrote out two copies of their history and instructions in his own hand and pasted them on the inside cover of each volume, where they remain. Since there was no common German language until Martin Luther translated the Bible into German more than half a century later, what Gutenberg wrote is very difficult to read. But sometime later one of the Bible's inheritors had it translated into modern German, and I have translated that into English.'" Knox paused, poured a glass of water from a silver carafe on the table beside him and swallowed most of it.

Randollph used the pause to glance at the various members of this heterogeneous congregation. Dr. Compton's face showed both hope and anxiety. Prior Simon appeared down-in-the-mouth, apparently resigned to the fact that if the Bible hadn't been included in the Order of St. Thomas Aquinas' inheritance, then someone else was going to get it. Robin Elder was staring glumly at something outside the window. J. J. Knox, the younger, was looking petulant. The representatives from the universities were obviously impatient to get on with it. Lieutenant Casey was relaxed and smiling. He had hold of the elusive motive in the Humbrecht murder.

"Ahem," J. J. Knox said. "I'll continue. Humbrecht was rather garrulous about his Bible—but then, I suppose he had a right to be."

"Can't we just skip all this history garbage and get down to the bottom line on the Bible," the university representative who wanted to be sure he got a fair cut said sharply.

"Oh, we'll get to the bottom line." J. J. Knox spoke with a cheerfulness Randollph supposed was calculated to irritate the university representative. "We do owe the dead something, though, don't you think? If you're bored, sir, there is no reason why you need to subject yourself to this. You may be excused and we can notify you by mail of any bequest to your institution."

Randollph wanted to chuckle. J. J. Knox was an artist at putting this chap in his place. The man muttered what sounded like a widely used four-letter scatological word, but was wise enough to mutter it very softly.

"I take it you wish me to continue, so I shall." Knox pushed his glasses a fraction of an inch farther toward the end of his nose, and resumed reading from the will.

"'This unique Bible, this very finest and most beautiful example of the printer's art ever created, was inherited by Else Gensfleisch Humbrecht, and has been passed down through her line ever since. It became a tradition in our family that possession of the Bible was a sacred trust, and that to sell it, or to neglect its care would bring horrible retribution on the guilty party. I inherited it as a young man while still living in Germany. I have been meticulous in its care and preservation, and it has been my most precious possession. Just looking at it, just gazing on this book of unmatched beauty, has renewed my spirits more times than I can count. I had hoped to have a child to whom I could pass it on, but unfortunately that was not to be. I am the last of Else Gensfleisch Humbrecht's line. It is now my duty to make provision for the disposal of the Bible.'"

Knox had everyone's attention now, Randollph saw. Except for Robin Elder, who was plainly bored and was still staring morosely out the window. Randollph assessed Elder as a self-centered man interested exclusively in what affected him personally. Since he could be sure he wasn't going to inherit the Bible, he probably had little interest in who did get it.

Knox began reading again. "He says, 'I have given long and careful thought as to the disposition of my treasure. My inclination was to will it to a museum.'"

Dr. Compton leaned forward eagerly. It was unthinkable to her, Randollph supposed, that Humbrecht would consider any recipient except her Art Institute.

"'However,'" Knox read, "'I couldn't decide in my heart which would be the one appropriate museum to receive it.'"

Dr. Compton slumped in her chair with a scowl and a grunt. It occurred to Randollph that she was a witness to the ugliness of the sin of greed—perhaps the ugliest of all the deadly sins. She'd already inherited a bequest worth many fortunes on behalf of her institution. But she would leave this room bitter and frustrated because the bounty she had received was not enough. No matter that it had not come to her personally. She identified completely with her institution. Perhaps the worthy use to which her institution's inheritance would be put mitigated somewhat the severity of the sin. Randollph didn't know. It was an interesting ethical problem. Were Andrew Carnegie's vicious and conscienceless sins committed in accumulation of his millions softened and excused by the wise and generous disposition of his fortune? It was a problem for the moral philosophers. Right now he'd better pay attention to J. J. Knox.

"'Nor did it seem appropriate to direct that the Bible be included in the corpus of the estate,'" Knox read. Scratch the universities, Randollph thought. "'So I have decided to put the problem in the hands of a wise and honest man. I therefore bequeath, without instruction or condition, my Gutenberg Bible to my dear friend and pastor, the Reverend Dr. Cesare Paul Randollph.'"

At first, Randollph didn't react at all. He thought

J. J. Knox had misread Humbrecht's words. He thought it must be a joke. He thought, well, he didn't know what to think. He suddenly realized that his mouth was hanging open like a hooked trout and that he was probably staring at J. J. Knox like an idiot. He was dimly aware that everyone was looking at him, expecting him to say something. He couldn't think of a thing to say.

Prior Simon broke the strained silence. With a wan smile he said, "I congratulate you, Doctor. I don't mind admitting that I wish it was the other way around and you were congratulating me. I thought for a moment that that's how it would be. When Mr. Knox read Professor Humbrecht's words about putting the problem of the Bible in the hands of a wise and honest man, I was certain he was describing me. Pride. Envy, greed, and now pride. I'm becoming quite a distinguished sinner of late, aren't I?"

"I can understand your disappointment," Randollph managed to say.

Prior Simon put a little more power into his wan smile. "I think I have enough Christian charity left to say that since Professor Humbrecht didn't see fit to bequeath it to our order, then I'm glad he willed it to you."

"Thank you for that." Randollph was beginning to recover his wits, though he was aware that he had not yet assimilated the reality of the situation.

Dr. Compton helped him. "Dr. Randollph, when you have a little free time perhaps we could talk about the Bible." If she couldn't inherit the Bible, then she meant to explore other means of obtaining it for the institute. She'd probably begin by suggesting he give it to the institute, he supposed. He could see his immediate future encumbered with fielding similar requests from every art museum in the country.

Lieutenant Casey spoke up. "Has it occurred to anyone that we don't know where the Bible is?"

J. J. Knox addressed himself to the papers on the table in front of him. "Perhaps Humbrecht tells us where to find it. Mm. Ah yes, here it is. 'The Bible, bound in two volumes, is kept in an insect-proof and properly ventilated compartment in the paneled wall below the bookshelves at the south end of the library and art room previously described. Count down four boards from the center of the shelving. Slip your fingers under the bottom of the fourth board. Though well-nigh undetectable by the eye, you will feel a small button. Press it, and the spring-loaded drawer containing the Bible will roll out.'"

Casey, Randollph noticed, looked unhappy. He was softly pounding his fist into his palm and muttering, almost inaudibly, "I should have insisted, I should have insisted."

"Insisted what, Lieutenant?" Randollph asked.

Casey, startled, looked up. "I must have been talking to myself." He paused as if reluctant to answer Randollph's question, then said, "I ought to have insisted we search Humbrecht's house from top to bottom. Captain Manahan said no, it would take a small army to go through the place properly and he couldn't spare enough men. Seal it up and let the estate worry about it, he said. Claimed there wouldn't be any clues in that mess anyway. I thought he was probably right. You've seen the place, Doctor. How would you go about searching through those mountains of junk looking for clues? Nobody even looked in the basement."

"How is the money divided?" one of the university representatives asked.

"Oh yes," J. J. Knox said. "It is divided equally between your two universities. You see, it was worth a trip downtown after all. And incidentally, Dr. Randollph is named executor—to serve without bond."

"I think I'd like to have a look at that room in the basement right away," Lieutenant Casey said.

13

THEY'D ALL ELECTED to be in on the discovery of the Gutenberg Bible—all except the two representatives from the universities who were anxious to be the bearers of good tidings of great joy to their superiors.

Lieutenant Casey said, "I'll phone my office and have the keys to Humbrecht's house brought over. But have you considered what you're going to do with all those books and paintings and, of course, the Bible? That's a lot of stuff, valuable stuff. You can't just toss it in a corner somewhere."

"I'm sure I could arrange to have the paintings transported to the institute this afternoon," Dr. Compton said.

"I suppose I could manage to transfer the library to our premises today." The prior sounded doubtful. "Though heaven knows where we would put it. Every item has to be carefully catalogued and the list is a long one. Hundreds of items."

J. J. Knox squelched those suggestions. "There are legal technicalities involved. The executor must make the distribution of assets, and Dr. Randollph has not yet qualified. A bit of legal red tape," he added, "but important for the protection of the beneficiaries. We'll be glad to get you qualified, Doctor, if you wish us to, and advise you as to your responsibilities."

"Yes, please do," Randollph answered absently. He knew he should feel honored by the trust Humbrecht had placed in him. And after all, he was a million dollars richer today than he had been yesterday because of Humbrecht's benevolence. But he could envision the amount of time his duties as executor were going to steal from the already too small pool of that precious stuff he had at his disposal. It would turn out to be a question of what regular responsibilities and duties he could neglect, slough off, load on others, and in various ways avoid. He hadn't been a pastor all that long, but it seemed to him that it was a profession in which the unexpected was the expected. Perhaps the devil cooked up these constant interruptions to a pastor's discharge of his normal duties. Maybe it was all a Satanic conspiracy to delay the coming of God's Kingdom. He had to admit, though, that these ceaseless interruptions added an extra flavor to the job. Maybe that was part of the Beelzebubbian scheme too. Wasn't the fallen angel supposed to be the acknowledged expert in the art of temptation?

"Why don't you just leave everything as it is in Humbrecht's house?" Casey suggested. "The room's supposed to be fireproof and theft proof. Where are you going to find a safer place than that? I think you ought to hire round-the-clock security service, though."

"Excellent!" J. J. Knox said. "Simplest way to solve the problem. I'm a great believer in the simplest solution. Nearly always turns out to be the best one. Oh, I'd better write down the combination to the lock on that room." He perched his glasses on the tip of his nose again, flipped through the will, then finding the page he wanted, carefully copied a series of numbers on a yellow ruled pad. He ripped the sheet off the pad, tucked it in his jacket pocket, and said, "I think we can go now."

J. J. Knox the younger and Robin Elder had volunteered their cars as transport to the Humbrecht house.

Randollph found himself in Elder's Cadillac Seville along with Dr. Compton and Prior Simon. Dr. Compton had hardly settled in her seat before she said, "Dr. Randollph, have you given any thought as to what you will do with the Bible?"

"There has hardly been time for me to ponder that subject, Doctor." It was obvious that Dr. Compton intended to get that Bible somehow. Randollph had a gloomy feeling that in the days ahead he was destined to become a lot better acquainted with this persistent lady than he cared to be.

Robin Elder swung the Seville toward Michigan Avenue. "You could sell it to her, Doc," he said.

Dr. Compton reacted quickly. "It seems to me that a gift of the Bible to the Art Institute—"

"What's it worth?" Elder interrupted.

"Hard to tell," Randollph chimed in quickly to cut off any further pitch for the Bible from Dr. Compton. "The best, most nearly perfect Gutenberg Bible is the one in our Library of Congress."

"I'll bet that irritates the Germans—the best Gutenberg in the U.S. of A. instead of Germany," Elder said. "What'd it cost us?"

"It was originally owned by a Benedictine monastery in the Black Forest. For some reason they sold it in 1926 to a Dr. Otto Vollbehr of Berlin. He paid then approximately $305,000 for it."

"Whew!" Elder said as he turned north on Michigan Avenue. "That was a lot of green in twenty-six! How'd we get it?"

"The Vollbehr collection came on the market in 1930. A United States Congressman from Mississippi named Ross Collins introduced a bill to buy the Bible, along with quite a number of other incunabula, for $1,500,000."

"A million and a half depression dollars." Elder shook his head in disbelief. "That's astronomical."

"It's printed on vellum, which makes it more of a rarity, of course. And vellum holds up better than paper. It is also the only extant copy of the Gutenberg Bible bound in three volumes—although this is not the original binding. It was originally bound in two volumes, as most of Gutenberg's Bibles were."

"You sure know your stuff about this Gutenberg and his Bibles." Elder turned at the street on which Humbrecht's house was located.

"It's my field of competence, church history," Randollph said with what he hoped was more modesty than he felt.

Elder was carefully nosing his Seville through the little business district not far from Humbrecht's house. The double-parkers made it next to impossible to thread a car through the narrow lane they left.

"Rich bastards!" Elder grumbled. "Think a Rolls or a Mercedes gives them the right to park anywhere they want." Randollph thought it was poor grace for a man driving a Seville to be complaining about the behavior of people who owned expensive automobiles—but then a Cadillac was a poor cousin in the family of costly motor cars. "How much farther is Humbrecht's place?" Elder asked Randollph, not concealing his ill-humor.

"Just a few blocks. You've never been there?"

"No, he was J. J.'s client, not mine. Though I doubt J. J. has ever been here either. No need."

"That squad car is parked in front of the Humbrecht house." Randollph pointed to the car.

"Yes, I see it. Big place."

"It looks a mite run-down," Prior Simon said. It was the first he had spoken since beginning the trip.

"Wait till you see it inside," Randollph warned. "Be prepared for a shock."

Casey and the others were waiting on the front steps, along with the uniformed officer who had brought the keys.

"I guess everyone's here now," Casey said. "O.K., let's go." He unlocked the front door. "I'll lead the way. Watch your step. The place is cram full of junk."

"Jesus!" a shocked Robin Elder exclaimed. "What a pile of sh—what a mess. All that dough and living like this."

"It stinks!" Dr. Compton pressed her handkerchief to her nose.

"My word!" Prior Simon said in an awed voice. "I'd no idea he'd come to this. The Professor Humbrecht I knew was a neat, clean man. He'd never have lived like this. What happened to the man?"

"Went queer after his wife died, I hear," Casey answered. "Let's see if we can find the stairway to the basement. Probably in the kitchen—if we can find the kitchen."

The stairway was in the kitchen, and—in contrast to the general condition of the house—was in excellent repair. When Casey found the switch it turned on a powerful light. They went single file down the firm broad stairs, Casey leading the way, Randollph right behind him. The stairs ended facing one wall of the basement, forcing anyone descending them to turn right for the main room.

They saw it as soon as they turned. It was a heavy white door with a combination lock protruding in the middle. The door was partway open.

"Hold it," Casey commanded the group on the stairs. "Stay where you are. Dr. Randollph, come with me. Don't touch anything." He advanced to the door, took out a handkerchief and pulled the door wide enough to let them in the room. "Be very careful not to touch anything, Doctor. Let's have a look." They stepped inside.

It was a very large room. Built-in bookshelves covered by sliding glass doors ran round the room halfway up three walls. Above the bookshelves hung several paintings of assorted sizes and framings. But both Casey and Randollph were looking at the south wall. Here the construction was different. The bookshelves began not at floor level but above about three feet of dark wood wainscoting. In the middle of the wainscoting a large drawer stood open.

"Let's go over and look," Casey said. "Mind your step." But both of them knew a look would only confirm what they suspected. The carefully constructed receptacle made to hold the two volumes of Humbrecht's Gutenberg Bible was empty.

14

After the technical crew had come and dusted and scraped and scooped and photographed and gone, Casey said, "Doctor, I took the liberty of asking the elder Mr. Knox to arrange for a private security agency to guard this place until you can dispose of the books and paintings. We've locked the room, and it would take a pretty good vault man to open it."

"Thank you for your thoughtfulness, Lieutenant. My mind has been preoccupied with the Bible, I'm afraid."

"Give you a lift home? I've got a squad car waiting. You, too, Bishop?"

Casey sat in front with the uniformed officer driving the car, but turned sideways in order to talk to Randollph and the bishop.

"This discovery just adds to your problems, doesn't it?" the bishop asked.

"It sure as hell—it certainly does." Casey did not look happy. "Now I've got to find someone who knew the combination to the lock on that door."

"Perhaps your men will turn up some fingerprints."

"Oh, they will, Bishop—and all of them will be Humbrecht's. I'd bet on it. Whoever did this was too smart to leave his fingerprints around. I'm looking for a murderer who knew that Bible was in the basement room, and who also knew the combination to the lock. You think of any candidates?"

"Is it possible that the thief forced Humbrecht to tell him the combination?" the bishop asked. "Tortured him, perhaps."

"Then stole the Bible, went back upstairs, and smacked Humbrecht with a baseball bat while having a nice cup of tea together?"

"Perhaps the tea came first," the bishop suggested. "Then the extraction of the combination from Humbrecht."

"Then the murder, then the theft?" Casey asked.

"It's a possibility." Randollph could see that the bishop was enjoying playing detective.

"And how did the killer find out about the Bible?" Casey asked.

"I haven't figured that out yet, Lieutenant. Perhaps he extracted that information from Humbrecht also." The bishop settled more comfortably into his seat with a self-satisfied smile.

"It won't play, Bishop. That would make the guy we're looking for a common thief who was prospecting for something valuable in that old house. But a common thief would also have extracted information about the value of the paintings. In fact, even under torture Humbrecht would have had no need to tell about the Bible. I'd guess he would have gladly sacrificed his paintings to protect his Bible. Just tell the bum that the paintings were valuable. Paintings are easy to steal. Cut 'em out of the frames, roll them up, stick the rolls under your arm and walk out. And don't forget the tea."

"Ah well," the bishop sighed, "I guess the Good Lord didn't cut me out to be a detective. The shoemaker should stick to his last. How I would love it, though, to perform a brilliant feat of deduction and name your murderer for you. Something to brag about to my grandchildren. 'Children, did Grandpa ever tell you about the time he solved a murder case?' Ah, well, I'd probably just turn into an old bore."

"Induction, Freddie."

"What did you say, C.P.?"

"You solve murders by the process of induction, not deduction. Deduction begins with an assumption that something is fundamental truth—like the literal inerrancy of the Bible, for example—and then arrives at other truth by inferring it from the fundamental truth. Induction reverses the process. It studies all the available evidence, forms a hypothesis which best explains the evidence, the tests the hypothesis to see if it will stand up under critical scrutiny. But you know that, Freddie."

"I read too many detective stories," the bishop replied lamely. "Detective stories always talk about deduction."

"I've got plenty of pieces of evidence in this Humbrecht business," Casey grumbled, "but they don't yet add up to a hypothesis. I'd welcome a brilliant deduction that'd give me the name of the guy who did it. It'd save me a lot of leg work."

Something was nudging at Randollph's mind—a thought, an insight trying to get in. Maybe this was how the Old Testament prophets received their revelations. Some remark, some observation, some idea nagged at them until it formed itself with such strength and clarity that they were able to speak it or write it preceded by "Thus saith the Lord." Randollph doubted that revelations from above ever arrived fully finished. However divine in origin, revelations were processed by the mind and personality of the receiver before public disclosure of what the Lord had said. Randollph didn't know if this gentle tapping at the door of his mind was a revelation or not, but he felt that if he could just let it in he'd be on his way to forming an hypothesis, at least, of what had happened at that crummy old mansion the day he visited Johannes Humbrecht and found the old man with his skull cracked open. But he knew from experience that he couldn't force whatever it was to come in. It would have to knock a lot louder before he could open the door.

Miss Windfall, Randollph thought, was a trifle less austere in her greeting, a jot less grim about the burdens she was waiting to heap on him. The change in her would have been imperceptible to anyone who did not have to live, day by day, tuned to her vibrations. But Randollph detected it. He read it as her way of saying, "I'm glad you're back, safe and sound."

She had a basketful of messages for him. "I've sorted these out in order of their priority," she stated firmly, as if her judgment in these matters was as infallible as the Pope's when speaking *ex cathedra*. "Every newspaper and magazine wants to interview you, but that can wait. Mr. J. J. Knox senior called and said he'd prepared a press release about Mr. Humbrecht's will and the missing Bible. He said he'd get Lieutenant Casey's approval, and I told him I was sure you trusted his judgment."

"Of course," Randollph assented.

"The Klines want to know if you can conduct the funeral of their son, Benjamin, Wednesday afternoon. He died early on the morning you were—you disappeared. The Klines were very understanding about your inability to call on them, and asked me to tell you how glad they are that you have returned safely. Mr. Gantry has visited them. I assured them that you'd be in touch today, and that you'd be able to conduct the funeral."

"Thank you," Randollph mumbled. Miss Windfall knew that almost nothing took precedence over a funeral in the list of a pastor's duties. She'd handled it properly and within the powers allotted to her.

"The coroner is releasing the body of Mr. Humbrecht. He understands that it is to be released to you, and would appreciate it if you could make immediate arrangements. I asked Mr. Knox if Mr. Humbrecht owned a burial plot," Miss Windfall related. "It seems that he does, next to his wife. And Mr. Knox has alerted a reliable mortician who is ready to carry out whatever instructions you have for him. And Mrs. Randollph asked that you call her at the studio as soon as you have a moment." Miss Windfall even managed to convey the order in which he should make his phone calls. He wanted to talk to Samantha first, tell her about the will and the missing Bible, hear her voice. But Miss Windfall was right, of course. Wordsworth, he remembered, had called duty the "stern daughter of the voice of God"—

an infelicitous metaphor but an accurate delineation of that taskmaster's character.

"I'll arrange to visit the Klines right away. We'll have Mr. Humbrecht's funeral in our chapel Wednesday at 10:30 A.M. We'll need to get an announcement about it in the papers, and notify Northwestern University. They will no doubt wish to send a representative, and perhaps some of his former colleagues will want to attend."

"I'll take care of it," Miss Windfall assured him.

Randollph went into his office, performed his manifest duty, and was rewarded with that sense of virtue which comes to everyone who resists the temptation to do what he wants to do before doing what he ought to do. Then he called Sammy. He told her about the will and the missing Bible, and she said, "Oh Lordy!"

"Meaning what?"

"Meaning, Cesare Paul Randollph, dear, that you were already the hottest news item in town. 'Con Randollph outwits kidnappers,' that sort of thing. People think your life lately reads like a movie script. This will only confirm what they already think."

"They'd think it even more if they knew the intimate details of my love life," he teased her.

"Oh, they can guess that. Everyone knows you keep a sexy bird like me in that lair in the sky. They don't imagine we spend all our time talking theology. And speaking of sex—"

"Yes?"

"I've booked you to be a guest on *Sam Stack's Chicago* Wednesday night."

"I fail to see what that's got to do with sex."

"Well, if you have objections, I'll offer you the unlimited use of my lovely body for the rest of the week."

"But I have that already."

"I know. But the offer would remind you how lucky you are, and then you couldn't turn me down."

"Your logic is somewhat convoluted, but the argument's persuasive. What's the topic for the show?"

"Since you probably didn't take time to read anything in the paper this morning but your own publicity, you missed the story about the cardinal and his new battle for tax support of, and I quote, 'Independent

Christian schools.' You're mentioned, though not by name."

"What am I called?"

"You're referred to as 'a prominent but misguided clergyman.'"

"I've been called worse."

"You'll probably be called worse on the show, since the topic is 'Should religious schools receive tax support?'"

Randollph thought he wasn't likely to enjoy discussing this topic on Samantha's popular weekly talk show. It was a no-win situation for him.

"Who else have you booked for the show, Samantha? The cardinal?"

"Tried to. But His Eminence, it seems, chooses to remain above the bloody street fighting. Got one of his minions, though. He's a monsignor from the Chancery."

"Who else?"

"There's a pastor of an independent Baptist Church who has the largest Christian academy, as he calls it, in Chicago. Name of Bottomly, Luther Bottomly."

"I've heard of him. It seems you are surrounding me with the enemy, Samantha."

"Not quite. I'll have a rep from the American Civil Liberties Union."

"You could find plenty of spokesmen, prominent ones too, for my point of view. Why me?"

"Because, Reverend dear, like I said, you're the hottest news item in town right now. People who don't give a hoot in hell about the topic will tune in just to get a look at the preacher who escaped from his kidnappers. And it'll be in the papers tomorrow about your inheritance, that Bible and a million bucks—hey, Randollph, we're rich, have you thought of that?"

"Not much. I'm already rich in everything that really matters. I've got you, haven't I?"

"Oh, Randollph, you do know how to melt a maiden's heart. But back to business. You'll boost my show's ratings."

"If I come on your show to help your ratings, I'll be guilty of nepotism. You know that, don't you?"

"If it helps my ratings, I don't care if you're guilty of antidisestablishmentarianism. I bet you didn't think I knew that big a word. See you tonight."

15

MISS WINDFALL regularly opened the church office at 9:00 A.M. This Tuesday morning Randollph was determined to be in his study hard at work when she arrived. This would demonstrate that contrary to her convictions he was capable of coping without her reminders with the holy flotsam and jetsam that, unattended, quickly cluttered the ecclesiastical waters lapping the shores of the Church of the Good Shepherd. Also, he had a lot to get done today.

If someone asked him, "What does a preacher do?" he wondered how he would answer. He could say, well, a preacher preaches, conducts public worship, baptizes, marries, and buries. But he'd have to add that a preacher also talks to people—maybe counseling them about a personal problem, maybe discussing with them the health and well-being of the church. A preacher also spends a lot of time in meetings. He also plans and studies and takes care of whatever comes along, not to mention such things as visiting the sick, devoting a certain amount of time to good works in the community, and—well, take a look at my schedule for today, he could say. Here it is as I wrote it out yesterday.

Item 1. Work on next Sunday's sermon.

Item 2. Write pastor's column for *The Spire*, Good Shepherd's weekly church newsletter. (Take care of item no. 2 before item no. 1 because copy for *The Spire* has to go to the printer by one o'clock so that the printer can have it back to the church sometime tomorrow morning so that one of the office girls who works under the chilly supervision of Miss Windfall can run the issue through the folding machine and addressograph in time to get it to the post office in time to get it mailed to the members of Good Shepherd so that they will receive it Friday or Saturday reminding them that the Church of the Good Shepherd is still doing business at the same old address and would welcome their presence come 11:00 A.M. on the Lord's Day.)

Item 3. Make out order of worship for Sunday morning (select hymns, prayers, etc.). This, too, needs to be in the hands of the printer today.

Item 3a. 11:00 A.M. regular weekly meeting with Tony Agostino, Good Shepherd's choirmaster-organist to discuss hymn selection and see if what Tony has in mind for Sunday's anthem fits—or at least doesn't clash—with sermon theme.

Item 3b. Also discuss with Tony music for Johannes Humbrecht funeral.

Item 4. Plan services and prepare sermons for Humbrecht and Kline funerals tomorrow. (Remember, because of funerals you won't have any time for sermon preparation tomorrow. Try to find some extra time later in week for sermon.)

Item 5. 1:30 P.M. Bertie Smelser explains church's monthly financial report to me. Could I skip this? Suppose not. He'd be offended.

Item 6. 2:15 P.M. Appt. Mrs. Jonathan Summers. Member of church. Know her slightly. Marital problem? Probably.

Item 7. 3 P.M. (Or whenever) make hospital calls.

Item 8. 8 P.M. Monthly meeting of church's governing board.

And that, Randollph could say, is what a preacher does. Except today is more crowded than usual because it isn't every day you have to get ready for two funerals, or even one funeral for that matter. But if it isn't that, it's likely to be something else. As you can see by this schedule, he would tell anyone who inquired as to how the clergy managed to occupy its time between Sundays, I need to have the skills of a scholar and orator, be able to write with at least a modicum of clarity and grace, understand institutional finance, have a grasp of psychology, possess the wit and charm of a diplomat, not to mention executive ability, decisiveness, emotional strength, and physical stamina to do my job properly. Some of these things I do well, he might go ahead to explain. Some of them I do adequately. Some I do poorly. I admit I procrastinate when it comes to the routines of running an office. I admit I wouldn't attend all the meetings I do attend if I could get out of going to them. But the parts of the job I like are more than enough reason for doing the parts I don't like.

He took a sheet of paper from a drawer in the big desk that his predecessor had installed as an appropriate symbol of the prestige and importance of Good Shepherd's pastor. He found a ball-point pen in another drawer. He wanted to have his column for the church newsletter finished and ready when Miss Windfall brought in the morning mail and told him what she expected him to accomplish before lunch. He was looking forward to seeing an astonished look flit across her face when he said, "Oh, by the way, here's my column for *The Spire.*"

But what to write? He stared at the blank sheet of paper. He was on the mailing list for quite a few church newsletters. He'd studied them. Many pastors regularly filled their weekly column with a mini-sermon. Helpful hints for improving one's devotional life, how your prayers can bring home the bacon, or perhaps a recommendation for a hot item in the inspirational book market. Other pastors filled their allotted space with touting some aspect of their church's program, or cheering a new denominational crusade guaranteed to resuscitate moribund congregations, fill empty pews, and transform worldly church members into zealous Christian soldiers.

Randollph had decided early that he just couldn't

manage this kind of pastor's column. He supposed it was part of any pastor's job to be an ecclesiastical huckster. Pews did have to be filled. People needed to be inspired. Church budgets required balancing. He didn't look down on the pastors who devoted their columns to holy hurrahs or soothing devotional instructions. Perhaps had he begun as a pastor instead of coming late to it he could have done it. But not now. He would have had to fake it. So what he did, as a rule, was to select some issue or event that was provoking public controversy and try to relate it to the Christian faith.

But what topic for this week? He chewed the end of his pen for a while and then it came to him. He needed to tell his church members something of his reactions to the recent days of his life. He pulled the sheet of paper in front of him and wrote across the top

THE UNHOLY BIBLE

My life in the last few days has been largely determined by a Bible. You have read about it in the newspapers, so I shall not recount here the unusual and frightening incidents in which I have been unwittingly involved. Perhaps some of you were struck, as I was, by the ironic nature of these events. Mr. Humbrecht's Bible was the cause of some most unholy happenings. It provoked acts of violence, perhaps murder. It unleashed the sins of greed, covetousness, and theft.

It occurs to me that we should detach the adjective "Holy" from the noun "Bible." The adjective is there to say that this body of literature we call the Bible is not like other literature, that it is stamped with the sacred, that it carries the authority of the Almighty.

But I am reminded by the recent events in my life that the holy can be made unholy if it is used for unholy purposes—as Mr. Humbrecht's Bible surely has been used.

There are any number of ways we can and do make the Bible unholy.

One way is by misrepresenting it. Some Christians contend that because the Bible is holy it is not for us to question anything the Bible says. To exempt the Bible from critical scrutiny means accepting its contradictions and some dubious concepts of God (such as we find in the Book of Revelation) among other things. That's dishonest, and dishonesty is unholy.

Then the Bible is often misrepresented by people who tell us that it says something it does not, in fact, say. Such people usually want the backing of the Bible for their personal and political advantage. Using the Holy Bible in this way makes it unholy.

Most Christians, though, make the Holy Bible unholy by neglecting it.

If Mr. Humbrecht's Bible is ever recovered it will interest millions of people because it is a superb work of art. They will be thrilled by the beauty of the book. And that is fine. We ought to be thrilled by it. But it is the use to which the Bible is put, not the beauty of its binding or its supposed inerrancy or theories of its divine origin that makes it holy or unholy.

Christians are people of the book. We do not follow religious ideas that somebody just thought up. Jesus did not walk the shores of Galilee spouting a lot of worthy suggestions about living that had come to him out of the blue. The religion of Jesus had its beginnings fifteen centuries or so before him, and its growth and development is recorded in that section of the Holy Bible we call the Old Testament. That part of the Holy Bible we call the New Testament is, Christians believe, the record of God's New Covenant with His people.

You have all read in the newspapers that Mr. Humbrecht bequeathed his Bible to me. I am humbled and honored by his kindness. But I had already inherited the Bible, an inheritance far more important than my acquisition of a unique copy of the Bible. It is a part of every Christian's estate. It explains us and defines us. Admittedly some parts of the Bible are more significant and enlightening than other parts. And even some of the best parts are easy to misinterpret and misunderstand. One responsibility of the faithful is to work at understanding what the Bible is saying to us as we travel toward that city whose builder and maker is God.

He just had time to sign the column, push it aside, and engage himself in leafing through the hymnal bearing the imprimatur of his denomination when Miss Windfall knocked once, then entered bearing mail and an aura of righteous efficiency. She knew what Randollph should be doing at any moment. Looking through the hymnal was something he ought to be doing about now in preparation for his conference with the choirmaster. Randollph could tell that she approved, and he'd be willing to bet she was thinking that his experiences of the last few days had sobered him, caused him to abandon his procrastinating ways, and otherwise improved his character. He waited until she said "hmmm" as a prelude to reciting his obligations for the day, then said, "Oh, before I forget it, here's my column for *The Spire*. I'm sure you'll want one of the girls to type it up right away." He was rewarded by Miss Windfall's openmouthed astonishment. But not for long. She quickly reset her mouth into its customarily purposeful line and said, "Thank you. It is nice to have it early. You're remembering the meeting of the governing board tonight?"

"Yes. I have it on the calendar."

Miss Windfall swept out of the office semi-triumphant. Randollph realized that Adelaide Windfall thought of herself as the very soul of the place, and pestering a procrastinating pastor was a drill she performed in order to confirm her self-image.

Since he had the hymnal in his hand, he thought he might as well make some selections for Sunday's service. This was one task he found frustrating. What you looked for were hymns whose texts reflected the ideas expressed in the sermon. At least the closing hymn ought to do that. Since he'd be preaching the introductory sermon to the series on the seven deadly sins this Sunday—that is, if he ever found the time this week to prepare it—he needed a hymn saying something about sin. He looked in the hymnal's topical index under "sin" and then read every listing. It appeared that there just weren't any good hymns on sin. They were superficial, sentimental, lugubrious. Someone, he remembered, had said that you have to be a fourth-rate poet to be a successful writer of hymns. He was reading:

> Jesus, the sinner's Friend, to thee
> Lost and undone, for aid I flee,
> Weary of earth, myself, and sin
> Open thine arms and take me in.

Now what normal person could sing that and mean it? he thought. He doubted that anyone in his congregation Sunday would be weary of earth. Some of them might be weary of their jobs, their marriages, their lot in life. But none of them would be weary of sin because they weren't the kind of people who thought of themselves as sinners. In moments of self-awareness they might think of themselves as damn fools, or victims of circumstances beyond their control, or guilty of poor decisions determining their destiny. But not as sinners. Randollph was wondering if a series of sermons on the seven deadly sins was the hot idea he'd thought it was when he'd first conceived it when the crackle of the intercom interrupted him.

"Lieutenant Casey is here to see you," Miss Windfall informed him.

"Send him in." Though Casey was a privileged visitor and always had immediate access to Randollph, he didn't abuse the privilege. He usually had something serious on his mind when he came to Randollph's study. Randollph got Casey seated and said, "Have you come to tell me you've arrested Johannes Humbrecht's murderer and recovered the Bible?"

"I wish to hell that's why I'd come," Casey replied. "What I came for is to tell you we now have another homicide possibly connected to that damn Bible."

"Who?"

"Robin Elder."

Randollph took a moment to absorb this news, then said, "Tell me about it."

"It didn't happen in my jurisdiction," Casey said, a little of the tenseness leaking out of him as he settled in the big comfortable leather-upholstered chair. "Guy lived in a big old house on the lake in Evanston. Fancy old place. Probably has riparian rights. Lives there alone."

"He's not married?"

"Married three times. Divorced three times. Must have alimony payments like the national debt. Anyway, he has one of those cleaning services that come in once a week. It's a big place, and he's—he was a fastidious fellow. Today was their day, they've got their own key to the place. He's usually gone by the time the crew gets there. This morning he's still there. Dead. Slumped over the desk in his study. Two bullet holes in the back of his head."

"You've been out there?"

"Yes. We get reports on homicides in the suburbs. They sometimes tie in with something we're working on. When I saw this report on Elder I got right out there. We have a cordial relationship with Evanston P.D."

"What makes you think this murder is connected with that damn Bible, as you put it?"

Casey grinned. "That wasn't any way for a good Catholic Christian to talk, was it? That Bible has turned into a great big pain in the neck for me. But I didn't say connected, I said possibly connected."

"You must have a reason."

"I've got some thoughts on the subject. I don't know how good they are."

"You want to try them out on me?" Randollph thought briefly of his day already too full and no time budgeted to discuss a murder that might or might not have anything to do with Johannes Humbrecht's Gutenberg Bible. Then he brushed the thought away as, he supposed, anyone who held down an executive's chair had to do frequently by telling himself he'd squeeze some extra time out of the day later on.

Casey glanced at his wristwatch, a sturdy-looking instrument that probably gave him the month, day, phases of the moon, and no doubt worked under water. "Almost time," he said.

"For what?"

"My mid-morning cigarette."

"Oh? You're on a schedule?"

Casey looked sheepish. "Yeah. I'm quitting by cutting down gradually."

Randollph found an ashtray and handed it to the detective. "Do you cheat now and then?"

Casey looked even more sheepish. "Pretty often. Actually, I've already had my morning quota. But I started the day very early, so I figure I'm entitled to an extra smoke before noon."

Randollph chuckled. "How we do rationalize our sins. Tell you what. If you'll give me permission to use you as an illustration—not naming you, of course—in one of the sermons I'm preparing on sin, then I'll absolve you of the sin of cheating on your smoking schedule, and you can really enjoy this one. I'll make the absolution good for the whole day."

"My pastor at St. Aloysius would say that since you aren't in the apostolic succession your absolution isn't solid. But I'm broad-minded. Make the absolution cover me until we clear up this Humbrecht business and it's a deal."

"Deal," Randollph said, watching Casey happily suck at his cigarette. "You were going to try your logic on me."

"First, coincidence. A partner in the law firm which handled Humbrecht's will gets himself murdered the day after the will is read and the Bible is found missing, stolen probably."

"But—"

Casey cut Randollph off. "I know what you're going to say. You're going to say that coincidences happen. But policemen don't believe much in them. Our experience teaches us to take a very hard look at a coincidence like this."

"So coincidence is your first reason for suspecting a connection between Elder and the Bible. What's second?"

"The place was ransacked. One hell of a mess. Every book in the library—can you imagine, the guy had a library, I don't know how good. Some pretty expensive pornography, I saw some of that. Anyway, every book was pulled out. Every drawer in every desk and bureau in the house dumped on the floor. Wall safe in Elder's study open and cleaned out."

"Sounds like a simple robbery murder."

"That's what it was meant to look like."

"How can you tell?"

Casey looked a little smug. "Amateur night. No forced entry. A window broken in the pantry and unlocked. Broken with a brick and from the inside. A pro would have used a glass cutter if he was trying to get in from the outside. Hard to tell what may have been taken. But expensive TV sets and stereos, stuff punks and hopheads always heist, easy to fence, not taken. And Elder still had his wallet on him with three hundred or so in cash and a flock of credit cards. Can you imagine a common thief dumb enough to miss that?"

Randollph admitted that he couldn't.

"No. It was amateur night. Whoever did it was just making a clumsy and probably hurried attempt to cover his real motive by faking a common robbery."

Casey was more intense now. He had the air of one who had at last seen the light and could hardly wait to tell what the Lord had done for him. Randollph invited him to testify.

"Well, here's my hypothesis." Casey absently lighted another cigarette. "Elder, we hear, needed money. He lived high. He supported three ex-wives and several expensive girl friends. Gambled some. Was in the market. Got all this from the Evanston P.D. He's got a couple D.W.I.'s on his record. They know him pretty well."

"If you live like that you're bound to need extra money every now and then."

"Yep. Even if you have one sweet income. Which he had. I've known people you give them ten million a year and they manage to spend eleven million. It often turns them into murderers. Most of them don't want to be murderers, it's just that they get in financial trouble and murder turns out to be the easiest way or the only way to lay their hands on a pile of kopeks in a hurry."

"But Elder was the victim, not the murderer."

Casey got up and began pacing the large office-study. Randollph guessed the policeman was smelling a solution to this pesky case and needed to work off some of the nervous energy the scent generated in him.

"Oh, Elder was a murderer."

Casey's flat statement startled Randollph. "Perhaps you'd better explain your hypothesis to me, Lieutenant."

Casey stopped pacing and stood in front of Randollph's desk. "O.K. Here's what I think happened. Elder had access to Humbrecht's will, right?"

"It was sealed."

"But seals can be broken. Remember, Knox broke the seal and told us that the will was sealed in the standard envelope the firm used for wills."

"I remember, yes." The scene came back to Randollph, and he also remembered that J. J. Knox had looked curiously at the seal before he had broken it.

"There'd be no problem for someone with access to the will breaking the seal, reading the will, then resealing it in another one of those envelopes. That's what I think Elder did."

"Why would he do that?"

Casey sat down again in the big leather chair. "From what little I know of the guy he must have needed money. Probably a lot of money. Quick."

"But why would he think that Humbrecht's will could help him?"

"I'm betting he opened a lot of wills. Most of them weren't sealed."

"I fail to see how that would produce quick money."

Casey was calmer now. This was familiar ground for him. "Wills contain a lot of information about people. Family feuds. People expecting an inheritance but have been cut out of a relative's will without their knowledge. Inside information is often marketable."

"Blackmail?"

"Sure. And remember that Knox, Knox, and Elder's clients aren't exactly on welfare."

"So Elder was prospecting to see what he could come up with. But why Humbrecht's will? Humbrecht was supposed to be a pauper."

"I think the seal intrigued him. He's bound to have heard the story about this old recluse who came in with a will already drawn, had it witnessed, sealed, and filed.

That doesn't happen every day in a law firm like Knox, Knox, and Elder. That kind of thing gets talked about around the office. Very peculiar for an old pauper to bring in a will to a fancy law firm, refuse to disclose its contents, and demand that it be sealed in his presence. I'll bet Elder thought there was no harm in having a look. Everyone knows about people like Hetty Green who lived like pigs despite their millions."

"And he recognized the Gutenberg Bible as described in the will as the solution to his financial problems. He has the information about the Bible, he has its location and the combination to the lock on Humbrecht's library and art room. He then goes to Humbrecht's place, kills Humbrecht, and steals the Bible."

"You've got it."

"That's your hypothesis. And you want me to help you test it."

"Can you see any holes in it?"

Randollph pondered Casey's story, then said, "What about the cups of tea? Why would Humbrecht offer hospitality to Elder?"

"I'm guessing that Elder passed himself off as a scholar in some field in which Humbrecht had some rare and hard-to-come-by books in his library. Remember, he had an itemized list of Humbrecht's library. He could do a quick study of the subject, enough to get him by with a few minutes' conversation. Enough to get him in the house. Elder's the type who could turn on the charm when it was to his advantage. Wouldn't Humbrecht offer tea to a charming fellow scholar?"

"Yes, I think so. But if he'd come to kill Humbrecht he'd have brought his own weapon. He couldn't have known that baseball bat would have been handy."

"I thought of that," Casey said, unperturbed. "I think he did have something with him. He probably carried a briefcase and had a sap or some kind of club like a blackjack in it. I don't think he intended to kill Humbrecht. Just knock him out long enough to heist the Bible."

"Then why use the bat?"

"Spur-of-the-moment idea. He saw it, it was handier to get at than whatever he had in his briefcase."

"If he didn't mean to kill Humbrecht, then why did he kill him?"

"Elder didn't know anything about knocking people out. People who don't know anything about it think it takes a lot more force than it actually does. They don't realize how easy it is to crack a skull. And that is a very heavy bat. He just misjudged, hit the old geezer a fatal blow. I'll bet it scared the sh—, I'll bet he was pretty upset when he saw what he'd done."

"But not too upset to steal the Bible."

"No. But he'd normally have shut the drawer to that bin or whatever where the Bible was kept. And the door to the room. The fact that he didn't is what makes me believe he was scared and wanted to get the hell out of there."

"And that's why he didn't steal any of the paintings? He must have known that they would fetch a good price."

Casey chewed at his lower lip, then said, "I doubt he ever intended to steal the paintings. Fencing them would have just complicated things for him. You see, Elder didn't think of himself as a thief. A professional thief would have planned to clean out everything of value in that room." Casey suddenly grinned. "I didn't think of myself as cheating on my quota of cigarettes this morning. I thought I deserved an extra because of a special need. Elder didn't think of himself as a thief. He thought of himself as a man with a pressing problem which he could solve by stealing that Bible. Amateurs, amateur criminals that is, well, their minds work in funny ways. You'd be surprised, Doctor, how many murderers—the kind of people who don't ordinarily go around killing people—how many of them don't think they're murderers. Their minds won't let them. They did it because, they say, as anyone can plainly see, it was the only thing they could do under the circumstances. Or that what they did was good for society and therefore not murder. Or they did it in a moment of justifiable anger. They didn't plan to kill anyone."

"You haven't yet explained—"

Casey finished Randollph's sentence for him.

"Who killed Elder and why. I'm getting to that. Elder had the Bible. By the way, what would it be worth? That's one reason I stopped by to see you. This is in your field. You ought to be able to give me a ballpark figure of what it's worth."

"Sorry," Randollph said. "I can tell you almost everything about that Bible but its price."

"Not even a good guess?"

"Not really. I assume that if it came on the market legitimately it would bring a substantially higher price than it could command if it had to be disposed of as stolen property." He thought a moment, then added, "Mr. Jones was willing to pay me half a million—tax-free as he put it—and hinted that he would go higher. And remember, he had me at a disadvantage. I'd guess he'd have paid a million or more. Of course, he was hoping to buy himself a good address in heaven with that Bible. But go on with your hypothesis."

Casey seemed glad to oblige. Randollph supposed the lieutenant wanted to hear how it sounded before he tried it on his superiors who would ultimately decide if all his assumptions made sense. A homicide detective probably had to sell his ideas just as an advertising executive had to sell a client on what the creative department had come up with. Casey leaned forward in his chair and spoke with a certainty he may or may not have felt. "Here's what happened. Elder has the Bible. He wants to sell it in a hurry. So what does he do?"

"I don't know," Randollph answered what he knew was a rhetorical question. "He could hardly advertise in the want ads."

Casey started to look pained, then changed his expression to a smile. "No, what he did was to make some discreet inquiries as to who handled that sort of merchandise. A big-shot lawyer like Elder wouldn't have any trouble finding a fence who specialized in stolen art."

"Everyone has to specialize these days, it seems. Go on."

"Elder describes the merchandise to the fence. The fence says give him a few days, he knows some parties who might be interested, but some of them live in other countries. He'll get back to Elder."

"Then what?"

"So now the word is out. Maybe the fence, maybe

one of the potential buyers, decides it would be a lot nicer to get the Bible for free than pay for it."

"No honor among thieves, eh?"

"None whatever. So this guy, whoever he is, sets up a meeting with Elder at Elder's house to negotiate the sale. Elder lets him in. The guy pulls a gun and demands the Bible. Elder, if I peg him right, would much rather have his life than the Bible. He wouldn't argue with a gun. Or maybe the murderer just said, 'Let's see the merchandise.' So Elder gets the Bible. If it happened that way, Elder probably just got one volume out of that wall safe—that's where I'm betting he kept it, that's why it was open. Then this guy inspects the volume and says, 'May I see the other volume, please—here, let me get it out of the safe.' Then he goes around behind Elder, pulls the gun, and shoots him before he can get out of the chair."

"Then ransacks the house?"

"Right."

"Why?"

"The guy doesn't want the murder connected with the Bible. He knows that sooner or later we're going to figure out that Elder stole that Bible and probably killed Humbrecht. Hell, the papers have been full of it. We get enough evidence to pull Elder in, he might crack and spill the whole story. That convicts the fence, and—unless the fence did it—leads to the customer who decided it would be easy to knock off Elder and get the Bible for nothing. Saves himself a million dollars or more. A million dollars is a powerful motivation. So he tries to make it look like an ordinary burglary. That's plausible. Plenty of them every day." Casey leaned back in his chair, relaxed, and waited for Randollph's verdict.

"Ingenious," Randollph commented. "I don't mean the crime, I mean the way you figured it out."

Casey looked pleased.

"But," Randollph went on, "it's pretty much speculation. It's like the doctrine of salvation by grace through faith. It makes a lot of sense. It is consistent with experience. But it isn't easy to prove." Randollph thought a minute about his analogy, then said, "Of course, St. Paul didn't try to prove the doctrine, only proclaim it.

You, on the other hand, have to back your proclamation, your hypothesis, with hard facts. Can you do that?"

Casey's pleased look faded. "I don't know. I will try, of course. I have to."

"I'd be interested to know how you'll go about it."

Back in the area where he was the expert Casey brightened up. "Procedure. Crimes are cleared up not by brilliant intuition—" he stopped and smiled "—not by an incredibly clever hypothesis like the one I've put together. They're finally nailed down by dull and dreary police routine."

"You have to test the hypothesis."

"That's right."

"How?"

"Well, first I'll run a thorough check on Elder. See if he needed a lot of money in a hurry like I think he did. Then I'll inspect his telephone records. If he talked to a fence, he probably did it by phone."

"You know the dealers who specialize in stolen art?"

"Oh sure. The ones in this area. There aren't many."

"Why don't you question them?"

"Oh, we will. Especially if we get a lead. But it won't do any good."

"I don't see why not."

"Because they know how to take care of themselves. They never keep the stolen stuff at their places of business—they are also legitimate art dealers. Sometimes they never see the stolen stuff, just act as a broker and take a commission. They aren't going to tell us about it. Why should they? We can't make them." Casey looked like he longed for the return of the rubber hose and knocking criminals around to loosen their tongues. "But following procedures, the routine, usually turns up something, leads you to people who point you in the right direction."

"You think there's a good chance of recovering the Bible?"

Casey said, "That's right, it's your Bible now, isn't it? To answer your question, I'd say there's a chance. If the guy that stole it from Elder—say it was the fence—wanted it to sell to someone, it may be in South America or Saudi Arabia by now. Not much chance of recovering it if that's the case. On the other hand, maybe the thief will try to jack up the price by getting potential customers bidding against each other. This is a pretty special item. If that's the case, it may still be here in Chicago. Then we've got a chance." He got up to go. "If the bishop makes that brilliant deduction he's hoping for you'll see that I hear about it, won't you?"

Randollph laughed. "I won't have to. You'll hear it from him."

Randollph was hardly back to the business of selecting hymns when the intercom sputtered again and Miss Windfall's voice informed him that the bishop was waiting to see him.

The bishop took the chair so recently occupied by Lieutenant Casey and said, "I know you must be up to your ears in work, C.P. I won't keep you long. I have a request."

It occurred to Randollph that if the bishop exchanged his oxford-gray suit and polished grained-leather black shoes for a brown habit and sandals he'd look enough like Father Prior Simon to pass as his brother.

"What do you want me to do, Freddie?"

"You have a meeting of your governing board tonight, I believe?"

"That's right."

"Would you mind if I attended?"

"Of course not, Freddie. Our board meetings are open to church members and members of the denominational hierarchy. You are our denomination's number one hierarch in these parts. You needn't ask. But you know that. You've got something in mind. Am I to be privy to whatever it is?"

The bishop smiled graciously. "Best that you aren't, C.P. Bishops, if they're any good at their job, need to know when to keep their own counsel." He pulled himself out of the deep leather chair. "I suggest, though, that if I should happen to say something which seems to you outrageous, that you don't go into shock."

"Don't be cryptic, Freddie."

"In this instance I'm afraid I must be."

Randollph sighed in what he intended to sound like exasperation. "I know better than to press you. It wouldn't get me anywhere. You'll just smile that inscrutable smile and turn on the charm."

"So I would."

"I'll forgive you if you can suggest a good hymn dealing with the subject of sin."

"I'm afraid there aren't any, C.P. At least none come to mind. Too many of them use blood atonement as their theme. I think blood atonement has no cogency for the modern mind."

"It's interesting that the church never did adopt an orthodox doctrine of the atonement. Did you know that, Freddie?"

The bishop opened the office door. "No, I didn't know that. Church history wasn't one of my strong subjects. It's a comfort, though, to know that my distaste for the doctrine doesn't make me a heretic. I'll see you at the board meeting."

Before coming to Good Shepherd, Randollph had seldom reflected on how the motor of a church was kept tuned up. He was occupied with telling future chief mechanics of spiritual service stations how the church had taken St. Francis of Assisi's order away from him for the best interests of God's earthly Kingdom, or why that seemingly dopey idea of the Crusades never achieved its avowed spiritual goal but blessed business by vastly increasing commerce. He knew that all churches, whatever their brand name, had some kind of official body charged with the responsibility of peering periodically into its holy machinery and deciding on what adjustments and repairs were needed.

As a pastor, short as his experience had been, he'd learned three things about the boards that governed the affairs of a church: that they were necessary; that their meetings were usually boring; and that you never knew when something unanticipated by the agenda would come up and provoke an unholy controversy.

The governing board of the Church of the Good Shepherd had an official roster of more than fifty members. It was considered an honor to be named to Good Shepherd's board because everyone in the city knew it was an old and prestigious congregation that traditionally only admitted those with a proper pedigree to its inner circles. Once admitted, however, board members did not feel it incumbent upon themselves to be totally faithful in attendance upon the board's meetings. Any number over thirty was looked upon as a good crowd.

Tonight there were few absentees. "Looks like everybody wants to see if you're any the worse for wear after your heroic exploits as reported so colorfully by the press," Dan Gantry said to Randollph. "What's the bishop doing here?"

"He won't tell me."

"He's up to something, or something's up. Got any guesses?"

"No."

Tyler Morrison, chairman of the board, rapped with his gavel. "My watch says eight o'clock. Let's take our places, get this show on the road, get it over so we can get home in decent time." People began to detach themselves from their conversational clumps and find chairs. They knew from experience that Tyler Morrison did not tolerate time-wasting. Randollph knew that Miss Windfall thought people like Tyler Morrison, who had made himself a millionaire with a chain of cut-rate drugstores, had to be regarded as second-class members of Good Shepherd. But Randollph liked him for his businessman's impatience with time-wasting and his salesman's unruffled good humor.

"'Fore we get to the agenda," Morrison said after whacking the table with his gavel again, "we are honored to have the bishop with us tonight. Like to say a few words, Bishop?"

The bishop stood up. Randollph wondered how a short man who looked like a chubby cherub and always presented an amiable expression could project an air of rock-hard personal strength and quiet authority.

"Thank you, Mr. Morrison. I'm here because your pastor and my dear friend has just come through a most difficult few days during which his life was endangered. I want to say that I'm overjoyed, both as his friend and his bishop, that he's safe and with us once more."

The group, led by the chairman, applauded the bishop's speech. Dan Gantry whispered to Randollph, "Nice speech, but five'll get you ten that's not why he's here."

"No bet," Randollph said. He'd been thinking the same thing.

"Sure we all join the bishop in those sentiments," Tyler Morrison said.

"Mr. Chairman, may I ask Dr. Randollph a question?" The would-be questioner was a portly man on the shady side of middle age. Randollph knew that his name was Franklin Culp and that he was a banker or securities broker, he wasn't sure which. He remade a resolution he made at every board meeting—to devise some method for getting better acquainted with the members of the board.

Tyler Morrison turned to Randollph. "Any objection, Doctor?"

"No, of course not."

"O.K., ask it, Frank."

Franklin Culp cleared his throat with an "ahem," then said, "What do you plan to do with the Bible left to you by the late Mr. Humbrecht?"

Randollph was startled by the unexpected question. He didn't answer immediately, and the room grew suddenly quiet. Finally he said, "Mr. Culp, I don't have the Bible."

"I know that," Culp said with an edge of irritation in his voice. "But I assume it will be recovered eventually. We have a very efficient police force. What will you do with it when it is recovered?"

"You askin' out of curiosity, or you got a point to make, Frank?" Despite his amiability, Tyler Morrison was quick to get at the heart of a matter.

"I have a point to make, Mr. Chairman. I want to say that the proper thing for our pastor to do is to give the Bible to our church."

The board members reacted to that. Muted "ohs" and "ahs" and even an "I'll be damned" could be heard among the exclamations.

"Let me explain my reasoning." Culp had to raise his voice to be heard.

Tyler Morrison banged his gavel. "I think you'd better, Frank. Quiet, let's hear the man."

Culp was not at all taken aback by the stir he'd created. "Dr. Randollph, in his capacity as pastor of our church, visited Humbrecht frequently and thus gained the old man's gratitude and affection. That's only natural. The old man was, I understand, friendless and lonely." Randollph felt the anger rising in him. Culp made it sound as if Randollph was after whatever he could get out of Humbrecht.

"Get t' th' point, Frank." Tyler Morrison had caught Culp's implication too and plainly didn't like it.

"My point is that had not Dr. Randollph been our pastor, which gave him the opportunity to get acquainted with Humbrecht, he never would have inherited that Bible. Since he visited Humbrecht as a part of his job—for which we pay him handsomely—he inherited that Bible in his capacity as an agent of the Church of the Good Shepherd. If a chemist discovers a valuable formula or process while working for a corporation, his discovery belongs to the corporation, not the chemist. I think the same principle should apply here." Culp sat down, satisfied that he'd explained an idea that only a moron could fail to grasp and only an idiot would challenge. Apparently, though, a lot of board members wanted to challenge it or at least discuss it. As soon as Culp sat down there were shouts of "Mr. Chairman! Mr. Chairman!"

The chairman whacked the table with his gavel. "Let's have order! This subject isn't on the agenda and I'm probably out of order to permit it. But since it's come up, I think we might as well clear the air. Chair recognizes Mrs. Sandifer."

Randollph dredged from his memory what he knew about Cornelia Sandifer. She and her husband owned and operated a respected and successful public relations business. A trim and stylish fifty or thereabouts. Miss Windfall approved of the Sandifers because the family had belonged to the Church of the Good Shepherd for generations.

"I'm not sure that Dr. Randollph has any obligation to give that Bible to our church," Cornelia Sandifer said in a husky, pleasant voice. "But if he decided to do that—" she turned and smiled at Randollph "—we'd become one of the best-known churches in the world. People would come from everywhere to see the Bible."

"Where would you display the Bible, Cornelia?" Tyler Morrison asked.

"Why, why, I hadn't thought about that. In the narthex, I suppose. Yes, that would be the best place, the narthex."

"How y' goin' t' protect it, keep it from being stolen?"

"Oh, why, well, I hadn't thought about that either." Mrs. Sandifer appeared slightly flustered.

"Got to think about that," Morrison said. "You'd need round-the-clock security service. That costs money. Plenty. You're talkin' upwards of six figures a year for proper protection. Where's it comin' from?"

"Oh, well, we'd have to think of something, wouldn't we? The idea's so new, well, we'd need to give some thought to the details." Mrs. Sandifer sat down. In her business, Randollph supposed, one learned when to back off gracefully without admitting defeat.

Franklin Culp was on his feet again. "I didn't suggest the church should keep the Bible. We ought to sell it. It'll bring millions. Think of what it would do for our endowment."

"Ah, the money changers in the temple," Dan Gantry whispered to Randollph. "Jesus drove them out, but they always come back."

"Chair recognizes Mr. Barnes."

Randollph did know about Whitman Barnes. He was the only black who was or ever had been a member of Good Shepherd's governing board. Only in recent years had Good Shepherd had any black members at all. It was easier for a church like Good Shepherd to accept blacks into membership than for the typical church which served a specific community. When a black joined Good Shepherd it didn't mean the neighborhood was changing and property values were being threatened, because Good Shepherd wasn't a neighborhood church. Some of the white members, in fact, took pride in belonging to a church with a handful of minority members. They felt they were being open-minded and liberal. Randollph thought of it as a costless liberalism and even spiritual pride. He had to admit, though, that he'd proposed Whit Barnes for membership on the governing board not so much because Whit was bright, educated, and presentable—which he was—but because he wanted to be able to claim that his church not only admitted blacks to membership but also to leadership. Another form of spiritual pride.

"Some of you know I'm an editor at the *Tribune,*" Barnes said. "So I thought you'd like to know that the *Trib* will be announcing a contest tomorrow for the best suggestion as to what Dr. Randollph should do with the Gutenberg Bible—once it's found, that is. Maybe Mr. Culp and Mrs. Sandifer will want to enter."

"So we're going public with your business," Dan Gantry whispered to Randollph. "Be a circulation booster I guess."

The bishop was on his feet. "Mr. Morrison, would you grant me the privilege of the floor to make a brief statement?"

"Course, Bishop. Go right ahead."

"I've been listening to these comments with considerable interest." The bishop, Randollph could see, was wearing his benign episcopal expression which he always assumed prior to uttering a clear and severe judgment about which there would be no debate. "I feel, as your bishop, I must make a point or two plain." He paused to look squarely at Franklin Culp, then continued. "First, Dr. Randollph has no moral responsibility, and assuredly no legal one, to give the Bible to the Church of the Good Shepherd. The decision is his alone."

"That ought to take care of that old fart Culp," Dan whispered.

"My second point is that if Dr. Randollph has an employer other than God it is not the Church of the Good Shepherd, it's me." This provoked a few surprised mutters. "Oh, you pay his salary," the bishop said. "But in our denomination the bishop has the final authority as to where a pastor shall serve. We try to be democratic about it, of course. We do our best to name a pastor who is acceptable to the church. But the final authority resides with me. I, then, have the prior claim on his loyalty. If he decides to give the Bible away for benevolent purposes, I am suggesting that he should give it to me. I would then sell it, and use the money to build new churches which we so desperately need in areas of population growth and for which the available funds are meager to nonexistent. The Church of the Good Shepherd already has an ample endowment. Our church building program has none. Thank you, Mr. Morrison, for the privilege of speaking."

That put out the fire.

"Neat, real neat," Dan whispered. "Got you off the hook, and you didn't have to say a word. Wonder how the bishop knew this was going to come up?"

"Divine revelation perhaps," Randollph whispered back. He noticed that Mrs. Sandifer was looking bemused, and Franklin Culp was obviously feeling surly. He supposed he'd have to find some way to placate Culp. He'd discovered that every now and then the shepherd had to soothe an offended member of his flock who better deserved a sturdy kick in the gluteus maximus. Maybe Culp would just be mad at the bishop, not him. But that was unlikely. Culp couldn't get at the bishop, but he could get at his pastor.

Tyler Morrison rammed the stated business of the board meeting through in what Randollph estimated was record time. Afterward most of the members expressed their happiness to Randollph that he had come through his kidnapping safe and sound. Some of them said how much they admired the ingenuity of his escape. When the members had cleared out, the bishop said to Randollph, "I'll buy you a cup of coffee. You come too, Dan."

The hotel, which occupied part of Good Shepherd's building, had a cocktail lounge and piano bar that appeared to be doing a brisk business. But the coffee shop was almost deserted. They found a comfortable corner booth and ordered from a tired-looking waitress.

"Now I understand, Freddie, why you wanted to be at the board meeting. What I don't know is who tipped you off about Culp."

The bishop pulled the top off a miniature carton of cream and dumped the contents into his coffee. "I believe I'll have sugar too, though I shouldn't have either sugar or cream." He ripped the ends off two packets of sugar and added it to the coffee. "To answer your question, C.P., no one tipped me off. It was a surmise based on experience."

"You'll have to explain that, Freddie."

"The boss here thought you'd had a divine revelation," Dan said.

"Bishops by tradition are expected to be in touch with the divine, and I hope that I am. But in this instance I needed no help from above. I've served as trustee of colleges, as dean of a seminary, and as a bishop. I've had ample opportunity to see the workings of institutional greed."

"I don't get it," Dan said.

"It works like this, Dan. When a person identifies himself or herself with an institution—a college, a hospital, a church—they become zealous for its welfare. They're supposed to. But over a period of time they come to view the welfare of their institution as paramount. Its claims take precedence over the rights and claims of other institutions or of people. They will work and scheme—as did Mr. Culp—for the advantage of their institution."

"Well I'll be damned," Dan said. "That's the way multinational corporations operate. Only they do it for the dough. But what's in it for Culp?"

"Pride in his institution, pride in his wit to think of something that will benefit his institution, pride in his power to pull it off." The bishop sipped at his coffee, then patted his lips with a napkin.

"It seems to me, Freddie, that your suggestion as to what I should do with the Bible could be construed as an example of institutional greed."

"Of course it could, C.P. It was meant to. My institutional greed took precedence over his. That was the point. It was the best way to settle the matter. This thing could have become a raging controversy in your congregation, even split it. Now you won't hear any more about it."

"For which I am profoundly grateful, Freddie."

"Nor are you to let my suggestion that you give the Bible to me be a constraint on your decision, C.P. Oh, I'm just as greedy for my institution as Culp is for his, probably more. But I recognize your rights, and he doesn't. However, C.P., you are going to be wrestling with that decision—or I hope you will. You've thought about it?"

"Not much, not until this evening."

"I've got to catch an early plane tomorrow," the bishop said, rising. "By the way, C.P.—"

"Yes, Freddie?"

"If you should feel inclined to donate the Bible to me for the purpose I mentioned at the meeting, I would feel duty bound to accept it."

16

ABOUT THE TIME Randollph, the bishop, and Dan were leaving the hotel coffee shop, a car pulled into the graveled parking area of a small public park on Chicago's northwest side. A chilly late September drizzle had set in, a message that summer was over and it was time for Chicagoans to realize that before long, blizzards and nasty winds off the lake would be making their lives miserable.

The park was deserted, except for another car in the parking area. The waiting car flicked its lights twice, and was answered by the same signal. The driver of the car that had just arrived turned up the collar of his dark raincoat, pulled down the brim of his black hat, and got out of his car. He reached back across the front seat to retrieve a heavy satchel. He shut the door, walked the few feet to the waiting car, and got in the front passenger seat. "Mr. Jones?" he asked.

"Yes, yes of course. Who else could it be?" Mr. Jones spoke with the irritability of impatience. "This is the merchandise?" He reached for the satchel, but the other man withheld it.

"Before I give it to you I want to review our business arrangements."

"What's to review? We've agreed on the terms."

"Because I'm a careful man, and because I'm taking the larger risk in this deal."

"You're taking no risk. I want that Bible, both volumes. Believe me."

"It is because I believe you that I suggested this arrangement. I deliver to you volume one of the Bible, which I have right here. You pay me nothing. You verify the authenticity of volume one. If you are satisfied, then you deposit half the purchase price in the Zurich bank I have specified to the account number which I will give you. I assume you are in a position to do this."

"Yes, yes, of course." Mr. Jones couldn't take his eyes off the satchel.

"After all," the other man said, "I don't know who you are, and I don't want to know. I'm gambling that you aren't a common crook. You could turn this volume into a lot of money. I'd have no way of getting it back. I think I've shown my good faith."

"Maybe so," Jones said. "But you aren't taking that much of a chance. You know something about how much trouble I've gone to over this Bible. Well, I don't need the money. I can make money. I want the Bible. I'm a collector. I want the only work of art of its kind in the whole world. Not just one volume, both volumes."

"I believe you. But when it comes to business I want both parties to be clear as to their obligations."

"Do you mind if I smoke?" Jones asked.

"Go ahead. You might crack the window a little."

Jones lit one of his slim cigars with the dashboard lighter. "Don't forget that I'm trusting you to deliver the second volume according to our agreement."

"I want the money just as much as you want the Bible. As soon as the Zurich bank verifies your deposit, I'll call you and specify how the second volume will be handled. And paid for."

"I'm satisfied if you are," Jones said. "Now, may I take a look at the merchandise?"

"Go right ahead," the other man told him, handing

over the satchel. Mr. Jones switched on the car's map light and fumbled with the catch on the satchel. His hands were trembling. After two attempts he got it open and peered inside. Then he gasped, looked up, and said with cold fury, "What are you trying to pull? There's nothing in here but—"

"That's right," the other man said and shot Jones twice through the head. He then carefully wiped the gun and every surface in the car he'd touched. Then, using the handkerchief, he placed the gun on the seat by Mr. Jones. He had no further use for it. He didn't want it in his possession a minute longer. He smiled to himself. The gun would give the police a confusing little puzzle to work out.

He was suddenly aware of a car turning onto the street that led to the park. It was four or five blocks away, but it might be a patrol car. He hastily got out of Jones's car, using his handkerchief to open and close the door, and hurried over to his car. Take your time, he told himself. Don't panic. Don't spin your wheels. He quickly started his car, turned on the lights, and forced himself to back out of his parking place at a normal speed. He shifted the gear selector to D and pulled away without spraying gravel. He passed the car entering the park and saw with relief that it wasn't a police cruiser. Just a teenage couple so engrossed in each other that they didn't even look at him. He was at least two miles from the park before it came to him that in his haste to get away he'd left the satchel in Jones's car.

17

THE CHURCH OF THE GOOD SHEPHERD had acquired a chapel through the generosity of a Mr. Jeremiah D. Pembroke, who wasn't a member of the church and didn't give a hoot in hell for its welfare. But his mousy wife, Lydia had been a devoted member of the church. Mr. Pembroke didn't give a hoot in hell about his wife either. He had neglected her shamefully during their long marriage, spending his time betting—with remarkable success—on commodities futures, and with high-priced ladies of the evening. After she had died as unobtrusively as she had lived, some tattered shred of conscience, perhaps, or maybe a self-serving wish to advertise himself as a grieving husband, prompted him to offer his wife's church a chapel if it could be named after her. Also, he'd just made a killing in soybeans and could use the tax deduction.

So an architect who specialized in ersatz Gothic was employed by the church's board of trustees, every member of which was under the impression that Gothic architecture was a style of construction, which it wasn't, instead of a solution to an engineering problem, which it was. Thus the Lydia Pembroke Memorial Chapel was built as a transept off the nave. It was inevitably referred to as the Lydia Pinkham Chapel.

But even though structural steel supported the roof rather than flying buttresses, and the stained glass windows derived their illumination from cold, unvarying fluorescent tubes rather than the uncertainties of the sun, it was still an impressive edifice, a mini-Chartres or Notre Dame. And useful. Splendid for small weddings. Randollph himself had been married to Samantha there not many months ago. And certainly preferable to a commercial funeral chapel for the rites which ushered a person of faith from this life to the next, when the anticipated attendance was so small as to be lost in the nave of the church.

The mourners for Johannes Humbrecht made a sparse congregation even in the chapel, Randollph noted. A few elderly gentlemen and a couple of white-haired ladies, whom he took to be former faculty colleagues of Humbrecht's. They had an academic look about them. Representatives of the institutions receiving largesse from Humbrecht, looking fidgety and wanting this chore over with. And Prior Simon. Randollph was at first surprised to see the prior, but supposed the monk was fulfilling what he considered a Christian obligation both to the late Mrs. Humbrecht, who had so generously endowed the Order of St. Thomas Aquinas, and to Humbrecht, who had bequeathed his not inconsiderable scholarly library to the order.

He'd had a little difficulty with the undertaker's assistant. He was a chunky young fellow with a brash manner who had presumed to instruct Randollph as to how the service would be handled.

"That chapel floor's stone, rough as a cob," he told Randollph. "We'll bring the casket in before the service, lots easier that way. Then you can come in from the side door whenever you're ready."

Randollph gave the fellow the kind of withering look he had once used on a rookie who'd spoken up in the huddle to tell him what play to call next.

"It is not a part of your professional responsibility

to instruct a pastor in the conduct of a funeral," he said coldly.

"But I thought—"

Randollph cut him off. "From this point on I shall assume the burden of the thinking. You are only obligated to do as I say. I shall precede the casket down the center aisle, reading from the service for the burial of the dead. Do you feel that this is beyond your firm's capabilities?"

The chunky young chap answered with a sullen "no." Randollph momentarily felt guilty for lacing into someone who was in no position to talk back, something he tried never to do. It was a measure of his nerves and their strung-out state. Funerals were hard on him. And today he had two. He wondered if, after twenty years or so at this job, he would develop a completely professional attitude toward sickness and death. He supposed one could, and it would save a lot of damage to his emotional system. He hadn't reached that level of pastoral professionalism yet, and he wasn't sure he ever would.

He'd told Tony Agostino to play mostly Bach because Humbrecht had apotheosized the works of Bach and believed his music would never be equaled. He'd often told Randollph that he looked forward to meeting Bach in heaven. The trustees of Good Shepherd, sagacious businessmen all, had realized that they had in Jeremiah Pembroke a pigeon in no position to protest a thorough plucking, so they stuck him not only for the price of the chapel, but also for a baroque pipe organ built especially for the chapel instead of a considerably less costly electronic instrument. The sound manufactured by Tony Agostino's skilled fingers on the kind of organ for which J. S. Bach had written the music was, even to Randollph's untutored ear, heavenly. He liked to think that Humbrecht and Bach were perched together on a cloud somewhere in the reaches of heaven listening.

Randollph believed that funeral sermons should be brief and should avoid excessive eulogizing of the departed. It wasn't always easy to pick an appropriate theme for a funeral meditation. But for Johannes Humbrecht it had been easy. Randollph chose a few words from Psalm 16, "The lines are fallen unto me in pleasant places.... Let us forget about Johannes Humbrecht's violent death. Rather, let us remember that he had a long, full and useful life. What more could anyone ask of life than the blessing of a keen mind, work in which that gift was fully employed to the benefit of people and society, and a happy and loving marriage?" He alluded to his friendship with Humbrecht, to Humbrecht's faith, the faith of a learned and highly intelligent man who found no conflict between science, logic and his religion. He spoke of Humbrecht's devotion to the Church of the Good Shepherd. He ended the service with a prayer which called to remembrance God's loving kindness and tender mercies to His servant Johannes Humbrecht, and for God's goodness that withheld not Johannes Humbrecht's portion in the joys of this earthly life. Then he pronounced a benediction and led the casket back down the aisle as Tony brought the organ to life again.

The mourners didn't wait to be ushered out. Normally, Randollph would have been in the vestry ridding himself of his ecclesiastical regalia before the mourners exited. But these people apparently wanted to be done witn the place and occasion, so he was caught. One of the representatives of an institution inheriting under Humbrecht's will asked how soon Randollph, as executor, planned to make a distribution to the legatees. "You'll be notified," Randollph told him curtly and turned away. Several people said, "Nice service, Reverend."

The last mourner to speak to him was Prior Simon. With a wan but friendly smile Father Simon said, "I thought you said exactly the right thing. I didn't know Humbrecht well, but I'm sure he was listening in heaven and appreciating your words."

"Thank you, Father," Randollph said, and meant it.

"Come out and see our establishment sometime soon. It's not much of a trip. I'd like to show you some of the work we're doing."

"I'll do that," Randollph told him, thinking it would be pleasant to play hooky and spend an afternoon with Prior Simon and inspect the scholarly endeavors of the Order of St. Thomas Aquinas. It certainly would be a lot more fun than the upcoming tedious ride to the cemetery where it would be his duty to consign the remains of Johannes Humbrecht to their final resting place. He hoped his chauffeur wouldn't be the brash young assistant undertaker he'd had to dress down before the service.

Miss Windfall never went out for lunch and didn't sully the office with crumbs from a brown-bagged sandwich and Twinkies. Randollph often wondered how she maintained her impressive girth on two meals per day. Perhaps she ingested rashers of bacon, numerous fried eggs, and a plateful of rich breakfast pastry before coming to work, then dined copiously on slabs of roast beef, or platters piled high with richly sauced pasta in the evening. However she managed her nutrition, she was always in the office during the luncheon hour, so after being deposited at the church door by the undertaker, Randollph thought he'd see if anything important had come up during his absence.

"Lieutenant Casey is anxious to talk to you," Miss Windfall told him. "He said to call him the minute you came in."

Randollph looked at his watch. "I'm on a pretty tight schedule, but if he's that anxious I'd better talk to him now." He went into his study while Miss Windfall began punching buttons on the phone.

"Doctor, we've got a new corpse, and he fits your description of Mr. Jones."

"Oh? Was he—"

"Yes. Shot with the same caliber gun that killed Elder. Whoever shot him left the gun, God knows why. We're checking it out. Probably untraceable. We're trying to find out who Jones—if it is Jones—really is. Can you come down to the morgue and have a look at him?"

"I've got a funeral this afternoon, and I'm scheduled on Samantha's television show this evening."

"Not much spare time?"

"Hardly any. Maybe I can squeeze it in after the funeral. I should be back here about five o'clock."

"I'll have a car waiting for you."

"It's that important?"

Casey chuckled. "Oh no. Just a service we provide for the clergy."

"Roll him out, Jimmy," Michael Casey commanded the white-coated attendant. The attendant pulled at a large drawer set in what looked like a giant filing cabinet. The drawer came out easily and almost without noise, and Randollph was suddenly looking at that too-large thin nose which gave the face, even in death, a look of menace.

"That's Mr. Jones," Randollph said, thinking he'd spent too much of the day looking at dead faces.

"No, that's Christopher Bart, born Cristoforo Bartelione in a little Sicilian town fifty-nine years ago."

"If you say so, Lieutenant."

"I don't say so. The FBI says so. Or rather, their fingerprint file says so. It never lies. Pack him back in, Jimmy. Let's get out of here, Doctor."

Outside, Casey indicated the blue unmarked Pontiac he usually drove. "Get in. I'll take you home. I know you're in a hurry."

"Who is Bart?" Randollph asked. "Or perhaps I should say what was he?"

"Top man in the Phoenix mob. That's about all I have on him yet. I could put it down as a Mafia hit and be done with it if it weren't for those telephone books and that damn gun."

"You've lost me," Randollph said.

"Remember, I told you that the guy who did it left the gun on the seat of the car beside the body?"

"I remember."

"A twenty-two. A favorite with the mob, only they use twenty-two long shells. Well, we ran a trace on it, and guess what we discovered?"

"I wouldn't even make a guess."

"It belonged to Robin Elder. He had a license for it. And," Casey said, coming to the main point of his peroration, "it was the same gun that killed Elder."

Randollph remembered to show the astonishment he knew Casey expected from him. It wasn't hard to do. "Well I'll be! That's quite a surprise, isn't it?"

"Isn't it, though."

"You mentioned telephone books."

Casey slid the blue Pontiac into a space reserved for unloading arriving guests at Good Shepherd's revenue-producing hotel, and waved away the doorman who had wasted no time in getting to the car. "There was a satchel on the seat of Jones's—Bart's car. Open. Two Chicago phone books—one of them the Yellow Pages—all that was in it. Figure that one out."

"I wouldn't pretend to try. I can tell you one thing, though."

"Any help I can get is welcome," Casey said.

"Jones was a very careful man. Very smart. He was killed by someone he had no reason to fear. Or thought he hadn't."

"That's right," Casey answered. There was a tincture of chagrin in his voice which meant that he hadn't thought about that. "Anything interesting turns up, I'll let you know."

Randollph wasn't looking forward to this evening's appearance on television, but decided it would be a welcome change from a day of dealing with death.

The studio was large, and every seat was filled. Tickets to Samantha's show were much sought after. It was an audience participation show, and if you were there you had a chance to be seen and maybe even heard by thousands of your fellow-Chicagoans having their second pre-prandial martini or munching TV dinners from a tray in front of their set.

Randollph and the other three guests sat in uncomfortable chairs which had been selected to discourage their occupants from slumping. The guests sat in a line on a platform high enough to make them visible to the studio audience, but low enough to make possible some kind of rapport between guests and audience. The TV monitor, having squeezed out the last of five commercial messages, switched to a montage of city scenes accompanied by a harsh rendition of "Chicago, That Toddlin' Town." Then a voice deep and pompous enough to proclaim the world would end in ten minutes and make you believe it, said, "Sam Stack's Chicago!"

The camera picked out a relaxed and smiling Samantha. She looked the part of a successful career woman, in a creamy yellow lightweight wool suit plainly tailored, with a narrow skirt and fingertip-length jacket. The skirt was slit on each side. "Have to have the slits or I couldn't walk in the damn thing," she'd explained to Randollph when getting herself into it. "I have to run around a lot on the show."

"You just want to display your legs," he'd said.

"All in the line of duty. Since I have to show them I'm glad they're nice legs."

"This evening we'll discuss the question, 'Should Religious Schools Receive Tax Support?'" Sam spoke into her cordless hand microphone. "Our guests this evening are: Monsignor Patrick Quinn, representing the Roman Catholic Cardinal Archbishop of Chicago, who recently announced a program to seek the city's financial support for parochial schools."

Monsignor Quinn had light brown hair, smiling blue eyes, and a black clerical suit that to Randollph's eyes looked tailor made. He was in his late thirties, and if the cardinal trusted him with this kind of task, the monsignor wasn't many years away from a bishop's miter.

"Our next guest," Sam said, "is Mr. Edward Cromartie, representing the American Civil Liberties Union. Mr. Cromartie has been a frequent guest on our show." Randollph had been on one of Sam's shows with Mr. Cromartie, and knew that the beefy, middle-aged lawyer's slightly dull look masked a mind that was as quick as a lizard's tongue flicking at flies.

"Our third guest is the Reverend Dr. Luther Bottomly, whose Calvary Independent Baptist Church operates the largest Christian Academy in Chicago." Pastor Bottomly, Randollph saw, was no red-neck Bible-thumper. A soft brown off-the-rack suit, but from the expensive end of the rack. Late forties. Thinning brown hair showing a little gray. He had the look of a successful hard-nosed business executive which, Randollph decided, was probably exactly what he was.

Randollph shifted his thoughts from the other guests in time to nod and smile as Sam introduced him. He was sure the nod and smile were perceived by the studio and TV audience as insincere because he didn't feel like nodding and smiling. Self-critical types like himself shouldn't expose themselves to the searching eye of the television camera, he thought. "I am surprised," Edward Cromartie was saying when Randollph once more refocused his thoughts on the program, "that the Christian academies would plead for tax support. I thought this was against your stated principle that tax support meant government interference in the operation of your schools."

"We are unalterably opposed to government interference in our schools." Pastor Bottomly had fielded this question before, Randollph guessed. "And that might happen if we received federal or even state tax money. But what we're asking is for a tuition grant from the city, which won't cost the city anything because it would have to pay for our students' education if we weren't here to educate them. We feel certain that the city won't interfere with us." Pastor Bottomly then recited the virtues of Christian schools—superior education, discipline, the inculcation of patriotism and moral values in their students, all to the end that instead of pot-smoking, fornicating, flag-burning slobs you had pure, polite, pro-American young people. The studio audience cheered. Pastor Bottomly had spoken in noninflammatory tones, but obviously he'd had plenty of practice in playing on the fears and loathings of middle-class America.

"Dr. Randollph, you are on public record as opposing tax support of parochial schools and Christian academies. But why would you oppose schools that offer superior education and teach moral values?" Samantha was playing the role of devil's advocate.

"I don't."

"You don't? But you're on record—"

"As opposed to tax support for any sectarian school, no matter how excellent it may be. The issue isn't good education. The issue is the Constitution of the United States. It prohibits the establishment of religion. Tax support is one ingredient in the formula for establishing religion."

"The cardinal archbishop has legal opinion which holds that this is not necessarily so." The monsignor spoke pleasantly, almost apologetically

"Then test it in the courts," Randollph replied, doubting that he sounded as tolerant and broad-minded as had the monsignor.

The monsignor sighed. "That takes so long, and our schools so desperately need help now." It was an effective plea judging by the nodding heads in the audience, Randollph admitted to himself. He revised downward the number of years he had estimated it would take Monsignor Quinn to make bishop.

"Dr. Randollph," the monsignor continued, "you were, I believe, raised as, ah, a Protestant in a small town."

"Yes, that's right." Randollph couldn't guess what this had to do with tax support for parochial schools.

"When you were growing up not many years ago, one characteristic of rural Protestantism was a strong anti-Catholic bias. Happily, this has all but disappeared. But was it present in your boyhood environment?"

Randollph had to admit that it had been very much present in the days of his youth. He hadn't a notion of what Quinn was getting at, but had the feeling that he was being led gently and politely into a trap.

"Yes, there was some of that in my hometown when I was a boy," he confessed, trying not to sound reluctant.

"We all admire you, Dr. Randollph," the monsignor continued. "Those of us who are sports fans have long admired your skills as a quarterback. Personally, I always tried to get out of any Sunday afternoon duties when you were on the tube. And Saturdays, too, of course, when Notre Dame was on national TV." The audience cheered. It was feeling warm and friendly toward this genial priest.

"And we admired your decision, many of us, anyway, to give up at great personal cost, your career as a professional football star to enter the Christian ministry."

"I did not look on it as a sacrifice," Randollph said.

"I'm sure you didn't," the monsignor hurried on. "What I'm getting at is this. No one would believe that your opposition to tax aid for parochial schools comes from any conscious bigotry. I know I wouldn't. Is it possible, though—just possible—that your boyhood environment planted deep in your subconscious mind a bias against the Roman Catholic Church? A bias which you, as an intelligent man of tolerant spirit would reject, but which gets out anyway disguised as a, shall we say, debatable interpretation of the Constitution?"

Randollph saw the look of alarm flit across Sam's face, banished quickly and replaced by her professional smile. So she'd recognized too how cleverly the monsignor had spitted him. After establishing himself as free of sectarian malice and an admirer of Randollph, he'd managed to call Randollph an anti-Catholic bigot who really didn't realize he was bigoted. There was no easy way out of this one. He didn't believe much in instantaneous inspiration from the holy spirit, but he'd have been glad for one right now.

Randollph would have been comforted a little had he known what Monsignor Quinn was thinking behind that relaxed and kindly gaze roaming over the studio audience. Father Quinn was, in fact, filled with self-loathing.

The cardinal had called him into his office and, in that abrupt way of his, had growled, "Patrick, I want you to go on that damn television program, you know, the one that redheaded woman runs—"

"'*Sam Stack's Chicago*,'" Quinn supplied.

"That's the one. She wants me to come on it. Can't, of course. Cardinal archbishops can't do that sort of thing."

"Quite so," Quinn had answered dutifully.

"They want to debate my proposal for tax-paid tuition to our parochial schools. I want you to go on as my representative. And, Patrick—"

"Yes, Your Eminence?"

"That Randollph fellow, the one who came out so strong against us, is going to be one of the guests on the show."

"He is?"

"Yes. And I want you to peel the hide off that skunk. Peel every strip of it off!"

Quinn was appalled. He was accustomed to the cardinal's intemperate tirades. The old man was senile, no question about that. Why Rome let him carry on was a mystery. There were days when Quinn felt like chucking his job at the chancery and finding a quiet parish. But there was that auxiliary bishop's job opening soon, and he was in line for it. He'd be the youngest bishop in the archdiocese, with a long, bright future ahead. Nonetheless, he had to get control of this situation.

"With all due respect, Your Eminence," he said as subserviently as he could manage, "Randollph is, well, I suppose the best way to describe him is as a folk hero."

"What do you mean by that?" the cardinal asked suspiciously. "You afraid to tackle him?"

"He's a famous professional football player—ex-player. He's just been kidnapped and made a daring escape from his kidnappers. He's inherited that Gutenberg Bible—Gutenberg's own Bible, if they ever find it—and everyone's wondering what he's going to do with it once he has it. He's enjoying a good press."

"And I'm not, is that what you mean, not enjoying a good press?" When the old cardinal got belligerent and his face reddened, the stroke which was always hoving near him came closer, and his aides knew that he had to be placated.

"Oh no, I didn't mean that at all," Quinn said soothingly. "What I meant was that I can't rush in and start calling Randollph an anti-Catholic skunk."

The cardinal was not placated. "I don't see why not. That's what he is."

"Perhaps so." Quinn didn't believe Randollph was an anti-Catholic skunk, but this wasn't the time to say it. "However, if we want to win points in this debate, Randollph will have to be handled with some care. A subtle approach is indicated, I think."

The old man seemed suddenly tired. "All right, Patrick, you're a bright young fellow and you know about these things. Do it your way. But strip the hide off him, subtly if you must, but strip it."

And that's what I've just done, Quinn was thinking, and I hate myself for doing it. But I'd hate myself even more if I'd refused to do it and blown my chance at that bishopric. This thought made him feel even worse.

At the moment Randollph was feeling something a long way from Christian charity toward Monsignor Quinn. Quinn was expecting a heated denial, which would contrast nicely with the ironic spirit in which he'd made his rather nasty point. A hot retort fairly leaped to Randollph's lips, but he choked it back. After all, the New Testament enjoined the children of light to be wily as serpents. And serpents were liars. At least the serpent in the Garden of Eden had told Adam and Eve a whopper.

It wasn't easy for Randollph to project a friendliness he did not feel, but this was doing the Lord's work, even if the method was a bit devious. So he let the studio audience see the kindliest smile he could summon up before he turned it on the monsignor.

"I want to thank you, Monsignor, for all those nice things you said about me. I have a weakness for flattery." This got a laugh from the studio audience. "Now you have suggested that my youthful environment has made me an anti-Catholic bigot. You were kind enough to say—and I believe you are sincere about it—that I am too decent to permit myself to be a conscious bigot, that if I am one the bigotry is lurking somewhere in my subconscious, that I am not aware of it."

Randollph paused to let this sink in on the audience and the viewers at home, then said, "Who can tell what lies in his subconscious? As I have said, there was anti-Catholicism in the town where I grew up. You may be right that it had an effect on me." He stopped long enough for what he hoped was a dramatic pause. "But I don't think so."

Quinn felt his victory slipping away. "Why do you think you were not affected, Doctor?"

"I'm glad you asked, Monsignor." Randollph felt he had drawn even in this game of wits. "I was quarterback on my high school team. And a good one, if I may be immodest. And my dream was—" here he paused a beat "—my dream was to play quarterback for Notre Dame."

The audience gasped, then cheered. This was Notre Dame country. Quinn looked like a batter who'd struck out with the bases loaded in the last of the ninth.

"I knew, of course, that Notre Dame was a Roman Catholic university, and I was a Protestant. But I also knew that the school would be glad to admit me, and the team would be more than glad to play me if I turned out to be as good as I thought I was." The audience roared. The momentum had swung to Randollph.

"But you didn't attend Notre Dame," Quinn noted. He knew he was grasping at straws

"No, I didn't."

"Why not?"

"Because Notre Dame didn't offer me a scholarship. And who could blame them? I played for a small high school in California. My reputation was local. Notre Dame wasn't the only school that hadn't heard of me. Apparently none of the larger universities in my own state heard of me either. None of them offered a scholarship anyway. And I needed a scholarship to have any hope of a college education. I finally got one to a small college. But I've always regretted that I didn't play for Notre Dame. Does that sound like a youthful anti-Catholic bias?"

Monsignor Quinn conceded defeat gracefully. "No, it doesn't. And, Con, since we're talking football, may I call you by the nickname of your playing days?"

"Please do."

"I wish you'd played for Notre Dame. It's my alma mater."

The audience clapped loudly. Sectarian rivalry as a burning issue didn't burn nearly as brightly—in these parts anyway—as the flame of loyalty to the Irish of South Bend.

Sam was smiling at Randollph, a smile which he read to say, "I'm on to you, Buster, but you skinned out of that one very nicely." Sam, of course, knew that it was the University of Southern California, not Notre Dame, where he'd dreamed of playing. He supposed he should feel guilty. But he comforted himself with the thought that he hadn't told a lie, at least not a total lie. He had thought of playing for Notre Dame, as every high school star with college potential did in those days. He'd just enhanced the facts. This smarmy rationalization, he knew, at least bordered on casuistry. But he was certain that heaven viewed a slight alteration of fact as inconsequential beside an attack on the Constitution of the United States.

"Is the caller there?" Sam asked.

"This is for Con Randollph," a disembodied young male voice came out of the speaker. "You there, Con?"

"I'm here."

"What you going to do with that Bible when you get it?"

Randollph hadn't expected that kind of question. To

give himself time to think up a proper answer, he asked, "What would you do with it?"

"Worth a lot of money, isn't it?"

"Yes."

"Sell it. I'd take the money and run."

When the audience quit laughing, Randollph said, "That's one possibility. I'd have a number of options open to me."

The voice came right back. "You made up your mind what you're going to do with it?"

"Yes. Yes I have." He hadn't been conscious that he'd made that decision, and was surprised at his own answer. Sam was looking at him quizzically. He'd have some explaining to do when he got home.

"You going to tell us?" the voice persisted.

"No," Randollph answered. "I cannot dispose of that which I do not possess."

"Thank you for calling." Sam wanted to be quit of questions not relevant to the topic under discussion.

The ACLU representative began to grill Pastor Bottomly about the curriculum in his Christian Academy. Randollph's mind wandered off to the murder of Humbrecht, the stolen Bible, and the shooting of Robin Elder and Christopher Bart or Mr. Jones. If Casey's theory that Robin Elder had killed Humbrecht and stolen the Bible, then been killed and had the Bible stolen from him was right, it was hard to see why Jones had also been killed. Where was the connection? Had Elder been in touch with Jones, or had Jones discovered somehow that Elder had the Bible? Certainly not before he, Randollph, had been kidnapped because Jones was obsessed with the belief that Randollph was the thief and the murderer.

Let's assume, Randollph thought, that sometime on Sunday or Monday Mr. Jones discovered that Elder had the Bible and had arranged to meet Elder and buy it. Was there any reason why Jones would have killed Elder? Randollph couldn't think of any. Jones was capable of killing. He would not be deterred from it by any moral squeamishness. Had Jones, in fact, decided to save the purchase price of the Bible by killing Elder and stealing it? Unlikely. Jones was willing to pay for the Bible, more than willing. And while murder would not bother Mr. Jones's conscience, it was against his principles of doing business. And if he'd meant to rob Elder and kill him, he'd have brought his own gun. Mr. Jones wasn't the kind of man who would count on finding a gun handy when he needed one.

Randollph recalled the scene at the reading of Humbrecht's will. Robin Elder, he remembered, seemed bored and maybe a bit down-in-the mouth. J. J. Knox the younger suppressing a strong resentment at his father's paternal bossiness. And also—

"...I don't have to prove I'm right about the infallibility of the Bible, Mr. Cromartie," Randollph heard Pastor Bottomly say. "I believe it. My faith tells me it's so. Nothing can shake that conviction. I live by it, and if necessary, I'd die for it."

And suddenly Randollph knew. It was that brilliant deduction that the bishop had sought. It came in a flash, like a vision, a shining insight. Or maybe it was induction, a lot of bits and pieces lying around in his mind and suddenly and unconsciously fused into a hypothesis. He knew he couldn't prove it, and maybe never could. But he knew, he was certain who had killed Elder and Jones, and why.

18

"IT'S PREPOSTEROUS!" Casey said grimly. "Preposterous."

"I know it is. But it's what happened."

"And there's damn little evidence. None really."

"I'll wager my chance at heaven that I'm right," Randollph told him.

That made Casey grin. "Not much of a bet, Doctor. You've told me that salvation comes from God's grace and not from anything we do to earn it."

It was Randollph's turn to grin. "That's correct."

"I like my way better. We Catholics know precisely what we must do if we expect to be saved."

"A tidier theology," Randollph admitted, "which is why so many Protestants put their faith in salvation by doing the right things. The disadvantage is that, while easier to grasp, it's incorrect. But let's get back to our problem."

"There isn't any problem. No grand jury would indict on what you believe to be the case. And that's about all you have to go on."

"There's the gun. It fits, substantiates my hypothesis."

"Any good defense lawyer could explain that away."

"What about the satchel?"

"Buy 'em at any Woolworth's. Untraceable."

Randollph thought for a moment before speaking again. "And the telephone books?"

"Just Chicago telephone books. One regular, and one Yellow Pages."

"Any marks on them?"

"Some doodling on the inside cover of the Yellow Pages."

"Enough to bluff with," Randollph said.

"What d' you mean? This isn't a poker game."

"Put yourself in his place, Lieutenant. If I'm right, he didn't have much time to plan the killing of Jones. He needed something approximating the bulk of the Bible, one volume of it. He wasn't going to take the Bible. So he grabs a couple of telephone books. But phone books aren't all that easy to come by when you're in a hurry."

"So where does he get them?" Casey was interested now.

"Perhaps his own books. More likely from somewhere else in his office. There must be dozens of them about in the office."

"And what do I do about it? Walk in and say, 'Pardon me, but have you had any telephone books stolen from your office recently?'" Casey was sarcastic.

"That's exactly what you do."

"Come on, Doctor."

"This is a bluff, remember. Take the books with you, show him the doodling, and ask permission to question everyone in the office if they recognize it."

"And if he refuses?"

"Say you'll get a court order."

"And then he'll break down and confess?" Casey snorted.

"He'll do something. I don't know for sure what. But he won't want you getting a court order. He'll do something that will, well, he'll try to stop you."

"And what does that do for me?"

"Tips you off that I'm right. Gives you a reason to dig for evidence."

Casey wasn't convinced. "I still say it's preposterous."

"Do you have a better idea?"

"You know I don't," Casey said gloomily. "I don't have any ideas at all."

"Then try it."

Casey got up from the big scruffy brown leather chair reluctantly. "All right. I'll have to go by the station and get the phone books. You going to be here the rest of the day? I'll call you and let you know what happens."

"I'll be here. It's Thursday, and my rule is that my sermon for Sunday must be finished before I leave the office—and I've hardly started on it."

"What's it about?"

"Sin."

"That ought to be easy. You've got plenty of material to work with."

"That I do. The problem isn't to find material, it's how to get it all in."

"My pastor at St. Aloysius would just think of sixteen ways to say he's against it."

"A simple homiletical method, but not very enlightening."

"How true. I'll call you if anything happens."

"It will, Lieutenant."

"I just hope to God you're right."

After Casey left, Randollph was fidgety. A man with sufficient mental discipline, he told himself, should have no problem putting Casey and his errand out of mind while he concentrated on writing a sermon, especially with Sunday almost upon him.

Randollph knew that in the vocabulary of most Christian laymen the word sin was a synonym for the external, the perceivable symptoms of sin—murder, rape, theft, etc. It wasn't going to be easy to convince a modern congregation that any sin, all sins, had roots in the universal human tendency to overestimate the importance of one's hopes, desires, welfare, success, personal gratification—overestimate their importance in the scheme of things. This overestimation caused a concomitant underestimation of the importance of other people's rights, aspirations, and well-being. This was original sin, which the story of Adam and Eve stated in beautiful picture-book fashion. He'd have to get this across in his introductory sermon or the series on the seven deadly sins would be a flop.

He'd been unable to discipline his mind to his task by an act of will. But becoming engrossed in the problem posed by his sermon had purged his thoughts of murder. He was picking up steam, writing more rapidly and with growing enthusiasm when the intercom squawked and startled him.

"Lieutenant Casey wishes to speak to you," Miss Windfall informed him.

"Yes, Lieutenant," he said into the phone.

"He wants to see you."

"He wants to see me? But whatever for?"

"He didn't say. Can you get right over here?"

"Yes. Yes, of course. Give me fifteen minutes."

J. J. Knox's private office had the same spartan elegance about it as his firm's conference room, Randollph noted, and carried the message of integrity, responsibility, and respect for careful craftsmanship. Knox didn't offer to shake hands, but invited Randollph to sit down politely enough. He then began stuffing a handsome Meerschaum with tobacco from an ornate wooden humidor. Randollph remained silent. Randollph noticed that Knox's hand did not tremble as he expertly flicked the head of a wooden match with his thumbnail and carefully lit his pipe. Satisfied that the pipe was properly lit, Knox spoke.

"Lieutenant Michael Casey has come to me with a fantastic notion."

"Oh?" Randollph answered.

"Yes. He thinks, or more likely has come up with a wild guess, that some telephone books left in that gangster's car, the fellow that was murdered, came from this office. He wants to question everyone here—lawyers, secretaries, cleaning people—to see if there are any phone books missing."

Randollph didn't say anything.

Knox sucked vigorously on his pipe for a few moments, then said, "Dr. Randollph, you are no doubt aware that a confession to a priest is inviolable, even to a court of law?"

"Yes, I know that."

"The law is not quite so clear about a confession to a Protestant clergyman, but it is generally held to have the same rights as a confession to a priest."

"In any case, I would claim that right and honor it," Randollph said.

"I thought you would. I don't know that I particularly like you, Dr. Randollph. But I respect you. I believe you to be trustworthy. I believe you to be a man who will keep his word. Anyone in my profession has to be a keen judge of character. I think I've judged yours correctly." Knox took time to relight his pipe, then continued. "I want your word that what I'm about to tell you will never be repeated—not to Lieutenant Casey, not to your wife, not to anyone."

"If it is a confession, you have my word."

Knox thought about that, then said, "We'll call it that. Technically I suppose that it is. I prefer to think of it as an admission. The word confession implies one is guilty of some sin. I'm guilty of no sin. But I did shoot my partner, Robin Elder, and that gangster, Bart."

"I thought that you probably had." Randollph hadn't meant to say it, and he wished that he hadn't said it. Knox might be furious. He might shut up. And he had information that Randollph very much wanted to hear, even if he couldn't use it.

A look of surprise quickly crossed Knox's face, then he suppressed it. "That's interesting. Why did you suspect me?"

"I suppose it started the day Humbrecht's will was read. You looked long and curiously at the was seal on the will before you broke it. I noticed, though it wasn't until recently that I realized why you did it. Somehow you detected that the seal had been tampered with."

"Very observant of you." Knox was now scraping the dottle out of his pipe. "I'd remembered that when we sealed that will the wax imprint was near perfect. When I went to break it, I saw that the seal had rough edges, little spiky projections from the round seal. That happens if you're a little careless or the wax is too hot when you press the seal."

"And you had a pretty good idea of who'd done it."

"Oh yes. It almost had to be Robin Elder."

"Why?"

Knox began the tedious process of reloading his pipe. "Robin Elder was what my grandfather called an off-ox."

"Peculiar term."

"Yes. Seldom heard nowadays. It originally meant an ox that was skittish, unpredictable, couldn't learn to work as part of a team. When applied to a person, it means about the same thing. Robin Elder was brilliant, a fine attorney, personable. But he had a flawed character. He couldn't stay married. He chased women. He lived beyond his means—and he had a large income. He gambled. He always managed to be in some kind of trouble."

"Why didn't you just fire him?" Randollph asked.

"I couldn't. The agreement drawn up when the firm was founded specified that any child of a partner who chose to become an attorney automatically inherited the father's partnership. But I'm interested to know what else led you to think I shot Elder and Bart."

"The clumsy attempt to make Elder's murder look like the by-product of a burglary. Amateur night, Lieutenant Casey called it. And the gun. It had to be done by someone who knew where Elder kept his gun. And you had a motive."

"And it was?"

"The protection of your good name—or, in this case, the protection of your firm's good name."

"You are keener than I imagined. You'd make a good criminal lawyer." Randollph supposed this was a compliment. "Yes. I knew Robin was desperate for money. He'd been embezzling from some of our trusts. I'll have to cover that, and it won't be cheap. But I suspected he was planning to go in the blackmail business. A firm such as ours has much private information in its files that could be marketed by an unscrupulous partner. I couldn't permit that, of course."

"And when you discovered that the Humbrecht will had been opened you suspected that Elder had read it, murdered Humbrecht, and stolen the Bible. That would solve his money problems nicely. But murder wasn't his business. You were afraid he'd botched it somehow and would eventually be exposed."

"Exactly." Knox was now tamping fresh tobacco into his pipe with one of the many instruments and accessories necessary to the convenience and comfort of pipe smokers. Randollph found this fooling around maddening. He wanted to get on with it.

Knox, the tamping completed, finally spoke. "That's what I thought. A partner in the firm of Knox, Knox, and Elder exposed as a murderer and a thief—well, that would have been the end of a fine law firm with a spotless reputation. I couldn't let a morally corrupt bum like Robin Elder do that to me, to the firm. I had to do what I could to head off that kind of disaster."

Now was the time to ask the question Randollph had been wanting to ask all along.

"And did he do it, kill Humbrecht and steal the Bible?" He waited breathlessly while Knox fired up his pipe again.

"Yes and no," Knox said between furious puffs.

"You'll have to explain that."

"I know. I confronted him with my suspicion. At first he denied everything. But I'm not easily put off when I'm determined."

Randollph had no difficulty believing this.

"So I finally wrung it out of him," Knox continued. "He admitted he'd read Humbrecht's will and copied out the combination to the lock on old man Humbrecht's strong room and where the Bible was kept. Xeroxed that page of the will, actually. Then he got in touch with some shady art dealer who specializes in high-priced stolen art. Described the Bible. Struck a deal with the fence."

"Did he then steal the Bible and incidentally murder Humbrecht?" Randollph tried to keep from sounding impatient.

"Claimed not," Knox answered. "Said he figured the Bible was in the safest possible place in Humbrecht's house. Said he planned to steal it as soon as he had a bona fide buyer. He almost had a heart attack, he said, when he heard about Humbrecht's murder and the Bible being stolen. Thought he had solved all his financial problems. By the way, he was asking two million for the Bible, minus the fence's commission. Or so he said."

"And you believed him?"

Knox looked meditatively at the bowl of his pipe. "Yes. Yes I did. I knew Robin, his moods, his weaknesses, when he was lying. I'm certain he was telling me the truth."

"Then why did you shoot him? He wasn't a murderer."

"No, but he had involved himself in crimes. Sooner or later Lieutenant Casey would have tied him to the Bible. And there was the blackmail he was planning. Shooting him was the best way to protect the firm's good name." He paused, then said, "Now tell me, Doctor, what led you to conclude that I shot that gangster?"

It seemed unreal to Randollph, this bizarre scene with an admitted murderer calmly talking about what he had done. Apparently the man felt no remorse, and betrayed no fear that he would suffer for his crimes.

"You will remember, Mr. Knox, that the gangster—actually Christopher Bart—kidnapped me."

"Yes. I'd forgotten for the moment."

"I was with him long enough to realize the power of his obsession to possess that Bible. You'll agree that an obsession can be a powerful motivation?"

Knox looked at Randollph carefully. "I think I know what you're saying to me, Doctor. But go on."

"If Bart had managed to discover the Bible was for sale—and the name of the seller—he'd have been frantic at the news of Elder's death. My guess is that he'd not had a chance to talk to Elder, but knew Elder was offering the Bible for sale. What would he do then?"

"Call me, hoping that I'd know something about the Bible."

"That's my guess."

"You guessed correctly. Jones called me. I didn't know who he was, of course. But I saw immediately that he represented a threat to me, to this firm. He knew one of the partners had been a crook. I suppose Jones thought, as I did, that Elder had killed Humbrecht. If he got to talking, well. . . ." Knox left the sentence for Randollph to finish in his imagination, then said, "It was essential that I silence him. Surely you can see that."

"I can see why you thought it necessary," Randollph

replied. "So you pretended that you had the Bible, and arranged to meet him."

"Yes. That's what I did."

"And put the telephone books in a satchel to simulate the bulk of the Bible. One volume."

"Yes. I agreed to let him see and have one volume to authenticate."

"I'm a little puzzled, Mr. Knox, as to why you are confessing all this to me." Randollph thought he knew why, but he wanted to hear Knox say it. Knox's answer surprised him.

"Because I'm a responsible citizen, Dr. Randollph."

"I'm afraid I don't follow you."

"Sooner or later you or Lieutenant Casey would conclude that Robin Elder had killed Humbrecht and stolen the Bible."

"Lieutenant Casey has already arrived at that conclusion."

"Oh? He's a bright young man. Likely to go a long way in his profession. The fact that he came to the obvious conclusion underlines my motive for admitting to you that I shot Elder and Jones. Without the information that Elder didn't do it Casey would assume Elder was guilty and close the case. I'd then be guilty of helping a thief and a murderer go free. By giving you this information under the seal of the confessional, I protect myself and at the same time discharge my duty as a responsible citizen and an officer of the court. By the way, I give you leave to tell the lieutenant that you have information that exonerates Elder—from Humbrecht's murder and the theft of the Bible."

Randollph did not doubt that J. J. Knox was convinced in his own mind that he was doing an honorable thing. Randollph, brief as his pastoral experience had been, had learned that nearly everyone who sought him out for counsel always painted for him a better picture of himself than the facts warranted.

"You would also like for the lieutenant to give up his plan to trace those telephone books to your office, I expect." Randollph tried to keep the sarcasm out of his voice.

"Yes. I would hope that he would. They did, as a matter of fact, come from this office. That was careless of me, but I hadn't planned to leave them in Jones's car. Just after I shot him another car turned into the park, and I had to leave in a hurry." Knox flicked on a half-smile. "You see, Doctor, I'm not an experienced criminal. I just forgot to take the satchel with me."

Randollph switched back to Knox's professed motive for making his confession. "So you want to help the lieutenant solve one crime at the cost of concealing your two crimes?"

"But what crimes did I commit, Doctor? Shooting a thief and an embezzler and would-be blackmailer? And killing a notorious criminal who had always escaped the consequences of his thefts, murders, and a long list of other transgressions? What I did, in both cases, was to mete out justice to two men who might never have suffered justice. What I did was a public service. No crime or sin was involved."

Randollph said, "The sin of playing God was involved. You arrogated to yourself a right, an action which is reserved for a higher court than your personal judgment. You committed the ultimate sin—the sin of spiritual pride."

"Theological twaddle," Knox said contemptuously. "The general public would look on what I did as a bold and courageous act of justice."

"The general public is not the final judge, Mr. Knox. I repeat my assurance that I won't disclose anything you've confessed to me—except that which you have said I may report to Lieutenant Casey. I can't promise, of course, that Casey will give up on his investigation."

"No matter," Knox replied. "He can, of course, cause me some inconvenience. But he has no real evidence. Telephone books from this office? That's not evidence that I was involved. The fact that I knew where Elder kept his gun? He kept it in his desk drawer where even the most casual of thieves could have found it. There are no possible witnesses. You divined my motive, but it would be impossible to convince a jury that it was a motive at all."

"That's true," Randollph said. "It isn't easy for people to understand the power of an obsession."

"Call it what you will, there's no way the lieutenant can get at me. He couldn't even get an indictment."

Randollph realized Knox was right. The lawyer would live out his life smug in his self-righteous conviction that he'd acted honorably.

"Lieutenant Casey said he would wait for you in the coffee shop next to this building on the north." Knox was dismissing him.

Randollph didn't rise. "Mr. Knox, let's carry out this business of a confession."

"You want to give me absolution, Doctor?" Knox was relaxed and smiling.

"No, I couldn't do that. Apart from the fact that absolution isn't a part of Protestant practice, you haven't met the conditions for the giving of absolution."

"I haven't?"

"No. Absolution must be preceded by repentance. You are not heartily sorry for your sins."

"True. I have committed no sin, so I can't repent of that which I have not done."

Randollph let that pass. "But I do wish to impose a penance on you."

"You want me to leave the Church of the Good Shepherd?"

"Oh no, not that, Mr. Knox. I hope you will remain a member. A church does not try to exclude sinners. It welcomes them. And you are a sinner, Mr. Knox. We all are."

Knox grunted.

"The penance I require of you, Mr. Knox, is to resign from the church's ushering corps." Randollph paused, then when Knox did not react, continued. "I admit that the penance is for my benefit, Mr. Knox, not yours. A weakness in me, perhaps. I'll be glad to see you sitting in the congregation. But to watch an undetected murderer carrying the offering to the altar Sunday after Sunday, Mr. Knox, is more than I can handle."

Randollph aimlessly stirred a cup of coffee he did not want. "All I can tell you, Lieutenant, is that Elder planned to steal the Bible from Humbrecht when he found a buyer, but that Humbrecht was murdered and the Bible stolen before he'd completed a deal."

"How can you know that?"

"You'll just have to trust me. I can say I'm satisfied that what I've told you is true."

Casey was thoroughly frustrated. "Was your theory right? Did Knox shoot Elder and Bart?"

"I'm unable to say."

"Unable or unwilling, Doctor?"

"In this case they amount to the same thing."

Casey exploded. "Oh come off it, Doctor." He slapped his palm on the tabletop, spilling some coffee out of his cup. "If you know, then you're obstructing justice by not telling me."

"Let me put it this way, Lieutenant. Imagine that I'm your pastor at St. Aloysius. If your pastor had just come from the confessional booth, and you had reason to think that he'd just heard a criminal confess to a crime, would you badger him to tell you what he'd heard?"

"No, of course not. He's a priest."

"Meaning I'm not?"

"Not a true, what I mean is, Catholics have well-established procedures and rules about the confessional. Protestants don't."

"Is a rule or a procedure more binding than a moral commitment?"

Casey was stumped. "Legally—oh, what the hell, did Knox make a confession?"

Randollph evaded a direct answer. "Anytime a Protestant comes to his pastor for confidential counsel, the pastor has a moral obligation to reveal nothing he's told."

"There's nothing to prevent me from figuring that Knox, well, that you were right about him, is there?"

"Nothing whatever."

"Then I can go ahead and try to link those phone books with his office?"

"Certainly. But let's assume that you do establish that they came from there. What do you have?"

Casey rubbed his chin as if there was a spot on it he'd forgotten to shave that morning. "You said when you sent me over here that if I could trace the phone books I'd know I was on the right track and could go after him."

"So I did. Let's assume you do trace the books to his office, then what?"

"I dig for more evidence."

"Fine. Where?"

"Well," Casey seemed uncertain. "Find witnesses."

"Yes, that's what I'd do." Randollph wished he could tell Casey about the car that turned into the park where Knox had just shot Mr. Jones, but he couldn't. "But that's a long, hard job, isn't it?"

"Usually."

"Meanwhile, what do you do about Humbrecht's murder?"

"Oh, Jesus, pray I guess. No, can't wait that long for an answer."

"The Almighty sometimes takes His time sending a reply, that's true," Randollph said.

"Somebody—and now we know it wasn't Elder—somebody knew the combination to Humbrecht's art room, and knew where the Bible was kept." Casey was talking to himself more than to Randollph. "And he left in one hell of a hurry, which suggests that he'd killed Humbrecht before stealing the Bible." Casey looked up at Randollph. "Who else besides Elder would have had access to the information about the lock and the location of the Bible?"

"Anyone else who had read Humbrecht's will."

"That's right." Casey was getting excited. "And Elder wasn't the only person in the office of Knox, Knox, and Elder. If Elder could get into that will, then why couldn't anyone in the office do it?"

"No reason why not."

Casey got up. "Come on, Doctor, I'll drop you off. I've got work to do."

19

RANDOLLPH DIDN'T manage to get his sermon finished until late Saturday afternoon, missing a football game between Penn State and Michigan that he'd particularly wanted to watch.

Also, he was assailed by doubts as to the sermon's merits. Was it too theological for a modern layman's taste? Modern congregations, the bishop had told him, preferred homilies on the positive—how, if they thought they could do it, they'd have no trouble getting a promotion, making a lot of money, becoming winners.

"Where does God come in?" he'd asked the bishop.

"Why, He's drug in," the bishop had replied. "He's almost an afterthought. The preacher needs to say a word about God in order to distinguish his sermon from a Rotary Club address."

Randollph recalled this conversation and felt depressed. People wanted to hear about the power of the positive. Well, that was fine. Randollph believed that faith, rightly understood, had a salubrious influence on the lives of the faithful. But he was too good a theologian to discard all the characteristics of the human species except its possibilities for the good, the courageous, the victorious. There were other possibilities that lurked alongside truth and goodness and winning the game. He'd be a sorry sort of preacher if he didn't tell them that part of the human story. Maybe they wouldn't listen. Maybe they'd yawn and whisper to their neighbor in the pew, "Wonder what's got Doc off on this negative kick?" Or, worse yet, "I don't understand what he's getting at, do you?" Randollph decided he'd have a martini before dinner.

The church was packed, as usual. Most of these people, of course, wouldn't be worshiping in this particular house of the Lord again until business or a convention brought them back to Chicago. Light bounced off the blue-and-gold crust on pillars which supported nothing but the illusion that this was a Byzantine church. When Randollph got up to preach he had to admit that a spectacular if spurious architecture, choir, organ, and a large and expectant congregation were an inspiring mix. It made preaching a lot easier. This scene stimulated the senses and the imagination. A preacher in a setting like this couldn't help but do his best.

He began by quoting Martin Luther. He supposed that was the professor in him, relying on recognized authority to make his point. Also, the quotation might startle a modern congregation into paying attention. It wasn't the kind of thing they expected from a classy, big-time preacher in a main-line church.

Luther, Randollph told them, once said: "The theologian is concerned that man become aware of this nature of his corrupted by sins." And that was his concern this morning, he said. We think of ourselves as decent, upright people. As essentially good people with maybe a few minor faults and areas of our lives that could stand some improvement. But we aren't aware, as Luther thought we ought to be, of the potential for evil present in the best of people.

Randollph didn't think of himself as a good person. But he thought of himself as one who was trying to be a good person. He did not look upon his religion as a means of getting himself to heaven. Many people did, he knew, but in his opinion that kind of faith was not only shoddy but also the product of misreading the Bible and bad theology. Let God look after the hereafter. He wanted to build into his life the Christian virtues of wisdom, justice, courage, temperance, faith, love, and hope. Build them into his life not in the expectation of earning a place in paradise but because these virtues, if one could manage to combine them in one's personality, produced a health of spirit, a wholeness of soul—which is what the New Testament meant by salvation anyway.

But his murderous rage at Mr. Jones and his two ragtag hoodlums had made him aware of the potential evil that resided in him, a man striving to be a good person. He supposed he hadn't been aware of it before—except theologically—because he'd not been so severely tested before. It was easy enough to be a nice person if nothing provoked you into becoming an ugly one. And there had been a moment in which he'd have taken savage pleasure in shooting Mr. Jones, or Pack, or Junior. So he was really preaching about a condition within himself, and of which he was now fully aware.

It was not unusual, he realized, to say something in a sermon that, as now, set his mind wandering. It had taken only seconds, and he'd gone right on preaching. He wondered if other preachers had the same experience and concluded that they probably did.

But then something unusual happened. The thought, or idea, or perception, or insight which a few days before had been gently nudging at the door of his mind suddenly kicked it wide open. Several scenes appeared and disappeared—a city street on a golden September afternoon; an open door in the basement of Johannes Humbrecht's old house; himself, gun in hand, snapping orders to Pack and wishing Jones would come in so he could shoot him. The door slammed shut quickly, erasing the scenes. He couldn't sort them out now and put a meaning to the experience. He had to finish preaching his sermon, and it took a powerful act of will to refocus his mind on what he was saying. But, just as surely as the Magi knew they were following the right star though they didn't know to what truth it would lead them, Randollph knew that he had seen the light, and that before long he would understand the nature of that revelation he had for one brief moment glimpsed.

Randollph was always ravenously hungry after he preached. Clarence Higbee knew this, of course. Clarence attended an early service at the nearby Protestant Episcopal Cathedral so as to have a hearty meal ready for the table when Randollph, benediction pronounced, hundreds of hands shaken, pulpit robe hung in the vestry, was free to take the elevator to the penthouse. Randollph was grateful for the proximity of the cathedral because Clarence considered it an acceptable substitute for the Church of England, especially as it was blessedly devoid of guitars and other ecclesiastical innovations which Clarence looked on as a stench in the nostrils of Jehovah. Thus Randollph never had to wait for his dinner.

Clarence set small plates in front of Randollph and Sammy on which he had arranged tissue-thin strips of pink smoked salmon dotted with capers and flanked by wedges of lemon. The simple artistry of the dish inflamed Randollph's appetite already stimulated by whatever it was about his Sunday morning duties that always stimulated it. He made a conscious effort to eat slowly and savor each small bite of this exquisite combination of flavors. He'd just finished when Clarence returned with a platter of thick brown-crusted slices of roast loin of pork arranged, like a shelf of oddly shaped books, on a bed of baked rhubarb. Randollph knew from previous experience with this dish how good it was going to taste.

Sammy watched him eat, then said, "Luv, how do you do it?"

"Do what?"

"Stow away the groceries like a lumberjack and never gain an ounce. Aren't you planning a sermon on gluttony in this series on the seven deadly sins?"

"Yes."

"How can a trencherman like you preach on gluttony?"

Randollph served himself another slice of roast pork. "Begin with a *mea culpa*, I suppose."

"What's that?"

"Latin for 'I am guilty.' Technically, though, I am not a glutton."

"You mean my eyes are deceiving me?"

"A glutton," he explained, "is someone who eats to excess. You said I don't gain an ounce. Therefore, I am eating only as much as my body requires. I hope Clarence made chocolate mousse. He usually does with this menu."

"How I envy you. I can put on pounds just looking at chocolate mousse. And I love it so."

"Envy is a deadly sin."

"Oh, shut up, Reverend. I thought ex-jocks always run to fat."

"Some do. I'm fortunate. And of course I work out regularly at the club."

"Not last week."

"No, but not every week is like last week." Then he added, "Thank God."

Randollph wished that he could tell Sammy about J. J. Knox. But he couldn't. Ever. He wanted to share everything in his life with her. But this barrier, erected by the traditions of his profession, could never be lowered. He decided that there were some rational or psychological arguments favoring a celibate clergy—although not many, and not worth the disadvantages, pain, and problems it created. He wondered if he should share with her the strange experience he'd had while preaching this morning. He decided against it. Not yet. He hadn't had a chance to figure out what those pictures were telling him, or trying to tell him.

Clarence placed bowls of chocolate mousse topped with swirls of buttery-looking whipped cream in front of them.

"Not for me, Clarence," Sammy said. "I don't want you to think I don't like it, or don't want it. I don't need it."

"Madam is the best judge of what she needs."

"Madam has a weak character when it comes to resisting chocolate mousse, especially yours, Clarence. Oh, leave it. Madam will permit herself one spoonful. The master here will probably finish it up for me." She spooned up a generous portion, making certain it was slathered in whipped cream. "Lordy, that's delicious!

And now, Reverend, while you gorge yourself, may I call your attention to some of the letters the *Trib* has received from people who are competing to tell you what to do with Humbrecht's Bible? There's a flock of them in today's paper."

"Please do."

"Here's one that says the only decent thing for you to do is to give it to the Chicago Art Institute."

"I'll bet I know who wrote that one—or saw to it that it was written."

"Here's a dandy. He says you ought to burn that popish Bible because popery is of the devil. And after his signature he writes 'no longer living in Ulster, but an Orangeman still.' And here's another one that isn't so nice." Sammy helped herself to a second large spoonful of chocolate mousse. "From the cardinal archbishop, no less."

"That's interesting. What does he have to suggest?"

"Here, let me read it to you. He says, 'If Mr. Randollph were a fair-minded man, he would know the only honest thing to do with the Bible, indeed the only Christian thing to do, would be for him to present it to the Vatican library where it belongs. However, since Randollph has made it plain that he is prejudiced against the Roman Catholic Church, and is indeed actively working against it in this city, we can hardly expect him to do the right thing. He wants to deny not only Roman Catholic children the blessings of a Christian education, but extends his prejudice to those Protestants who operate secondary schools. A man who is spiritually blind . . .' Oh, hell, Randollph, enough of that." Sammy threw the paper aside.

Randollph chuckled.

"What's so funny?"

"I'll bet he slipped that one by Monsignor Quinn. Didn't it strike you that Quinn really had no stomach for his job the other night? Oh, he was clever. He nearly boxed me in. But I'll bet he had orders from His Eminence to boil me in holy water. He could have gone after me with gloves off even though I came off the ropes in good shape."

"Then why didn't he?"

"Because he's smart. He knows a mean-spirited attack on me would do his cause more harm than it would do me."

"Are you going to answer the cardinal's letter? Answer it in print, that is?"

"No."

"Why not?"

"He's obviously a senile old man. Why devil him? Why play his game? Anyway, I expect that Freddie will take it upon himself to answer him."

"What will Freddie say?"

"Why, Freddie will use his affable style and a quiverful of sweet, kind, tolerant, understanding Christian words and phrases to shoot the old bigot down."

"Luck to him. I'm mad even if you're not. Come to think of it, I'm mad at you, too, because you haven't told me, your wife, what you intend to do with the Bible."

"Patience, Samantha. The only reason I haven't told you is that the answer involves a nice surprise for you."

"I'm still mad. I'm so mad that I'm going to eat the rest of this rich, fattening dessert." When she'd finished, she pushed her chair back and smiled at Randollph.

"There, Reverend, I feel better. I did enjoy that mousse. And I don't feel guilty over eating it because I needed it. I needed to get over being mad. It was like medicine for my soul." She got up, went over to him, and kissed him. "So I'm not mad at you anymore. Besides, I like surprises."

Randollph had discovered that his Sunday afternoons must be devoted to some undemanding mental activity such as reading a thriller or, in season, watching the succession of pro football games that dominated television on the Lord's Day. Television was occupied on Sunday mornings by preachers and afternoons by football. Both were essentially show business. But he was glad it wasn't the other way around. He didn't want to hear or think about preachers. He had a tendency to brood about his morning sermon. He suffered from a sort of postpartum depression. Had he gotten his points across in a clear and easily grasped way? Had the congregation reacted to his sermon as he had intended that it should? Was preaching a dying art anyway, no longer valued highly by the faithful? Had he sounded like a sage or a scold? Was he stepping in the pathway of the prophets, or was he just a posturing ass gratifying his ego? Watching burly young men bang into each other helped flush these thoughts from his mind.

But today he watched quarterbacks throw touchdown passes, interior linemen maim one another, and running backs savagely flung to the ground without seeing any of it. He was rerunning the pictures that had, unbidden, appeared on the screen of his mind while preaching that morning. He called for an instant replay of the street scene. He'd just come out of Johannes Humbrecht's house and was looking for the nearest telephone. He was able to conjure up the tableau, its busyness frozen, the people in it easy to pick out. He inspected each one carefully.

Then he changed to the picture of Humbrecht's art room. The heavy door was open. Inside, the large drawer which was the receptacle for the two volumes of the Bible was open. He flipped briefly to the picture of himself, gun in hand, full of rage. He thought he knew what that picture was saying.

He returned to the picture of Humbrecht's basement room. Someone had left it in a hurry. Someone who knew the combination to the lock on the heavy door. Someone who knew exactly where the Bible was hidden. Someone who was too scared to take the time to lock up properly. Or—

The television picture switched to the second part of Sunday's double-header. This one was between Dallas and Los Angeles. One Randollph particularly wanted to watch. He'd played with and against some of these fellows. Several of them had been good friends. He didn't even notice what was happening on the screen. He'd seen a light brighter than any a picture tube could emit. He'd seen the light of truth.

On Monday morning he was late getting to the office. He knew that many ministers took Monday as their day off. Like Sisyphus, they'd laboriously rolled that stone up the hill only to have it roll right down again. They'd huffed and puffed all week to get it to the top on Sunday morning, then had to do it all over again next week. Monday was their day to rest tired spiritual muscles. But Randollph found he usually needed every day of the week just to stay even. He put it down to poor organization of his time.

Miss Windfall was normally more merciful on Mondays, seldom plaguing him with the trivia of administration until the afternoon. This morning she had only one instruction for him. "Lieutenant Casey asked that you call him the minute you got in."

"All right. Will you get him for me please." He went into his office and shut the door behind him.

"I think I know the answer," Casey said without preamble.

"That's good news. Can you tell me?"

"Not on the phone. I'd like to run it by you. Can you get away?"

"I'd been thinking about playing hooky today."

"Pick you up in front in fifteen minutes."

"I'll be there."

"Any place you want to go?" Casey asked as he slid the blue Pontiac into the thick traffic with the careless ease of a man who did a lot of city driving.

"Yes, come to think of it. A little trip I've been promising myself for some time. Head south on Lake Shore Drive. Now, tell me the answer you've come up with."

"J. J. Knox, junior."

"Your reasons?"

"He had access to Humbrecht's will."

"Granted. But why? His motive?"

Casey swung the Pontiac onto Lake Shore Drive. Fall had not yet gotten a foothold in Chicago. Sunbeams danced on the harbor where Italo Balbo had brought down his fleet of flying boats, vastly impressing visitors to a now-forgotten world's fair. Sailboats bobbed gracefully as a brisk wind sent them scudding across choppy waves. Power cruisers arrogantly headed for open waters.

"I'm assuming that old man Knox did what you think he did, probably know he did—shoot Elder and Bart. But you think he did it to protect his good name, the good name of his firm. I asked myself, is that a strong enough motive for a couple of murders?"

"It would be for a man like Knox," Randollph said, then hastily added, "if, indeed, he is guilty."

Casey went right on as if Randollph hadn't spoken. "I assume, also, he confessed to you that he had done in both guys. I'm not asking you to confirm that. I don't have to. So I asked myself, why would he confess to you, even if you're pledged not to tell?"

"If he had, in fact, confessed to me," Randollph replied, choosing his words carefully, "it was to send you a message."

"What message? That no one in his firm had killed Humbrecht or stolen the Bible? That Elder had intended to steal it, but hadn't gotten around to it?"

"You'll have to interpret the message—if any, of course."

"I have, Doctor. And it reads like this. Old man Knox wouldn't have shot Elder and Bart to protect the firm. But he would have done it to protect his son. I think he discovered his son had gotten into Humbrecht's will, then stole the Bible and killed the old man in the process."

"Then why shoot Elder?"

"Because," Casey said, "Elder and Knox junior were in it together. Or Elder found out about it. Or it's possible Junior shot Elder. If Knox senior knew that, then confessing to you would be a great way to divert suspicion from Junior."

"Why? I couldn't tell you anything he said to me under the seal of the confessional."

"No. But he knows we're friends. If I got the idea Junior had done it, you'd warn me off because you wouldn't want me to make a fool of myself arresting the wrong man."

"Plausible," Randollph said. "Turn off here. Have you figured out why Junior did it?"

"Maybe for money. But I'll bet his real motive was a subconscious urge to get back at his old man for dominating him and humiliating him."

"So you noticed that too."

"Sure. The old man has Junior thoroughly cowed, but Junior hates him for it."

They passed the serene perfection of Frank Lloyd Wright's Robie House, and the huge gray mass of Rockefeller Chapel.

"It seems to me, Lieutenant, that for a policeman professedly dedicated to the virtue of police routine in homicide cases, you're launching out pretty far into the uncertain waters of psychology."

"It's that kind of case," Casey said. "If I'm right, I'll depend on routine to prove it."

"Oh, I think this is it. Pull over and park, Lieutenant. And come with me. My visit shouldn't take long."

Prior Simon seated them across from him at the long table he used for a desk. His office, or study, was walled with books. His table was stacked with books. This was a scholar's room. Put Bishop Freddie in a brown habit and subtract a few hairs from his head, Randollph thought, and he could pass for the prior. But the bishop, though widely read, was not a scholar. He needed an executive's desk, a telephone, and a secretary or he'd be lost. "Libraries," he had once told Randollph, "are not the natural habitat of bishops. Oh, we all complain that the pressures of office prevent us from keeping up on our reading. The truth is, most of my brethren in the episcopacy weren't great readers before they became bishops."

"How nice of you to accept my invitation to visit us, Dr. Randollph. And to bring Lieutenant Casey with you." He moved his chair from the table and stood. "Let me give you a tour of our establishment, then we'll have coffee and chat."

"Not today, Father," Randollph said quietly. "This isn't a social visit. We'd like you to tell us where you are hiding the Gutenberg Bible."

Casey said, "Ahumph," then cleared his throat. This was his way of choking off an exclamation, Randollph supposed.

Prior Simon looked at Randollph, then Casey. He sat down. He put his elbows on the table, lowered his face into his hands, and gave way to great, heaving sobs that thrashed his short, plump body. Casey started to speak, but Randollph motioned him to be silent.

Like a motor that has nearly spent its fuel, Prior

Simon's sobs gradually diminished, then stopped. He raised his red, wet eyes, looked at both Randollph and Casey again, then said, "I would have confessed. The monks were going to elect me abbot next month. I couldn't have borne that." He mined a big white handkerchief from somewhere in the folds of his habit and blew his nose. "Actually, I'm glad you found me out, Lieutenant." Again Randollph motioned Casey not to interrupt. "The burden of my guilt was becoming unbearable. I feel a great sense of relief. Can you believe that?"

"Of course we can," Randollph answered. "Why did you happen to visit Professor Humbrecht that day?"

"Our abbot had died. He visited benefactors of our order occasionally. As second in command, I assumed those duties on an interim basis." Prior Simon wanted to talk. Talk was a psychological analgesic, aspirin for the hurt in his soul. "I went through the list of past and present benefactors and came across Mrs. Humbrecht's name. I remembered her generosity and thought it would be nice to pay a call on her husband, let him know we still remembered her." He paused and smiled weakly. "Also, I thought I might encourage him to continue the patronage in her name. We always need more money to carry on our work."

"Most eleemosynary institutions do," Randollph said.

"I can't imagine how you came to suspect me. There was nothing to connect me with Humbrecht, with my presence there that day. Who would imagine that a mild scholarly monk would be guilty of violence and theft?" Prior Simon's face reflected the pain of remembering. "I thought I had nothing to fear from the police. The only threat to me was myself."

"How's that?" Casey spoke for the first time.

Prior Simon looked at Casey with faint surprise. "Why, Lieutenant, as a good Catholic you should understand that. In one insane moment I undid a lifetime of piety, prayer, faithfulness to my sacred vocation. I made it impossible to achieve the goal of my life's work, that of becoming abbot of the Order of St. Thomas Aquinas. And I lost my chance of heaven in the next life. In one moment of demon-inspired madness I violated everything I believe, everything I stand for, everything

I'd spent my life for. Catholic conscience, Licutenant. You ought to understand that no Catholic conscience, carefully nurtured as mine has been, could for long stand that kind of strain. The time was bound to come when I could no longer bear its accusation."

"Yes, I can see that."

"Will you tell me how you found me out, Lieutenant?" The father prior seemed reluctant to let the conversation lag, as if the sound of voices would protect him from the necessity of contemplating once more the awfulness of his own sins.

Casey made a harumphing noise. Randollph spoke quickly to explain to the prior and to Casey how Casey had solved the case. "Lieutenant Casey arrived at you by a process of elimination, Father."

The prior looked puzzled. "I don't see how that was possible. Surely I was never a suspect."

"No. Not until the lieutenant had to discard the idea that the door to Humbrecht's library and art room was opened, and the Bible removed from its secret drawer by whoever it was that, ah, killed Professor Humbrecht."

"I still don't see—"

"It then became apparent to Lieutenant Casey that one person who knew the combination to the door of the room, who knew exactly where the Bible was kept, was Humbrecht himself."

"But that doesn't involve me."

"No. But if Humbrecht left the door to the room open and also the drawer to the receptacle for the Bible, that meant that Humbrecht was going to replace the Bible shortly, that he'd only taken it out for a brief time—probably to show to somebody, since if he'd just wanted to look at it himself he'd have done it in the room. The conclusion is that he carried it upstairs."

"Yes. That's what happened. But why me?"

"Actually, I gave the lieutenant a little help on that."

"How?"

"By finally realizing that I saw you that day. After I found Humbrecht I went out to look for a phone to call the police. I had to go to that little business district not far from Humbrecht's home. In the distance I saw what I took to be a short woman in a long brown cloak and hood. She was carrying two unmatched bags and hurrying toward the el station. I suppose you found the bags in the rubble in Humbrecht's house?"

"Yes, yes I did. I had to have something to carry the two volumes. They're quite bulky. But what made you finally realize it was me and not some dumpy old lady you saw?"

"We began to wonder who might have persuaded Humbrecht to show him his precious Bible. We supposed that you and Humbrecht—two scholars—got to talking about ancient manuscripts, and he told you about his Bible."

"That's right." Father Simon was anxious to tell all, as if some measure of absolution awaited the end of his confession. "We'd been doing some work on the incunabula in our library. That excited the professor, and he couldn't resist telling me about his Gutenberg. What harm could come in telling a harmless monk about his treasure?" the prior added bitterly.

"And you persuaded him to show it to you," Randollph suggested.

"Yes, that's right. But you must understand that I had no thought of stealing it, or—" Father Simon put his face in his hands again, but quickly recovered.

"I'm sure you didn't," Randollph said gently. "We guessed that you acted on a sudden impulse when he told you what he intended to do with the Bible."

"How perceptive you are, gentlemen. That's exactly what happened. I suggested as tactfully as possible that he might consider leaving the Bible to our order. I was overwhelmed with its beauty, as you will be. It's in an unbelievably good state of preservation. Nearly flawless. Then he told me he was leaving it to you, Doctor, and I can't describe what happened to me. Blind rage, but that doesn't adequately tell it. Demonic fury. This, the finest, the loveliest, the most perfect printed copy of the Vulgate in existence—this official version of the Holy Bible for Roman Catholics being left to a Protestant clergyman. It was wicked, wicked! I could not allow that to happen." The prior's voice had risen, a little of the madness that had made him a murderer showed through. Then, just as quickly, it subsided. "Forgive me, Dr. Randollph. That's unworthy of me.

That's bigotry. My mind knows this, but my heart hasn't learned it yet."

"I doubt that you intended to kill Humbrecht, Father."

"I don't know what I intended. I honestly don't know. Except to possess that Bible. I was consumed with that passion. It was an obsession. I remember getting up from the table, seeing that bat, picking it up, and hitting Humbrecht with it. When you are in the grip of madness, you don't think, you don't plan, you act. Inhibitions are wiped out. Conscience is no guide. You just, just—" Prior Simon fumbled for the right phrase "—you just explode!"

"How well I know," Casey commented. "That's how homicides happen all too often."

"Still, it is unthinkable that a peaceful, mild-natured monk would do such a thing. How did you think the unthinkable, Lieutenant?"

"The lieutenant has learned to think the unthinkable," Randollph said hastily. "He's had enough experience with it. And he's had a good Catholic education, which means he knows something about theology. He was taught that the potential for evil resides in the best of people. Right, Lieutenant?"

"Uh, oh, yes, right."

"We all have our moral breaking point, Father," Randollph continued. "Fortunately, most of us never reach it. Unfortunately, you fell into a set of circumstances which pushed you past yours." Randollph did not think it necessary to state that the one clue which had enabled him to think the unthinkable and envision the little monk as a murderer was the experience of being pushed to the edge of his own moral breaking point by Mr. Jones and Jones's two young thugs.

Prior Simon looked at Randollph as if he couldn't tolerate a mitigation of his awful sin, and Randollph realized what the little monk desired, maybe needed, was censure and punishment. Being understanding about his crime hurt worse than a whipping.

"You didn't leave any fingerprints," Casey observed.

"No, Lieutenant, I didn't. We watch the cop shows on television here, and you learn about fingerprints from them. After I'd seen what I'd done, I carefully wiped the bat, everything I could remember touching, with my handkerchief. It was almost a reflex action." He turned to Randollph. "Do you know what I was thinking, what pictures were floating through my brain even as I was striking Humbrecht, stealing the Bible, and wiping off my fingerprints?"

"I have no idea."

"I was seeing a magnificent religious ceremony in St. Peter's. The Swiss Guards. Cardinals, bishops. Incense sweetening the air. Choirs chanting. And I was the center of all eyes. I stood before the Holy Father on his throne, I in my plain monk's habit, presenting the Gutenberg Bible, a gift, a priceless gift, to the holiest place in Christendom. That's what I wanted to do with the Bible, Doctor. Give it to the Pope."

After he'd booked the prior on suspicion of murder, Casey volunteered to drive Randollph home. Once he'd floated the car into the river of traffic, he said, "I'm mad as hell, Doctor. Why didn't you tell me before we went in what you planned to do?"

Randollph thought about how to placate the lieutenant, then decided he probably couldn't. "Because I wasn't certain. Oh, I had a strong hunch, an inner conviction that I was right. But it was all speculation. There's no real evidence. If you'd accused him and been wrong, you'd have looked foolish. It would have gotten around that Lieutenant Casey was, well, not entirely reliable. But I didn't have to worry about how I would look. If I was wrong, then I was wrong. No damage done to my career."

Casey was not entirely mollified. "I felt like an idiot, sitting there listening to you explain how I'd figured out it was Simon."

"You would have figured it out eventually—and using the same line of thinking I used. Remember, I had a piece of information you didn't have. I saw the prior that day. It just took me a long time to recognize who it was that I'd seen."

"I'm still mad," Casey said, but he didn't sound angry.

"One should avoid unchristian tempers," Randollph admonished him. "Anger is one of the seven deadly sins, you know."

"Of course I know." Casey was smiling now. "I've had an excellent Catholic education."

"So you've told me."

"Come to think of it, Doctor, I owe you. This case was going nowhere. Now it's solved. I'll get the credit for it and feel guilty for taking it—but I'll take it."

"And get over feeling guilty."

"Yep," Casey said, maneuvering around a pokey van.

"What will happen to Prior Simon?" Randollph asked.

"Probably not much. Manslaughter. Short sentence, considering who he is. Serve it in some comfortable slammer."

"He'll wish for the death penalty," Randollph said. "There isn't enough punishment to set his soul at rest."

"I know. Here we are." Casey swung the blue Pontiac to the curb in front of Good Shepherd.

"Thanks for the ride," Randollph said, opening the door.

"You're welcome. And, Doctor—"

Randollph paused, one foot on the curb. "Yes?"

"Now that you've got it, what are you going to do with the Bible?"

"I'll let you know after I tell Samantha. She'd never forgive me if she wasn't the first to know."

20

SAMMY GAZED with awe at the vastness of St. Peter's. "This is some cathedral," she said.

"It isn't a cathedral," Randollph said.

"What do you mean, buster? It's the biggest church I ever saw."

"Cathedral isn't a synonym for a large church—though many people use or misuse it to mean that."

"Then what does it mean?"

"The term is a Latinization of a Greek word which means chair."

"I don't get it."

"A cathedral is a church which contains a bishop's chair. It's the bishop's home church."

"Isn't the Pope a bishop?"

"Yes. He's the bishop of Rome. The bishop of Rome's cathedral is the Church of St. John Lateran."

"Then what do you call this?" Sammy gestured at the naves of St. Peter's.

"A basilica."

"What's that mean?"

"A church built according to a certain architectural design. Or it also means one of the seven main churches in Rome."

"Gee, Reverend, you're smart."

"So I am, ma'am," Randollph said. He was feeling frisky. He couldn't remember when he'd felt so good.

"It is big," the bishop remarked.

"Put Astroturf on the floor, and you could play two football games in here simultaneously," Randollph said.

"There is so much to see," the bishop said. "Michelangelo's *Pietà*, Bernini's holy water fount, so much. We'll come back later. We don't want to be late for our appointment."

The three of them were ushered into the presence of Pope John XXIV. He had been Paul Ignatius Terence Riley, cardinal archbishop of Los Angeles when, to break a ferocious deadlock between the Italian candidate and a third-world cardinal, he'd been elected the first American Pope. He was a big man, topping Randollph's six feet two inches, not fat, but large-framed and with a bulkiness enhanced by his papal white cassock. He advanced on Randollph and clasped him in a bear hug. "Con, Con Randollph. It warms my heart to see you."

"And mine to see you, Padre Paul."

"Haven't been called that since I last sat on the bench at a Rams' game. Sounds wonderful." He turned to the bishop and embraced him. "Ah, Freddie, we had some wonderful times together lighting fires under some of those ecclesiastical mugwumps, didn't we? Remember when I spoke to that interfaith conference at your seminary? Nearly started a riot."

Sammy stepped toward the Pope with arms flung open. "Me too," she commanded.

"Ah, may I present my wife Samantha," Randollph said in a hurry.

The Pope embraced her. "Welcome, Samantha Randollph, to my house."

"How nice," Sammy said. "It isn't every girl that gets hugged by the Pope. Aren't we supposed to kneel and kiss your hand or something?"

The Pope looked at Randollph. "She keeps you on your toes, I'll bet."

"She does indeed."

"No, my dear, you aren't obligated to kiss my ring. I'd feel uncomfortable if you did, just as I'd feel uncomfortable if my old friends Con and Freddie kissed it. Do they still call you Con, now that you're a man of the cloth?"

"I hope not. In the sports pages sometimes."

"Why do you call him Padre Paul?" Samantha asked Randollph.

"All the Rams' players called him that when he was Monsignor Riley. He was a kind of unofficial chaplain to the team. Protestant or Catholic or no religion, the fellows knew they could talk to him about their problems. He sat on the bench at home games. He was famous for it."

"I was a fan," the Pope said. "Con, I must confess, was just about my favorite player. He was a great one."

"Still is," Sammy said. "Not a great football player, a great person. I do try to keep him humble, though."

"A good work, that," the Pope told her. "Pride is the clergy's besetting sin."

"I'll protect him from it," Sammy promised.

The Pope turned to Randollph. "Con, I'm overwhelmed by this, by what you're proposing to do."

"You'll be more overwhelmed when you see it, or them. They're absolutely magnificent. We've two security men outside the door carrying them, if you'd care to send for them."

The Pope pressed a button on his desk. "One of the advantages of being Pope is that there are plenty of people around to go when I say go, and come when I say come." A young priest came in quietly and stood in front of John XXIV. The Pope spoke to him in Italian and he left. Shortly two husky men came in, each carrying a leather bag.

"Put them on the table there," the Pope instructed them. The men looked at Randollph and he nodded, then said, "Thank you, gentlemen. Your responsibility is now at an end. You are free to fly home whenever you wish."

Randollph then opened the cases and carefully extracted the two black Morocco-bound volumes. He opened one of them so the Pope could see it. Vivid red, blue, and green designs on the margins and in the space between the two columns of type fought for attention with the golden glitter of the illuminations heading the chapter. John XXIV gasped. "Incredible. It looks like it just came off the press."

"Gutenberg used an ink that is remarkable for holding that glossy black quality," Randollph said.

"Our librarians will go wild," the Pope said. "We have a large collection of incunabula, you know, including one two-volume vellum copy of the Gutenberg Bible, and one volume, Volume II, on paper. But nothing like this."

"There isn't anything else like this, not anywhere," the bishop said.

"Ah, Padre Paul, there are a few conditions to this gift."

"I was afraid of that," the Pope said. "They didn't name you Con for nothing." But he was smiling. "Name them."

"First, they must be on permanent display. One reason I'm giving you this Bible is that more people are likely to see it here than anywhere else in the world."

"Done. We'd want it that way even without the condition. What else?"

"That from time to time the Bible be exhibited in other parts of the world—times and places to be at your discretion, with one exception?"

"And the exception?"

"It must be exhibited in the United States every five years—in New York or Boston, Los Angeles or San Francisco, and Chicago."

The Pope frowned slightly. "That will take money—insurance, security, etc. And the Vatican is chronically short of money. With all our revenues, we don't seem quite able to make ends meet."

"I have the same problem," the bishop said.

"I've thought of that, Padre Paul. Professor Humbrecht, whose Bible this was, also left me a million dollars in his will. I wish to give it to you to endow the upkeep of the Bible, and care for the expenses involved in exhibiting it."

John XXIV looked at Randollph steadily as if he hadn't quite comprehended what he'd just been told.

"I hadn't expected that," he said finally. "I don't quite know what to say. Thank you, that's all I can think of, Con."

"It's enough."

"You aren't a wealthy man."

"We're comfortable. I've saved a little from my football days. Samantha and I both earn good salaries. I might add that she is in agreement with me on this. We want to do it."

The Pope said, "I'm surprised that Freddie hasn't persuaded you to give him the money for good works."

"Oh, I thought of it," the bishop replied. "We need to build new churches, and you know what building costs these days."

"Don't I, though," the Pope answered.

"But Professor Humbrecht kindly left me a million dollars to be used for good works. That's the way he worded it in his will—'for good works.' One oughtn't to be greedy, even for the church. No, I'm in agreement with C.P.'s decision to endow the Bible."

"There's another condition," Randollph said.

The Pope smiled. "Is there no end to the conditions, Con?"

"This is the last one, Padre. In my letter I told you of the stormy events precipitated by the Bible."

"You did."

"You remember the man called Mr. Jones? His real name was Cristoforo Bartelione."

"The chap who kidnapped you?"

"That's the one. He was a Roman Catholic. Not one you'd wish to point to with pride, but a child of the Church all the same. It was his intention to give the Gutenberg to you, to the Vatican. Not for the noblest of reasons. He wanted to mitigate the divine punishment for his many and scarlet sins and book himself a reservation in heaven. He thought the gift of the Bible would turn the trick. You have people or orders whose vocation is to offer prayers for the souls of the departed?"

"Yes."

"I want appropriate prayers said for the soul of Cristoforo Bartolione."

"A strange request, Con. I'm sure that kind of prayer has no place in your theology."

"If you mean do I believe such prayers are efficacious or even necessary to salvation, no I don't. But I'll feel better if they're said."

"You're being enigmatic."

"Jones believed in them. He would want them said. He was not a nice man. He provoked in me a murderous rage I did not know was there. I did not know I could possibly feel that way. I hated Jones. So by doing something that would be a comfort to him, even though he can't know about it, I am helping to cleanse my own conscience."

"I'll arrange for it."

"And Father Simon, the prior of the Order of St. Thomas Aquinas."

"The poor deranged monk who killed Humbrecht?"

"Yes. A fundamentally good man who for one moment gave way to an obsession. I want prayers said for him. His soul is in torment. If I can tell him that prayers are being said for his salvation, I'm sure it will help him find some kind of peace within himself."

"We can do that."

"He wanted the Bible in order to present it to you, Padre."

"Ironic, isn't it, that the Bible ended up where Jones and Father Simon intended," the bishop said. "And where the cardinal archbishop of Chicago has stated publicly that it should go, but wouldn't because its owner is a bigot and violently prejudiced against the Roman Catholic Church."

The Pope sighed. "He's an albatross around my neck. He'll be retiring this summer, heaven be praised, or I'd have to remove him from office."

"I'd be interested to know how you'd do that, Paul," the bishop said.

"Kick him upstairs. Give him some kind of fancy title and an office here at the Vatican with nothing of importance to do. Make it sound like a promotion."

"Yes, that's how I'd do it," the bishop agreed. "Save everyone's face."

The Pope addressed Randollph. "And now, Con, I

have a condition for you—for you and Freddie, actually."

Randollph couldn't imagine what the Pope wanted. "We'll do anything we can, Padre."

"Of course," the bishop added.

"This is an occasion that should be marked, this gift of the Gutenberg. I'd like to arrange a ceremony of presentation. Have it in St. Peter's. Freddie, as your bishop, can explain what is happening and then present you. You'll make a little speech presenting the Bible to me. I'll accept it on behalf of the Roman Catholic Church. We'll have television, radio, the press—"

"Padre Paul, don't the Scriptures enjoin us to give alms in secret?"

The Pope laughed, a deep rumble that shook his large body. "So they do, Con. But that was written before the days of organized public relations. You can imagine how much good this gift of yours will do for the cause of good relations between Romans and Protestants. And you know that is a cause dear to my heart."

"Yes, Padre, I know. But in my presentation I'm morally obligated to say that that isn't why I'm doing it. I'll be pleased, of course, if it has that effect. But I'm doing it because it belongs here. It is, after all, the standard Scriptures for the Roman Catholic Church. And also, more people will have an opportunity to see it here than in any other place."

"Fine, fine." The Pope seemed hardly to have heard Randollph. "I think we'd better have a choir, and a processional of some kind. Can't be casual about something of this magnitude. Maybe I can cook up an impressive Latin phrase or two for my acceptance speech. My Latin's weak. If the cardinals had known that they'd probably never have elected me. And, Con—"

"Yes, Padre?"

"I don't mind if you want to say something in your speech about how I used to sit on the bench at Rams' home games, and that you and the other players called me Padre Paul." The Pope had a faraway look in his eyes. "Sometimes I think those were the best days of my life."

21

"I HOPE YOU WON'T be offended," Clarence Higbee said to Randollph and Sammy as they locked the door of the penthouse behind them and signaled for the elevator. "Mr. Henderson insisted that I be a member of the party this evening."

"Why, for heaven's sake, should we be offended?" Sammy asked.

"It really isn't proper for the servants of a house to pretend to a social equality with the master and mistress of the house. It violates the proprieties of a well-ordered society."

"But Queen Victoria is dead," Sammy protested. "Social customs have changed."

"Worse luck for us, madam. Now there was a monarch! Everything done in order, everything in its proper place."

"You must remember, Samantha, that Clarence is a confirmed monarchist," Randollph said. "He's told me so. However, I should think you might set aside your convictions for one evening, Clarence, without undue damage to the proper ordering of society."

"I suppose so." Clarence didn't sound quite convinced.

Sticky Henderson's Auberge was plain and low-ceilinged with a bar running the length of one side. There were a few booths and banquettes, and several tables in the dining room. The tables were covered with coarse red cloths. A few paintings hung on the walls, all scenes of French life and most of them portraying the preparation or consumption of food and wine. The room had the look of a plain country inn or tavern.

The same people who had been guests at the Randollph table the day he'd discovered Johannes Humbrecht's body made up the dinner party this evening, Randollph noted. Except, of course, for Sticky and Louise Henderson, who were presumably in the kitchen. And Clarence Higbee, whose role this evening was that of guest instead of servant. They were no sooner seated than Sticky Henderson, garbed in white and wearing a chef's hat that looked like a prodigious mushroom, came out the swinging door to the kitchen and made his way to their table. He shook hands with Randollph, then said, "I have a little speech to make. This significant occasion, the opening night for Sticky Henderson's Auberge, should not pass without appropriate ceremony. I have invited you to share in this proud moment. It is good to have as guests distinguished clergy—Dr. Randollph, Father Purdy, M'Lord Bishop, the Reverend Mr. Gantry—" he nodded at each man as he named them "—and their wives and consorts."

"Am I a consort?" Thea Mason asked Father Purdy.

"Shhsh," he said.

"And, of course, that distinguished representative of law and order, Lieutenant Michael Casey and his beautiful wife, Liz.

"Now," he said, "we come to the guest of honor, the one without whose advice, instruction, and patient help none of this would have been possible—Mr. Clarence Higbee."

"Hear, hear!" Dan Gantry said. "What'd Clarence do to deserve this?"

"What Mr. Higbee did—"

"Clarence, Mr. Henderson, my name is Clarence."

"Not while you're a guest at my table. When I eat at Dr. Randollph's, I'll call you Clarence, and you can call me Mr. Henderson. But here, where I am proprietor, chef de cuisine, and your servant, I will address you as Mr. Higbee and you will call me Lamarr. It's the proper way."

"Good Lord, another monarchist," Sammy said.

"To answer your question, Mr. Gantry, Louise and I have long been fond of French cuisine. We're both good amateur chefs. We just decided to turn pro. Mr. Higbee has been tutoring us."

"He helped you clean up your language, Sticky, uh, Lamarr?" Dan asked.

"No, Mr. Gantry. Louise did that. Mr. Higbee advised us to limit our menu to a few traditional dishes from French provincial cooking. He planned our kitchen. He's taught me how to find the best meats, poultry, fish, and vegetables available. He's taught me about wines."

Randollph thought he couldn't have contrived a better way to put a period to the tumult of his recent days. A pleasant dinner party with friends. The promise of good food and good talk. One of life's common, unremarkable, and universal experiences. It annealed the spirit. It restored the soul. The Gutenberg Bible, a minatory presence in his life that had been the agent of his kidnapping and of three murders, an unholy Bible, had been resanctified by its disposition. He was once again living in the familiar world of Miss Windfall, committee meetings, Bertie Smelser's meticulous financial reports, sermon preparation, and listening with a pastoral ear to troubled parishioners.

Yet Randollph knew that he'd never be quite the same again. He'd understood with the insight of recent experience that good people can do unwise, even evil things without intending to, driven by the passion of a moment to sudden immoral behavior. He believed he'd be more compassionate in the future, more tolerant of human frailty.

Yet he knew he'd have to walk the tightrope that divided compassion from ethical flabbiness carefully. He thought the memory of J. J. Knox calling his own unrighteousness by the name righteousness—and believing it—would help him walk that line. It crossed his mind that God really has a tough job balancing judgment and mercy.

"So what's to eat, Lamarr?" Dan Gantry asked, jarring Randollph out of his theological reverie.

"Mr. Higbee has recommended that we offer fish, fowl, meat, and the specialty of the house. The first three will vary with the seasons, the specialty will be a fixed item."

"What's the specialty, Lamarr?"

"Let me describe the other dishes first. Tonight we have Chicken Normandy. The province of Normandy is noted for its apples. The chicken is stuffed with apples and baked with a liberal dousing of Calvados."

"What's Calvados?" Leah Aspinwall asked.

"Apple brandy," Dan told her. "Fiery stuff to drink, but no doubt a gentle benediction to this dish, eh, Lamarr?"

"I couldn't have explained it better myself, Mr. Gantry. We also have Halibut Provençale, a recipe—as the name suggests—from the Provence region. It is halibut baked with onions and fresh tomatoes, spiced with garlic, oregano, thyme, and vermouth. For red meat we have steak au poivre. You all know what that is, I expect. A good strip steak with crushed peppercorns worked into it, sautéed in oil and butter, served with a sauce of beef stock, shallots, and cognac. Not adventurous, but something most anyone would like."

"And the specialty of the house? That's what I'm waiting to hear," the bishop asked.

"Ah yes, m'lord, I'm anxious to describe it. It is called Cassoulet Clarence. You can guess why?"

"Did Clarence invent it?" Liz Casey asked.

"Well—Mr. Higbee, would you answer that? And while you're at it, would you describe the dish?"

Clarence Higbee seemed glad to oblige. "No, Mrs. Casey, I didn't invent it. There are those who claim the Arabs invented it, though in France that is considered heresy. It is fair to say, I think, that cassoulet is *the* provincial French recipe."

"Why?"

Clarence warmed to his subject. "Because nearly

every region of France has its own version of cassoulet. There is an endless argument as to what a genuine cassoulet must contain. People of the Toulouse area insist it isn't genuine unless the recipe includes preserved goose. But then, Toulouse has a lot of geese. I do not think goose at all necessary to a good cassoulet."

"But what is it?" Liz Casey persisted.

"Basically it is beans. Think of it as French baked beans. But much, much more."

"Such as?"

"A rich medley of flavors produced by cooking the beans with a variety of meats—pork loin, breast of lamb, salt pork, sausage. It includes tomatoes, garlic, a number of herbs, white wine."

"Sounds filling," Father Purdy commented.

"A hearty dish, Father. Not too well known here in the States. I know of no other restaurant in Chicago that offers it—at least not as a standard item on the menu. Henderson's Auberge may well become an oasis for cassoulet fanciers."

"Why is it called Cassoulet Clarence?" Thea Mason wanted to know. Randollph saw that she was making notes.

"Because I use Italian sausage cakes in my recipe—though I doubt that I'm the first to do so. I happen to like the anise flavor and aroma the Italian sausage adds."

After they'd ordered, Father Purdy said, "Dr. Randollph, you're the toast of the Roman Catholic community in Chicago these days, did you know that?"

"No, I didn't."

"They'd elect you bishop of Chicago by acclamation if things were done that way."

Randollph chuckled. "Interestingly enough, it has been done that way—at least once."

Father Purdy was surprised. "I can't imagine such a thing. Are you sure? When was this?"

"A long time ago—around 375. The see of Milan fell vacant, and the Trinitarians and the Arians couldn't agree on a candidate. Ambrose, the Roman governor of Milan, was present at the conclave and the people finally elected him by acclamation. He wasn't even a Christian."

"My word!" the bishop said. "I've seen strange things happen in ecclesiastical assemblies, but nothing like that. How did it all turn out?"

"They baptized him, ordained him, then consecrated him bishop—all in a week's time. Evidently he was a splendid bishop. He wrote so many theological works that today he is listed a doctor of the Church. And he's a saint."

"I'll be your campaign manager," Thea Mason said. "Maybe you could end up as a saint."

"A saint he's not—and he'd better not turn into one or I'll chuck him out. What healthy red-blooded American girl wants a saint for a husband? Ugh!"

"Sorry, Thea, I must decline. The uxorious aspect of my character takes precedence over my ambition for canonization."

Leah Aspinwall appealed to Sammy. "Did he just say something nice about you?"

Sammy gazed at Randollph fondly. "Yes, he did. Something lovely. The lad sometimes sounds like he's talking Swahili. But if you're around him enough you learn to translate it."

"Since I've been going out with Dan I've had, well, the most amazing experiences."

"Stick with me, sweetheart, there are wonders yet to come," Dan said.

Randollph wondered if Dan was making any progress in persuading Leah to become Mrs. Gantry. The bishop had given his blessing, Dan had reported, but Leah wasn't quite convinced. "I think she's weakening, though," Dan had said. "Hard to resist my charms."

"For example," Leah continued, "I've never been near a murder investigation. Now I know a homicide detective who solved what the papers called a near-insoluble crime. How did you figure it out, Lieutenant?"

Casey looked uncomfortable. "Actually, I have to confess—"

Randollph interrupted him. "The lieutenant is too modest. I think it was his good Catholic education that is responsible."

Leah was puzzled. "I don't understand what a Catholic education had to do with solving a murder."

"Look at it this way," Randollph explained. "The

ordinary policeman would never have suspected a gentle cleric of murder. But Lieutenant Casey has had some training in theology. He knows the potential for evil resides in even the best of us. That knowledge enabled him to entertain the preposterous idea that Prior Simon might have done it."

"I'd never have thought of him," Leah admitted.

Randollph could see Casey squirming. He knew the lieutenant wanted to give Randollph the credit Randollph had given him. But Randollph had made Casey promise to keep his mouth shut. Randollph could tolerate being known as a famous pro quarterback who'd turned in his jockstrap for a Bible. But a reputation as a clerical snoop, a holy Sherlock, was more than he thought he could handle. Casey would just have to suffer. This case was a particularly bright star in Casey's professional crown. That would eventually ease the lieutenant's pain.

"And going to Rome and meeting with the Pope, that must have been exciting!" Leah turned to Sammy. "I heard he hugged you, the Pope, I mean."

"Yes, Leah, he did."

"Tell me, Mike, have you made any progress in the murders of Mr. Robin Elder and that gangster, Bart, is that his name?"

"Bartelione was his real name." Randollph thought Casey sounded like a professor about to display his vast knowledge in his field of competence to students eager to be informed.

"I don't know if we've solved those murders, Thea," Casey said slowly, "but I've just come from booking a suspect."

Thea got out her notebook and pen. "Who? Same person kill both of them?"

"We think so."

"Seems strange. Who is it, Mike?"

"Robin Elder's law partner, J. J. Knox, senior."

That got an immediate reaction.

"My word," the bishop said. "That's hard to believe."

"Christ a'mighty!" Dan said.

"Old Mr. Self-righteous?" Thea asked.

"I see you've met him." Casey was working hard at suppressing a smug smile. Randollph looked at him pleadingly. Casey's expression was reassuring. Randollph interpreted it to mean, "Don't worry, pal. I've assured J. J. Knox that you didn't give him away, and I won't mention your involvement to these people or anyone else."

"How did you get on to him?" Father Purdy asked.

"Oh, this whole business about the Gutenberg Bible centered in the Knox office. I reasoned that someone in the office could easily have obtained the information in Humbrecht's will."

"Knox?" Purdy asked.

"No. Robin Elder. We were able to establish that. We also established that Elder planned to steal the Bible, but Prior Simon beat him to it."

"But I still don't see—"

"I know, Bishop. Why Knox?" Casey sat back in his chair, took out a pack of cigarettes, looked at his wife and put it back. "My theory was that Knox discovered what Elder was up to, confronted him, got him to confess, shot him, and made it look like a burglary."

"But why kill him?"

"I think Knox knew we'd get around to discovering what Elder had done and there'd be messy publicity that would badly hurt the reputation of the law firm. Knox was obsessed with the firm's spotless reputation. He'd do anything to protect it."

"What a creep!" Thea Mason said. "But why did he kill Jones too? Doesn't make sense."

"It makes sense, Thea, if Jones had been dealing with Elder and Knox found out about it. Jones, then, was also a threat to the firm's reputation. He knew something ugly about Knox, Knox, and Elder. To J. J. Knox that was intolerable."

Father Purdy spoke up. "If I may say so, Lieutenant, that's a theory that would be difficult to substantiate without some corroborating evidence. Yet you must have found some. As one who knows nothing about the methods of criminal detection I'd be curious to hear how you found enough facts to warrant booking Knox."

Randollph could see that Casey had been hoping someone would ask that question.

"I think you'll be interested to know, Father, that I had help from the Old Testament. From the Apocrypha.

I recalled the books of Bel and the Dragon, and Susanna. You know that these are considered the very first examples of the detective story?"

"Yes," Randollph answered. "I believe it was Dorothy Sayers who first pointed that out."

Casey, looking slightly annoyed, went on. "The Book of Susanna was especially helpful because it reminded me of a working principle every detective knows but sometimes is apt to forget."

Father Purdy chimed in with "The principle of separate interrogation of witnesses. Daniel destroyed the false witness brought by the two elders against Susanna by questioning them separately and their stories contained discrepancies."

"Exactly, Father. Only I used separate interrogation to substantiate a charge, not destroy one."

"How?" Thea asked.

"You read in the papers about the two telephone books found in Jones's car?"

"Yes. What's important about them?"

"I surmised that Jones—after Elder's death—had gotten in touch with Knox, hoping that Knox knew where the Bible was. My guess was that by this time Jones was frantic to lay his hands on the Bible and was being pushed by his obsession with it to take chances he wouldn't ordinarily take."

Randollph heard Casey continue to outline the theory he had laid out for him. He wondered if Casey's telling of it as his own theory was just good acting, or if somewhere along the way Casey had come to believe that the theory *was* his own.

"One of those phone books had markings, doodles, on the inside cover. Stick figures, little sailboats, stuff like that. So I took the book over to Knox's office, appropriated a conference room, and called in several of the secretaries. Called them in one at a time. Most of them immediately recognized the doodling as Knox's. He's noted for it around the office. Knox's personal secretary also admitted that Knox had had her get two new phone books the day after Jones's murder. Said someone had made off with his old ones."

"Is that all you've got, Mike?" Dan Gantry asked.

"No, Dan. I interrogated the switchboard operator.

She remembers a call from a Mr. Jones for J. J. Knox the day after Elder's murder. Mr. Jones, she said, insisted that he had to talk to Knox on a matter relating to his late partner. Knox took the call."

"Still not enough to put him in the slammer," Dan muttered.

"I know that, Dan. That's where the story of Bel helped me."

"How?" Randollph asked.

"By reminding me that in the long run solid police work, the collection of evidence, is the way to solve crimes."

"What's that got to do with the story of Bel?" Thea asked. "Whatever the story of Bel is."

"It's another story about Daniel as a detective, Thea. This heathen king and his people worshiped an idol called Bel. They set out sacrifices of food and wine before it every night, and the next morning all the food and wine were gone. The king said this proved that Bel was a living god."

"So?"

"Daniel said it's just an old idol, and he can prove it."

"Does he, as if I need to ask?"

"Yes. He had the food and wine set out before the idol, then put everyone out of the temple except the king and himself. He scattered ashes all over the floor, and had the king seal the door as they left. Next morning the king broke the seal, found the food and wine gone, but there were many footprints in the ashes coming from and leading to concealed doors. Seems the priests of Bel and their wives and children had been sneaking through the doors every night and eating the idol's food and drinking his wine."

"And that's the principle of collecting empirical evidence to solve a crime," Father Purdy supplied. "Even I can figure that out. But you already practice that principle in your work—practice it every day, don't you Lieutenant?"

"Yes," Casey admitted. "That's the basis of modern police work. I suppose you could say that remembering the story of Bel got me off my—er, stimulated me to try harder to find some empirical evidence to back up my theory. It's easy to doubt a theory, think you're just whistling 'Dixie,' and quit trying to dig out the facts that are there to be dug."

Leah Aspinwall had been listening carefully, but now spoke up. "Lieutenant Casey, you say these stories are in the Old Testament?"

"Yes, they are."

"Well, I studied the Old Testament in Temple Sunday School, I can even read it in Hebrew. But I never heard of Susanna and Bel and the Dragon."

"Smart girl, that one," Dan said. "That's what attracted me to her—her keen mind."

"Ha!" Sammy hooted. "Do elephants suddenly fly? Do leopards change their spots?"

Casey hastened to answer Leah before anyone else diverted the conversation into other channels. "You're right, Leah, the Apocrypha isn't included in the Hebrew Bible. For that matter, it isn't included in Protestant versions of the Old Testament. I guess you have to be a Catholic to be exposed to the Apocrypha." Casey looked at Randollph with a smile that said, "You're not the only one who can use the Bible and church history and theology to help figure out whodunit." Randollph suspected that Casey had done some hasty homework on the Apocrypha and wanted to show it off.

Casey continued his lecture. "The Apocrypha, which means hidden or secret, Leah, is a collection of Jewish writings produced probably during the two hundred years before Christ. The Greek-speaking Jews living in Alexandria accepted it as Scripture and incorporated it in the Septuagint."

"The what?"

"I'm sounding too academic," Casey apologized, but sounded pleased with himself. "The Septuagint was the Greek translation of the Old Testament. The Palestinian Jews never accepted the apocryphal books into their Hebrew Bible. That's why you never heard of the Apocrypha in temple school."

"And the Apocrypha isn't in the Protestant Bible, either?"

"It isn't in mine," Dan told her.

Randollph thought Casey was suffering from an overdose of intellectual pride. "Actually, Lieutenant, the Apocrypha was never officially read out of the Protestant Bible. Luther included the Apocrypha in his translation, but put it in separately from the Old Testament with a note that these books were not to be considered equal to Holy Scripture but were worth reading. The King James Bible followed Luther's pattern. Some Protestants objected to their inclusion and they were frequently left out by Bible publishers, then disappeared altogether. But they were never officially excluded by any Protestant ecumenical council."

"Then why are they in the Catholic Bible?" Leah persisted. "Catholics and Protestants are both Christians, aren't they?"

"Because the Roman Catholic Council of Trent, in 1546, declared all but three books of the Apocrypha to be canonical, that is, authentic Scripture. That's why these books are in Lieutenant Casey's Bible, but not in mine. But tell us, Lieutenant, did your scriptural inspiration lead to anything else?"

"Yes," Casey answered. "We asked the Evanston police to see if they could place Knox's car at Elder's house the night of the murder. He had a distinctive car. A Packard, not even one of the last models, which he kept in prime condition. He wasn't an auto buff, don't know why he kept it."

"Yankee conservatism," the bishop suggested. "Wear it out or do without."

"Maybe so. Anyway, the Evanston police finally found a kid who loves cars who noticed it at Elder's place. Even remembered the license number. And they also found plenty of Elder's friends who will testify that everyone who knew him knew he kept a gun, and where he kept it. Knox had to know that."

"And it was Elder's gun that also killed Jones, wasn't it?" Thea asked.

"Yes. That ties it all together."

"However," Father Purdy said, "this is all purely circumstantial evidence."

"So is most evidence," Casey answered. "But by adding circumstantial evidence you multiply the probability that it is factual."

"But is it enough to convict him, Mike?" Thea was skeptical.

"It's enough to indict. And we'll keep digging for more hard evidence, probably find some. It's like the sports announcers say, our team's got momentum."

"I imagine an indictment and a trial would be sufficient to serve the ends of justice whether you get a conviction or not," said Randollph.

"Yes, I can see that, C.P.," the bishop said. "A trial and all the sensational publicity surrounding it—" he looked at Thea scribbling away in her notebook "—would utterly destroy J. J. Knox and his beloved firm. What he had sinned to save he lost because of his sins. Poetic justice indeed." The bishop patted his belly. "I ate too much."

"I'd rather have a conviction," Casey growled. "And I expect to get one."

"Thanks to your good Catholic education, Lieutenant." Randollph was unable to quell a sense of relief that J. J. Knox was unlikely to be sitting in the Sunday congregation at the Church of the Good Shepherd ever again. He knew he should feel *agape*, a sense of Christian concern, no matter how unmerited, for the old sinner. He knew he should hope that J. J. Knox would continue to attend Good Shepherd, as he had said to Knox. However, he could feel nothing but relief. He recalled that one of the Greek words St. Paul used for salvation meant a process never completed in this life. Randollph decided he had quite a way to go, but was comforted nonetheless.

Father Purdy spoke up. "I have it from a friend at the chancery that the winner of the *Trib*'s contest for the best letter as to what Dr. Randollph should do with the Gutenberg Bible is the cardinal archbishop. The prize is a two-volume facsimile of the Gutenberg Bible. There were less than five hundred copies of it printed some years ago. Very beautiful, a faithful reproduction."

"Will he accept it?" the bishop asked. "I should think it would be most embarrassing for him considering the tone of his letter."

"He has to accept it or he'd appear churlish. The paper's planning to publish a picture of him accepting the prize. But he's expecting to be ill on presentation day and send Pat Quinn to accept it."

"What is the nature of the disease he's expecting to afflict him?" the bishop asked.

"He isn't saying. But my source at the chancery says around here it's known as the Randollph flu."

Sammy and Leah Aspinwall were carrying on a semiprivate conversation. "I loved the trip," Randollph heard Sammy say. "Everything about it. I'd never been to Europe before. Randollph doesn't know it yet, but he's going to take me to Paris. London, of course. And Venice. I must see Venice before it sinks into the sea. We didn't get to Florence on this trip, but we will on the next one. And then there's China. I simply have to see the Great Wall. And..."

Randollph wondered how he was going to placate his conscience and Miss Windfall for absenting himself from work to gad about Europe and all the exotic places Sammy was planning to visit. But he could deal with that later. Right now he wanted to preserve this serene moment. Such moments were benedictions, ointments for spirits abraded by the troubles and tensions which are life's necessary and inevitable afflictions. It occurred to him that this thought was good sermon material.